# SC

# By

# Kev Edwards

**Jacket Design**

**By**

**Fiona Scott**

## Copyright

## Dedication

I dedicate this book to my cousin, John Nicholls, who appeared as a fictional character in several of my earlier books and who died in May of this year after a short illness.

# Introduction

Scotty's War is a story based on events that actually happened, intermixed with what could have been and what might have been. It's possible that events which I have seen as fictional did occur but were never publicised. In short, this is a work of fiction with some "real people" woven into the fictitious story line .

The idea came to me when I started thinking about my Father's role in World War 2. He served aboard the Royal Air Force's Air Sea Rescue (RAFASR) launches, small vessels rather like the Royal National Lifeboat Institutions larger lifeboats of today. These launches rescued downed pilots, Axis as well as Allied, in a variety of places from Cornwall to the Shetland Islands and in the Mediterranean Sea from Gibraltar to Malta. The ASR launches were similar in size and speed to the Motor Gunboats (MGBs) featured in my book. But the MGBs were heavily armed and were deemed attack, not rescue, vessels.

My Father rarely spoke about his war service, preferring to focus on how fortunate he was to meet my Mother when he served in Cornwall's most westerly port: Newlyn, the home for my story and the place where I was born, grew up and finally left to join the Merchant Navy.

My Father married my Mother in 1944 and loved her till the day he died in 1991. And she loved him until her death three years later in what would have been their Golden Wedding Anniversary year.

All the above are facts. It is also a fact that the German Fieldmarshal, Erwin Rommel, fought an unblemished war in the North African Desert up to July 1942. This posed huge problems for the Allies, both strategically and from a public morale standpoint.

Strategically, North Africa was a springboard for the Allies to advance into the soft southern European underbelly. Forcing the Axis troops from North Africa would lead to the start of the Allies' invasion hopes, up through Italy, Austria, into Germany and the Balkans. Defeat, though, posed major headaches for the Allies. Their two major strongholds in North Africa, Tobruk and Alexandria, were strategically placed to protect Egypt from falling and the Suez Canal being closed to Allied shipping. And Suez was a vital lifeline for the Allies between the Mediterranean Sea and the Middle and Far Eastern trade routes.

As to public morale, after the Allied retreat from Dunkirk, it plummeted. When the German air force started their "Blitzkrieg" on UK cities night after night after night, the Government feared that morale would sink even further. And, German U Boats added to the mix by sinking hundreds of thousands of tons of merchant shipping, killing hundreds of seamen in the process. Their aim was to prevent vital goods and foodstuffs from reaching the United Kingdom and thereby literally starve Great Britain to death.

If the Blitz and U Boat packs succeeded, the Germans would have forced the British Isles into a negotiated peace or they may simply have invaded our shores. The wartime Prime Minister, Winston Churchill, recognised all this and that the country badly needed a victory, not further huge losses of life. With the heads of the armed services he developed a plan to change the fortunes of the Allies' war by enticing Rommel into one battle too many. If the gamble paid off, North Africa would be safe and our hopes of invading the southern Europe mainland would be preserved.

The plan started before Rommel's desert victory at Gazala in the summer of 1942. In this attack he captured Tobruk and many miles of land before the Allies stopped him barely fifty miles from Alexandria at El Alamein, an easily defended position. But also one that was almost impossible to attack without huge loss of life.

This defensive position could not be bypassed. Rommel had to attack and win to go any further towards Alexandria and Suez. To do so he needed reinforcements from other German and Italian theatres of war. The Allies' plan was to stop those reinforcements getting through and force him to attack before he was ready.

Many have heard of the Battle of El Alamein, a huge victory for General Montgomery and his hardened desert troops. Few have heard of the actual **first** Battle of El Alamein at Gazala which preceded it by a few months. My story explores what might have happened before that final battle took place.

It is where fiction merges with fact, a novel that tells the story of a group of Royal Navy sailors who take on the huge task of stopping German reinforcements getting through to North Africa after the Battle of Gazala.

I hope that you enjoy the story and forgive me for any liberties that I may have taken in telling a story that I enjoyed researching and writing. During the research I confirmed my admiration and respect for many of the war time leaders, civilian and military, who I mention. For them as people and for the tasks they carried out without thought of the harm that they might cause themselves.

I have, I believe, stayed with the truth and actual events where these happened. Where they did not, I have tried to be as realistic and as accurate in my descriptions as it is possible to be some seventy five years plus after the event.

I felt every nerve end in my body jangling, screaming for rest, telling me to close my eyes and sleep. Pins and needles made the tips of my fingers and toes tingle. I stood next to my Coxswain on the flying bridge of my Motor Gunboat, or MGB as the Royal Navy called her, and wondered how any of us had lived this long.

"How many days now, Coxswain?" I asked.

"Too many, Sir," David Williams replied, "nine, I think. Lost count a few days back. Have to check the log book," he laughed, though there was no humour in it.

"Nine bloody days and nine bloody nights. Thank God this is the last of the poor devils."

I looked down at the deck in front of me and turned to look astern towards the after deck. This deck and the foredeck were covered with soldiers, mostly British, but a few Frenchmen and Belgians, too. Not to mention a handful of Poles. There was no free space. Men lay where they dropped. Huddled together for warmth, perhaps comfort, too.

A sailor said that they shouldn't be smoking on deck as we were at Action Stations. I laughed aloud and told him that after the hell they endured on that open beach, attacked by German aircraft by day and German artillery by night they could do what they liked.

"They're pleased to be alive, man. God knows they've earned a cigarette or two."

"How many, Sir?" Williams asked, interrupting the train of thought.

"Another fifty this time. We'll have them home in time for tea."

We both looked up as the unmistakable sound of a Merlin engine roared overhead, the all too familiar and welcome sight of a lone Spitfire.

"No firing," I shouted into my loudhailer. Almost all my crew stood around the fast firing machine guns and the heavier anti-aircraft Oerlikon guns. At my shout they relaxed.

"They're dog tired, Sir. But, at least you gave them some time to get their heads down. When did you last sleep?"

"Plenty of time once we're back in Plymouth, Cox. Then I'll sleep for the rest of the month."

The boat rocked gently from side to side in the small swell. Williams eased the wheel through his hands looking all round, his eyes never still.

"HMS *Argyll's* signalling, Sir. Morrison," he shouted at the boat's signalman, "What's she saying?"

Morrison wrote on his pad and passed me the note. It was a short message, telling me to transfer this last squad of soldiers to them. Then leave for home.

I paused, before reading the last few lines aloud.

""Also, says, and I quote, Well done, Scotty. Sorry we had to keep you here for so long. God speed you home."

"You know the Captain, Sir?" Morrison asked.

"Old friend, Morrison. He's from Newlyn as well. We trained together at HMS Conway, then did our first trip together in the Merchant Navy. When we joined the Andrew he opted for the big boys, I preferred the gunboats. He's done well. He's a good skipper."

I looked back towards the beach of Dunkirk. When we first arrived over three hundred thousand men waited, desperate to get off and get home. German aircraft all over the place. E Boats by the bucketful. E Boats, one of our worst nightmares. They attacked in hordes, never fewer than five at a time. We saw most of them off, sank three. The bastards had fired on our soldiers as they waded out towards waiting boats. The sea was more blood red than grey.

I rubbed my fingers deep into my closed eyes, wiping the crusted sleep on my duffel coat.

"I wonder how many of them died before we could get them off?"

Williams eased the boat's twin engines back to Slow Ahead and crewmen on HMS Argyll held the two vessels together as the soldiers climbed the netting up to the destroyer's deck twenty feet above us. The last to leave, a sergeant, walked up to the flying bridge and threw a parade-ground salute.

"Permission to enter, Sir?"

"Granted, Sergeant," I replied, smiling at the formality. The man climbed on to the little flying bridge.

"I wanted to thank you, Sir. Not just for me and them," he nodded towards the last of his men climbing over the destroyer's rails.

"For all the others. I watched you these last nine days. How the hell you've survived with all those bombs dropping, I don't know. But I do know this. If it wasn't for you, hundreds of my boys and them from other regiments would be dead. Drowned in this bloody sea or shot or bombed by those bastards."

He stepped back, saluted again, turned smartly on his heel and climbed up to join his men.

"Makes it all worthwhile, Cox. Set course for home. Full Speed Ahead. Let's show *Argyll* what our MGB can do."

"Morrison, take the wheel from the Coxswain. I think we've all earned a tot of rum."

Williams told Morrison what course to steer and climbed down into the cockpit below, shaking his head as he went.

"We going home, Cox?" I heard a sailor ask as he went by.

"We are that, Son. But, first, the Skipper's just piped Up Spirits."

"Bloody hell, it's not even dinner time. Has he gone mad? If the Admiral gets to hear he'll be for the chop." I smiled despite my exhaustion at the reply.

"And who do you think will tell the Admiral?" Williams replied. "If they did, they'd be in for a long swim next time they were on watch with me."

He picked a microphone out of a handset on the bulkhead.

"Do you hear there? Up Spirits in the Crew Mess in five minutes. That is all."

When he returned to the bridge he passed me a huge enamel mug of tea. I lifted it to my nose and inhaled, almost choking when the smell hit my throat.

"I don't think I'll ever be able to drink tea again without a tot of your excellent rum, Dave."

I could see that Williams, as always, was thrilled at my use of his first name.

"You've earned it, Sir."

"I think we all have after this. I must say I'm looking forward to a spot of leave."

I finished the mug as an aircraft engine sounded overhead again.

"Enemy aircraft," I shouted into the PA system. "Emergency Full Ahead, Coxswain. Gun crews, fire at will."

The first bomb crashed into the sea less than ten yards away and the resultant wall of water heaved the small craft over almost on to her side. The second bomb landed just astern and lifted us out of the water. She somersaulted stern over bow, a feat the little boat was never designed to withstand. I remember landing heavily in the water then nothing until CPO Williams visited me in hospital a week later.

"I saw you face down in the water when I struggled back up to the surface," he told me,

"thought you were dead. I'd swallowed a lungful of water myself but threw it all back up as I swam towards you. I turned you face up and felt a small breath coming out of your mouth. Your head must have collided with the bulwark on your way over the side. You'd lost some blood."

He told me that the other survivors crowded around, keeping me afloat and one tied a wet and oily rag around my forehead to try to stem the flow of blood. Then they waited.

"How many survived?" I asked him.

"Six, Sir. Nobody below decks made it."

Six from the crew of twelve that we started the day with. Dear God, what a mess.

"Bloody water felt like concrete when I piled into it," I said. "I still ache all over."

"Me, too, Sir. But we made it. And I've never seen *HMS Argyll* move so quick, either. She was like a bloody greyhound coming back to get us."

He told me that we made good time back to Blighty and less than an hour later they transferred us all to waiting ambulances in Dover. *Argyll's* Medical Officer, a young sub lieutenant who'd been given some basic First Aid training stayed with me till they took me into the operating theatre.

Three weeks after Williams' visit I left the Royal Naval Hospital at Haslar and caught the train home to Newlyn in West Cornwall. Mother met me at the train station.

"You look a bit pale, Harry, Dear. And you've lost some weight."

She slipped an arm through mine and led me to her waiting car.

"We'll feed you up and get you well again. You'll see."

The next two weeks flew by and we were back at the same station.

"You shouldn't be going back, Harry. It's too soon."

I hugged her tightly.

"I'm fine, Mum. You've done a great job. I'm feeling as good as I was before Dunkirk. Anyway, I'll get bored if I sit round much more."

I climbed on to the train and waved goodbye. Before the train left the station I put my head in my hands and wept. Six men dead. How the hell could I have let it happen? And just when we were on our way home. I should have known the Germans would have had one more go at us.

The peacetime train services were bad enough but their wartime equivalent was even worse. It took us eight hours to get to Shoreham on England's South coast. And half an hour in a taxi to the harbour. When the cab pulled up I couldn't help but smile. Coxswain David Williams waited on the quayside looking down at *HMS Beagle*.

He turned as I got out, stood to attention and saluted. I returned the salute and picked up my bags. Williams stepped forward.

"Let me take one, Sir. And congratulations on the extra stripe. Captain Dennis told us about it when he came down yesterday."

I looked down at the two and a half stripes on my sleeve. Lieutenant Commander. After Dunkirk I felt lucky to still have a command.

"Thank you, Coxswain. Came as a bit of a shock I can tell you. What's she like?" I nodded down at my command.

"Lovely, Sir."

He went over the basic details with me and I couldn't help but feel the adrenaline flowing through my veins and a tingling feeling in my stomach. It helped me put aside for now the feelings of guilt over losing so many of my crew.

She was bigger than our last boat and, according to the briefing papers the Admiralty sent me, much faster, too.

"We got her up to thirty nine knots yesterday and Chief Mechanic Shaw reckons he'd get another three or four out of her if pushed."

Williams gave me a rundown of the boat's performance.

"She's straight out of the Fairwater Boatyard just up-river. She launched a month ago and we collected her last week for sea trials."

I knew Fairwater by reputation. A solid, traditional builder of small boats like this, fast attack craft.

"Who was in command?"

"Lieutenant Haywood. He was sub lieutenant when we last saw him."

I obviously looked a little vacant until he explained that Haywood was the young medic who escorted me to hospital. He wasn't' a trained doctor, just a junior officer who was told to help the wounded. The doctors told Williams that if Haywood hadn't staunched the bleeding I wouldn't have made it. And even though I was unaware of my surroundings at the time he kept talking and talking to keep me semi-conscious.

"The doctor at Haslar reckoned he saved your life,'" he finished.

I stared down at my feet, not wanting him to see the moisture in my eyes.

"He wasn't the only one, Coxswain. You kept me afloat in the water. I won't forget any of you."

I took a deep breath and even I heard the break in my voice as I spoke.

"Nor will I ever forget those who didn't come back. I'm not looking forward to Judgement Day, Coxswain. I'm pretty sure what Him upstairs will say. Just before he tells me to bugger off down below."

Williams did something he'd never done before. He was three inches taller than me, but he bent forward and put his hand under my chin and looked into my eyes.

"You, Sir, are the best skipper we've ever sailed with. You carried us through those nine days of Hell off Dunkirk. You saved us. And if you don't believe me, how many of those who came back to Blighty with you asked to be posted back to you?"

I shook my head.

"No idea. You and Morrison?"

He told me that it was all six survivors. How they wangled it I have no idea. It meant a lot right then. He turned away and shouted to Morrison down on the deck, ordering him to take my bags to my new cabin. Whilst Morrison did that we walked down the quay to a concrete shed. I looked at the sign and smiled.

"Our very own mess, Cox. That's a first."

"Well, we share it with the rest of your new flotilla. Six crews, almost eighty men. And the Wrens who work for Captain Dennis."

Morrison ran up as Williams opened the door, stood to attention and saluted.

"Good to have you back, Sir. We've missed you."

He walked inside and we followed.

"*HMS Beagle* Atten………shun," Williams shouted. All fourteen men stood at the same time, raised their right legs and slammed their feet into the floorboards as hard as they could with perfect timing.

"At ease, men," I said walking across to Morrison and accepting the pint of beer he thrust into my hands. I raised it to my lips and swallowed half of it in one. As much to hide my emotion at the welcome as to quench my thirst.

"It's good to be back. I never thought I'd miss such a motley crew as you. But I did."

I took another deep swallow and passed the mug back to Morrison.

"We sail out on final work-up at 0630 hours tomorrow. The rest of the flotilla joins us over the next three days."

I didn't pull any punches as I continued. They weren't fools and I always treated my men with the respect they deserved. They repaid it in droves. I told them that it was going to be tough, that the Germans were winning.

"But, one thing that I believe with all my heart is that they may win the battles today, but we will win the war."

They looked at each other and I wondered if they thought that the concussion had affected my brain.

"It won't be easy and it will take time," I finished, "but as long as we look out for one another and do as we're ordered, we'll win."

I turned to Williams.

"I'm going aboard, Coxswain. Meet me in an hour and we'll do an inspection of our new command.

Lieutenant Haywood," I said.

A tall young man, barely in his twenties stepped forward and saluted.

"At ease, Lieutenant." I held out my hand and shook his.

"I hear you, as well as this lot, saved my life. Thank you. Please join the Coxswain and me aboard *Dotty*."

Four days later, with sea trials completed and my other five boats in a V formation around us, I led my flotilla back to war. A war that was to be fast, violent and for some, fatal. A war that only MGBs could fight, hitting the enemy at high speeds, relying on the element of surprise, weaving amongst their ships, guns blazing, torpedoes racing, depth charges flying through the air before we escaped back out to sea. Usually.

# Chapter 1    Two Years Later March 1942, Scotty in Shoreham by Sea, Sussex

At last, we may get some leave. Since commissioning *Beagle* in July 1940 I'd had two spells of leave. Rumour had it that we'd soon get a third because the boat was overdue a refit. The whole crew's exhausted, I could tell just by looking at them. Even the Coxswain's on his last legs, and I've sailed with David Williams since the start of the war.

"Morning, Cox, anything interesting?"

I pointed at the letter that I'd watched him read three times as I walked down the foredeck. He would read it, look away, then re-read it. I couldn't see the words, but I could see that the letter was a short one. And the look on his face before he saw me come into the cockpit wasn't that of a happy man.

"Letter from the wife, Sir. Just a catch-up. Nothing much going on."

He put the letter in his pocket at that point and smiled.

"You sure you're all right, Cox? Looks like you've seen a ghost."

"She was never much of a writer, Sir. Just having a bit of a moan. You know what they're like when they're on their own for months. Can't see the wood from the trees. Everything's getting on top of her."

He grimaced as he said this. I walked to the corner of the cockpit and levered myself into the Captain's Chair, glad that I was only five feet ten tall. Any taller and my legs would have been bent underneath me.

"Orders for today, Sir?" Williams asked.

*Dotty,* or *HMS Beagle* as she was properly named, looked a bit the worse for wear. The storm in the Channel the last two nights when we'd been attacking German cargo ships off the French coast left the decks and ship's sides coated in salt. I told him to get the decks washed down. Our Senior Officer, Captain

Dennis, was lunching with me on board and he was a stickler for discipline and seaworthiness.

And *Dotty* deserved some Tender Loving Care. She'd carried us through two years of constant tension, leaving harbour in the early evening, attacking enemy ships in usually total darkness, speeding amongst them at almost fifty miles per hour. She hadn't let us down once.

And why *Dotty* outsiders asked? It was the crew's pet name for her. Morrison christened her after seeing the film star Dorothy Lamour at the cinema two years earlier.

He pinned up a newspaper picture of the lady in the crew mess and told his mates that "*HMS Beagle* may not be as beautiful as *Dotty*, but she moves through the sea like Miss Lamour dances in the movies."

Corny, but little things like that helped morale. And helped us take our minds off the horrors we saw almost daily.

That was back in July 1940 when I came back to sea for the first time since Dunkirk. I was passed as physically fit after three weeks leave at home, but I'd lost six men out of just thirteen crew.

When I joined *Dotty* I wasn't sure if I was capable of commanding a boat anymore. Until I stood on the deck that first day I didn't even know if I wanted to. I can still remember the doctor's words at Haslar.

"You'll be fine, Scotty. It was a concussion. We've checked you over. A few weeks leave and you'll be right as rain."

How the hell did he know that I'd lost six men, human beings who'd served with me since the outbreak of war?

"Sorry, Cox, what did you say? I was miles away."

"Do you think we're getting some leave, Sir?" Williams asked. "Seems that the rest of the flotilla's had their breaks from duty."

He was right, of course, but it's what happens when you're the lead boat and none of the other skippers was experienced enough to take over. Though of late, Lieutenant Adams on *Greyhound* had developed into a fine skipper. In the pubs around Shoreham his crew practically worshipped him.

"I may find out when the Old Man comes aboard for lunch later, Coxswain. You'll be the first to know." I left him to it after that and climbed down to the cubbyhole that passed for my cabin where I closed my eyes, sat on my bunk and put my head between my hands.

He was right, we needed a break. Non-stop for six months since our last refit. The strain was getting to all of us. Nightly attacks on German shipping across the Channel. When we weren't doing that we helped the Royal Air Force find missing pilots. God knows, the RAF's Air Sea Rescue launches were under pressure, too. But at this stage in the war there were fewer pilots ditching in the Channel. They could have given us the odd night off, but we always seemed to be the duty boat.

Still, I was lucky. We'd suffered no more losses, though it had been close more than once. Shrapnel from enemy shells re-opened my old head wound, but even that healed quickly. I sighed, stood and stretched, reaching for my uniform and toilet bag. No showers aboard MGBs but we had a decent enough toilet block on the harbour. Best to look the part of an officer when the Old Man arrived, even if I still wonder sometimes if I'd be better off ashore.

I touched the stripes on my sleeve. Lieutenant Commander, not bad for an ex-Merchant Navy third mate.

At noon on the dot, Captain Dennis walked briskly down the quay and climbed over the rail. Williams and I came to attention on the small deck.

"Lieutenant Commander Scott, Coxswain," he saluted back. "Show me around, Harry. Its been a while since I've been aboard."

Captain Robert Dennis (RN) had seen service in the Royal Navy in World War 1 and in the Merchant Navy between the wars. Holder of the Distinguished Service Cross and Distinguished Service Medal, he never spoke of his exploits. But, one of his Wrens told me that he'd captained a destroyer in the Dardanelles Campaign and at Jutland.

He was well into his sixties now but volunteered to come back into the Andrew when we declared war in 1939. And now he's Commandant of the Channel Approaches MGB Squadron. And *Dotty* was lead boat of the 18th MGB Flotilla, one of six such units under Dennis' command.

It didn't take long to give him the grand tour. Barely 75 feet from stem to stern and fifteen feet wide, like all MGBs *Dotty* was small but fast. And so agile, even at forty knots I'd turned her from hard a port to hard a starboard and she'd stayed upright. Well, that wasn't strictly true, her side rails went under the water when we turned at that speed.

More important, her small draft and low superstructure kept her under the radar of most enemy ships. At this stage in the war we had a much more efficient Radar operation than the enemy which made these boats ideal for surprise attacks. The evidence was plain to see. In the last two years my flotilla sank eight enemy warships and eleven merchant ships. Not to mention severely damaging God knows how many others.

Back in the wardroom I poured two pink gins and sat opposite Dennis at the small table.

"I'm sending you a new sub-Lieutenant, name of Hawes. He's good, just promoted from Midshipman with the 25th Flotilla based at Dover. Time for Lieutenant Haywood to earn his stripes."

"Thank you, Sir., that's good news. Haywood's done a great job and will do well with his own command. He's ready but I'll be sorry to lose him, just the same."

"You're not losing him, Harry. In fact, you're losing *Dotty*. We're getting a new breed of MGBs. The latest is 100 feet long. Faster, they reckon fifty knots. Extra guns fore and aft as well. You're taking over a new flotilla, Harry. Twice the size of this one. There's a big push coming before the end of the summer and you'll be part of it. You'll need an extra officer to help you run the show."

He paused as the steward brought in our meals before resuming, but in a quieter tone of voice. He leaned across the table. He told me some things that I already knew, that the war was going badly with U Boats sinking more of our ships in the Atlantic than ever before.

Even the Russian convoys were battered to hell and back. The only time that the U Boats didn't attack them was in bad weather; and the Arctic was known for its bad weather throughout the year. When the U Boats didn't batter the convoys, the weather took over.

"The papers tell the public that the RAF are pasting Germany every night and the Yanks are doing the same by day. But the losses are appalling. Churchill needs a victory to get the country cheering again. And you'll be part of it. Don't know what it is yet but the Prime Minister is keen to take the war at sea to the Germans. We've been on the back foot for too long."

"If we don't know what we'll be doing it's going to be difficult to train and prepare, Sir," I said with a smile on my face that didn't match the ball that formed in my stomach. That's when he dropped the next bombshell.

"I know, Harry. But we'll know soon enough. All I can tell you is that you'll be back in action fully by the summer. The good news is that you'll be based in Newlyn, close to your Mum. Still part of my command, but you'll have twenty four boats with you.

You'll have to train them, get them up to your standards."

We discussed the rest over lunch. More good news: we were getting two weeks leave. And I was getting an extra stripe to go with the job. A full blown Commander with Haywood getting an extra one, too which made him up to Lieutenant Commander.

As I escorted the Old Man off the ship my overriding thought was that you don't look gift horses in the mouth. But, extra stripes and a posting to my home town reminded me that some horses bite and kick. Would this be one of them?

I returned to my cabin and opened the package the Old Man had given me. A sheaf of papers; my orders for the next phase of war.

# Chapter 2    Captain Max Braun in Hamburg

I listened to the old idiots sitting across the railway carriage from me. From the conversation they were obviously veterans of the Great War, and veterans who had lost. They knew nothing about this war. In the end I lost my patience.

"Do you two know anything about this war? The Fuhrer is right. Churchill is quite mad. He is drunk on power and drunk on alcohol. We're beating him on every front. The sooner he surrenders the sooner he can join us to fight the Russians. If you don't agree perhaps I should arrange for the Gestapo to collect you when we arrive?"

They both stared hard at me, but three can play at that game. They left the carriage. I saw them again at the train station and called a police officer over.

"Those two," I pointed, "think that our beloved Fuhrer is mad to fight the British. Perhaps they need enlightening."

I thought he was going to ignore me but I held my hand up towards the Iron Cross at my throat and the Party badge on my uniform tunic before he clicked his heels and stalked off after the two old soldiers.

Half an hour later I walked down the jetty to my new ship. She looked beautiful in the late afternoon sunshine. A bit rust-streaked here and there, but I'd soon have the crew clean her up and paint her. It was irritating that the senior officer hadn't done it already. What was his name, again? That's right, Klopp.

I stopped at the gangway and the sailor on duty came smartly to attention. Traditional salute, though. Not a good start.

"Heil Hitler," I told him and waited. It took a second but at last he returned the proper salute and clicked his heels.

"Captain Braun reporting for duty to take over *Der Condor* and Gruppen 158 Escort Squadron," I said.

"Sir, welcome, Sir."

He called to a sailor on the upper deck who walked down the gangway, hefted my sea bag on to his shoulder and followed me back up to the main deck.

"Where is Commander Klopp?" I asked.

"He's on the Bridge updating the charts, Sir."

I left the sailor to take my bag to my cabin, climbed the internal companionway to the Bridge and walked into the chartroom. You could cut the air with a knife as the room was full of cigarette smoke. The smoker was a young man checking off navigational charts against a list. He was so absorbed in his work he didn't even look up. I coughed and he looked at me and smiled.

"Captain Braun, welcome aboard," he said, proffering his hand.

"Heil Hitler," I replied and he frowned.

""Do you see something puzzling, Commander?"

His smile stayed there, though it seemed frozen in place.

"Not at all, Sir. It's just that we have always used our traditional salute on *Der Condor* and the other ships in the squadron. The Captain was very clear in his standing orders."

"Well, your old Captain isn't here, Commander. He has left and I am in charge. So we will use the party salute in future. Make sure that all crews on all ships in the Squadron know. Punishment will be severe for non-compliance."

I turned and headed back below but felt that we should start off on the right foot.

"All ship's officers to meet in the wardroom in one hour, Commander. Full uniform, of course."

"Some are ashore, Sir. Enjoying a last spot of leave before we sail."

"Any officers missing will be posted as Absent Without Leave and put ashore, Commander Klopp."

I turned to face him and he took his hand from his mouth a little too quickly. It was clear that he was chewing something.

"Also, arrange for all ship's captains to come aboard tomorrow morning at 0800 hours. And if any are on leave, you know what their fate will be."

Once in my cabin I stripped off and showered. Someone once said that the mirror never lies and if that is so, I was proud of the reflection. Even the Fuhrer had said that I was a perfect example of German manhood: six feet tall, blue eyes, blond hair. Not an ounce of fat.

One hour to the minute later I entered the wardroom and Klopp introduced the officers. I had read their files, of course. Each stepped forward in turn and saluted. Properly. Klopp may not be as lax as I thought after all. Time will tell.

One person sat away from the others. I introduced him myself.

"This is Lieutenant Zirk, Gestapo Information Officer. I have asked him to sail with us. He will be my eyes and ears around the ship."

I looked at Klopp, daring him to contradict me. In his Navy the Captain's eyes and ears were the Commander. Not in mine. He said nothing.

Back in my cabin Zirk asked me for my opinion of my officers and I told him bluntly that not all were good Nazi Party sympathisers. However, if they were good at their jobs and did not make their sympathies known I would keep them.

"I agree, Captain. But being good at your job is not enough."

"You worry about their sympathies and report to me, Zirk. I will study their professional abilities. If both are not good enough we will get rid of them when we next dock."

After he left I reflected on what I knew about these men. Klopp seemed OK, perhaps a little soft. The First

Lieutenant seemed efficient. The two other watchkeepers were young, barely in their twenties but keen enough.

The engineers were older and would concentrate on their work below. I knew for a fact that the ship's doctor was a party member. He wore the badge. Time would tell whether these men were worthy of serving in a cruiser like *Condor*.

## Chapter 3     Chief Petty Officer David Williams in Cardiff

*Dear Dave, I've been in too minds about telling you this. Anyway, Mabel said I should. Your Agnes has been seeing another bloke. He stayed overnight every day last week. It might be innocent but when Mabel asked her who he was, she said it was her brother. But, she don't have a brother. Anyway, we thought you should know. All the best*
*Alf.*


That letter. The skipper didn't push it but from the look on his face he didn't believe me when I said it was nothing. Just a letter from the missus. Yes, when I told him that everything was getting on top of her I could have laughed. If I wasn't so bloody angry. She promised after the last time.

Still, two week's leave for everyone, then Cornwall. Skipper wasn't very forthcoming about the new posting. He usually shared what he knew. Ah well, find out soon enough. There's other stuff to sort out right now. If she's been at it again I'll bloody kill her. And him.

As soon as the train pulled into Cardiff train station I picked up my bag, walked off the platform and jumped on a bus. Never used to take half an hour to get from the station to Tiger Bay Docks. But the Germans had bombed the hell out of the city. God knows how many died. Hundreds, probably.

I got off the bus and walked the rest of the way. When I got to our street I couldn't believe it. One side almost disappeared, the other side of the street had gaps where houses used to be. I couldn't see far enough down to the end where we lived. I started running and came across some air raid wardens and fire brigade people. "Ah, it's the Navy come to save us, I do believe," one of them said.

"Too late, Mate. You should have been here two nights ago when they did this. Bastards bombed half the houses. Missed the docks and the ships."

"I live at 287. Left hand side."

The men fell silent and one looked at a list in front of him.

"Mrs Williams?"

"Yes, my wife."

The man looked down again and when he looked up he was frowning.

"There was a man killed. In the garden, he was. She said he was having a fag when the bomb dropped on the house two doors down."

I half ran the rest of the way down the street.

"Hullo, Dave," Alf, the letter writer said as I walked past.

"Thanks for the letter, Alf. Thought I'd come home for a few days. Make sure everything's all right."

I started to walk away.

"He was in the garden, I heard, when the bomb dropped on 283. Bit of bad luck, that."

"Depends what you mean by bad luck. If he was inside now I'd rip his bloody head off."

The door wasn't' locked so I walked down the hall into the kitchen. Nobody there.

"Agnes, are you home?"

There was a thud from upstairs and I took them two at a time. I slammed the bedroom door open and there she was. Alone, on the floor. Stinking of booze.

I picked her up and half carried her into the bathroom. I'd barely got out of the way when she threw up. I left her to it and went back downstairs. She needed to sober up before we could have any sort of conversation.

I put the kettle on, made a pot of tea and looked for the essentials. No bloody milk. What the hell's she been doing? I asked Mrs Jones next door if she had any spare and settled down in the kitchen with the paper.

"I'm sorry, Dave. I didn't know you were coming home. How long you here for?"

It was the following morning. I'd fallen asleep in the chair. At least she'd washed and cleaned herself up. Hope to God she's done the same in the bathroom.

"Who was he, Agnes? The fella who died in the garden."

"Oh, him. Just a bloke from work. His house was bombed last week and he stayed over. Slept in the spare room, of course."

I looked hard at her and she held my stare. She was always good at that.

"I got a letter. One of the neighbours said you'd been seeing someone."

"Nosy bastards. Why don't they mind their own business? You know I wouldn't do anything like that again. I love you, Dave. Come on, let's go upstairs. I've cleaned it all up. Made the bed. And I don't half fancy you. You know what you do to me."

She held out her hand and took mine, running it up the inside of her leg. All the way up, past the stocking tops to where her knickers should have been.

"You always said that I should be ready for you when you get home, Dave. Doesn't that feel ready?"

Back on the train I slept from Cardiff to Bristol. Then joined the Newlyn train and slept all the way down on that, too. Alf must have been wrong, I thought. She was never that good an actress. We did it in every room in the house. Every day. Twice. She was all right was Aggie.

# Chapter 4    Second Officer Annie Lenton at Newlyn in Cornwall

What a dump. Shoreham was bad enough, but this place stinks. I don't mind the smell of diesel, but when it mixed with the fish it was vile. And there was the dust. The local quarry was busier than ever before, producing stone to be taken by ship to the cities being bombed. They used it to rebuild.

All in all, not the prettiest town I'd ever visited. But, like everything else in wartime I'd get used to it.

"Biggest fishing harbour in the South West, second biggest in England," the Old Man told me yesterday, my third day down here.

And Captain Dennis knows his harbours. He'd been in and out of most of them either in the Andrew, as he calls the Royal Navy, or with the Merchant Navy. He's sailed small coasters in and out of this one, carrying stone away from the local quarries to London, Belfast, Cork, Edinburgh. Anywhere that built roads.

I liked working for him from the very first. Professional, courteous, rarely lost his temper and when he did it was time to take cover. When he said that he was moving his base down here, but he would understand if I stayed on the South Coast I didn't hesitate.

"The last thing you need is a new Wren learning the ropes at the same time as you're working up a new flotilla," I told him.

In truth, I love working for him so jumped at the chance to come down here from Shoreham to oversee the establishment and training of our new unit. We worked well together and I also got on with Mrs. Dennis.

"How are your digs, Anne?" he asked.

Never Annie, always Anne or Second Officer Lenton. Very old school, prim and proper, too. So was his wife. Though she was softer. And her friend, Mrs. Scott, seemed like a pleasant lady. More open than her son and so much a Newlyner. She knew so much about the village, its history, people and children. Mrs Dennis and she obviously got on and had known each other for years.

"Robert and I own a little cottage overlooking the harbour," she said when I asked. "We've been coming down here on holiday for many years. The boys grew up on the beach and played with Harry when he was younger."

She invited me round for dinner on my first night, which is when I met Mrs Scott, who coincidentally was a teacher at the local school. They both talked about their sons. Obviously I knew Mrs Scott's son. And I learnt that Mrs Dennis' were also in the Navy. One in submarines, one in destroyers. They seemed like nice boys. Not like my husband.

But that might be unfair. I haven't seen him for over two years. Not since I started at Shoreham.

His posting to the Mediterranean may have changed him. But I somehow doubted it. Once a womaniser always a womaniser, I'm afraid. I knew what I was marrying into. Should have seen it coming. And I haven't exactly been nun-like this last year. That young sub lieutenant from HMS Ark Royal was good fun for a few weeks. And the RAF pilot.

"Tin hats on, Anne, that's the air raid warning," the Old Man broke into my thoughts. "What the hell's going on? It's not even lunchtime. Jerry never attacks during the day."

Captain Dennis and I joined the throng of fishermen running down to the air raid shelter at the end of the quay. Just before I went inside I turned round and looked up. A huge bomber was flying in from the sea. I could see quite clearly those horrible black swastikas on its wings.

The explosion was huge. Well, there were five or six, but the bombs landed at the same time, so it seemed like one. They said later that the water shot high into the air, even higher than the Sea Road at the western end of the harbour. And that was fifty feet above sea level, I'd looked at the map.

The All Clear sounded ten minutes later and we all trooped out. Amazingly, there was little damage. Well, none to the scores of fishing boats tied up along the harbour wall.

"Did they know that oil barge was there?" I asked Captain Dennis as we went back to our office, the smell of burning oil pervading the air and even blocking the smell of fish. Right now I preferred the fish.

His face was grim. No smile, unsurprising as we'd just been attacked by an enemy aircraft. But, there was something else, something in his eyes. He shook his head and said nothing until we were back in the office with the clerks. He beckoned me into his office and closed the door.

"The flotilla starts gathering here tomorrow. Commander Scott collects his new MGB from Appledore shipyard and sails her around Lands End. The other boats follow over the next week or so." I nodded.

"Why did they attack right now. And why sink the oil barge? Do they know that something's starting down here? Has someone let the cat out of the bag?"

I told him that I'd get on to Royal Air Force Intelligence, though I couldn't see how anyone could possibly know about our new flotilla.

"Even Commander Scott's crew won't know their final destination until they leave Appledore tomorrow morning," I reminded him.

He drummed his fingers lightly on his desk, a habit that indicated a high degree of concern, before nodding and telling me to find out if any of the radar stations around the coast got a fix on the plane's course before and after the attack.

"Did you see what sort it was?"

I answered without thinking that it was a Dornier, probably one of the newer ones as it had a slim fuselage.

He stared at me and I felt my face turning red.

"I went out with a fighter pilot for a few weeks in Shoreham. He gave me a few lessons on aircraft recognition," I explained, without adding that I taught him a damn sight more about other things.

"They carry around 2,500 pounds of bombs. Usually 200 or 250 pounds each. So, if he dropped five or six here, he still had another five or six on board."

I walked back to my desk as a sailor came into our hut and said that one of the bombs skidded across the harbour before blowing the front wall off a house.

"Fire Brigade's there now with the ambulance," he added, "I think it might have been Commander Scott's house. If it wasn't it was the one next door."

I sent him back to confirm which house it was and find out if there were any casualties. I thought back to the dinner at the Old Man's house a few nights ago. She'd made an impression on me with her easy conversation and questioning style. The Commander Scott that I knew had certainly inherited his Mothers' deep brown eyes and dark hair but most definitely not her engaging and relaxed manner or smiling eyes.

I hoped that she was all right and it was the house next door before calling RAF Coastal Command Intelligence Section and waiting while they brought their information together.

Once I was sure of the facts I knocked on the Old Man's door and went in.

"RAF Intelligence just called back, Sir. They tracked the Dornier from forty miles out - the course she was flying most likely had her taking off from Guernsey in the Channel Islands."

I relayed the information the RAF had given me. There was enough to indicate that this was a hit and run raid, probably not aimed at our flotilla. When the bomber left Newlyn, it bombed Falmouth Harbour and sank an Air Sea Rescue Launch on her way into harbour through Carrick Roads.

"Everyone died, including a German pilot they picked up from the sea earlier this morning. Poor devil ditched last night after bombing Plymouth."

I paused at that and he tilted his head to one side.

"The house that was bombed. I sent Trenwith back there to find out if there were any casualties."

I stopped as I actually felt my throat constrict. What the hell was that all about? The Old Man was staring at me as tears rolled down my cheeks.

"It was Mrs Scott's house, Sir. They've just taken her body away."

He looked down at his desk.

"War is horrid, Anne. We both know that. Tell the Police that on no account are they to contact Harry. I will tell him when he arrives tomorrow. Let him enjoy one more day before he finds out."

As I opened the door he fired one more question.

"What's the story we're putting about in the local pubs about our flotilla?"

"We're saying that this is a new training base for the channel squadrons. It's quieter down here, not so much traffic. And the coastline's similar to the French coastline."

"Well, we'd best hope they believe it. We can't afford to have our true purpose get out. These chaps are already taking a hell of a risk."

"Do we know what they'll be doing, Sir?"

He shook his head before repeating the same thing he'd said many times in recent weeks.

"And we won't until the last possible moment. Careless talk costs lives. In this case, almost three hundred of them."

## Chapter 5    Fieldmarshal Erwin Rommel at German HQ, North Africa

"Do you see the way they drive those tanks across the sand dunes, Johann?"

"I do indeed, Sir. We have some of the best drivers in the whole of the German Army. They will annihilate the British troops. I almost feel sorry for them."

Johann Keller was a captain, ex-tank man himself. He was a good soldier, always obeyed orders and looked after his men. But, he was no strategist. Left to him we'd drive headlong at the enemy and use sheer force and numbers to overwhelm them. In the process many would die needlessly. And we would lose the battle.

"One thing I have learnt, Captain Keller," I used his rank and surname to make sure he listened and learnt. "One thing that I've learnt fighting the British is that you should never feel sorry for them. You knock them down and they get up and continue fighting. You think you've annihilated them, yet there are still more where they came from. Look at Dunkirk. What happened there?"

He was also too quick to believe the lies written by the Fuhrer's propaganda machine as he demonstrated by repeating their newspaper articles. I shook my head as he said that our Navy didn't attack in sufficient numbers and our air force didn't have enough planes.

"They allowed the Tommies to escape from the beach, Sir. Even though our army had them surrounded and cut off on shore."

He was still young and would perhaps survive the war. But he was my aide and I needed an aide who could think for himself so I thought carefully before reminding him that as I was neither a sailor nor a pilot I couldn't comment. But, as a soldier who's seen many campaigns in Africa as well as Europe what we lacked was belief. Three hundred thousand enemy soldiers escaped from Dunkirk because Churchill believed they could. And the crews of the boats that came from England believed it, too.

"Belief is a powerful tool, Captain Keller.""

I turned in my chair as General Schmidt came in to my tent. He saluted, properly, not the Hitlerite stab in the air, and stood to attention.

"At ease, Wilhelm. Come and sit. Keller, schnapps for the two of us. Then you may go."

When we were alone I relaxed. Schmidt and I had fought together since the start.

"Sometimes I think I'm getting too old for this, Willie." I felt a smile on my lips but I was only half joking.

"Good schnapps, Sir. Fresh from Germany?"

"Yes, my wife had a case sent out. It's a fine reserve."

"Too old you say. What then of me?" he laughed.

"Sixty five next month. You're a mere child, Erwin. I have fifteen years on you. And more important than that is that what you don't know about fighting the British isn't worth knowing. Have you decided when we attack?"

I don't know why, but I didn't want to fully commit to a date. Part of me wanted to wait and see if the Fuhrer would send me the reinforcements I'd asked for two weeks ago. But part of me was also undecided because we needed to win. And win at all costs. Our war was going well, but not well enough.

"Did I tell you what the Fuhrer told me when I was in Berlin last month, Willie?"

He shook his head, savouring the Schnapps. I told him about one of the more bizarre conferences I'd attended, though to be truthful, each one seemed to be stranger than the last. The Fuhrer ended up screaming at me that I should kick the British out of North Africa and drown them in the Mediterranean Sea. He ranted for fifteen minutes. And the Great Admiral Doenitz sat silently all the way through it. After the Fuhrer left Doenitz told me that they relied on me to bring the first real victory in this war. Bombing the English cities wasn't enough to win. Letting so many British soldiers escape from Dunkirk was more than a mistake. It was a humiliation."

"But it was his Navy that failed to stop the evacuation, Erwin," Willie said.

"I reminded him of that and do you know what he said? The Fuhrer thinks otherwise."

We were barely three years into a war that I doubted we would ever win. A war in which the Russians had already changed sides and started fighting against us.

"Those surrounding the Fuhrer, Willie, tell him that the Army is failing to give him the commitment he wants. Right now we're failing in Russia, still haven't destroyed Stalingrad. And Doenitz had the temerity to ask me these questions."

Willie was never an armchair solider. He hated Berlin and the senior staff officers who surrounded Hitler. Men like Doenitz and Himmler. Promoted because they told Hitler what he wanted to hear. I rubbed my fingers across my eyes.

"Come, Willie, look at the plans for our attack. You asked when," I led him to a map laid out across a big desk.

Working my fingers across the map I told him that we would start our attack on 26th May. The date itself had no significance except that it was far enough in the future to give us time to train the men that I hoped the Fuhrer would send in the next two weeks."

"Do we still not know if we're getting them?"

I shrugged my shoulders. I had no idea, even though I had flown back to Berlin to beg for more men and tanks. The enemy had already sent General Auchinleck twenty thousand men and extra tanks. I pointed to the map, at the road that took us across the desert from where we currently stood.

"That is an interesting ridge, just there, Willie. Just behind the enemy lines at Gazala."

"And why is it interesting, Erwin?"

Willie stared hard at it, even moving in until his nose was barely two inches from the desk top.

"Because, my dear Willie, that will be the direction from which we attack."

"But that will take us behind the enemy's lines. And the only way we can do that is to transport our thousands of men on a wide sweep to the south, into the desert."

"Which, my dear General, the British will not be expecting. Here let me explain."

## Chapter 6      Harry Scott in Newlyn

"How many times have you sailed into this harbour, Sir?"

My First Lieutenant asked good questions. Relevant, to the point, always building on what he already knew. Even though we'd sailed together for two years and knew each other well, he, like me, wanted to know more.

As is often the case in these small warships with just three officers aboard you either got on or the ship was damned. In James Haywood's case it was impossible not to like him. Two years younger than me, his boyish features and round face belied his twenty one years. At five feet eight and 160 pounds he was shorter yet almost a stone heavier than me. But the most striking physical differences were his blue eyes and red hair. God knows I had my own problems following *Dotty's* sinking off Dunkirk. My confidence was badly damaged, and at times I still doubted my own ability to command Yet, this was nothing compared to James'. He was blown up on his first ship, thankfully not bad enough to beach him. But the left side of his face bore the scars of deep burns. No amount of surgery could remove them.

"I've lost count, James," I replied. "Hundreds, probably, but always under sail."

I looked across the harbour and pointed towards a pub that stood fifty feet above our present position. The Fishermans Arms was my local and Mother and I always had lunch there on a Saturday. James and the Coxswain followed my gaze.

"There's an old harbour wall just below the pub. That's the Old Quay and my old Whaler is moored alongside it. We'll take her out if we get a chance. Cox, how long since you sailed a Whaler?"

"Longer than you've been in uniform, Sir. When I was at Sea School, I reckon, a long time ago. But you don't forget. They're lovely boats to sail."

I let my eyes travel the length of the old harbour wall and frowned.

"They've been bombed," I said looking at a gap where my Mum's front wall should have been.

I looked down the harbour almost to the end, the Royal Navy's moorings.

"Steer for the pontoon, Coxswain. Looks like we've got a welcome committee. Hope the Old Man hasn't brought that bloody Lenton woman down with him. Number One, men to the side, if you would."

I heard the Coxswain ordering his men to the bow and stern for coming alongside. And another group to the ship's side to welcome Captain Dennis and whoever else he had with him.

As we got closer I groaned.

"I do believe that Captain Dennis has brought Second Officer Lenton along with him, Sir."

I glared at the Coxswain, but with a smile.

"I thought he would. She's his right arm. And I have to say, as much as she looks down her nose at me, she is a good clerk."

My crewmen pulled our lines taut and I looked over my shoulder towards the stern of the boat. There was always that split second when the propellers were still turning, and we had three of the damned things, when you dreaded a badly handled rope wrapping itself around them. The pressure rose still further when you had an audience as you came alongside. Like now.

But, David Williams was a fine Coxswain and trained his men well. Harsh, he most definitely was, but fair. Unless one of his men crossed him deliberately. Then he used his six foot one-inch frame and one hundred and eighty pounds of muscle to set an example.

And that frame had come in useful ashore, too. I'd seen it in action. Not a pretty sight, and the sailor concerned, who was from a destroyer and had taken a dislike to one of our sailors stayed in hospital when his ship sailed.

"I know Morrison can be an idiot at times," Williams told me afterwards. "But when he's drunk he's a likeable drunk. And that matelot from *Illustrious* tried to break a bottle over his head. When he wasn't even looking."

I witnessed the incident and when the Shore Patrol tried to arrest the Coxswain I stepped in and told them what really happened. Which meant that I kept the Coxswain on board and he stayed out of prison.

I walked to the side and stood to attention as the Coxswain piped the Captain aboard.

"Welcome to Newlyn, Commander. You know Second Officer Lenton, of course."

I nodded towards her. She seemed different, somehow. Red eyes as though she'd been crying. Unusually she smiled, though it seemed forced.

"I'll take these charts to the First Lieutenant, Sir. Tell him where I've got to with the corrections."

She stepped across the rail and put her right foot on the deck where one of our mooring lines lay, dripping water on to the planks. Most of us wore boots with good thick, gripping souls. Shiny black uniform shoes had no grip. Which Lenton demonstrated when her foot slipped.

I stepped forward and grabbed her shoulder with one hand and the briefcase with the other.

"Sorry, Miss Lenton, we should have dried that up." When I looked into her face I knew that she'd been crying. Deep brown eyes, but red rimmed.

"Thank you, Sir. I should have looked before I stepped over the rail."

She took the case from me and looked directly into my eyes.

Later after they left, I told James about my Mother and asked him to keep an eye on things while I went ashore, back to where my home used to be. Some of it was still there and one of the neighbours said that a local builder had already inspected it and declared it fit to be repaired.

I had my doubts, but knew little about construction. I did know a lot about destruction, though and wasn't shocked at how much damage a single bomb could do. We were three years into the war and I'd seen plenty of ships wrecked, burning, sinking, men dying, men with lungs ruined for ever by oil and saltwater.

But, this was different. It was the house where I was born, where I lived, where I came back to spend my leave. After my Father died it was home to just the two of us. Now, it was home no longer. She was dead.

The builder returned and secured a tarpaulin along the front of the house. I walked inside and started tidying up, but soon gave up and walked down to Peakes, the undertakers.

"She's in the Chapel down there, Harry. You can go visit," Dicky Peake told me.

He'd buried my Dad after his accident and all my grandparents. Hardly surprising as he was the only full time undertaker in the village. One or two of the local builders did it as a side-line but Dicky put most of the dead villagers into the ground.

I looked down at my Mum. She looked asleep. Her hair was soft, brown, and neatly brushed. Her eyes closed, her skin pale. I stayed for twenty minutes and let the tears fall.

"Never had the chance to stay goodbye, Dicky," I said as he opened the door for me.

"I saw her day before yesterday, Harry. She told me you were coming home. She was so proud of you." He paused. I wasn't the only one who'd lost her. She was his sister as well as my Mother. His shoulders shook as I held him tight.

"It's war, Dicky. Doesn't make it any easier. But it makes it all the more important that we end it as soon as we can."

"Go kill them, Harry. For her and for us."

## Chapter 7    Prime Minister Winston Churchill in The War Rooms, London

I often wonder how the Cabinet Secretary manages to look so young. He's the same age as me after all and sixty-seven isn't old, although I feel at times closer to a hundred. Whereas Sir William looks barely fifty. He must have led a clean and sheltered life.

"You've seen the latest despatches from North Africa, Sir? Not good reading, if I may say so. We really could do with a win."

"I know, Cabinet Secretary, and it's deeply troubling." I looked up as the Chief of the Imperial General Staff entered the room. Why does the Army keep such verbose ranks and titles? What is wrong with plain General?

"Sir Alan. Good of you to come over. The latest news from General Auchinleck is not good," I said as I re-lit my cigar.

"No, Sir, it isn't. He's asked for another ten thousand troops and more armour. We simply don't have it. I spoke on the long distance telephone to him late last night. He is deeply concerned at the way that Rommel's marshalling his forces."

"What reinforcements can we get to him, General?" the Cabinet Secretary asked.

"Probably five thousand men, a hundred tanks and two hundred pieces of heavy field artillery. Another month and I could have doubled that. But we simply don't have the men and equipment available right now."

What exacerbated our situation in North Africa was a lack of decent air power and enemy superiority at sea. In the air, the RAF's heavy bombers weren't manoeuvrable enough for the close bombing needed to attack enemy positions at low heights.

And although our lighter aircraft were, our production lines couldn't keep pace with demand. In short, pre-war government short-sightedness and a lack of peace-time arms production meant that we started the war in a pitifully weak state and were still catching up.

I poured a small brandy and sipped at it. A thought was nagging away at the back of my mind but I couldn't grasp it.

"When do our agents expect Rommel to attack?" I asked, desperately searching for the elusive notion.

Sir Alan's view was that it would be within a month.

"*Enigma* messages between Russia, Berlin and Rome all say the same thing, Winston. Hitler wants a fast build-up of troops in Russia so he can destroy Russian resistance and transfer some of his best troops out of the North to reinforce Rommel in Africa."

*Enigma*, one of the few successes we'd had so far. When we captured the enemy coding machine it gave us the ability to decipher their military messages. Not all of them, but enough to give us a strength in intelligence that would soon turn the war in our favour. If *Enigma* said it was happening, it was happening.

"He'll have enough troops in place by the middle of May to launch a prolonged attack. Probably two weeks, maybe more."

I walked across the room to the wall map and slapped my walking stick across Egypt.

"If we can't beat Rommel in May, can we hold him for long enough to mount a counter attack later in the year? Say in September, even October when we'll have reinforcements a'plenty?"

The General stepped up beside me.

"If I may speak freely, Winston?"

"Of course."

He told me that our most senior officer in Africa was close to exhaustion.

"He told me himself, Winston. He's done well to hold the line as he has done, but tiredness often leads to mistakes."

This wasn't news to me, but the situation had deteriorated since we last spoke about it. The Auk, as he was known affectionately to his troops and in the press, had surprised us by defending the British positions against a much larger force. In the process he'd taken ground from the Germans. But it was clear from Sir Alan's tone that this could not continue.

"Do you have a replacement in mind?"

He said that the obvious choice was General Gott, the Auk's second in command who'd spent most of the war in the desert, but the idea of a change in command at this time concerned me. I said as much and he agreed.

"My choice would be late summer. Rommel will have attacked, we will more than likely have lost ground, but with his extra five thousand troops the Auk will hold Rommel."

"How much ground will we lose when Rommel next attacks?"

The old soldier looked decidedly awkward when he replied.

"We've been studying this for the past week and the news isn't good. But it could be a lot worse. We'll lose Tobruk. But if the Auk can hold the ground to the East, we'll stop Rommel in his tracks."

I could have wept. Tobruk. What a message to give to the British people. Singapore gone, the Japanese everywhere in the Far East. Germany marching through the Near East as though they owned it. Enemy bombers attacking our cities every night, U Boats pounding the hell out of our Merchant and Royal Navies. Stalin calling for reinforcements on the Russian Front.

"Yes, that's it," I shouted.

Sir Alan looked at me.

"If we hold Rommel, he'll call for reinforcements. Where will they come from?"

I answered my own question, repeating our own conversation minutes earlier. It was obvious that Hitler could only reinforce Rommel from Russia. The Fuhrer needed victory in North Africa.

"Rommel will attack us soon, Alan," I continued "and will gain ground, taking Tobruk in the process. We should plan to let him have it. But, after Tobruk, the Auk should choose his spot to stop and to defend. More important, to bring Rommel to a halt in the sand."

I warmed to my theme as the idea gained form in my mind. The Fuhrer was mad for a victory and it could only come in the desert and could only happen after he was sure about victory in Russia. With Stalingrad secure, he would release troops for North Africa.

"There is Italy, of course, Winston. Mussolini will have troops to spare."

"But how many, General? Not many, a few thousand at most. Most of his men are already in North Africa. We let Rommel take Tobruk, but then stop him dead. He'll need reinforcements to break out. Without them, he's stuck. But we'll be reinforcing our own Army while he's waiting for his."

"But what happens when Hitler transfers troops from the Russian Front?"

"Stalin will counter attack and push the Germans back. And we will destroy the reinforcements before they reach Egypt."

It sounded easy when I said it, straight forward, achievable. The looks on the faces of the Chief of the Imperial General Staff and the Cabinet Secretary said otherwise. In fact, I felt a little less confident in the success of such a venture than I sounded. Then again, deep down, I never doubted that we would save over three hundred thousand troops from Dunkirk in the dark hours of 1940.

"If we can save an entire Army from the clutches of the Germans we can destroy a few enemy ships in the Mediterranean Sea, gentlemen. That," I added, "is not an opinion by the way. It is an order."

## Chapter 8    Scotty in Newlyn

The funeral seemed to last forever. I carried the coffin, along with Uncle Dicky and four of his pall bearers. It was light, much lighter than I anticipated and I fancied I could smell her perfume on the wood.

After the service we drove her up to Paul Churchyard. Even in summer it was a bleak place with gates creaking as we carried the coffin through.

Afterwards we drove back into Newlyn and held the wake in the Fishermans Arms. It was the pub that I'd used since before I was old enough to drink. And where my Mother and I always went when I came home on leave. The locals were shocked at a woman being a regular customer, but they always made her welcome. As a teacher at the local school she knew all the customers - they were to a man and woman either parents or grandparents to her pupils.

Later I walked back down to the harbour and stopped at Captain Dennis' office.

"Is he in?" I asked Lenton.

"He's gone up to Portsmouth. Said they were trying to steal some of your new boats and he was damned if he'd let them get away with it," she told me before adding, "I am terribly sorry, about your Mother, Sir. I had dinner with her and Captain and Mrs Dennis just after I arrived. She made me feel very welcome in Newlyn. If funerals can be nice, though, her's was somehow, I don't know, nice."

"You were there?"

"Yes. I felt that I should. I hope you don't mind, Sir."

"No, of course not. I didn't see you. Were you alone?"

She said that she'd sat in the back row as she didn't feel that she had the right to be anywhere else. She sat forward in her chair and told me how the people around her chatted to each other after we'd left for the burial.

"Your Mother was very popular in the village. Before you arrived and after you left the people around me said so many things. I wish I could have known her better."

"Thank you, Miss Lenton. I appreciate that. She always saw the good in people. Goes with being a teacher, I suppose."

"Not always," she replied. "In fact, rarely. In my experience the truly good people always see the good first. It's the others who don't."

I nodded, wanting to avoid any further conversation. But that was not to be. Before he left the Old Man told her to brief me about the new flotilla while he was away so we could all get stuck in straight away. She smiled and I fancied that the smile was borne out of sympathy more than humour.

"If you don't feel up to it now, we could do it in the morning. He won't be back until later afternoon."

I groaned and she smiled again, this time I saw the humour in her eyes. Actually, she had a very pleasant smile and her eyes were deep brown, I could almost see my reflection in them.

"Actually, I could do with something else to think about. Let's go over it now."

For the next hour or so we sat in the Captain's office while Miss Lenton demonstrated, without realising, just how important she was to the Old Man. She had an infinite grasp of detail. Every question I asked, she replied to immediately or by going straight to a place in one file or another.

"You, your First Lieutenant and Sub Lieutenant need a refresher navigation course."

She told me that our new equipment was much more sophisticated than anything we were used to. A RADAR set that sees over thirty miles, a new navigation system that helps us plot a course without referring constantly to charts. And we'll have direct control of our engines from the wheelhouse and flying bridge. No more relying on the engineers to respond quickly when we're under fire and operating at speed."

"You know more about *Dotty* than I do," I said.

*"Dotty?"*

And I had to tell her about Able Seaman Morrison's notion of calling our boats after his favourite film star. She laughed. The first time I'd seen her laugh and it lit her face up. Maybe I didn't know this woman at all. I had thought her to be serious, distant, aloof.

She was looking at me.

"I'm sorry, I was miles away, Miss Lenton. Please forgive me," I told her.

"I will. You don't have to call me Miss Lenton. My friends call me Annie."

"Do you have many friends down here? You haven't been here long, have you?"

"It's difficult to make friends when you work for Captain Dennis. He is quite driven. There's not a lot of free time."

I was about to continue when the Coxswain walked in.

"Sorry to interrupt, Sir. Number One's ashore and the new Sub thought it best to check with you.

Harbourmaster wants us to move the boat fifty yards up the pontoon. Says all the boats can moor together if we're bow to stern and right up against each other. Helps him keep us apart from the fishing boats, too, he says."

"Right, Cox, I'll be there. Carry on."

I turned to Lenton.

"Sorry, is there much more to go through?"

"No, Sir, almost finished. Another half hour if you get a chance tomorrow morning. I'm here all day, so whatever time suits you best."

I told her that I'd be back later in the morning and returned to *Dotty*, where I donned a thick roll neck sweater beneath my uniform jacket. A chill wind blew across the harbour and it was getting colder by the minute.

"Single up fore and aft, Coxswain."

I looked at the bow where AB Morrison was looping a mooring line over his wrist before coiling it on the desk.

"Let go fore and aft. Morrison get that rope on the capstan and start heaving."

The theory was simple. One sailor on the pontoon at the stern holding a line tight so that the back end stayed close alongside. While Morrison, who had already secured a mooring line to a cleat further up the pontoon, attached the other end of the rope to the boat's capstan and fired that up to pull the boat along to its new position.

Easy in theory but also dangerous if you lose concentration. Which Morrison did as a Wren cycled by on the pier above. His eyes followed the movement of the Wren's legs on the pedals and he momentarily let the rope go slack.

Realising what he'd done he grabbed the rope too hard and a coil slipped off the capstan, went bar taut, parted under the pressure and threw him over the boat's side. Just as one of the fishing boats backed away from its mooring ahead of us and headed stern and propellers first towards him. My crew shouted at the trawler and pointed at the water, but the boat continued on its course.

"They're going to kill him," a sailor shouted which was when I dived overboard and grabbed Morrison's hair; the only bit of him above the surface. He thrashed around like an octopus in a fisherman's net, legs and arms everywhere, grabbing at my nose, eyes, mouth.

I heaved his face clear of the water and kicked out with both legs to get clear of the stern of the trawler, which was barely a foot away. Thankfully, someone on their bridge put their engine from astern to full ahead when one of my crew fired our deck gun to attract their skipper's attention.

"I've got you, Morrison, you're OK."

Which was when he went limp. I swam him back to the boat and willing hands reached down to drag him up on to the deck. I climbed up after him.

"He's not breathing, Sir. I don't think he's breathing," Williams said.

I knelt on the deck and put my face next to Morrison's. No movement, no sound, no breath. I rolled him on to his front and knelt on his back. I'd seen this done, but never done it myself. I placed my hands on his back and forced all my weight down on them before releasing the pressure and repeating. Time after time, I lost count. At last I heard a choking noise and what looked like half of Newlyn Harbour spewed out of his mouth.

I rolled him on to his side and he opened his eyes.

"Am I alive, Sir?" he asked.

"You're alive, Morrison. We'll get you under a warm blanket and get you checked over at the hospital."

I stood and looked down at the water dripping off my uniform.

"Ruined, I think, Sir. I'll arrange for replacements to be sent down."

Second Officer Lenton turned and walked up the quay.

## Chapter 9     Lieutenant Commander James Haywood at Newlyn Hospital

I'm not keen on hospitals, never have been. Too many reminders of people who are sick or dying. Well, more accurately, I'd spent more than my fair share of time in them while they patched my face up.

But, the ambulance crew who took Morrison to West Cornwall Hospital in Newlyn said it was a small place and not like the hospitals where they treated my burns. I walked down a short corridor and on to the men's ward.

"I'm looking for Able Seaman Morrison," I said to one of the nurses on duty.

"End bed on the left. He's perked up a bit since they brought him in," she told me as she walked down the ward beside me to the bed next door. She smiled as she drew the curtains round an old man lying there staring sightlessly at the ceiling.

"Wotcher, Sir. Good of you to visit. Those grapes for me?"

I handed Morrison the grapes and pulled a chair up to the bed.

"You were bloody lucky, Morrison. You need to keep your mind on the job and your eyes off the Wrens."

"Sorry, Sir. Couldn't help it. Is everyone else all right?"

"No thanks to you. You almost got yourself and the Skipper killed."

I could hear the nurse talking in a soothing voice to her patient before there was a phlegm-laden cough and silence descended. She asked if he was OK. I tried to turn my mind away from that cubicle and told Morrison what the skipper had done.

"I wasn't there but from what I've been told if the Skipper hadn't jumped in when he did you'd be dead.

That trawler had no idea you were in the water. You were already under the surface when he jumped in after you," I told him.

The Coxswain told me what happened and I recounted it to Morrison. By this time he'd swallowed so much water that he simply stopped breathing but we'd been told of a new technique to help sailors who'd been in the water for some time and the skipper practised it on his crewman.

"He kept pressing on your back until you spewed a load of Newlyn Harbour seawater up."

The sailor said nothing, but stared down at his hands.

"I'm sorry, Sir. I messed up. I owe him big-style. What with his Mum dying and all. I let him down. And you and the Coxswain," the boy said.

And a mere boy he was. Hostilities Only rating, recruited for war time service, not time served like the Skipper, me or the Coxswain. Jesus, poor kid.

I patted him on the shoulder and told him not to worry, that his wasn't the first life that Scotty had saved.

"What do you mean?"

I picked up a grape and chewed on it for a few seconds. What I was about to say could do a lot for crew discipline, one way or the other. But it wasn't fair to kids like Morrison to carry guilt about a simple mistake along with all the pressures he had to deal with whenever we went to sea.

"You joined *Dotty* just before Dunkirk, Morrison. I joined just after if you recall."

He nodded and I suspect we both thought back to those days in 1940 when Scotty was shaking down a new boat with a new First Lieutenant.

I'd come straight from a destroyer, and it was my first posting as a Lieutenant. I had so much to learn, but Scotty was always a good and patient teacher.

"We'd been out on a few raids when we got a day's leave," I told Morrison as my mind travelled back almost two years. A shiver still ran down my spine when I thought about that night. We hadn't talked about it with anyone since, not even between the two of us. We had an unwritten agreement that it happened and we moved on.

I scratched my face, a sure sign that I was tense, which I was whenever I thought back to the night.

"We'd had a few beers, it was the first time for ages that we weren't night duty boat," I said.

I felt the sweat running down my body as the memories returned. We were in a dockside pub, a few doors down from the local hospital. The bombers came out of nowhere, no air raid sirens going off.

Lieutenant Commander Scott, as he was then, and I heard the unmistakable roar of the engines above us as we finished our last pint of ale.

"The first bomb fell and landed on a house a few doors down," I said and Morrison sat up in bed. I picked at a grape and chewed it slowly.

"What happened next, Sir?"

I told him that the next million bombs, or that's what it felt like, hit the local hospital across the road. It was carnage. We ran out of the pub and heard screams all round. Bells rang as the fire brigade arrived, then the Police and the ambulances.

I looked up and saw a nurse on a window ledge two floors up, flames licking at the window behind her silhouetting her perfectly. There was a rusty old fire escape ladder pinned to the wall close by her and she was making for it.

"Go on, you can do it," the skipper shouted and she froze as she reached a hand out.

"I can't do it. I can't let go, I'm scared," she screamed. Next thing Scotty's shinning up this ladder like a bloody monkey. He got level with her and stretched his hand out, looking direct into her eyes. She was only a kid, barely out of her teens. I don't know what he said, but she stretched her arm out towards him, moved her foot a little and slipped. Harry took all her weight on one arm, the other clinging on to the ladder.

Even now I could hardly bear to think about it. I hated heights, always avoided going up the mast, and if I did I shook like someone with fever for hours afterwards. Scotty shouted down for me to help as she hung there in mid-air, her feet and legs flapping round. He couldn't move, not up not down. He could hold her but not for long.

Thank God the firemen got a ladder up to them and grabbed her while he climbed back down.

And do you know what, Morrison? He didn't say a word. Except to pat me on the shoulder when he got to the ground and say it's OK, James. I knew I could hold her till the fire brigade arrived. Didn't want you up there, as well. The ladder couldn't have held us both. You see, he knew I didn't have a head for heights. I told him when I first joined and he never forgot."

Morrison lay back down. He'd had a traumatic couple of days. I stood and put my cap on.

"We all make mistakes, Morrison. You'd best get some sleep. You'll be back with us soon enough."

I walked away from his bed.

"Number One," he said quietly. I turned around.

"Thank you for telling me. I'll not tell anyone else."

I gave him a wave and started walking back towards the door.

"Lieutenant Commander," the nurse said as I walked past the bed next door. "Was that really true?"

I nodded and she closed the curtain behind her.

"Dead?" I asked and she nodded.

"Cancer, we knew it wouldn't be long. It ravaged his body. Even took part of his face away."

She looked at me and smiled, looking directly at my own face and the scar that ran around the edge of my hairline.

"That doesn't look like cancer. More like burns?"

"Yes. I was lucky. I survived. Though sometimes I wonder if I really was lucky."

What she did next surprised me. She was shorter than me, and I'm not tall. But she gently took my cap off and looked directly at the scar. No woman has ever done that. Except the nurses who treated me.

"I suppose you've seen worse," I said.

She shook her head.

"No. But I'm glad."

"About what?"

"That you survived."

She replaced my cap at exactly the angle I wore it.

"Does it itch?" she asked.

"Yes, sometimes."

She stopped at a trolley and rummaged around.

"This is really good stuff. I heard one of our doctors telling a lady who'd burnt her hands that it stopped the itching and helped cool the scar tissue down."

I had no idea what to say as she walked down the ward with me.

"Your skipper must be something else," she said.

"All that and more, Nurse. Commander Scott's the best skipper I've ever sailed with. And he buried his Mum yesterday."

She looked down at the floor and I thought I heard a sob.

"I didn't realise that's who he was. Life can be so unfair, she said. "She taught me at Junior School."

## Chapter 10    Scotty in Newlyn

I spent half an hour with Second Officer Lenton going over the last of the records and requisitions we needed to build the flotilla.

"Thanks for your time, Miss Lenton," I said and she smiled.

I smiled back.

"Sorry, Annie."

She reached beneath her desk and passed me a parcel.

"Replacements for the uniform you ruined saving AB Morrison," she said.

The door flew open and Captain Dennis strode in.

"Commander, Miss Lenton. Glad you're both here. Got some information to share with you. Just between us at this stage. Nothing must get out."

He walked to a filing cabinet and took out a bottle of gin.

"A little celebration, I think. Managed to stop the Admiral from pinching our boats."

He poured three generous measures, opened a bottle of tonic and told me that I'd be going back to war soon. Before that I had to mould my boats into one single unit.

"All twenty three of them will arrive in the next few days, all part of a new Air Sea Rescue unit. That's the word going round the village, anyway."

"ASR, Sir? But we're clearly all armed to the teeth. And we're Royal Navy not RAF."

"Details, my dear Harry, details."

He paused to sip at his drink.

"Maud told me about the funeral when I telephoned her last night. Sorry I couldn't make it. Your Mother was a fine woman, Harry. The best."

He cleared his throat, the closest I'd seen him come to showing grief. Then again, he'd known her longer than I had.

"The RAF are withdrawing their boats from Newlyn as of tomorrow, so you'll do a few rescues in between training," he said, getting back into his stride and on to safer ground.

I took a sip of gin myself. I didn't like to tell the Old Man that I preferred beer. Wouldn't do at all for a Royal Navy officer to admit such a thing. He asked Annie if I was now fully briefed on the state of my new flotilla and she confirmed that we'd spent most of the last two days going over every detail.

She paused to sip at her gin and I took over, recounting what Annie had drummed into me. Twenty-four boats, five of them fresh off the stocks like *Dotty*, the others all refurbished and kitted out with two guns each fore and aft, heavy duty Oerlikon anti-aircraft abaft the wheelhouse, eight depth charges and four torpedo tubes. And all with the latest in radar, Asdic and navigational equipment."

Annie smiled across the table, clearly pleased that she hadn't wasted her time. Probably surprised, too.

"And you'll need all that before this war's over," the Captain interrupted.

We spent another ten minutes going over the flotilla's strength before the Old Man took a stack of files out of his briefcase.

I looked over them briefly, files on each of the skippers and their crews. Some pretty heavy reading, but it was the only way of getting to know these people before they arrived.

"Some good men in there," the Old Man said.

"And a few not so good, but beggars can't be choosers these days. I've done my best to weed out the real duffers, but couldn't get rid of them all. You'll make your own mind up."

He walked over to a map on the office wall.

"The north coast of Cornwall. From Lands End up as far as Bude. This is your new stomping ground. Where you'll put the flotilla through its paces."

"Bit open, Sir. Convoys up and down, in and out of Liverpool, Bristol, Cardiff, Glasgow. Not to mention Belfast."

"Precisely. That's why we're down here in Newlyn. We've got two months at the outside to be ready."

"Ready for what, Sir? I have no idea what I'm supposed to be planning for."

"Don't know yet," he said, taking another sip of gin and telling me that we would practise closing in on convoys without being spotted. And if we were spotted, our job was to get away without being tracked.

"But if we close in on our own convoys the escort vessels will open fire. Surely we can announce our intentions beforehand?"

"No, Commander Scott, you most certainly cannot. The whole point of the training is to get in, attack and get out before anyone knows you've been there."

I studied the map and guessed at distances. The Irish Sea was over a hundred miles wide at that point and Germany had spies up and down the Irish coastline. But, our convoys usually sailed close in to our coastline so we' could train somewhere in between the two countries but conduct fake attacks nearer English soil when we were ready.

The Old Man brought me back from my thoughts.

"Remember that the Royal Navy escort ships are particularly vigilant on this last leg of the journey with homeward bound convoys."

"And even more so with the outward bound convoys, Sir."

I walked slowly back through the streets of Newlyn. Twenty four MGBs, thirteen crew to a boat. Over three hundred men. All my responsibility. Good God above. I was just about managing my own life and boat. Even the six boats in my last flotilla occasionally proved to almost too much.

The streets were quiet. It was that time of the evening before the pubs opened when families were having their evening meal. The smells of home cooking permeated the air, mixing with the smells of diesel from the harbour and the day's catch from the fish market.

I found myself outside my Mother's house. My home. Looked as though the builder had come back.

Tarpaulin over the front as it was, but rubble piled in a heap waiting to be moved.

I suppose this would be mine now. Did I want it? Did I even want to stay in Newlyn now there was nobody left to come home to?

## Chapter 11    General Auchinleck at British Army HQ, Tobruk in the North African Desert

"Any messages, Smitty?" I asked as I walked into the tent.

"None, Sir. Well, nothing from Blighty. Couple of messages from General Gott. Could you telephone him when you're free, Sir? He's concerned about Rommel's build up. Wants to attack before the Germans attack him."

I felt my eyes raise to the ceiling. This wasn't India. You didn't go half arsed into attacking a soldier like Rommel. That was the trouble with Gott. Too used to fighting rebels with the Indian Army. Not fighting strategists who'd never lost a battle.

"I'll talk to him later. How well prepared do you think Rommel is right now?"

Smitty, or Colonel The Honourable Laurence Smith to give him his full name, walked over to the wall map.

"At the moment, according to our agents, he has seventy thousand men," he replied before going into the detail.

And he did detail well. All Rommel's men were experienced desert fighters, mostly German, but with four thousand Italians. Crack troops, not rubbish. He saved the best news to last.

"On top of that we estimate that he's got two hundred tanks, almost all of them Panzers."

I didn't doubt the intelligence. By this stage of the war we had a good network of spies, much better than when we started. When we added their intelligence to what *Enigma* gave us we could double check every piece of intelligence that came our way.

*Enigma*, Germany's code machine, certainly gave us an edge, the more so as the enemy didn't know that our boffins at Bletchley broke their codes and could decipher transmissions between the enemy's Army and

Navy headquarters on the one hand and the European countries they occupied on the other."

I sat back and thought about one other point. Whereas Rommel was getting reinforcements, we would not. The Chief of the General Staff was very clear when we last spoke.

"No reinforcements, old Man. Churchill is against it," he said. "We have to let Rommel think he's winning. It's the only way to give us the time to build up your troops and artillery."

Smitty and I walked across the parade ground to the Officers' Mess tent where my most senior officers gathered.

"We're getting reinforcements, Gentlemen," I said and they all smiled.

"But, not until July. We have to fight with what we've got."

They all started talking at once and I held my hand up for silence.

"We're getting the new Sherman tanks. The Americans have committed to sending us one hundred and fifty, but they won't be ready for whatever Rommel throws at us in the next month or so. We'll also get another twenty thousand troops. Some from India, Australia and New Zealand, the rest from Blighty as they come out of training."

"But not yet," one of my Colonels said quietly.

I smiled.

"That's' right, Hopkins, not yet. July."

"Gentlemen, we will beat Rommel. We will win the war. But to do it, we may have to lose a battle or two first. Let me explain."

# Chapter 12    Rommel at German HQ, North African Desert

We were barely a hundred miles from the British front line. Yet, if I am to succeed, many of my troops and tanks will have to travel over twice that distance to catch General Auchinleck unawares.

He is a good fighter and a fine strategist. But, he is tired, according to my spies, and needs a rest. The Auk, they call him. Not to his face, though. A strange nickname for an Englishman. Auk is old Germanic.

"Sir, we have a despatch from Berlin," Keller said.

"Ask General Schmidt to come in."

I held the letter in my hand. What would this one tell me? The Fuhrer's seal was etched on the envelope which meant that he personally authorised the contents.

"Good news or bad, Sir?" General Schmidt asked as he poured us each a glass of Cognac.

I sniffed mine. A deep sniff.

"Hine XO?" I asked.

Willie nodded, sniffing his at the same time. I rolled the brandy snifter around letting the deep bronze-coloured liquid ooze down the sides of the glass. I sniffed again and caught the hints of vanilla and oak.

"You can't rush a good cognac, Willie. How does it look, how does it smell. And of course, most important of all, how does it taste?"

I savoured and Willie beat me to it.

"I can taste toffee mixed with a hint of fresh fruit," he said.

I placed my glass on the table and slit open the envelope. If it was bad news we would share another brandy. If it was good news we would do the same.

"Four typed sheets of paper. All I wanted was a straight yes or no."

I read and smiled. I felt myself nodding.

"I take it back, Willie. It seems that Berlin do understand how important our campaign is."

I passed him the letter and rang the bell on my desk. Captain Keller knocked and entered.

"Johann, I would like to meet with all my generals tomorrow morning at 0700 hours. Please see to it."

Twenty thousand troops the letter said. I didn't know we had that many in reserve. Why haven't we had them before? We could have ended the campaign by now. Oh that our leaders understood the way wars should be fought.

Sadly, they believed that they would win by starving Churchill out and by sinking his Merchant Navy. If that didn't work, they would bomb his cities. Why didn't they understand that with America in the war neither of those strategies was possible.

I sipped some more brandy.

"They haven't said when they'll arrive. The last time I was in Berlin I told them exactly what was needed. Troops on the ground. Lots of soldiers, lots of tanks, lots of field guns. Heavy field guns. But guns that are mobile, that we can pull into place easily and deploy quickly."

"Twenty thousand extra troops," Willie said as he read the letter again.

"Many of them battle hardened soldiers from the Russian Front. They'll love the Mediterranean climate after that."

"Yes, Willie. And two hundred panzer tanks and a whole regiment of field artillery pieces." This was our moment. The next time we fight, we win. And win on Egyptian soil.

I walked outside to watch as the sun dipped below the horizon.

In less than a month I will raise the German flag in Tobruk. Nothing can stop me now. Provided the troops arrive in time.

## Chapter 13    Scotty in Newlyn

It was good to feel the engines running, the vibrations pulsating up through the deck, the lines taut fore and aft as Number One pushed the throttles fully forward then aft. Full Ahead to Full Astern. I watched the mooring lines tense as the immense pressures of holding the MGB to the land increased.

Haywood turned and smiled.

"Smooth as butter, Sir. I ran them up to 3,500 horsepower. Felt fine. Let's see what CPO Shaw makes of them."

Chief Petty Officer Shaw, our chief mechanic, hauled himself though the watertight door and into the cockpit.

"Marvellous, Sir. All three engines running like clockwork."

He turned to the First Lieutenant.

"You could have pushed a bit harder, Number One. Or were you worried that your lot hadn't tied the knots right on the mooring lines?"

Haywood laughed.

"Chief, the ropes were strong enough to lift the Titanic off the sea bed. I was worried about you chaps down below. Didn't want you burning all three engines out before we'd even left harbour."

Unusually, for commissioned and non-commissioned officers from different departments the two men got on well. When the Royal Navy Shore Patrol reported them for fraternising - they were drinking together in a local pub - I told them to go to hell. What my men did off watch was their own affair and mine.

"Right, Number One, time to go to sea. Well done, Chief. Engines in good order as is the rest of the boat."

He nodded and climbed down the short ladder to the engine room. Fifteen feet from the wheelhouse roof to the keel. Not like a destroyer or, God forbid, a battleship with ten or more different ladders to scale. If you fell here you'd be bruised. Fall down the ladders of *HMS Warspite* and you'd break your neck.

"Hands to stations for leaving harbour," the Coxswain announced over the PA system, after which he piped the same message. It may be 1942, but old traditions like the pipe were important in the Andrew. They gave us all a sense of belonging, of consistency, history and comfort.

The First Lieutenant left to supervise two crewmen on the after deck and our new Sub Lieutenant, Alfred Hawes, walked uncertainly up to the bow. I called him back and led him out on to the deck where nobody could overhear.

"Sub, I know this is your first trip as a fully blown officer. But, you've had two years as a Midshipman. They," I nodded towards the two crewmen on the forecastle, "will listen to you. They don't know that this is your first trip. And if they do, it makes no difference. When I give you the order to single up, tell them just that. When I tell you to let go, tell them that. Stand up straight, arms at your side, look ahead."

"Yes, Sir. I'm sorry, Sir, it's just that I feel as though I don't quite know it all, Sir."

I clapped him on the shoulder.

"Those are the most sensible words I've heard today, Sub. One more point. When they've finished coiling the ropes, check them. If they're not in round coils, tell them to do it again before they secure them for sea. And make sure they do. Carry on Mr Hawes."

"First trip sub lieutenants don't change, much, Sir," the Coxswain said as I walked back into the wheelhouse.

"No, but I'd sooner have them like young Hawes who's desperate to learn and do well. We'll take her out from the flying bridge, Coxswain. Fresh air and loads of sightseeing."

In fairness the flying bridge wasn't that much higher than the wheelhouse. It was a raised platform immediately aft. But I could see all round the harbour and amazingly I even had my own radar set up there built into a small wooden table.

I picked up the PA handset.

"Single up fore and aft. Morrison, stand by the flag."

As soon as we parted company with land we transferred the White Ensign from the jack staff at the stern to the small mast above the wheelhouse where it stayed from dawn to dusk till we came back to port.

"Let go forrad, Sub," I called and watched as he relayed the order to his men.

"Dead slow astern all engines, Cox," I said, watching the First Lieutenant for the signal that we were clear of the MGBs astern of us. He raised his arm.

"Let go aft, Number One. Stop engines."

Haywood raised his arm again. The signal that the ropes were out of the water and clear of the propellers.

"Slow Ahead, Coxswain. Starboard five."

With the stern now clear of the MGB immediately behind us we could show her skipper what we were capable of. I'd noticed him watching, wondering if his new Commander would give his boat a nudge.

"Midships the wheel, Cox. Increase revs for fifteen knots."

"Showing off, Sir?"

"Why not. The word has to go round that *Dotty's* not to be messed with. Nor her crew."

I felt the stern dig into the water when our three engines increased speed. As we passed the moored fishing boats, small launches to bigger trawlers, our bow wave caused them to bob up and down. Some of the skippers would be cursing the Royal Navy. But hopefully in a good humoured way.

"Slow Ahead, centre and starboard engines, Cox, half Ahead port and port fifteen the wheel."

This manoeuvre would take us through the mouth of Newlyn Harbour. Or The Gaps, as it was known locally. As we came neatly through the harbour mouth I gave one last order.

I glanced forward and saw Hawes pointing at the coiled ropes, using his finger to remind them how real seamen should do the job properly. As though he sensed me watching, he turned towards me and I nodded.

"All engines Full Ahead, Cox. Heading 135 degrees, South East."

*Dotty* raced over the waves, and more often through them, her wake bright white and frothy astern of us. She seemed excited at the prospect of getting back to the open sea, to show off what she was capable of. And her capabilities were her real strengths. She wasn't a big boat, some would say small by most standards. She was precisely one hundred and three feet long, barely three times the length of a double decker bus.

But what she lacked in size she made up for in other ways. Her four feet draft meant that we could get in and out of any harbour - friendly or enemy. No danger of grounding. And with a top speed of fifty knots she would show a fine pair of heels to her counterparts in the enemy camp: German E Boats.

Compared to her predecessor she was heavily armed. She had four 18-inch torpedo tubes, a 20 mm cannon at the bow and stern, two Vickers machine guns mounted either side of the wheelhouse and a 20 mm Oerlikon cannon immediately in front of the wheelhouse. And at the very stern she had two racks of depth charges.

As Able Seaman Morrison was heard to say before we sailed, "Lovely having all this ammo and stuff. We can blow anything out of the water. Mind you, let's hope the skipper don't let Gerry get the first shot in or we'll all be rocketing skywards like a bloody spitfire."

For the next four hours I put *Dotty* and the crew through their paces. Flashing through the growing waves at top speed, decelerating to bring her to a turning stop, skidding around in circles. She took it all in her stride.

Before sailing the Coxswain lashed a load of planks together on the deck. Now he cast them into the sea and each of the gunners took turns in firing at them. Once they adjusted to the movements of the heaving deck, they smashed the planks into splinters of wood washing away on the tide.

"I think that's enough for today, Number One," I said, giving the order to secure all guns.

"We're booked into the gunnery range off Lundy Island tomorrow. Depth charges first then torpedoes. Give the men the evening off. We sail at 0530 hours." I looked around one more time and yawned.

"Take her home, Number One. I'll write up my report." In my cabin I started writing but stopped after a few minutes. I should be delighted. The crew performed well, *Dotty* was a lovely boat. Everything working perfectly. Yet, I couldn't shake off a feeling of sadness. I lay on my bunk and closed my eyes. A picture of my Mother came unbidden and I felt the sob escape. Followed by another and another. And a flood of them. What the hell was the point? Why carry on? Haywood could take over. He was ready for command. And the Old Man could find another Commander. After half an hour I sat back at my desk and finished the report. Then wrote a letter to the Old Man telling him what I wanted. It was time to go ashore. I didn't want the responsibility any longer.

## Chapter 14    Captain Braun in Hamburg

My captains gathered in the wardroom with
Commander Klopp to one side, observing. And
chewing. He always seemed to be eating. I must ask
Zirk to study him more closely.

Thinking of our Nazi Party observer made me smile.
He's already walked all around the ship and visited
every department. His report is extensive. In his view
barely half the crew support the Fuhrer. I would have
to change that. Or change the crew.

"Gentlemen, your attention."

I stared as two of the captains continued a
conversation.

"Captain Mueller, Captain Schmidt. If you do not wish
to engage with this meeting return to your ships and
pack your bags."

There was an immediate silence around the room and a
tension that had not been there a few seconds ago.

"I apologise, Captain Braun. Your predecessor,
Captain Fischer, treated these occasional gatherings as
an opportunity to catch up with old friends between
convoys."

"I congratulate you on recognising that I am not my
predecessor," I said. "Now would you object terribly if
we continued?"

I didn't wait for a reply but turned to face the rest of
the room. Twenty captains from twenty ships. My
Group, Gruppen 158 Escort, to give it its full name.

"Gentlemen, for the next few months our task is a
straight forward one," I told them.

Actually, straight forward it might be, but it was far
from an easy task. Escorting slow, ponderous merchant
ships carrying men and armour to wherever it was
needed, long hours on watch, ever watchful for enemy
submarines, aircraft and ships. At least we had plenty
of firepower, but in reality over half my ships were not
only pre-war but almost ancient.

"We sail at 1800 hours this evening on the tide bound for Bergen in Norway. Commander Klopp, please pass around the sailing orders," I finished.

Whilst Klopp handed out the sealed packages I told them that they could read the orders at their leisure back on their own ships. That they should memorise them and react to them when instructed. Without hesitation, delay or question.

"Are there any questions?" I asked.

Captain Schmidt stood up.

"Would it be in order for us to read the briefings now, Sir? If we can see any flaws or can suggest other ways of doing things we can agree them before we leave."

"Captain Schmidt, this is not a democracy. I am your senior officer. I have looked at the convoy vessels and given my orders to the Commodore in charge. My way is the best way. Do I make myself clear?"

Schmidt sat down without another word but I can see from the way he avoids eye contact with me that he is not happy. Well, that makes two of us.

"We leave at 1800. Form line astern behind me for leaving harbour. We rendezvous with the convoy off Bremen Lighthouse at 2000 hours. You will take up your convoy positions as we collect the merchant ships."

At 1750 hours I walked into the wheelhouse.

"Are we ready to sail, Commander Klopp?"

"We are indeed, Sir."

"Why did you not report that to me in my cabin? Do you think that I am a mind reader, Klopp?"

He stared at me. The sailors on the bridge moved away. They have not heard an officer called by just his surname before, I guess.

"I am sorry, Captain. I assumed that you would be here for sailing. In future I will report readiness to you."

He saluted and turned to leave the bridge.

"Commander. That salute was not acceptable. Repeat properly."

He did so, raising his arm stiffly in the air and shouting "Heil Hitler" whilst clicking his heels together.

I raised my arm, as the Fuhrer does, in return, walked to the front of the bridge and gave orders for leaving Hamburg. Freed from all physical ties with the land I guided the ship to the middle of the outbound channel.

"Gruppen 158 Escort closed up in line astern, Sir," the watch keeping Lieutenant called out.

"Slow Ahead together," I ordered. "Midships the wheel. Steady on course 285 degrees, Quartermaster."

We left Hamburg behind and sailed almost due west to Bremen Lighthouse. Twenty one escort ships, I thought. My own cruiser and eight destroyers. Seven patrol boats - or corvettes as the English call them. Smaller but agile. Slower, too. Two guns, one fore one aft, fifty depth charges which we will use if we come into contact with enemy submarines. And five minesweepers.

All to escort seven ships. It seems a heavy investment. But these seven ships carry four thousand troops and their armoured cars, tanks, support trucks and field guns. The Norwegian resistance had got a lot braver of late and the Fuhrer is determined to break them.

"Message from Convoy Commodore, Sir," Klopp said looking intently at the Aldis Light at the top of the Commodore's mast.

"Message reads, *All ships on station and in position. Ready to proceed.*"

I studied the images in the radar screen in the wheelhouse. All my ships were in the positions I told them to occupy.

"Message to Convoy Commodore, repeated to Escort Group, *Course 020, make revolutions for twelve knots. Radio Silence.*"

I took my new group to war. For them it is nothing new. For me, this is a test. If I succeed in escorting these convoys Admiral Doenitz has promised me promotion to rear admiral by the end of the year. Well, let's start with the next two days.

# Chapter 15    Second Officer Lenton in Newlyn

God, it's busy. So far we've brought seven new boats into Newlyn to join the flotilla with another seventeen due any day. And each one has to be inspected and classified as ready for service, the crew fit and trained, the captains up to date with their certificates. The list is endless.

The office girls were not quite good enough, they kept missing things. And it's irritating to have to check every single thing they do. I looked down at the quartermaster's requisition for Commander Scott's boat and felt my fists clenching.

"Wren Harvey, in my office. Now," I called through the partition.

The girl, barely twenty years of age, walked in without knocking. Tall, over five feet ten inches. Long legs, long brown hair which should have been in a bun but hung loosely.

"When you're in uniform, Harvey, you wear your hair in a bun. And when you come into my office you knock at the door."

She looked back at me with an expression that verged on the contemptuous. It's difficult to read anything other than contempt when a person's eyes roll.

I stood and walked around the desk, closed the door and stopped in front of her.

"Atten shun," I said, quietly but emphasising every syllable and she flinches.

"I'm cancelling your leave this weekend, Harvey. You're on duty watch Saturday and Sunday. If you are stupid enough to challenge my authority, understand that there will be consequences. For you, not for me. And never give me that insolent look and wander in here as though you are walking up to a bar. Do you understand?"

"Yes, Ma'am. Was there anything else?"

I passed her the requisition.

"What's missing?"

She looked down and frowned.

"It's all there. It's what the Coxswain asked for."

"Ma'am," I added and waited. She repeated the word. "Since when do Coxswains submit requisition forms that have not been signed off by the boat's Commanding Officer?"

"But that's his job, Ma'am, not mine."

I took a deep breath before replying. It wasn't her fault at all, really, yet she must learn that part of our job is to make life as easy as we can for our sailors. They risk their lives, we don't.

I explained this as though I were talking to a child. "Do you understand that it is part of our responsibility? They go out and fight. We make sure they've got everything they need to win. Dismissed."

I sat down and looked at my own list of tasks, ticking those off that I'd completed when Captain Dennis walked in.

"I heard the lecture, Anne. Rubbing you up the wrong way?" he asked as he sat opposite me.

"No, Sir. The trouble with some of these girls is that they are careless. I know that Commander Scott's had his crew at sea constantly for the last forty eight hours and the Coxswain will be as tired as any of them. Our job is to help him. Not waste time by sending requisitions back and delaying the stores run. I'll take the form down the pier myself and get it signed."

Commander Scott was on deck when I arrived.

"Good morning. Miss Lenton," he said, stepping up on to the harbour wall.

"Good morning, Sir. I wonder if you'd mind signing your requisition off?"

"Good God, I thought that had gone off days ago," he said, his smile vanishing. "We sail for Falmouth in the morning. What the hell happened?"

"I know, Sir. There was a mistake in the office. It won't happen again I can assure you. And I've already

rung the order through and told them I expect it here
by fourteen hundred hours this afternoon."

He signed the form and handed it back.

"How did you get them to agree to that?"

"I know the First Officer in charge over there. We
trained together. It's quite a small world, the Wrens."

"Any more arrivals expected? Seven so far, but we
need to get the whole flotilla together so we can start
training. Even though I've no idea what I'm training
for."

"Admiralty says we'll have them all within the next
seven days, Sir. Two are finishing refits, five new off
the blocks and on sea trials and the rest are all sailing
south from their previous bases in Scotland. And the
new oil barge arrives tomorrow."

As I said that I saw his eyes darken.

"I am so sorry, Sir. I didn't mean to remind you," I
said as he looked down at the ground.

"Not your fault. It's good news, new oiler."

I looked across the harbour towards his Mother's
house. His now, I suppose.

"How are the repairs, Sir?"

"I have no idea. Haven't been up there," and he turned
and stepped back on to his boat.

## Chapter 16     Commander Klopp aboard *Der Condor* in the North Sea

One day out of Hamburg, one more day to Bergen. I have never known such a tense atmosphere on a ship. Captain Braun is a very serious man, never smiles, never cracks a joke. Doesn't even come on to the ship's bridge during a watch and talk to the watchkeeper. As his second in command I should know him well and trust him. But I have learnt nothing about him and from what I've seen certainly don't trust him.

And I'm not the only one. The Captain's Conference at the start of the voyage was a disaster. When I stood at the head of the gangway to see them off afterwards all the captains patted me on the shoulder with that look of, "Hard luck, Old Man. Maybe he won't last long."

I looked around the horizon before peering into the radar screen.

"Radar, Bridge. What's the blip dead ahead?" I said into the telephone.

"I can't see anything, Sir. You sure it's not dust on the screen?"

I looked again. Nothing. I frowned. I was sure that there was a contact there.

"Sir, got it. It's intermittent. There one second, gone the next. Submarine conning tower?" Becker asked.

I watched for a few more seconds. Yes, that must be it. I press the handle to sound Emergency Action Stations klaxon.

The Captain was the first to arrive and I told him what I've seen. He looked at the screen himself and picked up the phone.

"Captain, Radar. How sure are you that it's a submarine?"

"It's too small for a ship. Too big for a fishing boat. It can only be a sub, Captain."

Braun turned to me.

"How good is he?"

"Petty Officer Becker is highly experienced, Sir. Twenty years in. Man and boy, you might say. He has been our senior radar technician for the last two years."

"Who spotted it first?"

"He did, Sir," I lied.

What the hell did it matter, as long as one of us did. I caught the eye of one of the bridge lookouts and nodded towards the radar office. He knew what I meant and left quietly. Braun was bound to check and we'd both be in the smelly stuff if he gave the wrong answer.

"Make to Schmidt on *Prinz Rupert*." He told the signalman. "*Suspected submarine five miles dead ahead at position*," he paused and looked at me. "Give him the position."

Then resumed dictating, "*steer course parallel to mine on 035 until you pick up the contact.* And signal to Captain of the Baltic. *Am attacking a suspected submarine five miles ahead of the convoy. Assume command until I return.* Repeat both signals to the Convoy Commodore."

He walked to the front of the wheelhouse and pulled both engine room telegraphs to Stop, then Full Ahead, the signal for Emergency Full Ahead. We felt the vibrations through the ship as the engineers far below the waterline put the order into operation.

Back at my Action Stations at the Depth Charge Station on the after deck I smiled as the ship heeled over to starboard and steadied on her new course.

"Forty knots on her last attack, Ryker," I told the rating at the depth charge controls. "We'll be there in no time."

"How do we know it's not one of our U Boats, Sir?" he asked.

"We know where all our U Boat packs are - their HQ tell us before we leave port. There are none this far North and East. Prepare one rack for minimum depth setting. One rack for a hundred feet and a third rack for two hundred feet."

With Ryker getting his depth charges ready I picked up the phone.

"Commander Klopp, Radar."

"Radar, Sir. She's still on the surface. Be the fastest crash dive in history when they spot us. The smell will be awful."

I smiled. When their lookouts finally spotted us, there would indeed be an almighty rush to get below and batten down for attack. I looked at my watch. Another minute.

"Charges ready, Sir."

I rang the Bridge.

"After Deck to Bridge. Depth Charges ready. First rack minimum depth, second rack one hundred feet, third rack two hundred feet."

"Wait for my order, Commander Klopp."

I leant out over the rail, looking ahead to where the submarine should be. No sign, obviously seen us and dived.

"Stand by, Ryker," I said, holding the phone to my ear.

"Depth Charges away," came the order from the bridge and I waved at Ryker.

"First rack away," I said.

The explosions were almost instantaneous. Four huge pyramids of water rocketed into the air, high above the deck, almost to the top of the mast, a hundred feet above my head. Each of the four charges was three hundred pounds in weight, almost half of which was amatol high-explosive. If just one explodes within twenty feet of a submarine, the pressure hull implodes. I never think of the sailors down there when we fire the charges off the stern. Their death would be slow and horrible.

The ship came round on to the opposite course to pass back over the submarine's position. Braun ordered the second rack to be released and seconds later another four geysers of water shoot skywards.

This time the stern of a submarine followed, before it slapped down on to the surface of the sea. One hatch opened on the foredeck and another in the conning tower and men ran across the deck and jumped into the sea.

What happened next totally sickened me.

"All guns open fire. Klopp, minimum setting for your third rack of depth charges."

"But, Sir, they're abandoning ship," I said into the phone.

"Third rack, minimum setting," he repeated.

I stared at Ryker who stared back at me and said, "That's murder, Sir. They'll never survive."

"After deck to Bridge I can't hear. Repeat, please," I said.

He did so but as he started speaking the roar of our four inch guns deafened me. And we were past the submarine, out of range for our depth charge thrower. But then the machine guns started. Ours, not theirs. They never fired a shot during the few minutes they were above the surface.

I looked over the rail and saw *Prinz Rupert* stopping to lower their boats to the water. Our loud hailer came to life and Braun's voice reverberated across the water.

*"Prinz Rupert*, no survivors. It is too dangerous to launch your boats. I repeat, you are to leave survivors in the water. That is an order."

"Bastard," Ryker said.

"As you were, Ryker," I told him. I looked around. "Don't forget we have a Nazi Party official aboard."

"And you should not forget either, Klopp," Zirk said from behind me.

# Chapter 17    Scotty in Newlyn

The *Mission to Seamen* stands at the landward end of the North Pier in Newlyn village. The granite building opened in 1903 and between the wars was used solely by fishermen and other sailors coming into Newlyn. It had dormitories for shipwrecked mariners, a canteen and seating area and a small chapel overseen by a pastor. The atmosphere was always homely with the smells of bacon and eggs cooking in the kitchen, easy chatter amongst the staff and customers and the sound of waves lapping against the wall outside.

Today its big bar also served as the flotilla's briefing room and seven of my skippers joined me for an early morning meeting.

"We have to be ready for action within the next two months," I told them. "To achieve that we must act as a single, cohesive unit. When the rest of the boys arrive we'll continue to practise until I'm satisfied that we can do whatever is needed of us. But we'll start today."

"Do we know what the mission is, Sir?"

Lieutenant Norman Roberts had his own command for the first time and he was keen to get stuck in.

"No, not yet, Norrie," I replied. "Captain Dennis is operating on a strictly need to know basis and has told me that right now I don't need to know. Actually, he doesn't know either."

"How do we practise if we don't know what we're doing?"

Lieutenant Commander Eddie O'Leary was the most senior of skippers and would assume command if I was sunk or disabled.

"All I can tell you is that we have to attack from close quarters, against several vessels at once. And do it quickly before their radar picks us up. We'll be training in the Irish Sea," I replied, adding for good humour, "out of sight of Ireland so you won't be seeing your relatives, Eddie."

There was a touch of light laughter, always good for morale.

"More important," I continued, "the German spies dotted up and down their coastline won't see us. We'll practice in daylight to start but that'll soon change to night time runs."

I took a swallow of tea. The Mission made their tea strong enough to stand a spoon up in the mug. Just as I liked it. Just like my Mother's. My mind wandered off down a completely different path for a few seconds and I realised they were all staring at me.

I shook myself and shrugged my shoulders.

"God that tea's stronger than the Coxswain's rum," I said, smiling. "Sorry, what was the question?"

"When are the other boats joining? We're barely at 25% full strength."

That was O'Leary again.

"Latest from the Old Man is that we'll have a full complement by the weekend. Most of the boats are sailing south as we speak. They'll have an overnight in Portsmouth, Falmouth or Appledore for a quick overhaul before completing their voyages."

I finished my tea and pointed at a chart of the Cornish and Devonshire coastline that I'd placed on an easel in the centre of the room.

"We sail in twenty minutes. South around Lands End into the Gaelic Sea and on into the Irish Sea."

I tapped a point on the map.

"Almost exactly half way between England and Ireland. Maneuverers there. Today it's about getting the signals right and staying in formation. The wind's Force Four to Five, waves forecast to be around six to ten feet. If you've got any first trippers they'll be leaving their breakfast in Mounts Bay. If they've got any left by the time we get into position, they'll be lucky."

As soon as we left Newlyn Harbour I could tell that the weather forecasters were way out in their predictions.

"Force Four my arse, this is already Force 7 and we're not out of the bay yet."

James Haywood nodded and looked behind us.

"If we look anything like them, we make an impressive sight, Sir," he said and I followed his gaze, shaking my head in wonder.

"Well, we knew it wouldn't be a good day for it," I said as I watched the seven boats, one minute climbing the sides of the waves, the next smashing into another one before heaving the water aside with what I imagined to be a shrug. Well, some of the water. The rest dashed itself against, and sometimes into, the flying bridge.

"No point overdoing it on the first trip, Number One. Half Ahead all engines. Morrison, make to Flotilla *Reduce Speed to fifteen knots*."

We rounded Lands End and with the wind behind us sped up again.

"Good to be back in the open water, Sir," James said. "This little boat's a beauty."

He was right, she was a joy to handle. Responded to every order without fuss or delay. Her turning circle was the tightest I've ever known, her speed incredible. From a standing start she'd already worked up to forty knots in less than a minute.

We spent the next six hours on manoeuvres. I used each boat in turn as a target and the rest of us sped in towards her preparing the torpedo tubes every time to fine tune the crew's actions and reactions. We did the same with the depth charges, too, slewing our boats around at the last minute to simulate throwing the charges as close as we could towards the target. Finally we threw some old oil barrels overboard and used them as target practice for the gun crews.

"That's enough for one day, Number One. Take her home. Morrison, make to the Flotilla, *Enough for the day. You've done well. Set course for home. Last one in buys the beer.*"

I climbed down from the bridge and opened my cabin door.

"Captain to the Bridge. Repeat, Captain to the Bridge."

I could have wept. I was tired to the point of exhaustion. I couldn't recall the last night I slept for more than an hour without waking. I could barely stand. What the hell next?

## Chapter 18    Klopp aboard *Der* Condor En route to Bergen

"Lieutenant Zirk, I don't know what you think you heard, but we have nothing to hide. Do we, Ryker?"
Ryker swallowed and even in the dim light I saw his Adam's Apple bobbing up and down, working overtime like a tennis ball in a rough sea.
"No, Sir, Commander Klopp. Nothing to hide on this ship."
Zirk, I observed, had a nasty habit of smirking. He was doing it as he spoke, not an easy trick.
"I don't think that Captain Braun will appreciate being called a, what did you say, Ryker, bastard? Or do you think differently, Klopp?"
"If you had heard our entire discussion you would have realised that Seaman Ryker was not referring to our good Captain but to the English submarine captain. Ryker doesn't like submarines. Like me he has lost some good friends in sinkings."
Zirk stopped smirking and frowned, a shadow of doubt, perhaps.
"And by the way, Lieutenant Zirk."
He looked directly into my eyes, daring me to continue. I did.
"I always address my officers, whether they are senior or junior, by their rank and name. Especially when in the presence of crewmen. If you ever address me by my surname as you did a few minutes ago, I will have you court martialled for insolence. Even your Gestapo friends won't help you get out of that. We navy types are not afraid of people like you."
I took a step towards him, my six feet two inches towering over his five feet eight inches, placed my hand on his chest and pushed him towards the ship's rail.
"Look down there, Lieutenant. Tell me what you see."
He looked down quickly before looking back at me.

"I do not like the sea, Commander."

I pushed some more, this time grasping his arm.

"I cannot swim. Let me go. I will report you. You have not heard the last of this."

I turned him so that his back was now arched over the rail and he actually whimpered. I looked down and saw urine pooling at his feet. He'd pissed himself.

I pulled him back in.

"We are at sea for a long time, Lieutenant Zirk," I whispered in his ear and watched sweat rolling off his brow.

"You would be surprised at how the most unpopular of crewmen simply disappear without trace. Often at night. Do I make myself understood?"

"One day, Commander Klopp, I will have my revenge."

"Get off my deck, Lieutenant. And the next time you want to walk around my ship you will ask my permission. The Captain is in command of this ship but as his Deputy I decide where supernumerary crew members can and cannot go during Action Stations. You have just broken the golden rule of being away from your action station. That is regarded in the Navy as desertion and dereliction of duty and is punishable by death."

The smaller man turned on his heel and almost ran off down the deck, his gait more that of a dog with his tail between his legs than a proud German Shepherd.

"I think you've made an enemy, Sir," Ryker observed.

"No doubt, Ryker. But I've stopped him from roaming freely. For now. Put the word around that people should watch what they're saying."

I looked around and bent my head to his.

"The Captain is a stickler for the rules. He's nothing like our previous captain in that respect. But he is the Captain."

Ryker nodded and the PA system announced an end to Action Stations. I worked with Ryker to secure the depth charges and walked up to the Bridge to resume my watch.

Zirk was talking to Braun inside the wheelhouse so I stood outside and lit a cigarette. The door opened and I watched Zirk's back disappear down the ladder. Braun walked to my side.

"Commander Klopp, the lieutenant has reported that you assaulted him. Is that so?"

"Good heavens, Sir, of course not. The deck was slippery from the wash of water following our depth charges exploding. I helped him keep on his feet. These land-based people don't understand the laws of the sea as we do."

He smiled, though I didn't see a great deal of mirth in his face.

"I thought it must be something like that. These Gestapo people are quite sensitive, Commander. You should remember that."

He walked away but called over his shoulder, "Return to convoy and resume station, Commander."

I let out a large breath, until now oblivious to the fact that I had not been breathing. I felt the old pain below my right knee which was strange as there was nothing down there. I lost half that leg two years ago during a battle with one of the enemy's Motor Gun Boats.

I reached down to stroke the tin leg that sat in its place and grimaced. Jesus, some days the pain was worse than others. This was not one of the better days. It was the exchange with Zirk that caused it. Battles were easy, conflicts like those of the past few minutes weren't. I walked inside and poured a coffee.

"Steer due North, Quartermaster. Twenty knots. Let's get these bloody ships to Bergen."

I walked back outside and felt the wind around my face. My right hand groped inside my coat pocket and withdrew two small tablets. Nobody was looking as they disappeared into my mouth followed by a swallow of coffee. The relief was almost immediate.

How many a day did the doc say I could safely take? Eight, he said. Well, he was wrong. I was on double that and still doing my job as well as ever. As long as Zirk doesn't go prying in my cabin. I must get the spare keys from the Quartermaster. Tell him I've lost mine.

# Chapter 19    Scotty at sea off the Cornish Coast

As I walked back into the wheelhouse the First
Lieutenant smiled and put his head to one side. A
gesture of sympathy that I didn't need.

"This had better be good, Number One," I snapped.
His smile vanished and I immediately regretted the
outburst.

"Sorry, Sir, message from Newlyn. Downed German
fighter twenty miles off St Ives. Due west. I've altered
course and increased speed. Estimated Time of Arrival
1800 hours."

I looked at the clock on the wall.

"Almost an hour away. Do we know if they're alive?"

"There's a trawler standing by. They say that the two
crew are refusing to leave. They think the fishermen
will kill them. And they're armed. The trawlers'
standing well off but ready to move in if the plane
sinks."

"As well the weather's moderated, Number One. Get a
rescue party ready. And make sure they're armed. If
they want to start a fight we'll finish it for them."

The First Lieutenant opened the door to the
wheelhouse.

"And Number One."

He turned.

"I'm sorry. Was just about to get my head down. I
sometimes think I'm getting a bit too old for this."

He smiled and left.

"Emergency Full Ahead, Coxswain. Stay at Action
Stations," I said as I settled myself into the Captain's
Chair. I wasn't really joking when I said that I was
getting too old. Or maybe I was just sick of the whole
killing thing. All I want is to get back to Newlyn and
sleep.

"Got them on the radar, Sir," Haywood said. I looked
at the clock again. Must have dozed off.

"Carry on Number One. No risks. Are the gun crews closed up?"

"All closed up, Sir."

I moved up on to the flying bridge. With night falling I had a better view from up here.

"Coxswain, searchlight on the plane, please."

It was a Dornier, like the one that bombed Newlyn and killed my Mother. I felt my fists clench and my breathing speed up. I picked up the binoculars and looked more closely. Two figures sitting on the fuselage, holding on for dear life in the waves.

"Do you speak English?" I said into the PA. One of the men waved.

"This is HMS *Beagle*, Her Majesty's Royal Navy. If you have guns throw them overboard."

I watched as they exchanged looks and said something. They seemed to be arguing as their heads moved quickly and the hand gestures seemed aggressive. After a few minutes one threw something into the sea and grabbed at the other man's hand. There was a brief struggle then a shot. One of the men slid down the fuselage into the sea and the other slid down beside him.

"Coxswain, Slow Ahead, take us in."

I didn't need to tell Haywood what to do. He and his men were at the bow ready to grab the men.

The Coxswain nudged the boat into the wing tip then held her steady while Haywood and his men threw lines to the Germans.

They pulled the first one inboard and lay him on the deck. The second man climbed up himself. Haywood knelt beside the sailor on the deck and drew a blanket completely over him before looking back at me and shaking his head.

"Take us back out to sea, Coxswain. We'll use the plane for target practise"

We backed away from the bomber and stopped about a mile away.

"Gun crews open fire on my order only. Coxswain, Full Ahead all engines. Midships the wheel and steady on that."

We raced back in at over forty knots, the stern digging ever deeper into the sea as the three propellers churned their way through the seas. The bow was completely out of the water when I gave the order to fire.

The 4" gun crew told me later that they fired twenty-five shells from their position on the forecastle. They blew the bomber to pieces.

"Hard a starboard, full astern together. Depth Charges away,"" I called into the PA.

The charges flew across the six feet divide and slammed into the water where the bomber had been.

"Stop Engines."

I looked over the side at the pieces of canvas and wood floating on the sea and nodded.

"Sir, this is Lieutenant Hoffman. He tried to persuade his navigator to surrender but he wouldn't. When they struggled, well, we saw what happened."

"Very good, Number One. Get him some dry blankets and put a guard on him. We'll hand him over to the authorities in Newlyn."

The German made to speak but I waved him away. I had no desire to speak to a man who may have been responsible for the death of the only person on earth that I loved.

# Chapter 20    Scotty in Newlyn

"Ring off Main Engines, Coxswain. Port watch have the duty. Let Starboard have a run ashore. There won't be many more chances."

I buttoned up my duffle coat against the wind and walked slowly up the harbour. The First Lieutenant was already ashore. I'd given him two pounds.

"We were last boat in, Number One. My turn to buy the drinks. The skippers will be waiting at the Fishermans Arms. You go. Tell them the Old Man wanted to see me. Unless the Old Man's there in which case say that I've turned in."

Half an hour later I heard the crew going ashore. Laughing and calling to each other. Always the same when they had a run to the pub. They were good lads, but at least one would be on First Lieutenant's Report tomorrow. Perhaps even on my report if he'd been especially stupid.

I looked across the harbour. It was too dark to see my old home. But it was there.

This feeling of being alone was getting worse. But it wasn't just missing her. I didn't feel that I was up to whatever lay ahead. I shook all the way through the attack on the plane. For pity's sake, the plane was ditched. And if I hated the Germans for what they'd done to me, could I really be logical, calm under pressure? Would that hatred mean that my judgement was weakened?

I walked to the very end of the harbour and looked down at the waves ten feet below me. It was just after high tide, and I could see driftwood bobbing furiously in the current. I thought back to the days when Mum taught me to swim in this very harbour.

Three days, she said and you'll be swimming like a fish. I recalled laughing and telling her that I would be swimming that same day and she smiled and shook her head. She knew how to motivate me. It was a challenge and within an hour I was swimming alongside her. The next day and the next and the next I got stronger. By the end of the month I won every race we had.

I stepped over the low wall that acted as a barrier for the lorries that reversed after they'd loaded with fish from the trawlers below and took my duffel coat off. Despite the temperature I felt warm sweat trickling down my sides. I placed my cap on top and looked to the sky.

"Bit late for a swim, Sir," the voice was behind me, low, concerned, shaking a little.

I turned and looked at Second Officer Lenton.

"Miss Lenton, would you mind leaving me in peace. I have much to think about."

"If you're not using it do you mind if I put your duffle on? I saw you walking up here and for some reason followed you. But forgot my overcoat. I'm rather cold."

I waved my hand and she moved forward. I felt her hand on my arm.

"I know it's none of my business. But you're not alone in missing her, your Mother I mean. I spoke to Mr Peak this afternoon in the village. I didn't realise that he was your uncle. He's suffering, Harry, he needs you."

"I don't know if I can help him. I can barely help myself. Maybe it would be for the best if I just went ashore. O'Leary will do much better than me. He's younger, more enthusiastic."

"And hasn't been through half what you've been through, Harry. They need you. Whatever the job is, they need you to bring them home."

My cheeks were wet. I hadn't wept much since the day she died. I felt her turning my head towards her and she gently forced me to sit on the wall. She held my head to her shoulder as I cried like a baby. Sobbing and sobbing. At one point she picked up my duffel and held it tightly around the both of us. I don't know how long we stayed there but at last I stood, offered her a cigarette and lit them both.

"Voices, Harry, someone's walking up the pier. Put your jacket on. Here let me help."


It was an elderly man and a much younger woman in Air Raid Patrol uniform. Well, uniform was putting it a bit strong. Like all such wardens they wore armbands over their normal clothes which said ARP.

"Sorry, Sir, shouldn't be smoking outside. You know what them German pilots are like. Soon as they catch a glimpse of a light we get a load of bombs dropping. You know what happened a few days ago," the old man told me. He stepped towards me.

"Oh, sorry, Harry, didn't recognise you in the dark."

I looked intently at him until the penny dropped.

"Mr Tresize. I thought you retired last year."

"I did," he smiled, "but your Mum persuaded me to do this ARP thing when my wife died. Best thing I've done, apart from caretaking at your Mum's school. I loved that."

"Are you Commander Scott?" the girl asked and I nodded.

"I'm a nurse at West Cornwall Hospital. We had your AB Morrison in last week. I heard how you saved him. He is so grateful. I spoke with him after your First Lieutenant visited. He said that you cared about them all. Even when you should have been on leave after your Mum's death. You seem to have such a nice crew."

"Thank you, Miss…."

"Crebo, Carol Crebo," she paused. "I'm so sorry about your Mum. Matthew and I were just talking about her as we walked up the pier. She was a lovely lady. And a brilliant teacher. We all miss her. She spoke to everyone in the street."

I nodded, I couldn't say anything. But Lenton was on the ball.

"Thank you for reminding us about not smoking. Commander Scott was just helping me to find my way around Newlyn and we completely forgot. He was pointing out the quarry and how the boats come in to load stone. Well, we'd better leave you to it. You're in for a busy night. Thank you for what you do."

And she put her arm through mine and practically marched me back down the pier. We walked past my boat and on to her office. She looked hard at me before going in.

"Please, Harry, don't do anything rash. I know life must be hell right now. But think of all the people who depend on you. If you're not there what will they think? How will they cope if they feel they've let you down?"

"But they haven't. I'm the one who's let them down."

"No, Harry. When a nurse who doesn't know you tells you that your crew practically worships you, it's time to rethink."

She came back out and locked the door.

"Walk me home, please, Harry. It's getting late. My digs are near the Art Gallery."

Later, back on the boat, I slept. When I woke the next morning something had changed. Maybe I needed the grief to flow as it did last night. Maybe the sight of that German bomber in the sea had triggered something. God knows, I certainly didn't. But one thing that I was sure about. I had a war to fight and a crew to captain.

## Chapter 21   Braun approaching Bergen, Norway aboard *Der Condor*

"Commander Klopp, order the men to stations for entering harbour. Off duty men in full dress uniform to man the sides. We will show these Norwegian people what sort of sailors we are."

"We're still two hours from harbour, Sir. It's a biting wind out there. Shall we wait until we're closer?"

"No, Commander. The crew is slovenly. I need to stiffen them up. Two hours standing to Attention on deck will help. See to it."

He turned away.

"Commander, haven't you forgotten something?"

He looked a little bemused.

"Salute," I ordered. "Why isn't that second nature when you leave the bridge?"

I watched as his arm started to move before he stopped and gave me a real salute.

"As the Fuhrer would wish," I told him.

He must have realised what I was doing. His old Captain may have been pleasant. But pleasant doesn't win wars. Nazism does. I looked at the Quartermaster at the wheel without really seeing him. These men were a means to an end and were all expendable in order to win the war.

If Klopp continued to irritate and question my orders he, too, would have to go. I still did not altogether believe his version of events with Zirk.

"Crew to stations for entering harbour. Off Watch men to man the sides in dress uniform."

There was a pause in the public announcement before it continued.

"All men to stations in ten minutes. That is all."

Good. I picked the phone from its cradle.

"Master At Arms to the Bridge. On the double."

In all navies the MAA is the ship's senior policeman. And in all ships the MAA is universally disliked. Even more so on *Der Condor*. My MAA was a fully accredited Party member and knew exactly what I wanted.

"Ah, Master At Arms, you will have heard the last pipe. You and I will inspect the side parties. Any breach in uniform will be punishable by loss of one day's leave for each breach."

The door to the bridge wing opened and Klopp returned.

"Commander, the Master and I are going to inspect our side parties. You have the bridge."

It took us half an hour to complete the inspection. At the end of it we had walked up and down both sides of the deck. And of the three hundred sailors on parade, over half had uniform defects. Dear God, where had these men come from? What on earth had I done to deserve them?

Back on the bridge, Klopp listened as I summarised the disciplinary problems the crew demonstrated through wearing inappropriate or scruffy uniform.

"Sir, we've been in almost permanent combat since the start of the war. Most of these men have been on leave twice in that time. During our last mission in the Arctic we barely had time to eat, let alone press our uniforms. Perhaps a series of warnings on this occasion might be more apt?"

"Commander Klopp, I am not in the habit of issuing warnings. I gave clear instructions that the men should turn out in their No. 1 uniforms. They disobeyed my orders. Those that turned themselves out well will go on leave when we are next in port between missions. The others will go to the back of the queue. You will work with the Master At Arms to make sure this happens."

I dismissed Klopp to report to his own Station for entering harbour.

"And make damn sure you're in full dress uniform. Or you, too, will be missing your next leave."

I stared at the quartermaster who seemed to find something fascinating in the ship's compass in front of him. Most captains did not berate their juniors in front of ratings. But if they failed in their duty, they deserved that embarrassment. Besides, the word would very quickly get around that this was one captain who mixed neither his words nor his standards.

"Half Ahead both engines," I told the Quartermaster. *Der Condor*'s flotilla entered Bergen Harbour in line astern. The Commodore led the merchant ships over to the commercial docks while I led my squadron to the Navy pier.

"Signalman make to the squadron, *We sail for Hamburg at 0700 hours tomorrow morning. We have another convoy waiting.*"

There would be no slacking amongst the other ships. We all had a job to do. To beat the enemy we must allow nothing to get in the way.

## Chapter 22    James Haywood in Newlyn

"Thought I'd have a run ashore, Sir if that's all right."
The skipper seemed distracted, sitting at the stern,
chain smoking. Unusual for him.
"Carry on, James. I'll be staying board this evening.
Catching up on some rest. Doing anything special?"
"Might walk up to the Gaiety, see what film's on."
It was early evening and the sun was still shedding
some heat. I looked around me as I walked. This end of
Newlyn was given over almost entirely to small shops:
a butcher's, bakers, general groceries, barbers. And
places that supported the fishermen like the Mission,
net lofts, the ice works. And, of course, the Post office.
The smell was all pervading, but quite pleasant. A mix
of diesel oil, fish, tar used in waterproofing. Oh that it
was peace time. I could live in a place like this.
I was so busy looking around that I didn't even see her
walking in front of me. Thankfully, I grabbed her
before she fell over.
"God, I am so sorry. I was miles away. I didn't see you.
Are you all right?"
"Yes, thank you. Just a bit winded. You were walking
ever so quickly." She paused. "Oh, it's you, Lieutenant
Commander Haywood."
"How did you know my name?"
"I asked your seaman after we talked at the hospital."
I looked at her again. The nurse who had taken my cap
off and stroked my scar. The first woman ever to do
that. Including the ones I paid.
"That ointment works wonders, Nurse. It hasn't itched
once. Thank you."
"What's the hurry? Off to see a girlfriend. I bet you
have one in each port," she smiled.
I shook my head.

"Not really. Can't think why. You're the only one to have the courage to look at it, let alone touch it. Most of them just look and walk away if I'm at a dance."

I felt the bitterness in my voice. It was true. They were fine when they saw the uniform. Until they looked above it and saw the inch wide scar that ran from one temple to the other and the ravaged skin on my cheek. I couldn't blame them.

"Well, they're just stupid," she said. "None of us is perfect. We all have something that we don't like."

I stared at her. I hadn't really noticed her in the hospital ward. She was a few inches shorter than me, probably five and a half feet tall. Lovely soft blond hair which she must have had in a bun when we last met but it now flowed freely down her back. She had a coat on but I would put money on her having a lovely trim figure underneath.

But the most amazing feature was her soft, bright blue eyes which twinkled like diamonds. And her smile which seemed to be permanently switched on, the lips turning up at the ends. I can't remember the last time that I looked at a woman like this She must have a boyfriend. They'd be falling over themselves.

"You didn't answer my question," she said.

"Oh, I was going to the cinema. I read that The Road To Morocco was showing. Bob Hope and Bing Crosby. And our boat's named after the leading actress, Dorothy Lamour."

She laughed out loud. A lovely sound, almost more of a giggle. I laughed as well.

"Your boat is *HMS Dorothy*?" she asked and exploded into even more giggles.

"No," I explained, laughing at her infectious giggle. "Officially she's HMS *Beagle*, a canine-class Motor Gunboat. But each of the skipper's boats has carried the nickname *Dotty*. It's a tradition with him."

"I haven't seen that film either," she said and without thinking I blurted out "Would you do me the honour of accompanying me?"

God, how pompous that sounded.

"I mean," I began and she touched my arm.

"I would love to, but on one condition."

I asked what that was and she put an arm through mine and started walking towards the Gaiety.

"How can I talk to you and keep calling you Lieutenant Commander?"

She looked up at me and gave me a broad smile.

"It's James. Jimmy if you prefer."

"What do you prefer?" she asked.

"My family's always called me Jimmy, but my friends call me James."

"James it is, then," she replied.

I felt the biggest smile break out on my face and laughed.

"But what's your name. I feel as though I've known you for ages and I don't even know your name."

"Carol Crebo," she said. "And there's no shortened version."

As we walked she talked in that lovely soft Cornish accent that sounded friendly and warm.

After the film she said that she had to get home quickly as she was on ARP duty from ten until three in the morning. I walked her to her house, where she lived with her parents and we stopped at the end of the path leading to the door.

She turned and I realised that I wanted to kiss her. But daren't. She stood on tiptoe and brushed her lips against mine.

"So you know what to do next time, James," she smiled as she walked up the path.

"There will be a next time, won't there?" she asked, turning towards me.

I felt a lump in my throat. I nodded and waved while trying to swallow.

"How do I contact you?" was the best that I could get out.

"I'll keep an eye open for *Dotty*," she said.

# Chapter 23    Rommel at his desert HQ in North African

"Message from Berlin, Fieldmarshal, shall I open it?"
"Go ahead, Johann. I hope to God it's good news."
I watched Captain Keller slit the envelope and remove the thick document. He read the first page and smiled.
"Reinforcements, Sir. Arriving in Tripoli in two days and trains will bring them overland."
He passed me the letter.
"Twenty thousand men, two hundred Panzer tanks, two hundred field guns. This is good news, Johann. I think we may just have enough to beat the British into retreat."
I poured a coffee and walked outside. For as far as the eye could see there were hundreds of tanks and thousands of tents. None was of any use to me. The tanks were made of wood and the tents empty.
The real tanks were hundreds of miles away under camouflage netting. The troops moved them by night, wiping all traces of the tracks from the desert before daylight. It took a week, but we were now in a fine position to attack by the back door. The extra twenty thousand men and their armour practically guaranteed our victory in the next battle against the British.
"How long will it take them to get here from Tripoli?"
"Three days, Sir. They will be with us by the weekend."
"Tell the generals that we meet at noon tomorrow, Captain."

# Chapter 24     Scotty in Newlyn

"1800 hours, James, signal the flotilla *Time for some fun*."

We'd spent the afternoon going over the plans for this evening. The RAF had reported sighting a slow moving enemy convoy heading south down through the English Channel. Eight merchant ships, ten escort vessels.

"We could do with teaching them a lesson," the Old Man told me when he called me into his office.

"They might have invaded most of Europe, but it is the **English** Channel, damn it."

We had ten boats with us now. More than enough to play havoc with the German escort group. Four hours later we steamed out of Newlyn Harbour into Mounts Bay before heading north towards the English Channel.

"Good night for it, Sir," Haywood said as he sipped from a mug of boiling hot cocoa. The Coxswain always called it Kye - the traditional hot chocolate-type mix with a tot of rum. It brought the tears to your eyes until you were used to it. I smiled as I saw Sub Lieutenant Hawes retching after his first swallow.

"Take it easy, Sub. You'll choke if you're not careful," I told him.

"Get your head down for an hour Number One. Mr. Hawes and I will take the watch."

I finished my drink and took the mug down to the wardroom, turning to speak to Hawes as I left.

"Mr. Hawes, you have the watch. Course 095, Full Ahead all engines. I'll be in the wardroom. Call me if you need me."

He stared wide eyed at me before smiling.

"Aye aye, Sir."

Some might say it's foolish to leave the most junior officer on watch as you're going to war. But we had around 150 miles to travel on the outward leg. With clear skies, good visibility and a calm sea we'd see any other ship long before they saw us. We were that low in the water that newcomers to MGBs felt they were in a submarine.

And our radar sets were top of the range. We'd picked up an enemy aircraft a few days earlier at 100 miles out and frightened the life out of it when we had all guns blazing as they came in to attack. Ships weren't as visible, but our operator picked up a convoy a few days ago at almost thirty miles.

And with the Coxswain at the helm, perhaps there was a small degree of risk, but the young man's confidence would benefit hugely from an hour in command. I jerked my head up as Hawes spoke to the look-out.

"Keep your eyes peeled, Morrison. You haven't moved for two minutes. Jerry doesn't stay still on nights like this. And it's a long swim back to Newlyn."

He learnt quickly. We had the makings of a good officer there. Getting the job done with orders and humour.

I looked at the chart spread out on the wardroom table. In theory our plan was simplicity itself. We'd attack the convoy off the Cherbourg Peninsula. They would feel safe there, protected on one side by the French coastline, all of it occupied by the Germans and on the other side by the Channel Islands which they'd occupied two years earlier.

Only a bunch of fools would steam into their heavy shore-based guns. Or a flotilla of Motor Gunboats low in the water and speeding through the waves at over 50 knots.

An hour later I returned to the wheelhouse and felt the boat coming to life. I'd told the crew what we were doing, the timings, the target and where we were headed. Their response to a man was the same.

"Good to have a crack at the Germans. We've been practising for long enough."

Slowly the reports came in.

"Forrad gun closed up."

"After gun closed up."

"Depth Charges closed up."

"Torpedoes closed up.

"Oerlikons and Ack Ack closed up."

These two would be critical as they were our only defence should the Germans attack by air.

And finally came the last report.

"Coxswain at the wheel. *HMS Beagle* closed up at action stations and ready for orders, Sir."

"Very good Coxswain. Make to Flotilla, *attack as planned. Boats one to five break north, boats six to nine with me. All line abreast. Double check you're not showing lights. Radio silence until my order.*"

The last orders were important. At this distance a five second radio broadcast might be lost in the ether of other broadcasts but if the Germans were on the ball, they would be ready for us.

We'd use radio again once we were in amongst their ships.

But, chinks of light were always a danger. If the convoy or the land-based guns saw anything bright they would open fire. No questions. They knew their own shipping movements. We were not supposed to be here.

We crashed on in the darkness, *Dotty* cutting through the small waves but leaving a huge wake behind her.

"Bridge, Radar. Contacts dead ahead bearing 010, distance twenty five miles, Sir. Can't see Flotilla 2, Sir, they must be behind the convoy."

"Very good. Let me know the minute you see them."

We'd planned this to the minute, though plans often go awry. The idea was to split the escort vessels, confuse them by attacking the convoy on both sides at the same time. Or as near as possible.

"Make to Flotilla *Reduce Speed. Half Ahead all engines.*"

I sensed Hawes looking at me.

"We have a hell of a bow wave when we're ploughing along at forty knots, Sub. It's a giveaway on a still night like this. At half ahead, we're less visible."

"Radar, Bridge. Five miles and closing and Flotilla 2 are in position."

"Stand by torpedoes and guns. On my command."

Closer and closer. Still no shells from the convoy. Better yet, nothing from the shore batteries. Flotilla 2 were just ahead of us. I heard the first explosions from the torpedoes. Whether they hit the warships or the merchant men I had no way of knowing. Then it was our turn.

"Torpedoes away. Fire at will."

The sound was deafening. The four inch gun on the forecastle blasted its first shell straight into a destroyer barely half a mile away. The first four torpedoes were already half way to their targets. Two huge explosions forced huge flames high into the air.

"Full Ahead all engines, Coxswain. About turn and back down their sides."

We skidded around in a controlled turn, giving our Oerlikon on the after deck a turn at target practice. The gunner pumped a full round into a tanker's bridge. No flames, but she was clearly out of control.

The rest of the flotilla followed in our wake. Between my five boats we'd accounted for five merchantmen and two warships. I'd find out later how O'Leary's crews had fared.

One more blast down the side of the convoy was enough. The surviving warships had woken up. They were like a wasps' nest, firing shells at anything that moved. Thankfully most of them missed.

"Commander to Flotilla. Head For Home, Boys. We've done enough."

All five of my boats lined up alongside me, twenty yards at most between us. And two miles away through my binoculars I saw O'Leary follow suit. I was about to put the binoculars down when a huge explosion rent the night air and the boat next to O'Leary's simply disintegrated.

"Lieutenant Roberts, I think, Sir," said the Coxswain, adding a stream of curses showing what he thought about the enemy. The other boats slackened pace for a minute, but it was useless. When ammunition blew up like that the only thing you'd pick out of the water were bits. Better to leave them there.

"Didn't you know the Coxswain?" I asked.

I sensed Williams nod.

"We sailed together in the Merch. He was my best man."

# Chapter 25    Coxswain Williams in Cardiff

The train was packed, no seats from Newlyn to Exeter.
You couldn't get near the buffet car, either. Army types
everywhere. And I wasn't in the mood for their banter.
I took the letter out and read it again. Another short
one.

*"Dear Dave, sorry to do this again. But there's a
smarmy type, hair slicked back been visiting. Got a big
car. Been staying at your Aggie's for over a week now.
Mrs Barrowcliffe down the street said he ran a pub out
by the beach in Penarth. Not seen your Aggie for a few
days now. Yours, Alf"*

I thought we'd cleared the air after the last time.
The skipper was good about giving me a spot of leave.
I told him that I felt I should visit Trevor's widow, him
dying when Lieutenant Roberts' boat blew up. We
were all close and she didn't have anybody else in the
way of family. He said, fine, we're all stood down for
two days while the rest of the flotilla joined. Just going
out on the odd jolly, he said. They'd cope.
Bristol Station looked as bad as ever. Squaddies and
matelots everywhere. No signs up in case Jerry
invaded so how the hell did you find out which
platform the Cardiff train went from? And these
porters were bloody useless.
Eventually I found the right platform and seethed as
we puffed slowly down under the River into the Severn
Tunnel. Two hours later we arrived in Cardiff and I
spent a few hours with Elsie. Told her to contact me if
she needed anything. A few of her mates were with her
and they said they'd look after her.
I left her place and walked to the bus station where I
changed into civvies before catching the bus to
Penarth. Once there I walked to the beach. It was eight
o' clock and already fairly dark. No street lights in the
black out and with my black reefer jacket, I was almost
invisible to any passers-by.

There were three pubs by the beach and at the second I saw a big car outside. I pulled a woollen sailor's hat down over my forehead and shuffled in.

It wasn't that packed and I saw her sitting at a table by the bar with a chap with slicked down hair. They were drinking spirits, gin by the looks of it.

I ordered a pint and stayed at the bar, watching them in the mirror. They acted like man and wife.

"Who's the woman over there?" a squaddie at the bar asked a young barman.

"That's Aggie, Bert. Boss' new girlfriend. Old man's in the navy or something. Looks like she's desperate for it," he said.

He walked off to serve another customer and I finished my pint and left to stand in the shadows across the road. The place had seen better days I thought. The Germans must have off loaded a few bombs on their way home. Derelict houses down one side of the street. At Closing Time I heard them shout Last Orders and gradually they all filed out. I waited for the barman to leave, relieved that he didn't live on the premises, before waiting in the cold for another hour. A light came on upstairs and two figures walked across the window. An hour later the light went off and there was silence all around.

I walked around to the back door and listened. Nothing. I knelt down and looked at the lock. Old, probably rusty. I took out my knife and eased it between the door and the frame, working it up and down gently till I heard it click.

In the unfamiliar kitchen I took off my boots and left them behind the door. As I rested my hand on the kitchen table I felt a bread knife. As I started to move I heard moans from upstairs. Jesus, they were at it.

I crawled up the stairs as quietly as I could. Each time a floorboard squeaked I stopped, but the noises upstairs drowned everything else out. I stopped on the top stair and looked in the bedroom. The door was wide open.

She lay on her back with legs wrapped around his back. He was shoving hard against her and she moaned and moaned and moaned. Suddenly she arched her back and called out.

"Yes, Yes, Yes."

Hours later, it must have been two in the morning, I rose from the kitchen table and rinsed the knife off in the sink. I walked back up the stairs and sobbed at the sight. I loved her and thought she loved me. Why did she have to ruin it?

The seriousness of it hit me then. What the hell had I done. My heart raced and my breath came in short gasps. I raced into the toilet and threw up. Every part of me shook and I could feel sweat running everywhere.

Get a grip, Williams, I told myself. Think, man, think. The bodies, I must get rid of the bodies. I looked out the window across to the beach and the bombed out houses and it struck me. I'd have to be quick.

The walk back down to the harbour only took a few minutes and I found exactly what I needed, an old rowing boat tied to a wooden post on the pier. I rowed the short distance to the beach and loaded the bodies on board along with some old chain I'd picked up on the pier.

It took an hour to get far enough out into the bay, secure the chains around the bodies and dump them over the side. After taking the boat back to its mooring I returned to the pub and looked around the shed in the beer garden. He kept some empty cans there, probably for petrol. I took one of them and siphoned some juice out of his car.

Before the sun rose I walked away from the pub for the last time. Flames licked up the inside of the building around the downstairs windows. With luck the police would treat it as an arson job for insurance. But I didn't really care. For the first time in a long time I felt free. But a part of me wondered what the hell I'd become.

Was this what love did to you? Or was it what war did to you?

# Chapter 26    Scotty in Newlyn

"There it is, Sir. Away to starboard. The pilot's waving."

"Well spotted, Sub. Man the side. We'll get as close as we can."

RAF Coastal Command had reported the Messerschmitt ditching in the sea off Lands End and asked us to go out to rescue the pilot. Now, barely twenty minutes later we were in situ.

"Slow Ahead, Morrison. The Coxswain won't like it if you scratch the paintwork," I told our temporary quartermaster.

"Slow Ahead it is, Sir."

"Stop engines, Midships the wheel. Quick as you can, Sub," I shouted to Hawes as we drew close to the plane.

One of the crew threw a line across to the pilot who jumped into the sea and started swimming towards us. As he was climbing over the rail I heard the unmistakable sound of another Messerschmitt, but this one was still in the air.

"All guns enemy aircraft bearing 020 attacking. Independent fire at will."

"Morrison, Full Ahead, steer 090."

The roar of the Daimler Benz engine increased as the plane swooped down towards us, all five machine guns hurtling their 20 mm shells towards us at over three thousand feet per second.

"Morrison, zig zag every five seconds," I ordered, watching the once small dot almost obliterating our view of the sky.

"Hard a port, Full Astern," I shouted as I saw the first of the plane's bombs dropping.

We stopped dead in the water as the aircraft rocketed past barely a hundred feet above the mast. All my machine guns poured hundreds of shells into the underbelly of the aircraft as huge plumes of water exploded all around us.

The bombs missed, but the water soaked everyone on deck, including the newly rescued German pilot who was lying face down on the deck with his hands over his head.

"We've got him," one of the forward machine gunners shouted, pointing at a stream of white smoke coming out of the plane's engine.

"Stand by your guns, he's turning"'" I shouted, watching the aircraft's nose come round. "Open fire."

I willed the shells to hit home, every one of them. If he was daft enough to continue attacking when his aircraft was damaged, I was determined to destroy him.

Afterwards it was impossible to say which of my gunners stopped the plane in its tracks.

One second the plane was hurtling back towards us, the next it simply disintegrated in mid-air. A lucky shell into the petrol tank, perhaps, or a flame straight into the ammunition trays.

It didn't matter either way.

No parachute emerged from the flaming debris. No pilot to pick out of the water.

*"Dotty's* first aircraft shot down, Sir. And not a Possible but an absolute definite."

I smiled at Hawes who stood there with a camera in his hands.

"I think I captured the very moment, Sir," he said with pride.

I laughed and shook my head.

"If you did, Sub, we'll have it on the wardroom noticeboard," I told him.

I picked up the PA system.

"Well done, men. Good shooting. Our first aircraft destroyed."

The Military Police took our German captive as soon as we berthed. As they drove away I saw Lenton waiting.

"I heard about the attack. Is everyone OK?"

I nodded as I climbed up to the pier.

"Yes, a few scratches here and there but nothing serious. *Dotty* needs a bit of attention after being half drowned when the bombs dropped, though," I replied.

"And you, Sir? Are you OK?"

I nodded.

"Thank you, Miss Lenton, I am. We were lucky."

She hesitated before looking into my eyes. Once again I was struck by how attractive she was.

"Will you walk down the pier with me, please?" she said and we started towards her office.

"We had a phone call this morning from the Police in Cardiff. Didn't *Dotty's* Coxswain go up there a few days ago?"

I smiled at her use of my boat's name.

"Yes, he asked for some time to visit his chum's widow. Norries' Coxswain and Williams were good friends. Best men at each other's wedding, that sort of thing. The two grew up together, went to sea at the same time, sailed in the Merch together for a while. He said that the widow had no other close family. He had a few days leave owing so I sent him off. What did the Police want?"

"There was a fire in a local pub. Burnt the place down. Thing is, the landlord had a new girlfriend, Agnes Williams. I looked in the files and your Coxswain's wife was called Agnes."

"How can they be sure it was the Coxswain's wife?"

She told me that the Police had spoken to the regular customers. And the descriptions matched up. Also the barman said there was a stranger in the bar the night before, fairly tall, kind of windblown complexion like you'd get if you'd spent a long time at sea.

I felt a frown crease my brow.

"But presumably the wife can describe this stranger. If she was in the bar."

"According to the Police, she was. Along with the landlord. They were acting in quite a friendly way, they said. Well, they were a little more descriptive than that."

I smiled at her wording. I could imagine how the police might describe that sort of behaviour.

"What the police are more concerned about is where the landlord and Agnes Williams may be now. They haven't been seen since they closed the pub after Last Orders. And there were no bodies in the ashes."

"Well, I'll ask him about it when he gets back. His leave expires in a couple of hours and I haven't known him to be AWOL in the years we've sailed together."

"Will you tell him about the fire?"

"I'll play it by ear. He said he was going to Cardiff to see the widow. I suppose Penarth's just next door. But we don't know for sure that he got there. I'll see what he says."

"I think that's wise. If there's something fishy going on the police will want to see him, she replied. "I'll give them the details of Lieutenant Roberts' coxswain. Maybe they can check if he saw her."

She hesitated before blurting out a question.

"Please don't be offended but one of the Wrens is getting married on Saturday and she says that two of the guests have dropped out because they've been posted. She asked if I could make up the numbers and if so could I bring someone along. I wondered, if you're in port and you've nothing to do…."

I found myself smiling again.

"Miss Lenton, I would be honoured to accompany you to the wedding. I can think of nothing better to do."

She smiled in turn and blew a breath out.

"I think this is your office. What time shall I collect you?"

## Chapter 27    Klopp aboard *Der Condor* in Hamburg

Someone's been in my cabin. I always leave my things in pretty much the same place but someone had been in and moved things around. Almost certainly Zirk. Well, he'll never find the painkillers. Even I had to stretch face down on the floor to reach them under the bunk and I knew where they were.

I haven't spoken to Ryker since the incident with the submarine and he called Braun a bastard. I would have to remind him again about being in any way outspoken. Zirk and I, on the other hand have crossed paths. The man did not like me. That feeling was entirely mutual.

I had no love for anything to do with the Gestapo. There were too many stories about their atrocious behaviour for them all to be untrue. And I had seen the way they treated ordinary German citizens in Hamburg and in other ports. Zirk was no worse than many of the scum, but he was certainly no better.

One lunchtime Zirk and I dined together. Well, not exactly together. We were the only two at the wardroom table. He asked me how I had lost my lower leg and I told him that it was blown off during an attack.

"Do you suffer pain with it, Commander?" he asked

"Some. Not much. It's not a subject that I talk about with strangers."

The man obviously had a skin as thick as the walls of the vaults in the Reichsbank because he continued talking as though I had said nothing.

"I find that some men who have suffered injuries and continue to feel pain need something to help. Alcohol, drugs, medications."

I said nothing as I stood.

"Tell me, Zirk, what do you know of pain? Other than subjecting others to it?"

I swallowed two tablets and lay on my bunk. My eyes became heavy as I drifted off and the dream came back again.

I heard the explosions as the torpedoes crashed through the sides of the ship. Men screaming, huge clouds of steam flowing out of the funnel. Alarms ringing all over the ship.

I grabbed my lifejacket and ran up to the bridge.

"Johann, we've been torpedoed. Three straight into the engine room. Chief says we've no chance. Most of his men are already dead."

He paused as a messenger joined us.

"Commander says he can't close the watertight doors. Power's out. We're sinking fast, he said, Sir."

The Captain sounded seven short blasts on the ship's whistle followed by a single long blast. He picked up the tannoy and ordered all men to their lifeboat stations and to abandon ship.

"Good luck, men. We've signalled Fleet that we are abandoning ship. We will have rescue vessels with us soon."

"Good luck, Johann. You have been the best First Lieutenant a Captain could wish for. You will make a good commander. Now, to your station."

There was no panic because we had drilled many times for this moment. Hoping it would not come but preparing ourselves if it should. I ran down to the boat deck and took station between two lifeboats.

"Quickly now, men. Get those oars ready. Pull away from the ship as soon as you're in the water. Rescue any men who have jumped in. The water's cold. They won't last long."

With the boat loaded I gave the order for it to be dropped to the sea forty feet below after which I moved to the next boat. Once that was loaded and away I moved to the next.

The blast lifted me off my feet and blew me over the ship's rail into the water below. It was the last I remembered until I regained consciousness in one of the lifeboats. The pain was unbearable and I cried out loud.

"My leg. Help me. I can't stand it."

"Hold on, Sir, we've got some morphine. You've already had one dose," a sailor told me. "The pack says you can't have another for four hours."

I struggled to sit up but hands held me down.

"You don't want to look, Sir. It's a mess down there. The Doc's coming over from one of the other boats."

I felt rocking and heard the Doc's voice.

"Well now, Johann, let's have a look at what you've done."

He was silent for a few moments before he spoke again.

"How much morphine has he had?"

He listened to the answer.

"Nowhere near enough. I'm going to knock you out, Johann, until we can get you on the rescue ship. Then we'll sort you out."

The next time I was aware was two days later. The Doc told me they tried to save the lower half of my leg, but it was impossible.

"But look on the bright side, Johann, the artificial legs these days are marvellous. You'll soon be up and about again. And at least the pain will have gone."

The knock at my door woke me up.

"Who is it?"

"Ryker, Sir. Time for your next watch."

I thought back to the dream. The Doc was right on one score: I was up and about in a few days. The leg took longer as the wound had to heal and there were more operations to come. But, he was wrong about the pain. It started at the knee and shot down. On good days I managed it with the tablets they prescribed. On bad days I doubled and trebled the dose. The black market worked in Hamburg as efficiently as the Gestapo and I found willing suppliers.

Unfortunately, there were fewer good days now. And Captain Braun made sure that their numbers dwindled still further. I could cope with a hard taskmaster but his brutality and aggression in everything he did and said was wearing. And the crew looked to me to defend them against some of his wilder actions.

I swallowed another tablet and put on my cap. Perhaps he'd transfer me if I irritated him enough. And with that jolly thought and an idea forming in my mind I climbed to the bridge for my watch, a few spare tablets lodged in my shirt pocket.

# Chapter 28    James Haywood in Newlyn

As Spring turned into early summer and the days lengthened, we spent more time at sea practising attacks. And on occasions steamed up the English Channel to attack German shipping. We had a full complement of boats now and were used to working in small and large groups.

"Twenty four boats, James. A mighty fighting force," the skipper said as we returned to Newlyn after another exercise.

"Still no idea what we'll be doing, Sir?"

He shook his head.

"I've stopped asking. The Old Man says we'll find out when their Lordships at the Admiralty are ready. Just keep on doing what we're doing."

I thought ahead to the evening.

"Are you off ashore, Sir?"

"Yes, I need to see Second Officer Lenton. Catch up with the paperwork."

"Oh. Right."

"Something planned, James? Not with Nurse Crebo by any chance?"

I felt the heat in my cheeks and he smiled.

"Each time you've mentioned her name your eyes have taken you off to another planet, Number One. And I'm pleased for you."

"We've become quite good friends, Sir. First time that any woman's taken any interest in me since the accident. I can't say that I blame them."

He looked at me in that uncanny way that the skipper does sometimes. He'd never flinched, like some people do when they see the scar. Instead he patted my arm.

"You deserve it. Anyway, about time Sub Lieutenant Hawes earned his ferocious salary."

He picked up the bridge phone.

"Wardroom, is Sub Lieutenant Hawes there? Put him on."

"Ah, Sub. I am about to baptise you, Mr Hawes. You have the watch aboard this evening. Able Seaman Morrison is Duty Coxswain so will make sure that nobody throws you overboard."

As I left the boat to meet Carol, Coxswain Williams stopped in front of me and saluted smartly.

"At ease, Coxswain. How was the leave? How was Johnson's widow?"

"In a bad way, Sir. They've known each other since infants school. Married for ten years. I'm sure she'll get over it at some stage. And she's got some good friends around her."

"Did you manage to get home yourself, Coxswain? See your wife?"

There was a slight hesitation, unusual for Williams.

"No, Sir. Didn't really have the time. Came back here early and met up with some old chums instead. Well, one in particular. Known her for a long time. Needed to get drunk, tell you the truth, Sir. Are you off ashore?"

"Yes. See you in the morning, Coxswain. Carry on."

She waved at me from the end of the pier.

"I'm sorry, James, I know I said I'd meet you at the Mission. But I couldn't wait."

I took her arm and put it through mine.

"I'm glad that you couldn't. I've wanted to be with you since I last saw you."

She stopped and turned to face me.

"Do you really mean that?"

I swallowed.

"I did. I'm sorry, was that too forward?"

She stood on tiptoe and kissed me on the lips. I thought I was going to explode, I felt quite light headed.

"That was lovely," I told her. "We must do that again."

She laughed and hugged me. And that was the start of a wonderful evening. We walked towards Newlyn and stopped at the Mounts Bay Inn overlooking the sea.

The beer garden was empty and we sat and talked the whole of the evening.

On the way back to Newlyn she was quiet. When we got to her house she looked up at me and I knew that I was in love with this girl. I opened my mouth and she placed her forefinger on my lips.

"Hush, Darling James. Mum and Dad have gone away to stay with Mum's sister in Truro for a week as she isn't well. We have the house to ourselves."

She led me inside and up the stairs. I thought that I was hallucinating as she opened her bedroom door.

"Do you think that I'm being a whore?"" she asked and I took her in my arms.

"You see," she continued, "I've never done this before. I asked my friend in the hospital pharmacy about it and she gave me these and said if you're a real sailor you'll know what to do."

The tears ran down her face as she spoke, and I wiped them away with my finger.

"Darling Carol, I fell in love with you the first time I saw you on that hospital ward. I didn't dare hope that you might have some feelings for me. And by the way,"

She looked into my eyes.

"I am a real sailor, but not all that experienced in some departments, if you see what I mean. I think we may learn something new together."

The next morning we woke before the sun rose and made love again. And again. I had experienced nothing like it, had never felt so elated, so fulfilled.

As we ate breakfast we said little. Words did not seem necessary.

We walked back down the hill to the harbour.

"Will you be going to sea today?"

"Yes, we're due out on exercises. Should be back by tea time. Can I see you if I can get away?"

"With all my heart, James. But I'll understand if you can't make it."

We kissed goodbye and she started to walk away.

"James, before we met last night a man came out of the pub. You spoke to him."

"That was David Williams, our Coxswain."

"Oh. He was with a woman. One of our local floozies, if you know what I mean."

I smiled.

"There are always a few prostitutes around when the Navy's in port."

"Yes, I know that. But they were talking and he said something about remembering what to say if the police came calling. And he gave her a thick envelope."

# Chapter 29    Rommel at his HQ in the North African Desert

"It's going to be a long day, gentlemen so let's get started."

Looking back over the last twenty-four hours I thought that was the biggest understatement of all time. My generals and their deputies crowded into the largest tent we had. The heat was suffocating but I needed absolute secrecy. I had guards posted in a tight circle one hundred yards away with orders to let nobody in or out.

At the end of it all we had our plans and everyone knew their role.

"We are putting our ninety thousand troops against General Auchinlek's one hundred thousand. But, we have more tanks and ours are also bigger and better. Our spies have done well. We have more information about them than they can possibly have about us. We must win this battle. We must push into Egypt. We must take Tobruk."

Ah, Tobruk. I lit a cigarette and poured a Schnapps. Tobruk, the jewel in the British crown. Alexandria would have been better but that was too far away. We will take that next time. I'll settle for Tobruk instead.

I sat at my desk and looked at the map. We had all our men and artillery in position. In one hour they would advance while it was still dark. When the sun rose, the attack would begin. The British would expect an attack from the front or from the flank. But our artillery would pound the enemy's lines from their rear.

We had marched twenty thousand troops hundreds of miles through the desert, avoiding British lines and spies. When this battle ended, Tobruk would be ours. And Alexandria, the enemy's other key stronghold would be within our grasp.

The Suez Canal would be next and once we had that we had control of all shipping from the south into the

Mediterranean Sea. The British had nowhere else to turn and we would drive them out of Africa.

But, so much depended on stealth and deceit. We were feeding information to known local agents that indicated an all-out, full frontal attack. Would the enemy believe it?

Two days later I had the answer. The British fought as only the British can fight. They made us work hard for every inch of ground we advanced. But, advance we did. Soon, they were in full scale retreat and we pressed home our advantage. The extra twenty thousand men were the difference between victory and failure.

"Gazala, Sir," Keller told me, looking at the map. "We advanced over a hundred miles. And this," he pointed at the map, "is where we are. Gazala."

"Yes, Johann. The question is how long do we stay here before we get our reinforcements for the next big push?"

"Do you think Berlin will send more reinforcements, Sir?"

"Yes, Johann, I believe they will. We must wait until later in the summer when the Russian campaign will be well under way. The Fuhrer himself promised me the troops and he has never let me down."

# Chapter 30    Coxswain Williams in Newlyn

The skipper and I did Rounds this morning. He warned the crew beforehand that he wanted the boat ship-shape and ready for sea at any time of night and day and told the other skippers that they should each carry out their own inspection at the same time.

We started on *Dotty* directly after breakfast and visited every part, from the engine room to the sailors' quarters in the forecastle. It never took long but the skipper used it as a chance to talk to every man aboard. I'm sure he did it more to get to know his crew than to make sure the boat was always sea-ready and shipshape.

After inspecting men and boat we walked along the quay to see how *Dotty* looked from ashore.

"A coat of paint wouldn't go amiss, Coxswain."

"Will do, Sir. I'll get the hands on it straight away."

"How was the run home?"

"It was sad, Sir. She's not taken it well. Luckily she's got some good friends around her."

"Yes, the First Lieutenant told me at breakfast. Also said you didn't see your wife."

"No, Sir. I didn't really feel like it. I suppose seeing Edith in a state made me wonder how Agnes would be if I bought it"

"Wouldn't it have been better to see her and reassure her? Not that it's any of my business," he added. "I'm no expert in the romance department."

"I wanted to forget for a couple of days. I came back here and…"

I had to get the lie out there, but my voice choked. God knows why.

"I spent the night with a woman, Sir. Someone I've known for a while. She came down here a few weeks ago. It's nothing serious. Just a one night stand."

He didn't say anything at first. We were looking down at the stern and he seemed miles away.

"Was Agnes seeing someone else, David? You can tell me if she was. It'll be between us."

As always the use of my first name took me by surprise. Normally I would have been pleased. It was his way of sharing a confidence, telling me he trusted me. Right now it made me feel guilty as hell.

"Not that I knew, Sir. She was always a bit flighty but it ended at that. Why do you ask?"

He turned and looked straight into my eyes and I wondered if he suspected something. His next words confirmed it.

"The Cardiff Police rang HQ yesterday. A pub caught fire a few nights ago. They suspect it was arson. The firemen found a strong smell of petrol and an empty can lay on the ground at the back."

Thank God I wore gloves. At least they couldn't get any prints off it.

"What has that got to do with Agnes, Sir? I don't understand."

He told me that some witnesses had seen someone called Agnes getting very friendly with the landlord. According to them she was staying at the place overnight. I felt the colour drain from my cheeks and swallowed, before kneeling on the quay and vomiting my breakfast into the sea below.

The skipper put a hand on my shoulder and kept it there until I stood up.

"Was it my Agnes, Sir? Was she in the pub when it caught fire?"

"They don't know who it was for sure. But, no, they haven't found any bodies. The place was empty. Look, I'm really sorry, David. I didn't mean to shock you. The thing is that the Police haven't heard anything from the landlord. And neither have the pub's locals. They're treating the whole thing as suspicious."

"And they don't know where Aggie is?"

"No. and they have no witnesses and no idea who might have done this. The landlord didn't have any real enemies as far as the police know. Well, a few shady deals, but most landlords in those sorts of areas are the same. Buying cheap booze where they can, bit of black market whenever they can get away with it, lock-ins for the locals. But nothing serious."

He changed the subject then and asked me about the woman I'd been with. He told me that Number One's girlfriend had seen me come out of The Dolphin with her.

"She's a prossie, Sir. Been on the game for years. She said she was broke, hadn't enough money for the rent and the landlord was threatening to throw her out. I first met her in Plymouth when we berthed there back in 1939 for a few months. She moved down to Newlyn last year. I bumped into her on a run ashore when we first came here."

After that he said that the police would probably want a word with me and that I should tell him if Agnes got in touch.

"She was never a great letter writer, Sir. I think I've had three since the war started."

Now, walking back down the pier towards the boat I wondered if I did the right thing. Not in killing her. And the bastard who made her do it. But, in dumping the bodies at sea. Did I use enough chain to weight them down? What happens if they come to the surface? Will the police be able to see how they died? Did I leave anything behind that could pin their deaths on me?

I'd have to see Madge again tonight. Make sure she won't let me down. Jesus I gave her almost a year's wages to keep her quiet. What if she blagged? How could I stop her?

## Chapter 31    Winston Churchill in The War Rooms

The news was as bad as any we'd had since the first day of the war.

"Are you sure that Tobruk has fallen, Alan?"

The Head of the British Army nodded his head slowly.

"General Auchinleck sent word an hour ago, Prime Minister. He has ordered a full scale retreat to El Alamein."

He walked to the wall map and placed his finger on a dark spot in amongst a host of yellow.

"A railway halt, Sir, not even a full blown station. But the area is perfect for the next stage in forcing Rommel's hand. He'll be cocky. Want to follow up on his success. But the Auk's already got his men digging in. Rommel can't get past them. The terrain's a nightmare to attack. But easy to defend."

"The papers will have a field day. Losses mounting at sea, Singapore gone, thousands captured by the Japanese."

"But we do have Enigma, Prime Minister. We know what the Germans are planning. We've broken the codes and they don't know it."

"I know, Alan, I know. But that doesn't make it easier. In fact, because we can't say anything it makes it all the more difficult."

I relit my cigar and sipped at a brandy. At least we were destroying more U Boats than ever before. And our shipping losses were down slightly. Not growing as much as they were. And the Americans coming into the war was good news and gave us more ships to fight with.

But, we needed to win the North African desert campaign and put pressure on the Germans and Italians who thought the territory was theirs.

"How long can the Auk hold out?"

"Supplies-wise, four months. That gives us time to get reinforcements in place. Our intelligence will pick up when Rommel plans to attack. It won't be soon, he needs reinforcements to replace his losses. This battle was bloody but the next will be worse. According to MI6 Rommel has already told Berlin he can't attack until he gets more troops and tanks. Auk will hold him off if he decides to attack in the next few months."

We had spoken before about General Auchinleck and recognised the need to replace him as soon as possible. But now was not the right time.

"Alan, we must visit the Auk. Not now, perhaps in about a month or two. Will you tell him that he will be replaced after the next battle?"

"Already done, Sir. One other thing, Winston."

"Don't tell me there's more bad news."

"I am afraid there is, thought we expected it to happen. The German Luftwaffe have sent reinforcements to support Rommel. I've spoken to Sir Sholto and he is adamant that his flyers can defend our positions. But without more planes he cannot go on the offensive. It looks like we'll need the Navy to attack any reinforcements sent to support Rommel."

Sir Sholto Douglas was Marshall of the Royal Air Force. If anyone knew their capabilities it was him.

"Talk to Admiral Cunningham, Alan. Tell him he's to start preparations immediately. Though knowing him of old he's already started."

Sir Andrew Cunningham, one of our greatest admirals, in charge of the Mediterranean Fleet since 1939. If anyone could do it, his boys could.

The conversation ended there and my thoughts turned to Rommel. He'd got his reinforcements for this battle. We must inflict a good deal of harm on him in the next. And stop him from getting any more reinforcements. It would have to be the Royal Navy's responsibility to do that. And right now, though I didn't rate their chances highly, they were our only chance.

## Chapter 32    Scotty in Newlyn

I haven't been to many weddings but from what little I
knew this one was good fun. The Wren looked
beautiful in a white dress with some sort of lacy veil.
The groom was in his RAF dress uniform. I learnt that
he was an engineer on one of the RAF's Air Sea
Rescue launches based at Newlyn.

After the wedding in St Peter's Church there was a
short reception at the Chypons Hotel, barely two
hundred yards away. Not many guests but those that
were there were mainly servicemen and women with
their husbands, wives or boyfriends.

Lenton, I have to say, looked simply delicious. I hadn't
seen her out of uniform, but today she wore a very
simple knee length blue dress with a white jacket. Her
hair was jet black and almost down to her waist.
Normally she wore it in a bun.

But, it was her face that captivated me. She told me
that her Mother was Chinese and had left Hong Kong
to come to England after World War 1. She had met
Lenton's father in the colony when he served in the
Army. They married, against the wishes of her parents
and his senior officers and she had quickly become
pregnant.

From that moment onwards they had little peace and
Mrs Lenton quickly agreed to move back to London
with her new husband. That was as much as I knew.
Except that today I realised how beautiful her only
child was.

She held my arm as we walked back down to the
village centre.

"Have you been out to Lands End?" I asked.

"No, it's supposed to be quite rugged."

"It is. But on a day like this with the sun high in the sky and no rain it's also quite beautiful. What do you say?"

She smiled, which lit up her face even more.

"I would love to. But how do we get there?"

"I've got my car. Well, it was Mum's, but I've always driven it when I've been on leave. The Navy police let me keep it in their yard at the end of the pier."

We drove out of Newlyn along the long, winding Coombe Road, the trees either side providing shade from the bright sunshine.

When we arrived at the rough ground around the Lands End Hotel I parked and we walked the few yards to the very end of England. The wind was little more than a gentle breeze and it blew her hair out from her back. She took a scarf from her handbag and tied it around her head.

"You have the most wonderful hair," I told her. "I didn't realise how long it was."

"We have to keep it short. It's one of those rules they have to try to make us look like Plain Janes."

"I don't think any rule could make you look like a Plain Jane, Annie. You have the most beautiful face."

"Thank you, Harry. That's a lovely thing to say. Most people look at me and wonder where I'm from."

"You're obviously English. And you told me that your Mum was originally from Hong Kong. Where is she now?"

"Mum and Dad settled in East London. With more and more Chinese coming here to escape persecution they got enough money together to open a restaurant. Well, they called it a café when they first started. My Dad's quite a businessman and Mum's a really good cook and they expanded and expanded. Six restaurants and a shop as well."

"Did they approve of you joining the Wrens? Most parents would have been aghast at the thought of their daughter joining up. It's hardly a woman's world."

"My brother was in the Merchant Navy when war broke out. He was torpedoed on his way back from Norway. He drowned. It didn't seem right to work in an office after that."

"I'm sorry. I had no idea."

I took her arm and walked her away towards the Hotel. "Let's have a drink. They serve residents here out of hours. I'm sure they'll serve Royal Navy types, too. Tell me about the Wrens, what made you choose them?"

The barman brought us two gin and tonics and we talked for over an hour.

We walked back to the car and I opened the door for her. Before she got in she turned towards me and took her scarf off, shaking her head as she did so. The hair cascaded around her shoulders and I inhaled deeply, barely able to catch my breath.

"Thank you for steering me away from my brother, Harry. That was kind of you."

"I didn't want to ruin a perfect day, Annie. I haven't relaxed like this for, I don't know, ever."

"No more evil thoughts? No more doubts about you and being a captain?"

"No. After that night, I think I realised that none of us is perfect. Although you look more perfect than anyone I've ever known."

She laughed and her dazzling smile was captivating. I held her hand and lifted it to my lips. As I kissed it I smelt her perfume. She squeezed my hand and leant forward.

"I think we can do better than that," she said and we kissed. I felt my heart banging in my chest.

I don't remember the drive back to Newlyn. It went far too quickly, that I do remember. When we arrived at her billet, a house owned by an old lady close on the outskirts of Newlyn, we kissed again.

"Can I see you again, Annie? If you want to, that is."

"I would love it, Harry."

She pecked me on the cheek and got out of the car before bending down and looking into my open car window.

"Mrs Richards is looking out of the window. She'll want to know all about my day. I don't want to give her too much to gossip about. We'll save that for another time."

# Chapter 33    David Williams in Newlyn

I waited till Morrison walked to the stern to check our moorings. Once he was out of sight, I slipped over the side and in underneath the pier. There were wooden pilings all the way down to the end of the harbour. They were slippery because at high tide the sea water covered them and the diesel oil that floated on the top turned the pilings into a mini ice rink. I was careful; if I fell in, the splash would echo around the harbour at this time of night and the thought of swallowing mouthfuls of diesel and salt water was not a welcome one.

At the end of the pier I hopped down on to the beach and crept over to the shadows thrown by the offices. Good thing about the blackout was that nobody could see more than a few feet in front of them.

I knew Madge's place well enough to find it in the dark. Her light was on upstairs so she was probably entertaining, but there were no lights downstairs. The back door wasn't even locked and I put on my gloves, eased through it quietly and left it on the latch. Her room was on the left at the top of the stairs and the room next door was empty. She'd told me that a new lodger was due to move in next week.

I listened at Madge's door and heard the usual noises for a few minutes before they started talking.

"He gave me two hundred quid. Said there could be more if I told the police we'd been together that night."

"Two hundred don't sound much, Madge. Tell him you want more. Get another two hundred and we can get back up to Plymouth. It's bloody boring down here and we're not earning a lot of money. You can get a proper job up there and come off the game. I'll help you out, I got loads of contacts up there. What's his name anyway? You never did tell me."

"He said if anyone ever found out who he was he'd kill me, Sammy. I'm scared. He's big. Didn't tell me his name. You know what they're like. Just said to call him Will. We met in Plymouth in 1939, he was there on one of them MGBs, that's all I can tell you. I was surprised when I saw him down here. He was in the Fishermans Arms and I recognised his accent. Welsh it was."

She didn't tell me her pimp had come down with her. This could be more awkward than I thought. I heard the sound of mattress springs moving and slipped into the empty room.

A few minutes later the door closed quietly and I listened as footsteps echoed down the stairs. When I looked out the window he was leaving through the front door. He stopped and looked up towards Madge's room and lit a cigarette. That's what he looked like. I'll remember that. I wonder where he's staying. Madge'll tell me.

Why are women like that? First, Agnes now Madge. Was I that bad a man? The toilet flushed and Madge's bedroom door clicked shut. I waited half an hour and slipped into her room. It stank of old perfume, stale sex, sweat and booze. A half empty bottle of gin stood on the bedside table.

I stepped over to the bed and wondered about one last time, but she stirred and opened her eyes. She opened her mouth to scream and I grabbed the pillow from underneath her and slammed my open hand against her mouth before pressing the pillow down hard over her mouth and nose. I waited till she stopped kicking then dressed her as best I could.

I tipped the gin bottle into her mouth and she gagged on it before swallowing. Now to get her down to the harbour.

I held her under her arm as though I was helping her along and staggered out of the house and down to a small beach just outside the harbour wall. The tide had just turned and was going out. I laid her on the pebbles and rolled my trousers up. I put her face down in the water and held her like that for a few minutes, not pressing too hard, then walked her out till I was up to my thighs.

She floated off slowly. With luck she'd be treated as a drowning. And with even more luck wouldn't be found for a month or two.

I dried off as best I could and went back to her room. I went straight to the mattress. There was my money. I looked through her handbag but couldn't find an address for the pimp. Newlyn wasn't a big place. I'd do a pub crawl tomorrow and find him. His type were always in pubs looking for punters for their girls.

# Chapter 34    Scotty in Newlyn

The Old Man was particularly jaunty this morning.
"German convoy heading from St Nazaire. Likely destination Channel Islands according to Enigma."
"What did we do before we captured that machine, Sir? Good old fashioned spies with binoculars up and down France's Atlantic coast I suppose."
"Yes, well we don't have to bother with that now. Those people who decode the messages are first class. Had some excellent intelligence on German shipping. Now, Harry, this next raid's important. Six ships in all but a big escort again. We must destroy the ships to show what we're capable of."
"I don't need all twenty boats to attack this convoy, Sir. How many escorts?"
He looked down at the file on his desk.
"Twenty one according to this. They say it's a newly formed group: Gruppen 158 Escort."
I smiled at his attempt at German. It sounded like he was clearing his throat.
"Something funny, Commander?"
"No, of course not, Sir. Just a passing thought. Do we know the makeup of the escort group?"
"One cruiser, eight destroyers and twelve smaller ships. A lot of firepower. Average speed currently ten knots."
I walked over to his wall map.
"Where are they now?"
He pointed and I picked up a pair of dividers and a parallel ruler.
"Midnight tonight they'll be fifteen miles off Brest. That's a hundred and fifty miles from here. Weather forecast for the next twenty four hours is fair. Leave here as the light's failing we'll be there in five hours."
We spent another hour working up a rough plan. Anything could happen between now and midnight to

scupper any thorough planning. We would have all the info we needed once we got closer.

I led the flotilla out through the Gaps at 1830 hours. Daylight practically gone, the moon rising into the clear night sky.

There was no need for contact with the other boats. The two hours planning earlier in the afternoon was enough. Radio Silence all the way there. And with luck fighter cover from the RAF on the way back.

"Steady on 140 degrees, Coxswain. Revs for thirty knots."

There was no reply and I turned towards him.

"Coxswain, are you all right?"

"Sorry, Sir, 140 degrees and thirty knots. Aye, Sir."

I'd have to keep an eye on Williams. He wasn't the same man. Even Morrison said to one of the crew that the Coxswain was awfully quiet these days. Mind you, if his wife's done a bunk, it's not surprising. Perhaps the Cardiff police would have some information when they see him tomorrow.

"Boat's closed up, Sir. Not a light showing anywhere."

"Thanks, Number One. And where's our sub lieutenant this evening? Curled up in his bunk fast asleep?"

"No. I've got him on the radar for the trip out. He's picked it up well."

I nodded. Hawes settled in well. Even the oldest of our crew respected him. If he didn't know something, he asked. And he grasped the theory of discipline quickly, too.

"Ready for his full stripe, James?"

"Not yet, Sir. Another couple of months."

We drove through the night at thirty knots, rather like driving a car on an unlit road in pitch darkness at seventy miles per hour. Except that I had radar to guide me as long as we were within thirty miles of the coastline as it showed me the outline of the nearest land. But, it was a backup system to the eyes and ears in the wheelhouse.

"Almost time, Sir," the First Lieutenant said.

"Radar, anything on the plot?"

"Nothing, Sir," Sub Lieutenant Hawes replied. A minute later he spoke again.

"Radar, Bridge, we have a group of twenty six ships moving northwards in formation."

"Give it two minutes and tell me their exact course and speed."

"Coxswain make to Group 2, *stand by to break away.*"

"Radar Bridge. Twenty six ships confirmed. Course 020 degrees, speed twelve knots."

He gave their present position and my group of twelve decoy MGBs reeled away on a southerly heading to approach them from the rear. That left my remaining twelve MGBs to attack from the east - closer into the French coastline. A coastline held strongly, of course, by the Germans. And I hoped a direction that would be completely unexpected amongst the escort group.

"Increase revs for fifty knots. Full Speed Ahead. Make to Group 1 *Maintain Position. Break off for attack on my order.*"

They knew that. I knew that they knew. But this was twenty-four boats working together for the first time in action. It did no harm to remind the skippers. And the enemy rarely picked up on the short messages.

I walked aft to the Radar desk and looked down over Hawes' shoulder. Good, Group 2 exactly where they should be.

"They'll make their turn in a few minutes, Sir," Hawes said.

"And Group 1's exactly where I want them, too, Sub."

"As soon as we fire our first shell, Sub, signal Newlyn. Tell them the time and give them the message, *Attack started, Await cover.*"

I hoped that the RAF were on time. There were lots of airfields around Brest and the Channel Islands weren't that far away. I could do with a squadron of Spitfires to keep the Germans away.

I looked at the small blips on the radar screen. How many would be there in five minutes time. More important, how many of my boats would return to Newlyn?

## Chapter 35    Braun Aboard *Der Condor* off the French coastline

The Action Stations klaxon sounded as I turned over in my bunk. I was upright and into my boots within seconds and on the Bridge before a minute passed.

"Radar contacts ten miles out, Sir, astern of us and closing. Twelve vessels, their course is 090 degrees and they're closing fast, estimated speed 30 knots."

A good report, Klopp, I thought but didn't say it. I liked to keep him off guard.

"Make to destroyers: *Twelve enemy vessels astern, ten miles away. Leave the convoy and engage.*"

"All destroyers, Sir? These are small vessels, probably Motor Gunboats. What if there are more ahead of us?"

"Make to all escorts except destroyers, *All remaining escort vessels, close up on convoy. Sharp look outs. All go to Action Stations immediately.*"

"Mr Klopp. What I see is an attack from astern. An unusual manoeuvre to be sure, but one that could have come off if we had not seen them on our Radar. You are dismissed."

Zirk came over from his position at the rear of the bridge.

"Commander Klopp does not seem to learn, Captain."

"No, he doesn't, Zirk. Perhaps you would be good enough to follow him to his Action Station. To make sure that he follows orders."

"But he told me that I should not leave the Bridge during Action Stations, Captain."

"The last time I looked, Lieutenant Zirk, I was the Commanding Officer of *Der Condor*. Go."

"All departments are at Action Stations, Sir."

"Good."

The English didn't have enough fast gunboats to mount an attack here. We have them now. The destroyers will blow them out of the water. There was a series of explosions from astern.

"Sonar Bridge, sounds of a ship breaking up. Maybe two."

I grabbed the telephone.

"What do you mean, Maybe? Be specific, you fool."

"Sorry, Sir, it's too far away to be sure."

I walked on to the Bridge wing and looked out over the stern. Another series of explosions. Then the radio squealed to life.

*"Condor* from *Brummer.* Two destroyers sunk. Mines. The English have laid mines. All the way across our course."

Another explosion.

*"Condor* to *Brummer.* Are you receiving?"

Nothing.

*"Condor* to *Brummer.* Are you receiving?"

Nothing.

"Radar Bridge, fast moving vessels to starboard. Two miles out, forty knots, twelve ships in total."

"How the hell did they get there? Why didn't you see them earlier?"

I picked up the handset. Too late for radio silence.

"Gruppen 158 enemy attacking from the east. All guns fire at will."

I looked down at my hands, both gripping the handrail in front of me so tightly it looked as though the blood vessels were outside my skin. I realised that I was holding my breath.

I could see the wash from the bow waves. My God, they were almost on top of us.

The ship directly ahead of me exploded in a flash of intense light. One second there, then gone.

"Hard a starboard, emergency full astern," I shouted. We heeled over to starboard as we smashed through the debris in front of us, steaming over the upturned faces of the merchant seamen who seconds earlier had been safe on board their ships. I fancied that I heard the screams as our huge propellers turned those men into mulch, bloody mulch.

"Wheel amidships, full ahead both engines."
Another set of explosions from the other side of the convoy.
"It's *Axel*, Sir. She's stopped in the water."
My God, will this night never end? *Axel* was one of my corvettes. Our forward guns blasted out shells as fast as they could. They rained down on one of the enemy boats and it disintegrated. I cheered.
"More like that."
Flames shot into the sky from all directions. We were now in the middle of the convoy and fires raged all around us. Gradually, we pulled out on to the eastern side and at last I saw one of their gunboats turning away from us. But not before Klopp sent four depth charges flying over the rail towards it.
Four explosions, all set for minimum depth lifted the boat out of the water. And dropped it back in tatters.
"Machine gunners, fire at will."
They needed no further bidding. Those English sailors who survived soon died as hailstorms of bullets flew across the divide between us, blasting their way through human flesh.
"Sir, another merchant man has been torpedoed. It's the Commodore's ship at the front of the convoy."
"Quartermaster, set course for the head of the convoy, emergency full ahead."
I looked at my watch. Three minutes, only three minutes since we spotted the contacts. And how many ships would we lose before the next three minutes ended?
We were passing our sole tanker when the next explosion happened. I looked around but could see nothing. We were barely a hundred yards away when the fuel aboard the tanker ignited. Thank God the force of the explosion went skywards.
The tanker stopped dead in the water, flames leaping into the night sky. She settled deeper in the water,

burning oil oozing down her sides and into the sea.
And that oil was coming towards my own ship.
"Starboard twenty, Quartermaster," I said. I had no
intention of risking *Der Condor*.
"Bridge, men in the water."
"Leave them. They'll be dead soon enough."

# Chapter 36    Scotty aboard *HMS Beagle* off the French Coast

Four minutes since we started the attack. Three merchant men destroyed so far. For the loss of one of my boats. Lieutenant Green, barely out of his teens. We spoke before sailing for the first time since he arrived. I looked at my watch. Yesterday morning. And he was married last month.

Three of their destroyers down as well.

I saw the silhouette of another freighter barely half a mile away.

"Number One, torpedoes at the ready. We'll fire from the port side."

"Half Ahead all engines, steady as you go."

Even at half speed we were travelling too fast to launch the fish with any degree of accuracy. But the Germans were already regrouping and I didn't want to stay for much longer.

"Stand by, Number One. Wait, wait, Fire."

"Full ahead all engines, steer 300 degrees."

"Sub Lieutenant Hawes, make to flotilla *That's enough for one day. Head for home. Maximum speed.*"

"*Greyhound* to *Beagle*, I'm sinking. Sorry, Sir, Good luck. See you after the war."

I raced back to the Radar desk and looked at the plot. Hawes pointed at a stationary blip.

"There she is, Sir."

"*Greyhound* stay where you are. We're coming back for you."

"Coxswain, reverse course. 090 degrees. Emergency Full Ahead."

"Sub, take over aft. We'll get alongside and take them straight off."

"Leader to all boats. Head for home. Repeat head for home."

A huge fireball rocketed into the sky.

"We got her, Sir. Must have been carrying ammunition to go up like that."

"Good shot, Number One. Get the men to the sides, we won't have much time."

I picked out *Greyhound* silhouetted against the burning freighter and told the Coxswain to steer towards her. The First Lieutenant had his men getting ropes and grappling hooks ready. We were cutting it fine.

"Dead Slow all engines, Coxswain,"

As we slowed down to come alongside the stricken and obviously sinking MGB the rest of the flotilla sped by, all guns blazing.

"Looks like they'd didn't hear your last order, Sir," the Coxswain said, without any sign of a smile.

I shook my head and prayed that we'd all make it back safely, watching as the last of *Greyhound's* crew stepped over the rail. O' Leary, her skipper and my second in command came into the wheelhouse as I ordered withdrawal at maximum speed.

"Thanks for coming back, Harry. Thought we were in for a bit of a beating from the Germans before they put us ashore. They can't be very pleased after what we did to them today."

I shook his hand.

"Glad you made it, Eddie. Any casualties?"

"Nothing serious. It was a lucky shell that got us. One of the corvettes, I think. Took most of the bow off."

He looked back at the spot where we'd picked him up.

"Not my first command, but definitely my best. She was a lovely boat. Handled so well. Never let me down."

"There'll be other boats."

I looked at the Coxswain who nodded.

"You'll get another boat soon enough, Sir," he said. "And you'll get as attached to that as you were to *Greyhound*. The skipper and I have been through it."

"Make sure your men are OK, Eddie. They need you right now. They've been through a hell of a fight. Tell them well done from me."

"Are you as attached, Coxswain? You've been a bit distant these past few days."

"Losing my mate was bad enough, Sir. Then seeing his missus and my own wife being missing hasn't helped. I'm getting through it."

"Mr. Hawes. I think we could all do with a mug of the Coxswain's infamous Cocoa. Relieve him on the wheel while he makes it."

The rest of the flotilla were closed up around me. Arrow head formation we called it. A huge roar sounded overhead and a squadron of Mosquitos dropped out of the sky. They gave us one of their infamous salutes as they swooped over us and headed for the German ships chasing us.

I saw the waterspouts as they dropped their bombs or torpedoes and zoomed high into the sky.

"Germans turning about, Sir. Must have heard the RAF's reputation for daylight bombing."

The First lieutenant continued to watch as we put a greater distance between the destroyers and our own flotilla.

"Looks like the Mossies are staying with us for a while, James. Long enough to get us closer to home."

Four hours later we steamed back through the gaps of Newlyn harbour. I saw the Old Man and Annie waiting at our berth and handed the mooring over to James. As we came alongside I stepped over the rail and saluted. Captain Dennis returned the salute before stepping forward and slapping me on the shoulder. I looked at Annie and she smiled, though I could see a tension in her eyes that I hadn't noticed before.

"Well done, my boy, well done. Just had confirmation. Four merchant men and three destroyers sunk. The Admiralty are beside themselves with joy. The First Lord himself sent me a note. Get some rest, you'll be back in action soon enough. Sorry about Green. Good man. Will you write to his wife?"

I nodded and he walked back up the pier towards his office.

"I'm so glad you're all right," Annie said and it was an effort not to reach out to her.

"We caught them by surprise. They were close to home, not expecting an attack. But I lost two boats this morning."

"And you went back for Lieutenant Commander O' Leary. We listened in on the radio. They wouldn't be alive now if it wasn't for you."

"I know. And the whole of the flotilla followed me. I really must tell them not to disobey orders in future. The RAF turned up on schedule. Those Mosquitoes were the most welcome sight. The Germans could have blown us out of the water."

"I'd best be getting back. Captain Dennis will want a full report as soon as you can get it to him. The phone's been ringing non-stop since your first reports came in."

"Can I see you tonight?" I asked. She looked into my eyes and smiled.

"I would be very annoyed if you didn't. Come round at 7 and I'll cook dinner. My landlady's out at some sort of social event."

# Chapter 37    Annie in Newlyn

*"My dear Anne,"* I read for the third time. *"I'm sorry that I haven't written before but we've been rather busy out here. Anyway, I'm due some leave and thought that we could get together. I know things weren't too good between us before I was posted but I've had a lot of time to think. And I want to make a go of it. Anyway, let me know when you can get some leave.* With love, Roger"

If half the tales people told me were true my husband certainly had few spare moments. A Wren friend stationed in Malta told me that he propositioned every woman he met. Not all of them had her moral standards and he bedded quite a few.

That was the problem throughout the three years of our marriage. I wasn't as pure as the driven snow. I had three affairs, one night stands every one. Never serious. And all three after someone had told me yet another tale of his philandering. I put the letter in my bag.

When Harry left Newlyn last night I stayed in the office. I couldn't face the thought of going home. I dozed fitfully on the couch until the signal came in that they were attacking. After that I was almost sick. I knew Morse Code well enough to interpret the fact that one of the MGBs sank. Then I heard about *Greyhound* and Harry returning for the crew.

At that I ran outside and vomited over the wall. Thank goodness nobody was around to see. Yet the strange thing is that I never once felt any sense of foreboding about Roger. I realised that I had never thought of where he was or what he might be doing. The last time he wrote over a year ago he was in the Mediterranean Sea on patrol commanding a frigate. I supposed he was still a Commander as I always kept an eye on the promotion lists for Captain Dennis. And the list of ships and crew members lost.

We married in a rush, I suppose, whirlwind romance, he was waiting for his next posting. It wasn't as though the sex was great either. He was as selfish in that as he was in most things. I didn't hate him, but I know now that I didn't love him either.

I thought about Harry and how much I felt about him in the early hours of this morning. And I don't know how I stopped myself from throwing my arms around his neck when Captain Dennis left us.

I would reply to Roger telling him that I didn't want to see him. There was too much open water between us.

And I must make sure that I have everything I need for this evening. We may not have long together but we would make the most of every single second.

I looked up as two men walked into the office.

"Cardiff CID," the older of the two said and showed me his warrant card. "Detective Sergeant Brown and Detective Constable Jones."

"I suppose you're here to see David Williams?"

They nodded.

"He's just got back in. They attacked a German convoy last night. Why don't you use the spare office? Better than trying to interview him on an MGB," I pointed at a doorway behind them.

"Wren Harvey, would you get these officers some tea and biscuits, please? I'll fetch Williams."

Williams walked back with me without saying a word.

"Do you want me to come in as a witness, Chief Petty Officer?"

"No thanks, Ma'am. I've nothing to worry about."

From the quiver in his voice I wondered if that was true.

An hour later he left the office without another word and the two officers came out behind him.

"Thank you for your hospitality, Miss and for the tea and biscuits. Can you organise a taxi. We need to stop at Newlyn police station to put them in the picture. Just a formality."

I phoned the local taxi company and arranged for them to collect the officers. And that was an end to that, I thought. When the two officers left I looked down the pier towards the MGB berths expecting to see Williams but there was no sign of him. I looked in the other direction towards Newlyn and saw him just before he turned the corner by the Post Office. How strange; why isn't he going back to his ship?

Shaking my head and thinking that I'd ask Harry about it later I sat down, wrote the letter to Roger and put it in the Out Tray. I did not want him coming down here. I hadn't even told Harry I was married and it would be just like Roger to ruin whatever relationship I wanted.

# Chapter 38    Klopp aboard *Der Condor*

In all my days of fighting for the German Navy I don't recall a night like this. The MGBs were everywhere. The decoys laid their mines accurately right across the path of the destroyers. And Braun, the great Captain Braun, fell for it.

"How many have we lost, Sir?" Ryker asked as we stood at the depth charge racks waiting for an end to Action Stations. The attack finished over an hour ago and we should already have been on normal watches.

"Four merchant men I think, Ryker."

"And three destroyers mined, Commander. Don't forget them."

I nodded, turned away and popped two painkillers into my mouth. I didn't need anything to wash them down. I was used to taking them dry now. The pain spread from my knee downwards, and was agonising. It got worse each day.

"Those men in the water. Do you think that any survived?" Ryker asked.

I shook my head. There was no chance for any of them. What the sea didn't kill our own machine guns finished off. I felt sick.

"It's not war, it's murder"," I said aloud.

"No, it is war, Klopp. And that was mutinous talk. I will report you to your Captain. You'll be off the ship as soon as we dock. And I will look forward to seeing you at Gestapo Headquarters within hours."

Lieutenant Zirk stood before me, an evil smile on his lips but no humour in his eyes. Before I could reply Ryker strode up behind him and gave him a huge shove. The RAF Mosquitoes had hit nothing during the few seconds of their attack but their bombs brought tons of seawater on to our decks. Most of it rolled back through the scuppers into the sea again. But it left large patches of slippery decking.

Zirk stood on one when Ryker pushed and he skidded towards the ship's rail. Because this was where we fired our depth charges the rail at this point was merely a simple chain linking through stanchions at around thigh level. And Zirk's thighs smashed into the chain before the simple laws of gravity took over and he somersaulted over it. His scream was like nothing I'd ever heard before.

"I'm sorry, Sir. I couldn't let him do that to you," Ryker said. "The captain would be even worse if you weren't here. And he deserved it. Gestapo vermin."

My hands shook and my stomach felt decidedly queasy. And at that moment the klaxon sounded. Action Stations was over.

"Ryker, we mustn't tell anybody what happened," I said, feeling foolish as I uttered the words. Why would either of us mention it to anybody? But a thought occurred. I picked up the phone.

"Man overboard, starboard quarter."

Ryker's mouth dropped open.

"Think, Ryker, think. We saw a figure up on the poop leaning over the rail, probably being sick. The ship pitched and the figure disappeared. We don't know who it was."

He smiled and nodded his head.

"When we get to port the Gestapo will come aboard and ask questions. All we have to tell them is what we saw. Nothing more, nothing less."

We both felt the deck heave over as the ship turned violently to starboard. I ran to the rail and pointed in the opposite direction to where the strong current took Zirk. I looked up towards the bridge wing and as I expected Captain Braun was already there. He waved at me and shouted towards the wheelhouse. Good, directing the helmsman in the right direction. Right for me, wrong for Zirk.

An hour later Braun called the search off.

"Do you have any idea who it might have been, Commander?" he asked.

"No, Sir. All I saw was the outline of a figure. Have we done a roll call?"

The First Lieutenant arrived on the bridge before he could answer.

"Been right the way through the ship, Captain. All crewmen accounted for. But there's no trace of Lieutenant Zirk. I've told the Chief to perform one more search, stem to stern, keel to crows nest. But we were very thorough first time round."

"Could he swim, Sir?" I asked whilst looking out across the sea. The waves were growing in height and the sky was black. Braun walked to the front of the bridge.

"Sir, we could transmit a request to look out for a man overboard in the vicinity. You never know," I said.

"Do it," he replied. "I am going below, Commander. You have the ship."

"Not the most popular of men, Zirk," the First Lieutenant said.

"Didn't know him," I replied.

"Didn't you have a run in with him, Johann? That's the word in the wardroom."

"Come on, Herman, you know how the men always exaggerate. Someone obviously misheard a conversation he and I had. I reported it to the Captain. He had a job to do the same as me and you. Off you go. Get some rest. We'll be back at stations for entering Jersey in an hour."

I wondered how Braun was going to explain the loss of most of our convoy. Not to mention three destroyers. The First Lieutenant returned to the bridge.

"I thought you were going to put your feet up, Herman?"

"So did I, Johann. Captain wants to see you. Told me to take the watch."

"Ah, Commander, come in. Have a seat. Here,

schnapps. I don't often drink at sea but we've had a tough few hours."

I took the glass that Braun offered and sipped the Schnapps.

"I prefer this peach variety," he said, sniffing it appreciatively.

"Yes, I like the acrid sweetness of it," I agreed.

"The admiral has asked for a report. From me and corroborated by you, Johann."

I noted that this was the first time he'd called me by my first name. The man was utterly transparent.

"That is usual, I believe, Sir, in cases where ships have been lost. What will you say?"

He actually had the grace to look awkward.

"I was to be promoted to Admiral after this command. Probably in a few months time. Depending on what I say, that may not happen."

I said nothing but sipped at my Schnapps.

"The radar warning us of the boats astern of us was very late. I had to defend the convoy against attack. The best way with fast moving boats was to use our fastest ships: our destroyers."

I nodded.

"And there were a lot of boats, Sir. Don't forget. Could have been forty, fifty even," I suggested, knowing as he did that there weren't. But I had a feeling I could turn this to my advantage.

"Of course, Johann, how could I forget? And the main attack, the enemy clearly have fast moving patrol boats that we weren't told about. Why weren't we told?"

I nodded in what I hoped was a wise manner.

"Naval Intelligence clearly wasn't at its best. And why did our shore radar stations not warn us of such a large number of enemy ships in our area. And alert the Luftwaffe, Sir?"

"Will you confirm such a report, Johann? I will, of course, write it in my own hand when we arrive in Jersey."

"Naturally, Sir. May I ask a question?"

"Of course. Ask away."

"What will you tell the Gestapo about Lieutenant Zirk?"

I take my hat off to Braun for what he said next.

"How many times did I tell him not to go out on deck during attacks? He would have fallen overboard once before if you hadn't saved him. The man was a fool."

I felt a huge burden lift from my shoulders. I had already searched the Gestapo man's cabin and found his report. That was safely at the bottom of the English Channel. Perhaps at long last the Captain and I understood each other.

# Chapter 39    Coxswain Williams, Newlyn

After I left Lenton's office I checked my watch. Pubs were open. Time to look for that pimp. Already been in two boozers and now here he was in the Swordfish. I was sure that he didn't know me and I didn't know any of the other girls who worked for him.

"You sure you haven't seen her?" he asked.

"Come on, Sammy, I would tell you if I seen her. Anyway, she don't normally surface in the day. She's best on the evening shift. You have been up to her place?"

"Course I have. Went up an hour ago. No answer. Her landlady says it looks like she hadn't slept in her bed. Which is strange cos I was there last night. And she hasn't been in none of the local pubs neither. I've been in every one."

So far so good. All we need is the tides to do what they should and keep her out to sea. Not that I trust that to happen.

I thought back to the interview with the Welsh Police. They didn't seem overly interested in finding Agnes. Another tart giving it away while her old man's at sea. They didn't actually say that but they've clearly made some enquiries and put two and two together. I hope that stays the same.

And Madge wouldn't blab now. Well, she couldn't. After I pushed her body out to sea I worried about a lack of an alibi. Then I thought, why bother? Nobody saw me leave the boat and nobody saw me return either. As far as the crew were concerned I was aboard all night.

The pimp got up to get some more drinks and I looked closely at the woman. About forty years old, dark haired with some grey showing through. Nice face, and from what I could see good figure, too. She turned and caught my eye and I smiled. She raised her eyebrows and I mouthed "tomorrow." She nodded.

I finished my pint, walked outside and waited for Sammy. Wonder where he's billeted? Wonder why he's not been called up? Doesn't look too old for service. Another bloody coward or chancer. They made me sick. We go out like we did last night and risk our necks. For what? So he can shag who he likes and stay safe ashore.

Half an hour later the landlord called time and he staggered out. God knows how much he'd drunk. He could barely stand. The woman came out after him and left him to it. Probably still had business to do. Sammy started walking along the road, stopping to lean against a wall every so often to get his bearings. By the time we got to the top of the hill above the harbour it was dark. He crossed the road and lit a cigarette.

He smoked it and resumed his stagger, turning into Trewarveneth Street. It was steep, like all the roads above the harbour and he took an age to get to his billet half way up. I watched from the shadows as he put his key in the lock. He had a few tries before the door finally opened and he went inside.

I gave him half an hour, waiting, an idea forming in my mind. When I walked over to the door it was unlocked. I looked around, nobody in sight, and walked in. It was an old two up two down fisherman's cottage. Sammy was unconscious, head slumped on the kitchen table.

I checked the rest of the house wondering if anyone else stayed here. Only one of the bedrooms was in use. Perfect. Back in the kitchen Sammy hadn't moved. It didn't take much to drag him across to the oven and lie him down on the floor.

He stirred once and I left him alone and waited till he drifted back into an alcoholic stupor. God, his breath stank. I opened the oven door and switched the gas on, then the burners on top. I lifted his head into the oven and walked back to the kitchen door. I waited until I could smell the gas fumes, stepped outside and took a few deep breaths.

Back in the harbour I slipped back aboard without anyone noticing and quietly eased my cabin door closed. Chief Petty Officer Shaw always slept like a log and he was certainly doing that now. I could have slammed the door shut a hundred times and all the crew would hear was the CPO giving it some z's.

Up until now the only people I'd killed were Germans. In the last month I'd murdered my own wife, her boyfriend, a whore and now a pimp. Did that make me so very bad? I didn't have the answer to that and didn't much care. I felt somehow cleansed. Funnily enough, though, sleep simply didn't come and I spent the rest of the night tossing and turning.

When I finally got to sleep the same four faces came to me, one after the other. I woke up with loads of questions racing through my head.

What the hell have I become? Could I have done things differently? And perhaps worst of all, how could I look the skipper or Number One or Morrison squarely in the eyes again?

# Chapter 40    James Haywood in Newlyn

"When do you go back to sea?"
It was a simple question, but I didn't have the answer.
"I don't know, Carol. The skipper shares most things with me, but he's been quite cagey on that. We're doing another attack run tomorrow. But so far I've no idea where."

We were sitting on the Promenade, a long and wide expanse of pavement that ran at the back of Newlyn Beach. At this time of the evening there were a few people pushing prams and some couples walking arm in arm.

"Let's walk down to the swimming pool. See if anyone's mad enough to be in there at this time of year," I said.

The sun was still above the horizon, but there was a slight breeze blowing. Carol shivered beside me.

"I'm sorry," I told her, "Let's go into the Yacht Inn for a drink instead. They'll have their fire burning."

We settled at a table by the fire and the colour soon returned to her cheeks as she sipped her gin and tonic. My pint of St Austell Ale didn't warm me up. But it tasted good after a few days of watchkeeping on a strictly no-alcohol basis. The skipper was very strict when it came to drinking aboard.

"When I was on air raid duty last night we noticed a light on in a house in Trewarveneth Street," she said, pushing her drink away.  I must have frowned because she smiled and said,

"It's the first street after you climb the steep hill opposite the small Memorial."

"Oh yes, close to where the skipper's mum used to live."

She said that they were almost at the end of their air raid patrol and noticed a light coming from a small cottage.

"That was unusual, as after the raid that killed Mrs Scott everyone's got so much better," she said before continuing the story.

They knocked on the door but there was no answer so they went in. And the first thing they noticed was an overpowering smell of gas.

"It was horrible. We were worried that the place would explode," she told me, shivering with the memory.

They walked carefully into the kitchen and saw a man on the floor with his head practically in the oven. She ran over and seeing that all the gas taps on, switched them off and helped Matthew drag him out into the street.

He was barely breathing but she kept his head steady while Matthew went off to phone for an ambulance.

"When I went on duty this morning," she continued, "he was on my ward. He was linked up to oxygen and seemed to be breathing a bit better."

"Does anyone know why he tried to kill himself?"

She shook her head and looked concerned. A little frown creased her normally smooth forehead and she had a very thoughtful look in her eyes as though she was remembering something.

"No. He came round a little just before I finished my shift and I helped him drink some water."

According to the man, whose name was Sammy, he couldn't remember much at all. Except being quite drunk and staggering home before collapsing at the kitchen table. The only other thing he could remember was someone coming into the cottage and helping him lie down on the floor.

"Perhaps he was putting the kettle on for a cup of tea before going to bed," I suggested.

She suggested the same thing to this Sammy but he said he never drank tea. Didn't agree with him. Before she went off duty she told the ward sister, who dismissed it.

"We've got enough to do without trying to work out what these foreigners are doing down here instead of fighting like our men do. Anyway, Nurse, the police are coming to see him tomorrow. Let them sort it out."

I smiled at the term.

"Foreign is he?" I asked.

Carol laughed.

"He's from Plymouth. Anyone from outside Cornwall is foreign to our Sister. And anyone young enough to be in uniform but not fighting gets very little sympathy from her. He's both."

"Did you know him?"

She shook her head telling me that as a local girl she used to know everybody. But not any longer. Too many people coming and going.

"Sister said that he had lots of cash on him when they brought him in. She thinks he's black market or something similar. Too much money to be legal."

We walked back to her home while she finished the story of her night on ARP patrol: before they arrived at Sammy's house she was sure that she saw someone walking further down the street. They seemed to come out of one of the houses around Sammy's.

# Chapter 41    Rommel North African Desert

"I have reminded Berlin about our reinforcements, Willie. They say that it may be weeks before they can get enough men together. Things are going well on the Russian Front just now and they anticipate improvements in a few weeks as the weather improves."

"It will take them many weeks to move south, Erwin" Willie replied. "It's a two thousand mile trip and moving that number of troops can only be done by train."

I couldn't disagree. I was frustrated at having got so far and Berlin not seeming to understand the urgency, despite Hitler's promises. Morale amongst my troops was high at the moment but if the men could see no further progress in our campaign they would soon be disillusioned.

"Tell the men that we won't be staying here for long. Keep them busy, Willie. Keep them practising for our advance."

I pointed at the map. Our next step would be to attack the enemy at El Alamein. It was the way to Alexandria and the Suez Canal.

"Once we have Alexandria and Suez, the English will retreat. They will be finished in Egypt, Willie. We will have won."

Deep down I wondered if that really was true. Auchinleck maybe was an old dog but he's managed to learn some new tricks. He may have lost the last battle, but I was sure that he would do his utmost to stop us winning another. The reinforcements were essential for our success. As well as bringing fresh blood they would reinvigorate the rest of the men who were exhausted.

"What will you do if the reinforcements don't arrive?"

I lit a cigarette and smiled, though I felt no humour.

"We may have to attack without them, my dear General. Our spies say that even as we speak the British are sending the Auk fresh troops and new tanks. And the tanks are American Shermans. We can't afford to wait for the numbers to build. I estimate that we have between six and eight weeks before we must decide."

Willie left and I poured a coffee. If I decided to attack and lost, it wouldn't be the British leaving Africa with their tails between their legs. If the Nazis back in Berlin had their way I probably wouldn't have any legs to hide a tail.

## Chapter 42    Winston Churchill, 10 Downing Street

"Auchinleck is worried that Rommel will spring an early attack to take his present position. If El Alamein falls, there is little to stop the Germans from reaching Alexandria. After that all is lost. There is nothing between Alex and Suez."

"We expected this to happen, Prime Minister," Sir Alan Brooke told me as we debated our trip to Egypt to see the General. "We knew that Rommel could take Gazala but the Auk could hold him off until we sent reinforcements. Most are on their way as we speak. Some have already arrived, albeit not in large numbers."

"And what chance do we have of getting the troops to him that he needs? God knows the German Air Force seems to have complete command of the skies in the Med."

Sir Alan was irritatingly calm. I suppose it went with the job. As Chief of the Imperial General Staff he could hardly start tearing his hair out and weeping into his brandy.

"Five fast ships carrying our armour and troops protected by half the Home Fleet as far as Gibraltar. Where Admiral Harwood will meet them with the Mediterranean Fleet. And the Germans won't have it all their own way in the skies. The total escort group includes two aircraft carriers. *HMS Ark Royal* and *HMS Glorious* will fly sorties day and night to keep the Germans away."

I knew the plans inside out, but it didn't stop me worrying. We needed a victory in North Africa. It would pave the way for invading Italy and working our way up into France, Austria and Germany. Until we secured Southern Europe there was no point in invading Northern Europe from the English Channel.

"What intelligence do we have? Any movement of troops anywhere in Europe?"

Sir Alan said that we were picking up a considerable amount of traffic between Rommel and Berlin through Enigma. What we would do without that machine? Ever since we captured the German cypher machine from a sinking U boat we had access to much of their coded traffic. Enigma helped us to decipher it, and the incredible thing was that nobody knew we had it apart from a small handful of specialists at Bletchley Park to the North of London. And the Chiefs of our services.

"Hitler's desperate to help Rommel. With the summer starting in Russia he seems prepared to remove regiments from Northern Russia and send them south. We don't know exact timings yet. But we'll get them," he continued.

"And no doubt the Fuhrer has told his little Italian puppet to release Italian troops as well?"

"He has. We are a little clearer on that. It seems they'll be shipped out of Trieste as part of a fast, well-armed convoy. And will be landed on the Egyptian coast a few miles from Rommel's headquarters."

I relit my cigar and drew heavily on it. I felt the smoke sink deep into my lungs and breathed it back out in a steady stream. The smell was strangely comforting. I felt on the verge of an epoch-making battle.

But not the next one. It would be later in the year when we had our reinforcements settled and ready to fight. The Auk would bear the brunt of defending his position and bringing the Germans to a halt. It would be for a new man to beat the Germans into submission.

"Make the arrangements for you and me to fly out to Egypt as soon as you can. All other diary appointments can be re-scheduled. We must prepare him for the coming battle."

"And his transfer, Sir?"

"Yes. And his transfer."

After Brooke left I looked at my map again. Trieste, in Northern Italy. If Mussolini's troops left from there, it would make sense for the German reinforcements to do likewise. Why pull together two convoys when one would do?

The Germans didn't have enough spare ships in the Med for this. Well, I didn't think they did. We needed more intelligence.

The following day was the weekly meeting of the Service Chiefs.

"Gentlemen, we must gather as much intelligence as possible about troop movements, particularly withdrawals from the front line," I said by way of opening.

Our discussion was wide ranging. Enigma could give us details of shipping movements but we needed more than that. By the end of the morning the chiefs went off to put their people to work. Berlin Navy Command and the main German ports would be put under close surveillance, as well as the port of Trieste.

I had one other problem to deal with and it would require a most sensitive conversation. Marshall Stalin, the Russian leader was already highly critical of the Americans and ourselves for not launching a Second Front in Europe. Now I would have to persuade him to insert spies close to the German lines around Stalingrad to find out if and when the German High Command gave the order to withdraw troops.

Before the meeting ended Air Chief Marshall Douglas, head of the RAF, turned to his Royal Naval counterpart, Sir Dudley Pound.

"Dudley, Old Boy. We will have to attack this German convoy by sea. I've looked at an air attack from all angles. We cannot guarantee getting through without huge losses. In fact, I don't believe our aircraft will penetrate their escort fire cover."

Pound simply nodded.

"We've already had a few thoughts, Sholto. We guessed that the German air cover would be too strong. We've got a surprise or two up our sleeve."

He looked at the calendar on the wall.

"Our problem is getting into position exactly on time. A day either way will wreck our chances of destroying the convoy at the same time as putting our own ships in huge danger."

# Chapter 43    Scotty at The Admiralty, London

Captain Dennis and I left Newlyn on the Paddington train at 0730 hours. A good run would get us to London by 1530 hours that afternoon.

"We're due to meet CinC Western Approaches tomorrow morning at 0900 hours. The plan is to be back in Newlyn the following morning on the overnight sleeper."

"Why didn't we just drive up, Sir? Damn sight faster."
I felt a little annoyed as Annie and I had planned a visit to the Gaiety Cinema tomorrow evening and that would now have to be postponed.

"Because, my Boy, it is normal for relatively junior Naval officers like us to travel on the train. It is not at all common for mere Captains and Commanders to commandeer chauffeur driven limousines."

Part way through the trip we walked up to the buffet car and bought a sandwich and beer. Neither of them did much to lift my spirits.

Promptly at 0700 hours the following morning we left our hotel after a breakfast that matched Great Western Railway's luncheon yesterday. Barely edible and not even pretty to look at. Neither of us cared much for London's Underground Railway system so we walked the two miles from our hotel in Hammersmith across the River Thames to the Admiralty. The Great Admiralty Arches seemed to dominate the skyline in Central London, though in truth Lord Nelson's statue was much higher.

"Now there was a sailor, Harry. A hero to all his crews. And to England and Great Britain. Not many like him left now."

This area of London with office buildings serving all three armed forces was a magnet for sandbags. They were everywhere. Quite what protection they gave against German bombs I had no idea. Perhaps you buried yourself underneath them and prayed.

A smartly turned out Able Seaman stood at the doorway of the Admiralty building and came smartly to attention when we arrived.

"At ease," the Old Man told him. "We have an appointment with the Commander in Chief Western Approaches."

The seaman studied our passes and told us to go to the reception desk inside the foyer from where a Wren led us through the building to a huge conference room at the rear. She poured coffee and left us alone. A minute later the door opened and the Old Man and I both stood to attention.

"At Ease, Captain Dennis, Commander Scott. Please sit."

The three men in front of us had more gold braid on their sleeves than all the officers in my flotilla put together.

"Good to see you again, Robert. How's Dorothy? Long time since we saw you."

Admiral Sir Dudley Pound, First Sea Lord, the man in charge of the whole of the Royal Navy was on first name terms with the Old Man! Just wait till I tell Annie. The two carried on chatting about old times and the ships on which they served together. The First Lord clearly had a good memory, but the Old Man matched him ship for ship and memory for memory.

"Right, gentlemen. Let's get down to it," Pound said at last. "Sir John will give you a more detailed briefing but I wanted to paint a wider picture."

He pointed at an Admiralty chart on the table.

"You'll have heard that Rommel's made considerable headway in the Desert. He's in sight of Alexandria and if he takes that, we lose Egypt. And, worse still, we lose Suez and that huge trading route we depend on for moving men, cargo, armour, pretty much everything around the world. Malta will be finished as will our chances of getting a toehold in Southern Europe."

He went on in similar vein for a few minutes before pausing once more.

"What I'm about to say must go no further. Not to your officers, crews, wives or girlfriends. If this got out the Government would fall."

I listened as the country's foremost sailor told us how the government decided to let Rommel take Gazala and move into Egypt. And how we would fight him now on grounds, and at a time, of our choosing.

"But surely, he could attack at any time, Sir?" I asked without realising I'd interrupted him mid-flow.

He smiled and nodded.

"Yes, Commander, he can attack whenever he chooses. But to succeed he needs reinforcements. He can't move any further towards Suez unless he replaces the men and armour he lost at Gazala. There is only one direction that those reinforcements will come from and it is our job to make damn sure we destroy them while they're travelling."

As he explained that the next land battle in the desert would bring the German advance to a standstill I thought of the loss of lives that this would cause. Avoidable? Perhaps, perhaps not. But telegrams would come through the letterboxes of many soldiers" families sometime soon announcing the death, injury or capture of another husband, son or grandson.

"Are you with us, Commander?" Pound said.

"Sorry, Sir. Yes, just starting to picture our role, Sir."

He smiled again and I wondered if he knew that I lied. I somehow thought that he did.

"Commander, your flotilla has been put together for one job and one job only. To destroy the convoy bringing these reinforcements to the North African campaign. The RAF were to bomb them, but have admitted that German air power is too strong. Your Motor Gun Boats are the only weapon left to us. Fast, agile and armed to the teeth. With, of course a fine Commander and first rate skippers and crews."

He left the room soon afterwards and Admiral Sir John Cunningham, CinC Mediterranean Fleet, finished the briefing.

His final words before we left for Newlyn echoed in my ears.

"You will take all twenty four MGBs out with you, Harry. Sadly, I strongly suspect that not all will return. I have one final order and it is non-negotiable. Until you have completed your attack and are returning to Alexandria you will on no account stop to pick up any unfortunate boat crews who've been hit. After the attack, yes. Before, no."

He passed me a thick envelope.

"Your orders are all there. Guard them with your life, Commander. If the Germans are ready for you, well, I don't need to spell it out."

# Chapter 44    Annie, Newlyn

He rang from Paddington station.

"We're getting the 1530 train, Annie. Won't be back till almost midnight. Can I see you tomorrow evening?"

"No, you can't," I told him and I heard him breathe in deeply. "You will see me tonight. I've missed you, Harry. I don't want to wait until tomorrow. I'll look out for you."

I left the office at 1800 and went back to my digs. Or billet as the Navy called it. Mrs James prepared a nice stew and we chatted until 2100.

"Would you like a nightcap, Mrs James? I have some gin and tonic upstairs. I don't normally but I've so enjoyed our chat this evening and it may help us sleep."

I'm sure she swallowed it in four or five gulps. Anyway, within ten minutes she started yawning and went upstairs to bed. After she left I made some sandwiches and took them upstairs to my room. He would be hungry when he arrived. I knew what the food on trains was like.

I put the bottle of gin and some tonic water on my dressing table, settled by the window and thought about the letter from Roger. My reply was succinct:
*Dear Roger, thank you for your letter. I am surprised at you contacting me after such a long time. I have a new job and am enjoying it hugely. I have no desire to pick up where we left off. Nor do I wish to make a fresh start. At some convenient point we should divorce. Good luck, Anne.*

I heard footsteps outside and opened the window, waving to him to be quiet. I listened at Mrs James' door and almost giggled out loud at the snores coming from within.

A minute later we were in my room and I was in Harry's arms.

"I missed you so much, Annie. I really wanted to see you tonight but daren't say anything in case you thought I was only after one thing," he whispered.

"I missed you, too, darling Harry. I couldn't possibly wait another day. Here, have a sandwich. It's all I could get together, I'm afraid."

He laughed quietly and I relaxed a little.

"Are you sure your landlady won't hear us and come to investigate?"

"I gave her a double gin a few hours ago. She always sleeps through till morning after one of those. And I don't want to sleep, not tonight."

He put his plate to one side and moved closer to me on the bed.

"Are you quite sure, Annie?" he asked and I nodded as I let my hair down from its bun.

We undressed each other slowly, kissing all the while. I will remember the night for as long as I live. Nobody ever made love to me like Harry. He was gentle, warm, loving. And talked quietly to me, telling me how beautiful I was, how soft. I wanted the night to go on forever. But of course it didn't.

After the second time I lay in his arms as though we were an old married couple.

"Harry, I had a letter a few days ago from my husband. Well, ex-husband in many ways."

He sat up quite suddenly.

"I didn't know you were married. Why didn't you say? I shouldn't be here."

"Harry, wait, listen to me. Please" He stayed sitting while I explained my rather odd married life to him.

"We never loved each other. I felt sorry for him as he was about to be posted overseas and we had a good time. But as soon as he left I realised what a huge mistake we'd made. We haven't seen each other for three years and when his letter arrived I was stunned. I wrote back and told him that I wanted a divorce and I never wanted to see him again. He's had so many affairs and I realised when I was with you that I was falling in love."

I stopped and for some inexplicable reason started to cry. He lay down next to me and held me again.

"Say that again," he said.

"What, that I didn't love him?"

"No, the other bit."

"I love you, Harry. I knew it the night we talked at the end of the pier. I could see how upset you were, how guilty you felt about the men who died. But I often heard the men talking when you came back from a raid. Not just down here but in Shoreham, too. And some of the Wrens went out with some of your crew as well. They said that the men adored you. Men being men, of course, they'd never say anything. Roger never had things like that said about him. Your crew would do anything for you, follow you anywhere. And so will I."

I sobbed more than spoke, looked at him through tear filled eyes and he put a finger on my mouth.

"Where is he now?"

"Somewhere in the Mediterranean. But he's commissioning a new ship back here. I don't know when but I think soon."

"I love you, Annie. With all my heart. But if he comes here you should see him. If you love me, we'll be together. But you must be absolutely sure in your own heart and mind that you do not love him."

He got dressed after that and before he left he said one of the loveliest things I have ever heard. And one of the most frightening.

"I felt something tonight that I have never felt before. And don't expect to ever again. Let's make the most of the time we have."

## Chapter 45    Scotty in Newlyn

"Read that, Harry. Looks like we're on our way."
The Old Man passed a sheaf of papers across.
"Pages three and four are the most interesting bits," he said. "I've read the rest. It's irrelevant."
I skimmed the first two pages, read the next two rather more slowly and skimmed the remaining three before passing the papers back.
"Well, looks like you're right, Sir. No dates in here, though. Would be good to know when we'll be leaving."
While he filled his pipe and went through the ritual of damping down the tobacco, lighting and relighting it, sucking hard to get it going I thought about the intelligence in that report. A small number of enemy troops withdrawn from the Russian front line. Not many, and not enough to be sure that they would be sent south.
Some jumbled radio messages referring to Gruppen 158 and a Board of Enquiry investigating the disappearance of an officer overboard.
"The last page of the report talks about Gruppen 158, Sir. A large escort group, ten destroyers. How many escort groups do the Germans have, do you think?"
He shook his head.
"No idea, why do you ask?"
I told him that when we attacked that convoy off the Channel Islands there were around twenty escorts defending just five merchant men. That was a large number of escorts in one single group. He raised an eyebrow and I wondered if I was reading too much into an insignificant detail.
"Is it important?" he asked.
"It could be. The CO of *Der Condor* has been recalled to Hamburg for a Board of Enquiry. You don't recall

an entire group just so that one commanding officer can be investigated. What would you do if one of your COs had to be investigated?"

"If the group was in service I'd leave them where they were, tell the second in command to take over and bring the CO back."

I had no idea if it was important, or whether I was simply seeing ghosts where none existed. But I did know that if we had indeed attacked Gruppen 158's convoy, barely a few weeks ago, their CO reacted too quickly to a feint attack. That was how we managed to destroy most of the merchant ships. Plus some destroyers. It could give us an edge in the Mediterranean.

"You've got one more job before you leave," he continued, pointing to his wall map.

"We've got a German convoy heading north up the west coast of Ireland. Due in a few days. Be a good bit of practice for your boys."

I frowned. That was almost four hundred miles away and our maximum range was barely five hundred miles.

"I take it that the Admiralty has a plan to get us back? Or is this a one way trip?"

"You can hardly attack the enemy in the Mediterranean if you're interned in Ireland, Harry. Anyway, you're far too valuable to allow the Irish to lock you up after they've rescued you. And we wouldn't want them getting their hands on our MGBs. Work your way round the UK coast, attack off Londonderry."

He handed me a thick envelope containing my Orders and answered my one unasked question. Why us?

"Yes there are ships closer than you. And they could probably do the job. But, this will be a practice run, dress rehearsal for the real thing. And it's important."

His explanation was clear and concise, but I felt the hairs on the back of my neck rise when he spoke of the cargo the merchant ships carried. Hitler's scientists had developed some new bomb material, more destructive and longer lasting than anything that's gone before.

"The War Cabinet is worried sick that once this bomb is in Hitler's hands he'll use it to devastating effect. Not only is it powerful, but the chemicals would render wherever it was dropped uninhabitable for decades."

I stood to leave and he gave me one final order.

"The Prime Minister has promised Ireland that we will not carry out attacks on enemy shipping while they're within their twelve mile limit. Therefore, we expect the convoy to stay within Irish territorial waters for as long as possible because they will deem themselves safe. But, they will have to leave Irish waters to take a more easterly route which gives you about a two-hour window of time to sink the merchantmen. The detail, positions, timings etc. are all in your pack, Commander. Good Luck."

I left his office, deep in thought.

"Penny for them, Commander," Annie said as I almost walked past her desk. I was unaware of anything except how the hell I was going to lead my entire flotilla north through the Celtic Sea, into the Irish Sea, around the tip of Ireland into the North Atlantic. And that was before we attacked a German convoy, a heavily protected convoy with escorts all over the shop. All at the end of Spring in one of the roughest oceans in the world.

"Sorry, Annie. Just been given a job and the logistics are a nightmare."

"I know. I checked your orders when they came in," she paused. "Sorry to break in, but I wondered if you saw Chief Williams come back aboard after he saw the two Welsh policemen?"

"That was a few days ago wasn't it?" I said, surprised at the change of conversation and feeling a frown deepening on my forehead while thinking of the job ahead.

"The day before I went up to London?" I asked and she nodded.

I thought hard and felt the frown gather strength as I told her that I hadn't seen him return aboard.

"He told me that the police wanted to see him about his wife's disappearance and I assumed they took a long time over the interview. Why do you ask?"

"He wasn't with the police for that long. Barely two hours. But when he left the office he turned right and went into Newlyn."

I thought back to the night we'd attacked the last convoy and how his concentration had momentarily vanished.

"Don't be too harsh on him, he may be struggling with his friend's death, Harry. We all deal with these things differently. Be careful. It might be as well simply to ask him how the interview went and take it from there," she said quietly so nobody else could overhear.

I couldn't help but smile.

"You're very thoughtful Second Officer Lenton," I said loudly enough so the other Wrens could hear. As I said it I put my hand over hers on her desk and squeezed it.

Back on the boat the Coxswain was on deck with some of the crew checking our guns and torpedoes. In port this was a daily affair. Making sure the guns were loaded and ready to fire, the torpedoes and depth charges stored securely but ready for immediate release during an attack.

"Coxswain, could you spare me a minute, please? On the harbour wall if you would. Carry on, men. You all know what to do. The Coxswain will check what you've done in a moment."

I started walking down the pier towards the village.

"Anything I can do, Sir?"

I stopped and faced him.

"I haven't had time to ask since I got back from London. But I understand from Second Officer Lenton that the Cardiff police came down to see you."

His eyes glanced away momentarily before he answered.

"That's right, Sir," he said before telling me that they were investigating his wife's disappearance along with that of her publican boyfriend.

"How was it left?" I asked and he said that they would let him know as soon as they had any news.

"Long interview?" I asked.

"Quite long, Sir. Lost track of time and when I came out I popped into the village for a pint before coming back aboard."

"I don't recall seeing you come back aboard, Cox. What time would that have been?"

"Not sure, Sir," he told me.

Which was strange as everything this man did was by the book and to the letter. I started walking back to *Dotty* with the distinct feeling that CPO Williams was lying.

"Let me know if you get any word about Agnes, Cox. I'm sure she'll turn up."

# Chapter 46    Coxswain Williams, Newlyn

A few days after talking to the skipper about the police interview, I stood on Newlyn Fish Market watching the trawlers getting ready to unload their catch. This had become a regular event after breakfast and I found that listening to the auctioneers speak in their strange language took my mind off other matters. One of the fishermen had become quite friendly and explained the different species of fish being landed and how much they were priced at.

He pointed towards the latest arrival, a boat that was perhaps fifty feet bow to stern.

"Awful sea boat," the fisherman said. "Rolls her guts out in any sea at all."

I could believe it. This one wasn't even as long as *Dotty*, and I knew first hand that she could hold her own in any pitching and rolling competition.

I noticed that the auction had stopped and sellers and buyers alike were moving towards the new arrival. I looked more closely and saw the name on the stern, *Our Boys*.

"She only put to sea yesterday," my fisherman friend told me.

I remembered seeing her as she left harbour. It was odd for a boat that normally stayed out for three or four nights to return within twenty four hours.

The fisherman nodded in response.

"It is strange, Coxswain, but the trawl picked up a body off the Scilly Isles and when he tried to land it on St Mary's they told him to bring it back here."

I moved closer to see if I could recognise anything but blankets covered the corpse. An ambulance arrived and when the attendants transferred the body to a stretcher I thought I saw a ring on one of the fingers.

Madge wore a ring, I recalled, but on which finger I had no idea. The ambulance drove off and I walked back to the auction. The fisherman joined me and leant against a railing. I offered him a cigarette and he lit mine then his.

"I picked one out the sea once. A few years ago but I remember it like it was yesterday. Not much left of the face and precious little flesh anywhere else. But the police reckoned it was a fisherman from St Ives. He wore a Saint Christopher medallion and his missus recognised it."

I couldn't think of anything to say in reply so stayed silent and wished I'd checked Madge's ring.

"Strange thing was, he went overboard off Lands End and we found him off The Scillies weeks later. Funny old world."

"Do you think this was a fisherman?" I asked.

"Twas a woman. Who it was I have no idea."

Back aboard *Dotty*, Morrison looked up from scrubbing the foredeck.

"You look like you seen a ghost, Cox. You all right?"

"Just seen a body brought ashore from one of the trawlers. Been in the sea a while. Not a pretty sight," I told him before going down to my cabin.

I felt my stomach churning and just made it to the toilet before I threw all my breakfast and last night's beer up. What had I done to myself? And how much more could I take before someone put two and two together?

# Chapter 47     Scotty, Newlyn

I looked down at *Dotty's* foredeck and smiled with pride at how clean she was. She still sparkled like the day she came out of the boatyard, which she should as she was still barely a couple of months old. Morrison had painted the German merchantman symbol on the outside of the wheelhouse: our first kill since the German bomber.

"Deck's looking good, Morrison. Why are you on your own?"

"The others have just gone below, Sir. I was finishing off. My turn at night-watchman tonight. They're all off ashore."

"Very good. Is the Coxswain aboard? I need a word with him."

"I'll fetch him, Sir. He's not been back aboard long himself. He didn't look too good, tell you the truth, Skip. Said he'd watched a body landed from one of the trawlers over there."

He pointed towards the fish market the other side of the harbour.

I shook my head in disbelief. We've seen enough bodies these last three years. And body parts as well. Corpses without heads. Unattached arms and legs after a depth charge attack. Why should Williams be affected by this?

The First Lieutenant was in the wardroom pouring a cup of tea.

"Make that two, James. We have a long session ahead of us."

There was a knock at the door and Williams put his head around.

"You wanted a word, Sir?"

"Yes, Cox. Pass the word to the Chief Mechanic. We need full tanks and all engines at readiness. On a little mission in two days' time. But, we've also been asked to stand by as rescue boat tonight. Then ask all MGB skippers to meet me in the Seaman's Mission at 1700 hours this evening."

He nodded and started to walk away.

"And, Cox, could you ask the Mission Superintendent if his big room is free at that time? I meant to do it on the way back to the boat but an ambulance raced past and I forgot."

"Must have been the one from the market, Sir. One of the boats brought a body in. They think it was a woman."

He swallowed heavily and ran for the toilet.

"What was that all about?" Haywood asked.

Instead of answering I rolled the chart out across the wardroom table and took pencil, paper, dividers and parallel rule from the drawer.

"No idea, but we have bigger things to sort out than the Coxswain's queasy stomach."

Thinking back to my meeting with the Old Man I told James that we had to get the flotilla from Newlyn to Londonderry to meet a northbound German convoy and do our best to destroy it.

"Why us, Sir? Half the fleet's based in Londonderry. Some of those old battleships need to get out and do a bit for the war effort. If they can lift their anchors with two years' worth of rubbish tipped overboard on top of them."

It was the same argument that I'd used with the Old Man but the plain fact was that the fleet was there to prevent the German Fleet breaking south into the Atlantic. I repeated that answer and brought us back to the pressing problem.

"How do we get from here to there, attack and get home?"

"Has to be in stages, Sir. When will we attack?"

We spent the next hour working out the logistics. By the time we got into position for the attack we would have travelled almost seven hundred miles. That made a round trip of one thousand four hundred miles.

It was a logistical nightmare but we split the flotilla into pairs of MGBs and identified twenty possible refuelling ports between our base and Londonderry, the southernmost port in Northern Ireland.

"Shame the Irish aren't more co-operative, Sir. They seem quite happy to have German spies based along their coastline but completely against giving us any help."

"I know, James, but they keep telling us they're neutral and there's nothing we can do about it. Besides, even if they offered us help we couldn't make it across the Irish Sea without running the tanks dry."

Gradually, the picture emerged. Pairs of boats leaving Newlyn at half hour intervals and travelling between three and four hundred miles at thirty knots.

"That gives us a safety margin of over a hundred miles before the tanks run dry. No speeding, enough fuel in reserve and provided the weather holds and everyone sticks to the timetable we'll hit the convoy before first light the day after tomorrow."

We walked up the quay to Annie's office and she gave us two Wrens to ring each of the twenty ports and ask them to refuel two MGBs whenever they arrived. While they made the calls, another Wren typed up copies of our Orders. We finished just in time to walk down to the Mission to brief the flotilla skippers.

"Gentlemen, in two days' time we leave Newlyn for Londonderry."

I passed out envelopes to each of them and stayed silent as they read. After ten minutes I called them to order.

"The Admiralty want a convoy destroyed. One that is transporting chemicals that Hitler intends to use in a new type of bomb. If it gets through, it could spell disaster for the Allied war effort."

There were many furrowed brows as I summarised what the Old Man told me, interweaved with what I had read before this briefing. It was certainly a frightening scenario. A new bomb with new explosives and new chemicals in the hands of the German dictator. I explained that should the Germans drop a two hundred and fifty pound bomb on Newlyn it would kill everyone within a mile radius and cause the land to be unusable for years to come.

"Gentlemen, there are twenty two ships in the convoy but sixteen of them are escort vessels; destroyers, corvettes and minesweepers. The other six are the freighters we're interested in: the ones carrying the chemicals."

"Why are they transporting the stuff by sea? Why not make it in Germany?"

"There's a Nazi laboratory in Argentina that's beavered away since the start of the war."

I smiled as hands went up around the room.

"Yes, I know, Argentina's neutral. Except we know they're not. But, they're far from Europe and our bombers. And, Germany reckons their secrets are safer out there than in Germany where our double agents could uncover them."

"Is this why we've been brought together, Sir?" another skipper asked.

"Partly, yes," I replied, a half-truth, perhaps.

I explained that the attack would help us hone our skills at getting in close to the enemy before they knew we were there. That it has to become our second nature that we can swoop in and launch our torpedoes and depth charges before the escort screen sees us

We spent another two hours going over the plans for our journey north around the top end of Ireland, with each pair of skippers planning their own voyages.

Finally, we were all clear on our own movements as well as those of the boats around us.

"Starting at 0100 hours tomorrow morning we leave in pairs. Half an hour between each. Rendezvous twenty miles due west of Londonderry at 0230 hours the day after tomorrow."

I pointed at the chart on the table.
Right there, gentlemen. And one hour later we'll be up with the enemy."

## Chapter 48    Carol Crebo West Cornwall Hospital, Newlyn

Matron called me into her office when I arrived for my shift.

"Nurse Crebo, the police will be calling in to see Mr Smith and he has asked for one of my staff to accompany him. It seems that he doesn't trust police officers."

"Of course, Matron. I'll ask Sister Mary if she can spare me."

"No need, Crebo. I've already done it. Wheel him into Sister's office. They can see him there."

We had a few minutes to spare before the officers arrived and I used them to make a pot of tea and ask Mr Smith how he felt.

"Not bad, Nurse. Still got a bit of a headache. Can't wait to get out of here. Got loads of work piling up."

"Oh, what do you do for a living?"

He was quite vague about that. Just a bit of this and a bit of that. What with the war, he told me, everyone wants something from him.

At this point two plain clothes officers arrived. I poured their tea and sat down next to Mr Smith.

"Right, Mr Smith. My name is Detective Sergeant Warner and this is Detective Constable Dixon. Let's start with your full name and address."

The sergeant did all the talking and every so often Mr Smith shuffled in his wheelchair as though he was trying to get comfortable. I noticed that he rarely looked at the sergeant when he answered the questions.

"How long have you been in Newlyn?"

"About three or four months. My rent book will tell you exactly."

"And where you were before that?"

"Hard to say. I move about a lot in my line of work. Do a lot of travelling selling stuff here and there. Spent a lot of time in Plymouth."

"How well do you know Marjorie Bennett?"

"Never heard of the woman? Should I know her?"

"Perhaps you knew her by a different name, Mr Smith? Do you recognise this woman?"

He held out a photograph and I was sure I knew the woman, but couldn't place her. Next he took a ring, quite a distinctive one with a jet black stone in the middle from his pocket. He told Mr Smith that the stone was, in fact, Jet.

"Quite an expensive piece of jewellery, I'm told."

Mr Smith's face lost all colour and he looked quite ill.

"Do you want a glass of water?" I asked him and he nodded.

I poured some out of a jug and passed it to him. He downed it in one.

"Where did you get that?"

His voice was barely a whisper and it cracked slightly as he spoke. A tear appeared in the corner of his eye and rolled down his cheek. Others followed.

"Let's stop playing now, Sammy. We know who you are and what you do."

The constable looked at a sheet of paper in his hand.

"Samuel Walter Colton. Date of birth sixth December 1912. Previous address, 29 Union Street, Plymouth. Occupation: Pimp. What did she do to you? Start getting serious about another bloke? Tell you she'd had enough and wanted out?"

"I don't know what you're talking about, Constable. I haven't seen her for days. She disappeared after we spent the night together. Me and one of the girls looked all over Newlyn for her but couldn't find her. Where is she?"

"In the mortuary. What's left of her. A fisherman dragged her out of the sea yesterday morning. Looked as though she drowned. Except that the doctor reckons she was dead before she went into the water. Suffocated, he reckons."

"No," he howled. "No, there's got to be a mistake. She can't be dead. She was a good girl, never hurt anyone in her life."

"I know, Mummy's little girl, went to Church every Sunday," the Sergeant interrupted.

"Come on, Sammy, just tell us what happened. She was just a whore."

And that's when it happened. Sammy launched himself out of the wheelchair and grabbed the Sergeant by the throat, crashed his knee in between the officer's legs and fell on top of him where he started beating him with his fists.

The Constable tried to get Sammy off, but he was like an enraged bull and wouldn't let go. I joined in and between us we managed to drag him off and back into the wheelchair where the constable handcuffed him.

I knelt beside the sergeant and helped him sit up.

"Stay where you are, I'll get some towels and clean you up," I told him.

He shook his head, rose unsteadily to his feet and sat in his chair.

"I don't care what you do to me," Sammy shouted, "but don't you dare call her a whore. We moved down here to get away from the bombing in Plymouth. She hated it. She shook every night when the Nazis came over."

"So why did you kill her?"

"I didn't kill her," Sammy ground out, hissing more than talking.

"I loved her. We were married."

The sergeant's head rocked back and he looked as though Sammy had hit him again.

"When? Before you strangled her?"

"Six months ago. Before we left Plymouth. We were going to do this for another few months then start afresh. She was always careful, see. Only did it with people she knew, or one of the other girls knew. Always wore something, too. We wanted children."

"So, if you didn't do it, who did? She make a mistake? Get with a stranger?"

Sammy shook his head.

"No, she would have told me. We made some money, had almost two thousand pounds put aside."

The officers exchanged glances and asked where she hid the money. He said that it was in an old suitcase in her room, under the bed. He looked at the sergeant and asked him why he was looking at him like that.

"We searched her room last night. There wasn't any cash there."

Sammy's eyes filled with tears and he wept. Huge sobs racked his body. I stood in front of him and held him as tightly as his wheelchair and handcuffs would allow.

"When will he leave hospital, Miss?"

"I don't know. Not today. The doctor has already done his round. Maybe tomorrow or the day after."

"Will you find out and let me know at Newlyn police station? We'll arrest him before he leaves."

They started to leave the room.

"Wait, Sergeant. Please remove his handcuffs."

"I can't do that, Miss. He'll run off."

"You will remove his handcuffs or I will come down to the police station and complain personally how you goaded and goaded him. And after that I will go to the local paper and tell them how you arrested an innocent man."

He tried to argue but he knew it was pointless. And I remembered where I saw the woman.

# Chapter 49   Annie in Newlyn

There was another letter waiting for me when I arrived at my office.

*"Dear Anne,"* it read, *"I am due back in England for a while next month. I don't have the exact date yet but will be home for two or three weeks commissioning a new ship. She's being fitted out in Falmouth so I won't be that far away. We need to talk and though a lot of water has passed under the bridge and I haven't been the most attentive of husbands, war has changed me and I value those aspects of my life that I treated so badly before. I will let you know when I'm in Cornwall."*

Harry handed it back to me without a word.

"Will you see him?"

"You suggested that I should, if only to end the marriage," I replied. "And he is so maddening. Nothing in the way of apologising for not keeping in touch. No apologies for the affairs he's had. Not even a "looking forward to seeing you." I will see him, but it will be the last time."

Harry took my hand as we walked along the promenade at Newlyn towards the Yacht Inn. The pub had become our local and the regular customers now smiled and nodded when we walked in. This evening was no different.

"I'm glad that you will see him. Not because I want you to realise that you love him," Harry said as we sipped our drinks. "You have to be absolutely sure in your own mind that if you tell him goodbye and something happens to him, you will have done the right thing. None of us knows what's around the corner, Annie."

I felt the tears at the back of my eyes but would not let them come. This was our last evening for a while and I refused to ruin it with stupid tears.

"What time will you leave tomorrow?"

He told me that they would leave in pairs starting just after midnight.

"We rendezvous with the convoy between 0400 and 0500 the next morning. Still dark, so we should be almost invisible. The early hours of the morning are good times to attack. We'll have the element of surprise with us."

I finished my drink and held his hand.

"We should go. You'll need to get some sleep if you're leaving just after midnight. Come back safely, Harry."

I woke early the next morning and heard the roar of Harry's engines starting up but managed to get back to sleep eventually. Finally, at 0530, as the last two boats left Newlyn, I got up, washed, dressed and had breakfast. At 0630 I walked into the office to relieve the night shift early.

"There's a nurse in your office, Ma'am, name of Crebo," Wren Harvey said as she made me a cup of tea. "She says she's due to start her shift at the hospital in an hour."

I took my tea into my office and introduced myself to the young woman sitting at my desk.

"I am sorry to bother you so early in the morning but I needed to talk to someone and James mentioned your name last night when we were having a drink."

"James?" I replied before smiling. "Oh, you're that Carol Crebo. Now I'm with you."

"James has spoken about me?" she gasped.

"Don't worry, Nurse Crebo. James Haywood and Commander Scott have worked together for a long time. They don't have any secrets. And men are worse gossips than women," I told her. "Harry tells me that James is really fond of you. *He's never known anyone as lovely inside and out.* They were James' words, not Harry's."

She relaxed a little at that and we chatted about the men in our lives for a few minutes. I found myself liking her almost immediately. There was a genuineness about her that you could almost reach out and touch.

"Wren Harvey told me that you're due on shift at the hospital soon. How can I help you?"

She told me about the police officers' interview with one of her patients and how she thought that they suspected the wrong man.

"I watched his face while he spoke and I don't believe he did it. You see, the woman who died was a prostitute and I saw her with one of the sailors off the MGBs. I told James and he said that it was the Coxswain off his own boat."

I felt as though someone had knocked the air out of me for a moment as I thought back to the Welsh police interviewing CPO Williams in this office.

"Are you sure that you saw CPO Williams, Carol?"

"Yes, I am, Miss Lenton. Quite sure."

"Please, call me Annie. I feel as though I've known you for ages," I said, my mind racing with my own suspicions that Williams was not as innocent as he pretended to be.

"How can we prove that your patient didn't do it?"

"Well, there is one person who may help. When I wheeled Sammy back to his bed he said that he wished he could talk with Eileen because she knew that he hadn't killed Madge. If we could find this Eileen, we could ask her."

She stood and put her cape on.

"I have to go, Annie. Could you think about how we might find her?"

"Of course I will. Are you free tonight?"

We agreed that we would meet in the tea room at the Seamen's Mission at six o'clock that evening and start a pub crawl around Newlyn. If Eileen was still here she would almost certainly be in one of the local hostelries. Later that afternoon Wren Harvey put a telephone call through to me.

"Lady on the phone for you, Ma'am. Says she's your Mother."

My breath caught in my throat and I felt my chest tighten. Mum never rang me at work.

"Mum, what is it? Is everything all right? Is Dad OK?"

"Of course, Anne, we're fine. Even though the Germans try to kill us every night," and I could tell by the humour in her voice that she had a smile on her lips.

"We are perfectly safe. When the air raid sirens sound we go down into the shelter with everyone else. We're Londoners, we're used to it. How are you?"

We spent the next five minutes gossiping about Mum and Dad and their business. I hadn't been entirely honest with Harry about their Chinese restaurant business. They owned a chain of ten now plus a large grocery shop which sold lots of Chinese goods.

On top of that when other nationalities left mainland Europe ahead of Nazi Occupation they expanded and catered for Polish, French, Dutch and many other tastes. I never asked where Mum and Dad got their stuff from, but they were certainly very far from ordinary shopkeepers and restauranteurs.

"We had quite a shock last evening, Anne," my Mum said at last. "You'll never guess who came round to our home."

I laughed. It could have been anyone, they had a huge circle of friends.

"Go on. Uncle Wang has come back from Shanghai?"

"No, he'll never come back here. He's doing far too well in the Black Market. Even the Japanese don't touch him because he has information about some of their top people out there. It was Roger."

I couldn't believe it and it took me a moment to realise what Mum was saying.

"He said that he never realised how big our business was. And laughed when Dad said that when he retired it would all be yours."

# Chapter 50    Scotty in the Irish Sea

We rounded Lands End in virtually flat calm seas, easily maintaining our thirty knot speed limit. Young Hawes took the first watch with me as we entered the Celtic Sea, the stretch of water that separated the Atlantic Ocean from St George's Channel and the Irish Sea.

"Course due North, Coxswain. Sub, ask the First lieutenant to relieve us at 0600 hours. He can get his head down until then."

The Coxswain and I stood close together in the wheelhouse, braced against the movement of the sea below us. Though the sea was indeed far from rough, a chilly Force Four wind kept us inside although the lookouts were on the open flying bridge from where they had a better view.

"Any more news from Cardiff, Coxswain?"

"Nothing at all, Sir. I rang them yesterday before we left but they said there'd been no developments. Don't know why they use those big words, Sir. Could just have said, nothing to report."

"Ah well, we all have our little foibles. First Lieutenant mentioned that a local prostitute was brought in on a fishing boat a couple of days ago. Local police interviewed some chap about it at the hospital yesterday."

I could have sworn I felt the man twitch. I only said it as something to chat about on a night watch.

"I didn't know that, Sir. Who was she?"

"No idea. Didn't you say that you knew one of the local girls? Moved down from Plymouth?"

"That's right, I did, Sir. But that was ages ago. Haven't seen her since. Didn't seem right what with Agnes disappearing and all."

Hawes came back into the wheelhouse at that stage so I took him to the chart table and talked through what we would be doing on our journey north. I enjoyed teaching him the tricks of the trade as he had a passion for everything he did. He loved the sea and was never happier than when he learnt something new.

"Mr Hawes, you have the exuberance of youth. But you need to balance that with the experience of a mature officer. Now set a course from Anglesey to Londonderry. Let me see how much of your navigation training you're retained."

I left him at the table and walked to my chair at the back of the wheelhouse. In reality there was no distance between the front and the back of the tiny cockpit. But there was enough room for me to sit and place my feet on the shelf at the foot of the reinforced glass windscreen.

"Wheelhouse, Radar. Aircraft bearing 045 degrees, closing," Morrison reported.

I pushed down hard on the Action Stations klaxon and within a minute all guns were manned and all crewmen in position.

*"Flotilla Leader to Greyhound,"* I radioed to the MGB somewhere on my port side. *"Aircraft approaching bearing 045 degrees."*

"Got it on the Radar, Sir. Is it friendly do you think?"

That was the all-important question. At this time of the early morning with darkness all round us, it was impossible to say. Most aircraft had distinctive engine sounds, but that could be misleading.

*"Don't know, Greyhound. Hold fire. Let's not give our position away."*

I joined the two lookouts on the flying bridge.

"Jones, check we're showing no lights.""

I picked up my loud hailer.

*"Captain to crew. Do not fire unless I give the order."*

Morrison reported the aircraft closing, but maintaining a height of around five thousand feet which was low for an enemy aircraft.

"Don't sound like one of ours, Sir. Sounds like one of them Dorniers what attacked Newlyn."

"You may be right. Let's hope they don't see us. I would like to make the trip without having to fight an enemy bomber."

"Radar, bridge. Aircraft losing height rapidly. Closing on us."

The plane's engine tone changed and I fancied I could feel the air parting before it as it dived down towards us.

"Jones, man the searchlights," I ordered.

One piece of equipment added after we took *Dotty* over from the shipyard was a pair of searchlights fixed to the front of the wheelhouse. They could light up a ship a mile away, showing every detail of its hull. According to the fitters who'd rigged them up, they could easily blind a pilot if aimed directly into the cockpit.

The lights picked out the shape of a Dornier barely half a mile away. First one light, then the other. And Jones was nobody's fool. He had them both on full power.

"All guns, fire at will," I called.

*HMS Greyhound*, half a mile away on our port side, had the same idea. The German pilot was just pulling out of his steep dive when both sets of searchlights caught him like an actor on a stage trapped in the spotlights.

Except no actor was ever blinded by the equivalent strength of twenty lighthouses burning their route through his eyes. Afterwards it was impossible to say what exactly happened. I saw our guns gouging chunks out of the plane's fuselage, a string of bombs dropped from the bomb bays and fell harmlessly into the sea in front of us.

Flames crawled from one of the starboard engines before licking back along the length of the plane itself. Next the aircraft simply blew itself apart. Thank God just after she'd passed over us.

The heat from the explosion was quickly dissipated as the sea swallowed plane and crew up.

*Greyhound, any damage?"*
*"No, Sir, no damage, no injuries."*
We arrived in Anglesey six hours later, where each of us, *Greyhound and Dotty*, painted half an aircraft on our wheelhouse bulkhead.

# Chapter 51    Carol Crebo Newlyn

I knew all the people who worked in the Mission and had no problem ordering tea for Annie and me before we started our pub-crawl. When I told our waitress what we would be doing that evening she shook her head.

"Don't know what your mum and dad would say, Carol. Good job they're away, that's all I know."

Annie arrived as Betty told me what she thought about young women who went on pub-crawls.

"It's not at all like that, Mrs Pentreath," she said. "We're looking for a young woman who has been missing for a few days."

When the waitress left to tell her colleagues that there was yet another missing woman we finished our tea and sandwiches and decided on our strategy.

"We'll start at the Tolcarne Inn down in the village itself and work our way along Fore Street," Annie said.

"Good idea. That way we can finish up here at the top of the village where we both live," I agreed.

And that is what we did. The Tolcarne was a nice pub, very popular with office workers and managers. The landlord made our shandies and we took them over to the table. When he came over to clear the glasses from the table next to us I asked him a question.

"Do you know a lady called Eileen? She's not local, well at least, I don't think she is. Probably in her twenties and thirties."

"The only Eileen I know is over there with her old man," he pointed.

I looked over and giggled. Annie did, too.

"No, she is a lot younger than that," I said.

Annie was staring out of the window.

"They'll be all right," I told her. "James said that Harry never takes unnecessary risks."

"I know," she replied, "But you can't help worrying."

I took the chance to study her properly. Her long black hair hung loosely almost to her waist. She was a little heavier than me but had a lovely figure underneath her jacket and skirt. I knew she was a couple of inches shorter than me as I was five feet six inches tall.

She turned and looked at me.

"You're wondering about my parents?" she asked with a slight hardening of her tone.

"No, I wasn't. I think your hair is beautiful and you are very attractive. I can understand why Harry must be in love with you."

"I'm sorry, I didn't mean to be abrupt. It's just that with a Chinese Mum and English Dad people often get the wrong idea. I was brought up to respect people for who they were, not where they were from. Sadly, too many people believe it should be the other way around."

"I can assure you that I liked you from the minute we met. It feels like I've known you for ages," I told her and she smiled.

We finished our drinks and moved to the next pub. Three hours later we'd visited the Swordfish, the Dolphin, the Star and the Red Lion. With no trace of Eileen in any of them. Certainly, some of the regulars knew of her. But none had seen her in the past few days.

"I'm beginning to get a little worried," I said as we walked to the very last pub: the Fishermans Arms.

"So am I," Annie replied.

Pat, the landlady asked what we wanted.

"I am so fed up with shandy," I said. "Shall we have a gin?"

Annie nodded.

"I don't think I could look another shandy in the face."

We paid for the drinks and I asked Pat if she knew Eileen.

"Yes, she normally comes in around now if she hasn't found a customer. You do know what she does for a living, Carol?"

"Oh yes. We just want a word with her. Do you know where she lives?"

"In the cottage at the back of the pub. Been there for almost six months. She's a quiet enough girl, keeps herself to herself. Well, apart from, you know…"

We sat in the little lounge bar. There were only two or three customers in as it was getting close to Last Orders and most of the regulars were either fishermen who'd be out early tomorrow morning or retired and liked their early nights.

The door opened and a young woman in her thirties walked in. Pat smiled cheerily at her and the two chatted before Pat pointed over towards us. The woman picked up her drink and brought it over.

"Pat says that you've been asking about me," she said in a Devonian accent.

"Have a seat, we're not police or anything like that," Annie said.

She was good at getting people talking and soon Eileen chatted along about Newlyn and the people and I had the chance to look her over. I don't know what I expected but she seemed normal. Pretty face, not much make-up. Short fair hair and short finger nails. Her skirt was just below her knee and I could see she wore no stockings.

"You don't think I look much like a prossie?" she asked and laughed. "We're not all the same. Up in Plymouth the sailors expect something different. Down here, it's quieter."

"I'm sorry, I didn't mean to stare," I told her. "Do you know a gentleman called Sammy?"

"Gentleman? Well, I suppose he is. He looks after his girls. If anyone tries any funny business he soon sorts them out."

"Did you know that he was in hospital?"

"Why? What's happened? Is he OK?"

"He's fine now. I found him face down in the kitchen with his head in the gas oven," I told her.

She dropped her glass and it shattered on the floor. Annie started to gather the pieces and I placed my hand over hers.

"He's OK, honestly. But the police think that he killed Madge."

I really shouldn't have said it, and I don't know why I did. At this she howled and put her head between her hands.

"No, No. Madge can't be dead. We were only looking for her two days ago. Sammy was really worried about her. They were moving back to Plymouth together and had almost all the money they needed," she said.

She was almost hysterical by now, shouting all this out between sobs. Pat came over and placed a brandy glass in front of her.

"Get that down, Eileen. You need it. Don't argue with me, just drink it."

She did so and started to calm down.

Annie shuffled along her seat and sat next to her and I did the same on the other side. Between us we told Eileen all that we knew.

"It couldn't have been Sammy. He loved her. I know it sounds funny, but she loved him, too. They got married just before we came down here and had everything planned."

"Can you tell us anything else?" Annie said but she shook her head.

"The only thing I know is that Madge told me that some sailor gave her a load of money to give him an alibi but it wasn't enough to risk her being killed."

When I asked if she knew his name or what he looked like she shook her head before collapsing into even more hysterics. We left soon after.

# Chapter 52    Scotty in the Irish Sea

We left Anglesey Harbour and set a course around the northern tip of Ireland before taking a southerly course towards Londonderry. It was my first time in this part of the North Atlantic Ocean and I was surprised at the effect of the sea as we passed between the Scottish mainland to starboard and the Northern Irish coastline to port. *Dotty* didn't as much pitch and roll as corkscrew the conflicting currents.

"How are you, Sub?" I Asked Hawes.

"Fine, Sir, can't wait for the action to start."

"You might be thinking otherwise if the German escorts get wind of us, Mr Hawes."

I looked at my watch and told him to take a star sight.

"Good practice, Sub. Take the sights then check the position you get with Radar."

Hawes climbed on to the flying bridge with his sextant and came back down a few minutes later, pad and pencil in hand. He asked Morrison to record their position by taking a radar bearing on the two nearest headlands on each side of our boat and walked back to the chart table to calculate the boat's position from his star sights.

What position do you have, Morrison?" he called out and the sailor told him.

Hawes walked back to my chair and held out his pad with the Longitude and Latitude he'd calculated.

"Well done, Sub. Spot on. Now we know where we are. Coxswain, steer Northwest by west."

An hour later *Dotty* and *Greyhound* had full fuel and water tanks and we waited alongside Londonderry's harbour wall listening for the messages that my other boats had completed their own refuelling and were under way.

Three hours later all boats were within thirty minutes steaming and I led *Greyhound* away from Londonderry due west towards the incoming German convoy. Long before they arrived at the rendezvous point Morrison had all the flotilla's boats on his radar screen.

All circling nicely, Sir, as per your orders."

*"Flotilla Leader to Group 2, break off and assume new course. Forty five minutes to attack."*

Ten boats wheeled away under the temporary command of Lieutenant Commander O'Leary, my second in command. They would attack from the west, hopefully leading some of the escort ships away from the convoy. Whether they succeeded was largely immaterial. I would rely on the element of surprise to lead the rest of the flotilla past the escort ships on the eastern side of the convoy and in amongst the merchant ships.

I thought back to the conversation with the Old Man just before we left.

"Even if you sink half the merchantmen, that won't be enough. You must scupper at least five out of the six."

With barely two minutes to go before Group 2 started their attack run, one of the lookouts called out from the flying bridge.

"Ships ahead, Sir. Five degrees to port."

"Just where you said they'd be, Sir. Well done," James said as he left the wheelhouse for his Action Stations position at the torpedo tubes.

I looked all round the boat, sensing the tension as men braced themselves for the attack.

"Explosion almost dead ahead, Sir. Flames, too. Looks like a ship on fire," the lookout called.

"Message from Group 2, Sir. *Starting attack*," Hawes called out.

"Emergency Full Ahead, Coxswain. Wheel amidships. Fire when ready, Number One. All four tubes. Reload as quickly as possible."

O'Leary's group had done well. There were two ships already on fire and they provided the perfect silhouette for my targets. My group of MGBs broke away from each other as we'd planned and selected their own targets.

So far the German escorts had focused entirely on Group 2 but now fire started coming towards us. Because the MGBs were low in the water the shells flew overhead at first.

"Torpedoes away," James shouted as we slewed broadside on to a huge freighter. Twin explosions signalled a hit and flames shot into the air as the freighter rolled over on to her side.

"Destroyer to starboard," the lookout called and James raced over to the starboard torpedo tubes. The sailor manning the controls looked for the signal and brought his hand down on the levers sending four more torpedoes flying through the air before disappearing beneath the waves. We were barely one hundred yards away when at least one of the torpedoes slammed into the destroyer's side.

I gave the order to turn about and we headed at maximum speed into the heart of the convoy posing a dilemma for the German warships: if they opened fire they risked sinking their own freighters. If they didn't, the MGBs would attack those same freighters.

I had no such fear as we raced down between two lines of ships with the other MGBs doing the same. When we reached the end of the line we turned and made one more pass. James, now out of torpedoes, came back into the wheelhouse.

"I counted four merchantmen on fire or sinking, Sir." I gave the order for Group 2 to re-join through the centre of the convoy and attack again if they could while I led my boats in towards the destroyers.

*"Leader to Flotilla, any of you got torpedoes left?"* None did so we withdrew to Londonderry to refuel for the journey home while *Dotty* waited for O'Leary and his boats to return. Of the twenty four boats that left Newlyn, twenty two made the journey home. *HMS Greyhound* and *HMS Terrier* didn't make it.

*"Greyhound copped it from one of the destroyers,"*
O'Leary said over the radio. *"Not sure what happened to Terrier, but there was an almighty flash from where she should have been. Could have been her ammunition going up."*

Twenty six men dead.

"I hope it was worth it," James said.

Before we docked at Anglesey on the way home a radio message arrived from Captain Dennis in Newlyn. "Reconnaissance aircraft flew over the convoy half an hour ago. Reported thirteen escorts and no freighters. Well done. Godspeed home."

# Chapter 53    Annie in Newlyn

Newlyn police station was not the most hospitable of places and when Carol Crebo and I told the sergeant at the desk that we wanted to see Mr Samuel Smith the atmosphere turned even colder.

"Why do you want to see him?" the sergeant asked, rather brusquely I felt.

"To ask him some questions," I replied.

"You have to tell me the questions first then I can decide whether to let you see him."

"Does he have a solicitor?" I asked.

The sergeant burbled, quite literally, and his face turned red.

"That, Miss, is none of your business."

"Oh but it is my business. He is a resident of Newlyn and Newlyn is in the charge of the Royal Navy, as you should know, Sergeant. If you are holding Mr Smith without charge and without access to a solicitor you are acting illegally and I will have to report you to the Port Captain, who I happen to work for."

After a little more bluster he showed us through to the cells and took a seat by the door.

"Can't let you see the prisoner unattended. Against the law," he told me.

I pointed out that if I were his solicitor a police officer would most certainly not be allowed to attend an interview with my client. And I stared at the door to the outer office. He left.

"Is that really right, Annie?" Carol asked. "That Captain Dennis is in charge of the whole of Newlyn?"

I told her that he was, though we didn't broadcast the fact. In times of war the senior military officer in the area has extraordinary powers. Usually, we don't need them, but it's handy to remind people like the sergeant occasionally.

I walked across to the cell and looked through the little window in the doorway. Sammy lay on a metal bed frame on what looked like a paper-thin mattress between him and the steel below.

"Mr Smith," I said and he sat upright.

"Who are you?"

I told him who I was and Carol came forward so he could see her.

"Mr Smith," I began, "we have been making some enquiries about you and your late wife. May I say how sorry we are about her death? It must be horrible for you."

"Came out of the blue, Miss. We were going to move back to Plymouth and start again. We had some money saved up. Not enough, but we knew where to get more. Well, Madge did."

He started sobbing when he mentioned her name and Carol left to ask for some tea. She came back with water and shrugged her shoulders.

I told him that we'd spoken with Eileen and she wanted to visit him. Would he mind?

He shook his head.

"Not while I'm in here. It's a horrible place. Tell her to wait till I get out. But if she leaves Newlyn ask her to let me know where she goes. I'll find her."

He stayed silent after that and stared at the cell walls. It wasn't a big room, I would guess that it was barely eight feet square with a bucket in one corner and a wash basin on a little shelf next to it. I didn't blame him for not wanting any visitors.

"Mr Smith, do you have a solicitor?" Carol asked and he shook his head.

"But everyone's entitled to a solicitor," she told him. "I shall have a word with that sergeant before I leave. You shouldn't say anything to the police unless your solicitor is with you. I saw that in a film the other day and it's true."

I smiled for the first time since entering the police station.

"Do you have any idea who would do this to Madge?" I asked.

"No, she didn't have any enemies. If she was ever worried about a customer she told me and I kept an eye on things. I do the same with Eileen and the other girls."

"But why would anyone do this? I don't understand," I said.

"I don't know, Miss. I do know that it wasn't me. And I also know that if I find out I'll kill him myself. And it won't be a quick death. I'll make him suffer like Madge did."

We sat in silence again for a few minutes.

"I know it sounds like a silly question, but how much money did you need to move back to Plymouth?" I asked.

"About two thousand pounds. We had almost eighteen hundred saved up, some of it from Madge's job, some of it from mine. I can put my hands on most things that people can't get in the shops. The black market's stronger than you think down here and there aren't many with my contacts up country. Between us we did all right."

I thought he was going to continue but he stopped and looked away.

"What were you going to say?"

"Nothing. Whoever did it, they took the money. The police searched her room and it was gone."

The sergeant came in behind us and made a show of holding the door open.

"Visiting time's over, miss. I'll show you out."

I turned back to Sammy and asked him to let us know if he thought of anything else.

"Just ask the sergeant to pass a message to me at Royal Navy HQ in Newlyn."

We walked back to the front desk where I turned to the sergeant and told him that if Sammy didn't have a solicitor the next time we visited I would make sure that the sergeant was demoted.

Outside I stopped and looked at Carol. She had one of those thoughtful looks on her face.

"How much do prostitutes, you know, charge for..?

I smiled at her discomfort.

"I have no idea. Why do you ask?

"Eileen said they'd only been down here for six months. Yet Madge had eighteen hundred pounds. It seems like a lot of money for just doing…"

This time I didn't laugh.

"We need to speak to Eileen again. You may just have helped us prove him innocent."

## Chapter 54    Churchill at General Auchinleck's North African Desert HQ

"Well, Claude, you seem to be well dug in. Can you hold Rommel when he attacks?"

"We can and we will, Sir. I chose this place because it's virtually impossible to attack and win. The terrain favours the defenders. Look around you, Sir."

I didn't need to do that as our pilot circled the area before landing. Hills, ditches, sand as far as the eye could see then more hills and ditches and even more sand. An almost impossible place to attack and win. But infinitely easier to defend and beat the enemy off.

"I want you back in England before the summer's over, Claude," Alan Brooke told him. "The PM agrees. You have done a first class job here, but it's time for a rest and for someone else to take over."

The Auk looked at his CO with his eyebrows raised.

"Gott's not ready, Alan. He thinks he is. I know he isn't, too traditional. The man to beat Rommel must be sly, cunning, prepared to think the unthinkable. That simply isn't Gott."

Although I agreed, this was neither the time nor the place for this particular conversation.

"Rommel has asked for reinforcements and it looks as though the Wehrmacht has agreed," I told him, explaining that the Germans were pulling troops out of the Russian Front.

"It's summer and if Hitler doesn't take Stalingrad now, he never will. Another winter will annihilate his troops."

And it was true. Enigma messages flowed freely between the German Navy and the Wehrmacht, their army.

Brooke went into the detail of how the Germans planned a fast convoy to sail south from Trieste down through the Adriatic Sea, into the Ionian and finally into the Mediterranean Sea."

At this stage we didn't know where along the Egyptian coast they would land the troops, but we would attack them when they were close enough. And I hoped that the closer they got, the more relaxed they became. Our Navy boys needed every advantage they could get.

"Our spies also tell us that the Mussolini is pulling Italian troops out of frontier guard duties and transferring them to the North. Probably Trieste again," Brooke added.

The Auk wiped a hand across his forehead, a habit Alan Brooke told me that meant he was thinking carefully. I said nothing, simply waited. I had to know that he could hold the line here before we made one huge attack later in the year. One last offensive against an unprepared and demoralised Rommel.

"If German reinforcements get through, I cannot guarantee holding out, Prime Minister. At the moment we have more troops than Rommel if I am to believe my spies. Even though he has more armour, he won't be able to move it quickly enough during his attack."

I exchanged looks with Brooke.

If they don't get through, or if only some of them are able to land, what are your predictions?" Brooke asked.

The Auk picked up a piece of paper and read it.

"This is the latest intelligence report. You gave it to me yourself when you arrived."

I knew what it said. It was deciphered from Enigma and told us that Rommel's reinforcements amounted to twenty thousand troops, two hundred panzer tanks and hundreds of pieces of field artillery.

"If half of it gets through, El Alamein will fall. And after that Rommel will have an open road into Alexandria and the Suez Canal. We must destroy those reinforcements or we lose North Africa, gentlemen," he told us.

Those words echoed in my head during the whole of the flight back to London.

Back in Downing Street I called Sir Dudley Pound, First lord of the Admiralty to Downing Street to meet with Sir Alan and me. Sir David Petrie, Head of MI6 and the operation that deciphered Enigma coded messages joined us.

"Gentlemen, the campaign in North Africa has not gone as well as we would have wished. But we believe we have an opportunity to reverse our fortunes in the autumn and throw Rommel and his troops out of Egypt."

I reminded them of the intelligence that Enigma had given us but the most critical intelligence we needed now was confirmation of when the reinforcements would land, the precise route they would take and how the Germans intended to escort the troop and tank carriers.

"Time is of the essence, gentlemen. We still don't know when the Germans intend to attack El Alamein." I looked pointedly at Sir David, who had been in post barely a year.

"I give you authority to use whatever means you can to bring us that information and quickly. If we are to attack the German convoy it must be in the next six weeks. That's forty two days."

Sir Dudley coughed gently before interrupting.

"Prime Minister, if we are to get our MGBs in a position to attack we must get them loaded on to a Mediterranean bound convoy within the next week. When I received your signal from the desert I requisitioned four of our fastest cargo ships. The Merchant Navy is not happy, because they were supposed to take supplies to Russia. But, we need them more."

"Comrade Stalin will no doubt be on the telephone before the day is out," I smiled. I was used to dealing with Russia's President. One more argument would not unduly dent our relationship.

The Admiral outlined his plans for the convoy with each ship carrying six MGBs below decks, out of sight to any who would wish us harm.

"Thank you, Admiral. Please convey my personal gratitude to the owners, masters and crew of the merchant ships. And tell the Flotilla Commander that we must destroy these German troop carriers if we are to stand any chance of retaking North Africa and throwing the Germans into the sea."

I didn't dare voice my final thought before the meeting ended. Without the destruction of this convoy we could well see Mr Hitler cutting off one of our most important supply chains before he marched down the Mall to Buckingham Palace within the year.

# Chapter 55    Annie in Newlyn

Carol and I went our separate ways after our visit to the police station and I spent the rest of the evening wondering how Harry was, temporarily forgetting the dilemma of Sammy and the missing money.

I did get to sleep eventually, but was up early the next morning and in the office by 0600 hours. Once again, Wren Harvey was surprised, and I daresay delighted, to finish her shift early.

There was a note from Carol on my desk apologising that she would not be able to join me in another pub crawl that evening: "*Dear Annie, I am sorry but I must cry off this evening,*" she wrote. "*I have a long double shift today and an ARP shift when I finish at the hospital. With luck I may just get three or four hours sleep before my early shift tomorrow. If you would rather wait for my company I will quite understand.*"

The phone rang at that moment.

"7 Squadron, Second Officer Lenton."

"Anne, it's Roger. How are you?"

"Oh, it's you. Where are you?"

"Just landed. I'm in Falmouth. When can I see you?"

"I told you that I didn't think that was a good idea," I reminded him.

"Look, what about a drink. Say on Friday night. One drink for old times' sake. What do you say?"

I didn't say anything. Harry had said that I should see him one more time. Perhaps I was worried that I might still feel something for him and might take him back. But I didn't think so.

"No, I'm busy on Friday. Make it Saturday. We'll meet in Newlyn at the Fishermans Arms. I'm on duty on Sunday so I won't be late. Let's say 7 o'clock."

"Right. I can't wait to see you. I've really missed you. And, I love you."

"Goodbye, Roger."

I made a pot of tea and thought about our marriage. It wasn't much of one, maybe we never gave it a chance. And the thought of him having affairs right now had no effect on me. At one time I felt angry, hurt, let down. But not now. I really didn't care. I would see him, but only for one drink.

The phone rang again and I wasn't at my friendliest when I answered it. I half suspected it was Roger.

"7 Squadron, Second Officer Lenton."

"Is Captain Dennis in? It's Western Approaches Command Centre."

"No, I'm afraid not. Who is this?"

"Commander Aston, duty officer. I really need to speak to Captain Dennis urgently. When will he be in?"

My blood felt like an icy river, the cold seemed to start from my chest and work outwards. My breath caught in my throat.

"I'm Captain Dennis' assistant, Sir. He should be at his desk in an hour. Can I give him a message?"

There was a delay before he replied.

"You have a flotilla on the way home, I believe?"

"Yes, are they all right?"

"This is an open line, SO Lenton. I can say no more than that. Have Captain Dennis ring me the instant he gets in."

That hour was the longest of my life. So many questions ran through my mind. Was Harry OK? Was he sunk? Was he injured? Why hadn't he radioed before now? At last the Old Man arrived and I gave him the message.

He went into his office and closed the door. Minutes later he called me in.

"Anne, the boys are on their way home. Two losses, I'm afraid."

I felt the colour drain from my face.

"Harry's OK. They want him to detour. They've had a report of an enemy submarine in the Irish Sea. One of our Catalina flying boats bombed it an hour ago and it dived. But the Catalina picked up its trail. Harry's boats are the closest to its last known position. Western Approaches are diverting him now."

I looked at the wall clock as the Old Man walked to his chart.

"Between Fishguard and Wexford," he said pointing at the two ports, "the former in Wales, the latter in Ireland. One of the narrowest parts of the Irish Sea. Harry must be within a few miles if he's on schedule."

"How many boats will he take, Sir?"

"One other. We can't afford to lose any more with the mission coming up."

Our signalman came in at that point with the post for the day. I gave him the outbound packages and started sorting out the envelopes that had just arrived.

While I was doing this the day shift of Wrens arrived and soon there were the usual sounds of a kettle boiling, chatter as the Wrens caught up on who'd been doing what to whom the previous night and phones starting to ring. A typical busy day in our office. But my mind was over a hundred miles away.

"Annie, are you all right?" one of the Wrens asked.

"Of course. Why do you ask?"

"I've asked you twice if you'd like a cup of tea and you didn't hear me."

"Oh, sorry, Jean. Miles away. We have to start planning for the flotilla to leave."

"Will you miss him?" she asked.

My look made her step back from my desk.

"I'm sorry, Annie. We've worked together since the start of the war and I've never seen you this happy and relaxed. I didn't mean to offend."

I stood and touched her on the shoulder.

"It's me who should apologise. Yes, I'll miss him terribly. I think he might miss me, too. Just a bit."

"Huh, Miss Lenton. More than just a little bit. I've seen the way he looks at you when you're together. He's besotted. Wouldn't be surprised if he asked you to marry him."

I picked up two cups of tea and the morning's mail and walked into the Old Man's office. As I slit the envelopes he removed the contents and skimmed the first few lines before putting them to one side.

He stopped after skimming the fifth or sixth pack and his brow furrowed, as a frown crept along it. At last he looked up.

"Well, there it is. Harry's orders. He sails from Devonport in three days. Their Lordships at the Admiralty have pulled out all the stops for him. Fast convoy south, around the Horn of Africa and up through the Suez Canal. Very special treatment."

Very special treatment was right. Provided they made it without being torpedoed or bombed, provided they got past Suez without being found out, provided there were no leaks. I was more interested in the voyage home than the outward bound trip.

# Chapter 56    Prime Minister Churchill in London

"The Head of MI6 is here, Sir," my secretary announced. "Shall I show him in?"

"No, I'll come through and fetch him," I replied, following her from my office at the back of the War Rooms to the waiting room at the front.

That was no mean feat, I can tell you. The place was a rabbit warren with offices, briefing rooms, plot rooms and, of course, canteens dotted all over the place. All beneath the ground close to Parliament Square.

Sir David Petrie and I walked into the Map Room where Admiral of the Fleet Sir Dudley Pound, Marshall of the Royal Air Force Sir Sholto Douglas and Sir Alan Brooke, Head of the Chief of the Imperial General Staff waited.

These meetings were regular affairs although today's would focus on one topic only instead of the usual four or five. Most theatres of war right now presented plenty of challenge but no change. North Africa and Russia were different. And at this moment intertwined, though thousands of miles apart.

"Sir David, please bring us up to date on the intelligence you've gathered," I ordered.

Petrie was a smallish man, no more than five feet six inches. According to his file he'd served behind enemy lines in France in the last war, avoiding capture for two years. In that time he'd sent huge amounts of information about German troop deployments back home. For the final two years of the war he headed up the unit responsible for identifying German spies on the UK mainland.

I knew him to be fastidious in his manner, his speech and his dress. Today he wore his customary black bow tie with a dark blue double breasted suit and shiny black shoes. He sipped a glass of water - I had never known him to drink anything stronger - before opening a small notebook.

"Prime Minister, gentlemen," he began, "since our last meeting MI6 has expended the maximum effort possible to secure further intelligence about troop movements. Only two hours ago I received a personal radio transmission from our top agent in Stalingrad. This confirmed the picture that we have built in recent weeks."

Annoyingly, he stopped to take a further sip of water, patted his lips dry with the whitest handkerchief I've ever seen and referred once more to his little book. He told us that there were sure signs that German were leaving the front line. And that there were large build-ups of German soldiers and Waffen SS in a holding area some hundred miles from the city

"Enigma has intercepted messages from Berlin that paint a strange picture. Hitler wants to over-run Stalingrad this summer - in other words within the next three to four months. But, he has ordered ten thousand troops to be kept back from the front line pending orders."

"Do we know what those orders might be, David?" the Admiral asked, in a somewhat impatient tone of voice.

"Not precisely, my dear Dudley. But that same holding ground houses several hundred Panzer tanks and other pieces of artillery. Unusually, the trains that have transported German troops and machinery into Northern Russia are still there. Normally they are withdrawn back into Germany for further transportation duties. "

I drummed my fingers on the desk and asked about troop movements in Italy, especially whether there were signs of Mussolini taking troops out of his front line.

"We have seen nothing out of the ordinary, Prime Minister. But, we have intercepted messages ordering an unusually large German navy escort group to sail from Hamburg to Trieste."

"So we have an escort group sailing to Trieste, German troops being pulled out of the front line in Russia, trains being kept in Russia instead of going back to Germany. We must be right in our assumptions. Hitler's agreed to Rommel's request for reinforcements. Why hasn't Enigma picked anything up between Berlin and Rommel?"

"Enigma will only intercept radio messages, Prime Minister. It is entirely plausible that Rommel received his orders in a written letter."

Pound walked across to the huge wall map.

"Trieste down to the Egyptian coast isn't a long journey," he said quietly.

"How long?" I asked.

He used his forefinger and thumb as a pair of dividers and walked them across the map.

"About five to six days, Winston."

"What happens if that convoy sails before we can get our boys into position?"

"We lose North Africa. Alexandria falls and the Nazis take control of Suez. We're damned," Brooke said in as sombre a voice as I'd heard since 1939.

I looked at Sir Sholto but he shook his head.

"I know what you're going to ask, Winston and it can't be done. If I send any of my bombers over Northern Italy they will be shot out of the sky within half an hour of take-off."

"I will brief my agents, Prime Minister," Petrie broke in. "We have partisan groups in Czechoslovakia, Poland and Hungary. The trains must move through at least one of those countries."

He smiled at this point, unusually for him. "If the troops move towards Trieste too early, we'll slow them down. We are quite the dab hand at blowing up railway tunnels."

"Please keep us informed of your intelligence," I told him. "And let me know if you need any extra equipment or personnel."

After he left, Pound, Brookes and I discussed the operation ahead. At the end of the meeting it was clear that we would need an awful lot of luck to have our MGBs in position as the convoy came into the Mediterranean Sea.

"The tide is turning, Winston," Pound said.

"But is it turning quickly enough, Dudley? Even if the MGBs leaves on time, it will be almost three weeks before they're in the Med. And that's without any sort of delays, U Boat attacks and sinkings."

"I've given them the biggest escort I've ever allocated, Sir. Though there are never guarantees in life, we would have to be damnably unlucky to lose any of our ships on this run."

"But there's the Med, Admiral. And we know what hell that has been for our convoys breaking through to Malta."

"We've routed them around the Cape and up through Suez. Barely any Med to go through. And Henry will lead them the whole way, Winston."

Sir Henry Turner, one of our finest admirals, was C-in-C Home Fleet Battle Squadron. If anyone could get those MGBs from England to Suez and on to Alexandria it was Turner and his battle-hardened ships and crews. They'd been together since Dunkirk, had patrolled the deadly waters off that beach for days on end. With Turner, so his crew said, sitting in his chair on *HMS Ganges'* bridge for the whole of that time. When the Battle Fleet with Turner's aircraft carrier, *HMS Ganges,* started a mission, they always finished it. They had yet to fail. I hoped that this would not be the first time.

I walked back through the War Rooms and up into the street. I needed fresh air and space to think. Most of all I needed time and luck. I lit my cigar and leant against a lamppost on Whitehall.

"Give Hitler one for us, Winnie," a passing taxi driver shouted and I waved and laughed. If we pulled this off we would indeed wipe the smile off that Nazi bastard's face.

# Chapter 57   Commander Klopp in Hamburg

Since we arrived two days ago the Captain has spent every waking hour at Gestapo Headquarters. They called me in yesterday and some of the other officers, but we weren't there for long. As the Captain and I agreed, we told the investigators that Lieutenant Zirk disobeyed orders several times by going on to an open and very wet and treacherous after deck. Even hardened sailors took extra care in those conditions, particularly in the midst of a battle.

Whether they believed us I couldn't yet say. What was interesting was that they seemed more interested in Zirk than in the loss of part of our destroyer screen off the Channel Islands. Even Admiral Meyer remarked on it.

"Three destroyers sunk with five hundred sailors drowned and all they're worried about is one snotty little Nazi who couldn't keep his footing on a wet deck."

But he said it quietly and only when there was just him, the Captain and me in the room. It was not sensible to voice such thoughts in Gestapo HQ.

The Captain returned aboard just before dinner. I was at the top of the gangway when he boarded and the side party came smartly to attention.

"Welcome back aboard, Sir. Can I buy you a drink in the wardroom? The officers will be pleased to see you."

"No, thank you, Commander Klopp. I will join you all for dinner but I don't think we should celebrate the death of a colleague just now."

I felt as though I'd been slapped in the face, and watched as he disappeared up to his cabin just aft of the bridge. Perhaps our understanding was one of convenience after all. And, worryingly, perhaps, he thought that I knew more than I let on about Zirk's disappearance. I felt the old pain in my leg and retreated to my cabin.

The painkillers were where I hid them so long ago and I withdrew two from the bottle, chasing them down with a shot of Schnapps. A knock at the door startled me and I quickly straightened the sheets on my bunk. "Come in."

Captain Braun stood there with a bottle in his hand. "May I come in, Johann?"

He closed the door behind him and sat at my desk while I sat on the bunk. He pointed at my glass. "Started already?"

"Just a small one, Sir. Steadies the nerves. Thought you might be bringing the Gestapo down to arrest me for not looking after Lieutenant Zirk."

He laughed and I laughed with him.

"I am sorry if I was abrupt when I came back aboard. We must all be careful what we say in future. You never know who's listening. Anyway, back to the events of the last few days. You know what they said in their summing up? Let me tell you."

He poured two glasses of Schnapps and described the events of the past week. The first day was more of an interrogation of where everyone was when Zirk disappeared. No mention of the British attack on our convoy at all. At the start of the second day they went over the same ground again until the Admiral interrupted them.

"I have been talking with Berlin," he said quietly.

"And Berlin is not happy at the way you're treating one of our next great Admirals. The Fuhrer himself has asked for a report on today's proceedings."

After that, Captain Braun said, the tone changed. They asked more questions about the attack, helped by the Admiral's coaching about maritime matters. Finally, they announced their verdict and declared it a shame that Zirk had not listened more to Captain Braun and his officers.

They went further and ordered that all Gestapo officers serving on German Naval ships should adhere to the orders, not the advice but the orders, given by the ships' officers.

"The finest conclusion," Captain Braun said, "was to investigate why German Intelligence didn't warn us of this new type of fast patrol boat and the numbers that lay in wait for us."

"A good and fair outcome, Sir," I raised my glass. "To *Der Condor* and Gruppen 158, Sir. And to our next mission."

After dinner the Captain returned to his cabin, but before he left the wardroom he asked me to arrange for all Captains to meet aboard *Der Condor* at midday the next day.

"We have our next mission and it is vital that we succeed. The future of the war may depend upon it."

At exactly noon Captain Braun strode into our large wardroom and looked at his captains. The Admiral had replaced the destroyers we had lost on our last convoy and their captains sat amongst their more experienced colleagues waiting for Braun to brief us on our next mission.

"Good afternoon, gentlemen and welcome to *Der Condor*. I start by congratulating you on our last mission. The Court of Enquiry concluded yesterday that we should have been given much better intelligence about the size of the fleet that attacked us and their speed. They asked me to pass on their thanks to all of you for the part you played. We lost many ships, but we did save the troopship."

Some of the captains exchanged looks, but none held anyone else's eye and none said anything. They were probably as relieved as Braun and me at the thought that there would be no further Gestapo enquiry.

"Now to our next mission. We are to bunker all ships for a fast passage south."

He passed envelopes around and indicated that they should open them and start reading.

"I will be brief because before you leave today I want you all to have read your orders and when you have done so to assure me that you understand what Germany requires of you."

He paused and for the first time smiled. He should try that more often, I thought, it really makes him look almost human.

"Let me summarise the task ahead of us before you start reading," he told them.

What he said sounded entirely plausible. We would sail to Trieste in Northern Italy and pick up a convoy of troopships and freighters bound for North Africa.

"These are the reinforcements that Fieldmarshal Rommel needs to throw the British out of Africa once and for all."

So far, so plausible, I thought. A small convoy of merchant ships with a large escort of warships. His voice quickened as he talked about how we were all that stood between a certain German victory in North Africa and a humiliating defeat. As he spoke, I wondered how he could exude such confidence and not challenge the implausibility of it all.

A four thousand mile sea journey through the Atlantic Ocean and the Mediterranean Sea before we even arrived at Trieste. Followed by a further thousand miles to the North African coast. Through Atlantic waters inhabited by British submarines and into the Med where anything could happen. I felt the pain start and willed the meeting to end.

# Chapter 58    Scotty in the Irish Sea

When Western Approaches ordered us to stay in the area and find an enemy submarine, I thought it would be like looking for an upturned rowing boat in mid-Atlantic. Or a grey pebble on a shingly beach.

With the rest of the flotilla homeward bound, *HMS Bulldog* and *Dotty* started a box search. The Catalina stayed with us for a while, flying in ever-increasing circles. An hour into the search the ping of the ASDIC set woke us all up.

Our anti-submarine detection devices had improved immeasurably since the start of the war, and our operator could identify targets beneath the waves five miles away. And our latest set told him not only the distance, but also the bearing and depth.

"Four miles, Sir, bearing 045 degrees," he said, adding a few minutes later, "she's heading due north."

I ordered *Bulldog* to approach the U Boat from the North West to reduce the chances of the sub escaping and slowed *Dotty* down to give them time to get into position. When *Bulldog* told us that she was in position, I ordered *Dotty* to increase revs for twenty knots, the maximum speed at which ASDIC could continue tracking.

The operator called out the distance, bearing and the sub's heading as we closed and I warned the First Lieutenant to stand by.

"One hundred yards," the operator called and I gave the order for the first rack of depth charges to be catapulted over the side. Four huge underwater explosions followed with four towers of water leaping into the air.

"Lost contact," the operator reported, a common outcome when the seas below the surface boiled and raged.

"*Bulldog* closing, Sir" Morrison reported at the same time as ASDIC regained contact. I ordered *Dotty* out of the area to give her space and watched as the waters boiled and seethed again.

The operator lost contact once more and I held my breath until I heard the next Ping. This U Boat was either very lucky or was good at anticipating our movements.

I changed tactics and ordered *Bulldog* to run parallel to us but two hundred yards to port.

"Keep the U Boat between us," I told her CO, Lieutenant Williams. "Fire on my order."

We took a long sweep around and *Bulldog* took station off my port side.

"How many charges left, Number One?"

"Two racks, Sir."

"Full rack on the first pass."

"Aye aye, Sir."

We sped in once more, again at twenty knots, with the operator calling out the reducing distance between the target and the two MGBs.

On his last call I gave the order to fire and eight depth charges, four of ours and four of *Bulldog's,* plunged into the seas. The impacts of the explosions sent both MGBs heeling over on their sides but we soon swept back up to the vertical and waited to see the U Boat. She popped out of the sea bow-first like a champagne cork out of the bottle before falling under the waves once more. My crew gave a huge cheer but kept their eyes clearly focused on the spot where she vanished.

"Sounds of vessel breaking up, Sir," the operator said. I went out on to the open deck and looked around. Death by drowning was bad enough; I'd seen more than enough of that myself. But a slow death trapped inside a metal hull while it broke up around you and sank down through the murky waters was horrid. Goodness knows these U Boats had killed thousands of our own sailors since the start of the war. Even so, it was not a good way to go.

James joined me and I could see his nostrils twitching.

"Oil, Sir, I think."

The light was still good enough for us to be able to see the surface. Long streaks of oil merged in with the sea and bits of wreckage: lifejackets, lifebuoys, and limbs. "Bodies, Sir," a lookout reported and I gave the order to move slowly towards them.

One seemed to be moving and a group of my crewmen pulled him aboard.

"He's alive, Sir," one said and they wrapped him in blankets and carried him below where it was warm. We left the others covered in blankets on deck.

*"Beagle* to *Bulldog,"* I radioed, using *Dotty's* official name. "Good shooting, Peter. We share the kill."

*"Bulldog* to *Beagle*, and you, Sir. Any survivors?"

"One sailor. Two other bodies lashed to our deck. Time to go home."

It took us almost four hours to get back into Newlyn as the weather started to turn for the worse. By the time we tied up there was a full gale blowing and the seas were mounting. We'd been lucky.

The rest of the flotilla stood on the quay as we came alongside and gave us a rousing cheer. I looked for the one person I wanted to see more than anyone and there she was, at the back, behind the crews. She gave me a quick wave and walked quickly away.

Captain Dennis stepped down on to the deck and slapped me on the shoulder.

"Good work, Harry. One convoy wrecked and a submarine destroyed."

I wasn't sure what to say, so smiled instead.

"Thank you, Sir. The flotilla acquitted themselves well. I think we're ready for whatever's next."

"Just as well, my boy. Your orders came through. Day after tomorrow you leave for Plymouth. A fast convoy awaits you in Devonport. I'll have you stored and refuelled tomorrow ready for an early start."

James Haywood walked over to me after the Old Man left.

"Tell Sub Lieutenant Hawes he has the watch, James. Time for you and me to get ashore. I imagine someone's waiting to see you."

"I felt exhausted when we came through the Gaps, Sir. But right now sleep is the last thing on my mind."

We walked up the quay together and I saw Carol Crebo waiting at the barrier, her face lit up with a huge smile.

"See you tomorrow, Number One," I said as I walked into Annie's office.

She stood and ran over to me and her kisses were the sweetest ever.

"I've booked a taxi. We're staying at the Queens Hotel tonight. And I don't want to waste a single second," she said as she locked the office door and gave the driver our destination.

# Chapter 59    Annie in Newlyn

With our two boyfriends working into the evening to
get the boats ready for departure Carol and I walked
around some of the pubs which we thought Eileen
might frequent. We started at the Fishermans Arms
where we'd talked with her before. But after half an
hour there was no sign of her.

Neither of us wanted to miss being with the boys
before they sailed so we decided to walk along to the
Red Lion. And there she was, talking to one of *Dotty's*
sailors at a quiet table towards the rear of the pub.

"Excuse me, I am sorry to interrupt, but would you
give us a few minutes with Eileen, please?" I asked the
sailor as politely as I could.

"She's not your type, Darling. More mine," he replied,
rather drunkenly I thought.

"You do not address an officer in that tone. Apologise
and move away. Now," I hissed at him.

His eyes widened and I wondered if he was going to
hit me, but another sailor came over and whispered
something in his ear.

"Sorry, Ma'am. Drink talking," he said as he went up
to the bar with his friend. Eileen's eyes narrowed.

"I was on to a good thing there," she said. "Drunk
enough to pay but sober enough to perform."

"This won't take long," I told her as Carol and I sat at
her table.

I asked the question that Carol asked me after we saw
Sammy.

"Why do you want to know that?" she asked frostily.
"You from the tax people or something?"

I explained that Sammy said that he and Madge had
saved around eighteen hundred pounds and only
needed another two hundred before they could move
back to Plymouth. But the money was no longer in
Madge's room.

"So, why do you want to know what we charge? We charge as much as we can. Or as much as they give us."

"Could you earn almost two thousand pounds in six months?" I asked. She laughed.

"You got to be joking. That bloke," she pointed at the sailor by the bar, "we just agreed to five pounds. And that's a good night."

According to Eileen, some customers only paid three or four and some nights they didn't get any customers. We got up and thanked her.

"How's Sammy? Can I visit him yet?"

I told her what he'd said and she looked down at the table before pulling a white handkerchief out of her bag to wipe her eyes.

On the walk back we did some arithmetic. The result was that even if Madge had been busy every night she wouldn't have made much more than a thousand pounds at most.

"And Sammy said that he'd made a bit but nothing like eight hundred pounds," Carol said. "Where did the rest of that money come from?"

"As important, where did it go?" I replied as we said goodnight.

I unlocked the office door and thought that I might as well do some work until Harry arrived. He'd booked us into the hotel for a further night and we were due to have dinner there in just over an hour. As I opened the door, Chief Petty Officer Williams walked by and I called out to him.

"Chief Williams, can I have a word?"

He walked over and saluted. I returned the salute and asked him if he'd heard from his wife.

"No, Ma'am. Nothing at all. And the police haven't been in touch either."

I don't know what made me do it, but I asked him how well he knew the prostitutes working in Newlyn and I could have sworn that his head shot up in some sort of sharp reflex action.

"Only one, Ma'am. The one they say is dead. Knew her from Plymouth. She went with some of the lads. But, I'm a married man I don't need nothing like that." He paused before asking, in quite a shaky voice, "Why do you ask a question like that?"

I shook my head and for the first time looked down and saw his hands clenched into fists.

"I met a man in the police station who's being charged with murdering the lady that drowned. Only she didn't drown. Someone killed her."

He stepped towards me.

"What would that have to do with me?"

"Well, you look like someone who knows what's going on. You're an experienced chief petty officer, you listen to men talking. I wondered if you'd heard anything."

I swallowed heavily, not liking the way he was edging closer to me.

"I haven't heard anything, Miss Lenton. And you shouldn't assume that all sailors are the same. Not all of us go with prostitutes."

He turned and walked away. Well, in truth he stalked off, arms swinging forcefully at his side as though he were purging demons. I walked into the office and locked the door behind me. I felt quite confused. On the one hand, pleased that I asked him the question. But, on the other hand, surprised and frightened at the way he responded. It didn't seem at all right that he should react so aggressively.

I should mention it to Harry but I didn't want anything to spoil our last evening together before he left tomorrow.

I saw the door handle turn and breathed in sharply. Was it Williams returning? A voice called out, "Annie, are you in there?" and I ran to the door.

He came inside and I hugged him tightly.

"Are you all right?" he asked.

"Of course I am. Come on, the taxi'll be here in a minute."

I have never felt as loved as I felt that night. We had a delicious dinner. I didn't dare ask where the chef had got the steak or the delicious ice cream we finished with. Neither of us knew a lot about wine so we let the waiter decide for us. All I can say is that it was red and it was delicious.

After dinner we went to our room. The last few times we'd been together we had got to know each others' bodies and what we liked. This time our love making was sublime. We barely slept a wink all night.

"I've got weeks at sea to catch up on my sleep," he said before we did at last fall asleep in each other's arms. We walked back to Newlyn in the morning and Harry kissed me slowly and with love, not passion, before he waved goodbye and walked down the quay. When I heard the roar of the flotilla's engines starting up an hour later I didn't go out to wave him off. I knew he would come back.

# Chapter 60    Annie in Newlyn

The Fishermans Arms was a pleasant pub and one that I could almost call my local after the number of times I'd been in there with Carol. I'd also been in there with the Old Man for lunch once or twice as they served the most delicious home-cooked Cornish pasties.

Roger rose from a table at the rear of the pub and strode to meet me at the door. He put his arms around me and tried to kiss me on the lips but I turned my head.

"Sorry, Anne, got quite carried away at seeing you again. You look absolutely smashing. The Cornish air must agree with you."

He ordered me a gin and tonic and one for himself. From his reddened cheeks this was far from his first.

"How have you been?" I asked.

"The Med has been pure hell. They outnumber us in the air and at sea. Their submarines hunt in packs like they do in the Atlantic and in the Arctic. They've decimated most of our convoys. We're getting perhaps two out of every ten merchant ships through to Malta. Aside from when I've been on leave I don't think I've slept more than three or four hours out of every twenty four."

This was not what I wanted to hear with Harry about to leave for precisely that region.

"It must be tough out there," I said. "But I thought you were there for just a few months before they sent you into the South Atlantic to escort convoys around the Cape of Good Hope?" I asked.

"Well, yes, they did. But it's still quite harrowing. U Boats operate down there as well, you know.""

This was the man I knew. Not the hero of the Mediterranean Fleet. One of my friends told me that he'd done just three trips in the Med before wangling a transfer to quieter, and safer, waters.

"I've missed you, he said, lunging forward and grabbing my hand. "Their Lordships are posting me and my new ship to the Far East. We'll be leaving in a few weeks. It's unlikely that I'll be coming back to Blighty for a long time. Maybe not until the war's over."

I withdrew my hand from his.

"Roger, we have nothing in common. You never loved me. You had affair after affair. Don't you think I don't know that?"

He looked down at the floor and I thought that he sobbed before telling me how much he'd changed and how much he realised he loved and missed me.

"Please give me a second chance."

"Why? What is so important that you want to stay married? Surely it would suit you better to be single so you're free to do whatever you like?"

I sipped my drink and looked at him. He was handsome, of course. One or two of the younger female customers at the bar couldn't keep their eyes off him."

"Have you seen my parents?" I asked.

"I popped into see them when I went up to the Admiralty last week. They insisted I had dinner with them," he said taking quite a large gulp from his glass.

"What will you do after the war, Roger?" I asked.

"Hadn't thought about it, Old Girl. I might try my hand at something different."

"Pimping? You should have the experience." I couldn't help myself.

He laughed, but it was very much a forced laugh.

"Or shop keeping, perhaps? With a restaurant thrown in? Mum said that you became quite animated when Dad started talking about his business. Especially when he said how much they earned from all their interests. How much was it?"

"I don't recall. I was more interested in what they were selling, not how much they made," he said, emptying his glass.

"Would you like another Gin?" he asked standing up.

"No, thank you, Roger. My Mum is a terribly good judge of character. We had quite a heart to heart this evening before I came here. She also has a photographic memory. She remembers every question you asked that evening. And was amazed at you not drinking once Dad started talking business and money. Did you write it all down after you left so you could be sure that it was worth staying married?"

His face was a picture. He was clearly very angry and put his glass down on the table with so much force it broke. The landlady looked over from the bar and started walking towards us.

"Look, I was interested because when this is all over I won't stay in the Navy," he said hurriedly, which took me by surprise. "I have no skills to offer any employer other than being captain of a ship. I'm scared about the future, Anne. Your parents made me think that perhaps I do have some skills after all. Being a captain means heading up your crew, looking after them, pushing them to do things. I could help with the restaurants, start at the bottom and be ready to help you when you take the business over."

I was quite taken aback. This was a different sort of man to the one that I thought I knew.

"Look, I have to leave now. I came here to beg you for a chance to save our marriage and you treat me like some sort of thief or scoundrel."

He finished his drink and stood.

"We're working the new ship up before we leave," he said before adding that he would be completely immersed in his new destroyer for the next six or seven weeks.

"Just think about what I've said. If your answer's still no, you won't see me again. I promise."

And he left. Gave me a peck on the cheek and walked out. I left the pub and walked back to my room.

# Chapter 61    Harry in Devonport

We arrived in Plymouth Sound in mid-afternoon after a quiet voyage north from Newlyn. As ever, the Sound was full of ships of all types. The aircraft carrier, *HMS Ganges*, sat at anchor with her squadron surrounding her. If any U-Boat or mini-submarine tried anything here they'd be blasted out of the water.

The Old Man told me before we left that *Ganges* would lead the escort group. Which was something of a relief as funnily enough I felt somewhat nervous at the thought of being just a glorified passenger on someone else's ship. At least the escort would give us the protection we needed on this trip.

And what a trip it was going to be. Convoys normally travelled at the speed of the slowest ship and that could be anything between seven and ten knots. Ours was classed as a fast convoy, average speed around fifteen knots.

"What a glorious sight, Sir," James observed from the flying bridge. "If anyone can get us through it's old *Ganges* and her chicks."

"Don't get romantic on me, Number One," I smiled. "*Ganges* was built in the early nineteen twenties. I'd rather have the *Ark* but beggars can't be choosers."

*HMS Ark Royal* was one of the best known ships in the Royal Navy. The public loved her and whenever she came home to Plymouth or Portsmouth thousands of people turned out to cheer her.

But her home for the foreseeable future was where we were headed: The Med. And her job as flagship of the Mediterranean Fleet made her even more popular. Admiral Cunningham, CinC Mediterranean had already won two huge battles against the Italians and Germans. I hoped he was on hand if we needed him.

"I did a month on the *Ark* when I was at Scapa Flow just before the war," James continued. "My last posting as a midshipman," he went on. "We were sent into the Arctic to help a destroyer. It was mid-winter, temperatures never above freezing."

"I didn't know that," I said. "Good trip?"

"Actually, no. When we got to the destroyer's last known position the skipper flew one of our Walruses off to see if they could spot her."

The Walrus was an old bi-plane, the Fleet Air Arm's mainstay during the early years of the war. Slow and ponderous, what they lacked in speed and mobility the pilots more than made up for in courage and sheer human grit.

"A young lieutenant and his observer took off, spotted the destroyer and guided us in," James continued, his eyes narrowing.

"But when the Walrus landed back on the deck, everything had frozen. She skidded sideways all the way down the flight deck until she crashed into the superstructure. Pilot and observer both died."

"No ice this trip, Number One. We're headed south into warm waters."

"That's what they said on the *Titanic*, Sir," he said before walking up to the bow for our entrance into Devonport Dockyard.

"Number One's in a strange mood, Sir. Reckon he's missing someone," Sub Lieutenant Hawes said as he took his place at the engine controls. "Or something."

I laughed, though I knew the feeling well. I wondered how Annie's meeting with her husband had gone. Maybe there would be a letter waiting when we arrived in Cape Town.

"Have you looked at our course, Alfie?" I asked the sub.

"Naturally, Sir. West south west to Cape Verde where we leave two of the merchant ships. Then almost due south crossing the Equator and into Cape Town. Refuel, up to Suez and arrive Alexandria two weeks after that."

"Very good. You listened to me at our briefing. Five weeks from now we'll be back in the water in our own boats. Provided nothing goes wrong. Provided we're not torpedoed."

"Not a chance of that, Sir. Old *Ganges'* Battle Squadron will get us through. Look at how many of them there are."

I looked across as we passed through the squadron on our way into the Dockyard, dipping our ensign to these more senior ships and captains.

"My word, Sir, I counted ten destroyers, four frigates, seven corvettes and one other carrier. All to escort ten ships," Alfie said, the awe in his voice almost touchable.

"Their Lordships at the Admiralty have really pulled out the stops for us, haven't they Sub?"

"Devonport Dockyard to *HMS Beagle*, come in," an officious sounding voice sounded through the tannoy.

*"Beagle* to Devonport, orders, please," I replied.

*"Proceed to Tamar Basin where the Harbourmaster awaits you."*

The flotilla formed up in line astern as we moved slowly through Plymouth Sound's anchorage into the River Tamar itself. I couldn't see into the Dockyard itself from here but could make out the funnels of eight merchantmen berthed bow to stern around the jetties. The Harbourmaster did a magnificent job of guiding my twenty-four boats to their respective transporter ship and as soon as we were alongside and securely moored we closed *Dotty's* engines down.

The crew climbed up the rope ladder on to the *SS Pacific Liberty*, a former American freighter now on Lend Lease to the British Government. She would be our home for the next five weeks.

Those five weeks would seem like an eternity to men used to constant watch keeping and ship maintenance. Luckily, *Liberty* had plenty of deck space for exercise and lessons - we'd brought plenty of paper and pencils and I planned a rota of lessons, teaching some myself, but using individual crew members to teach others.

I was the last to leave *Dotty* and climb the ladder to the deck along with CPO Shaw who was responsible for shutting down the engines.

"Can't wait to get back on her, Sir," he told me when we stood on *Liberty's* deck. "Always hated someone else looking after the engines."

"I know the feeling, Chief. Have you decided what you'll be teaching the crews?"

"Chess, Sir," he replied and I found my eyebrows rising to the sky.

"It's a wonderful pastime, Skipper. Makes you think about the future. Not the here and now, but longer term."

"Didn't know you played," I said and he frowned slightly.

"Used to play with the Coxswain every night. But just recently he's not been interested. Think he's got problems at home."

I put the thought out of my mind for now and climbed up to the bridge.

"Permission to enter, Sir?" I asked the ship's master who was also the commander of all the convoy's merchant ships, known in the jargon as ComConvoy

"Come on in. I suppose you want to watch while we bring your flotilla aboard. Make sure we don't drop any," he smiled.

I smiled in return as we shook hands. For some reason my feelings of trepidation subsided. They didn't disappear entirely, as I still felt uncomfortable at being a mere passenger. But this merchant sailor had an aura of quiet confidence and ability. His skin had the look of one who'd sailed the world's oceans, brought his ships through storms, hurricanes, mountainous seas. Looked after his crew but applied a keen discipline, too. In the weeks to come I found all this to be true.

But that afternoon we stood on his bridge wing, smoking cigarettes, sharing bottles of beer and watching as he and his fellow masters loaded twenty four MGBs into four ships. Six boats into each hold, three on the upper deck, three on the lower.

When the last MGB was safely secured in the hold we walked below and he pointed to the Owner's cabin.

"It's a kind of tradition in the Merch that there's a cabin put aside for the Owner. Not that many owners ever sail on these ships. They prefer the big liners," he told me as he left me to unpack.

"Dinner at eighteen hundred hours. We sail at twenty hundred on the tide. Come up to the Bridge if you like."

And I did. I stayed up there as the sun went down and I could feel rather than see *Ganges* and her offspring take station all around us. Eight merchantmen surrounded by twenty three of the most heavily armed ships in the Andrew. I hoped that was enough to protect us. But I wouldn't bet on it. We had a long journey ahead of us, too much of it through waters that were far from friendly.

# Chapter 62    Klopp in the North Sea

Captain Braun lowered his sextant and walked to the chart table in the wheelhouse.

"Right, Commander, let's see how close our fixes are," he said as he hung his duffle coat on a hook and bent over the table.

Separately we worked through our calculations and straightened up at the same time.

"You first," he ordered.

"45°24'12.2' N and 15°10'26.5 W, Sir" I replied.

"Excellent, Johann, we know exactly where we are," he replied pointing at his own full page of calculations and plotting the Condor's position on the chart.

"Another twelve hours and we'll be out of range of the RAF's long distance aircraft," I observed

"RADAR Bridge, aircraft, bearing almost due East, range twenty miles."

The Captain's hand pressed down on the Action Stations klaxon, one of the most spine tingling noises known on surface ships. Nobody could ever sleep through the horrendous rattle.

Within minutes the ship was closed up and the Captain spoke to the crew through the PA system.

"Aircraft due east of us. In these waters it is most likely to be British. We are still within range of their long distance bomber bases."

"There he is, Sir," a bridge lookout called, his arm extended and pointing away to our port side.

We all looked and saw the speck in the sky, a speck getting bigger by the second.

"Escort Group closed up for Action," I called out and looked to each side of *Der Condor*.

In line with the Captain's orders we travelled in an arrowhead formation with *Der Condor* in the lead. This gave us the advantage of both undersea and surface surveillance through the ships' radar sets and the human lookouts.

At times like this it also gave us the opportunity to turn to meet the aircraft head on, presenting a smaller target for them to bomb but using the enormous firepower from our fleet of twenty one well-armed fighting ships. "Each ship fire at will," the Captain ordered and I relayed the instruction via the radio. Up to now we'd kept radio silence but the aircraft would have radioed our position back to its base.

I squinted into my binoculars and after a few seconds announced that it was an American Liberator, probably almost at the limit of its range.

Braun ordered our guns to start firing and I felt my ears buzzing as the firepower killed off any other sounds.

"My God, how can anyone survive that?" I asked, watching the airspace around the Liberator fill with huge clumps of black smoke as our ships fired four-inch shells, two-inch shells, rapid-fire Oerlikon anti-aircraft rockets at the incoming aircraft.

The plane roared overhead at less than a thousand feet and dropped an entire stick of bombs across the flotilla.

"Missed, you bastard," Braun ground out before staring at one of our corvettes with acrid black smoke pouring from its funnel. Without warning the ship exploded amidst huge flames and disappeared beneath the waves.

"Either a bomb went straight down the funnel or they caught the ammunition stores," Braun said in a sombre voice, but one without emotion. No cracks in his demeanour even though he had just lost one of his ships and over a hundred men.

"Make to the squadron, do not stop. No survivors," he said as we steamed on. "Let's give the after guns a chance, Commander."

We kept to our course and waited as the Liberator turned in a tight circle and started back in towards the flotilla.

Our ships held their fire until the aircraft was barely five miles away. At three hundred miles per hour the plane would be on top of us within sixty seconds. I saw the open bomb doors at the same time as the Captain gave the order to open fire again. This time the filthy black smoke hid the Liberator from our view.

As the aircraft sped towards us I saw tiny flames licking around the engines on the wings and the nose of the plane dipped violently. Afterwards none of us knew whether it was by design or by accident, but the Liberator kept falling from the sky and stopped when it smashed into the bridge of *Der Prince Friedrich*, one of our beloved destroyers.

I stared, open-mouthed, as the Liberator slipped off the side of the ship and disappeared into the sea.

"Looks like she's still under control," I said and Braun gave the order to turn *Der Condor* and go back to the destroyer.

Fires raged on the deck and the bridge and superstructure had all but disappeared.

The Captain brought *Condor* to a stop and picked up a megaphone.

*"Friedrich*, who is in command?" he asked.

An officer on the foredeck raised his hand and shouted through his own megaphone.

"Huber, Lieutenant, Sir. The Captain and First Lieutenant were on the bridge. All dead."

I heard the catch in his voice.

"Get your men into the lifeboats, Lieutenant, you can't save her," he ordered.

Within half an hour we were back at full speed and heading south once more. Two ships down, almost three hundred men dead. And not a quarter of the way to Trieste.

"This was supposed to be the easy part of the voyage, Johann," Braun said as we stood on the bridge wing watching the scenes below us where the crew hosed down the debris left by the *Friedrich's* crew when they came aboard. Not all had survived. Some died in the lifeboats, some on the deck itself. Of the fifty or so that survived, many would die of their injuries and burns before the night ended. Many of them in uncontrollable agonies.

I hoped it was worth the sacrifice. I said nothing. Although Braun seemed to have changed, I didn't know by how much.

# Chapter 63    Winston Churchill in The War Rooms

"Sir David Petrie to see you, Sir," my secretary said, interrupting a particularly irksome train of thought. The Labour Party had already started to make noises about what our country should look like after the War and their leader, a man for whom I had great respect, gave me an early look at some of their ideas about education and health. They were certainly fascinating and if implemented would be hugely popular with the ordinary citizen. But there was a war to fight and win before that.

I put the papers down and stood to welcome the Head of MI6. We sipped at our coffees, though he declined any additional flavouring in his.

"Prime Minister," he began, straightening his shirt cuffs and checking that each one showed exactly the same amount of material below the end of his jacket sleeve as the other, "Prime Minister, two days ago the first train left Stalingrad for Trieste. Much earlier than we had anticipated."

"Why was I not informed about this? This could wreck all our plans for the North African campaign," I said, a little louder than I should. I know that I should control my volume, but at times there is no other way to express my anger.

"Because Prime Minister, you did not need to know. My agents have kept the train under constant surveillance along its journey. At no small risk to themselves and our entire network of spies and resistance fighters. There are times, Sir, when the need to know is kept within a tight circle. This is one of those times."

Are you implying that I can't keep a secret?" I demanded, thumping my walking stick into the linoleum floor. "Good God above, Man I am the Prime

Minister of the United Kingdom. I must know everything."

He stared back at me with an amused expression on his face.

"But, why, Prime Minister? If I bombarded you with every small detail of my operations I could hardly call myself the Head of the Secret Intelligence Servicer, could I? Especially the Secret and Intelligence bit. And this country relies on you to lead us, Sir. You cannot do that with your head full of trivia. We need you to look up and outward. Not down and inward."

I sat back in my chair and tried, unsuccessfully, to smile.

"You are right, David. But this development is deeply worrying nonetheless."

"Well, it is and it isn't, Prime Minister," he replied, before telling me the obvious: that if the train were to reach Trieste it would be worrying. Whereas if it didn't, there was little to worry about except how soon the next train could leave Russia.

"Are you telling me that the train will not arrive in Trieste?"

"Precisely, Sir. Exactly six hours ago, the train entered a mile long tunnel near the town of Tankow, just inside the Polish border."

I frowned as he explained that this tunnel was formed by tunnelling beneath a series of hills. When the men and women from the Polish Resistance judged the train to be more or less half way between the entrance and the exit points they set off a series of bombs.

"They've been wanting to do this for some time because the tunnel is not overly distant from Krakow."

I breathed in deeply. Krakow, we knew at this stage of the war, was home to one of Hitler's concentration camps and his beastly troops took many innocent citizens there from all over Europe by train. We didn't know exactly what happened there, but many of us suspected the worst.

"The local population is sparse in that area,"" he continued, "so the Nazis' usual threat of reprisals amongst local civilians is little more than sabre rattling."

"And the train?"

"We don't have any details, but five hundred feet of rocks and soil fell on to the tracks. It is highly unlikely that anyone could survive. At any rate it will be many months before the tunnel can be used again."

I walked over to the map and found the town of Tankow.

"And what are the alternatives for transporting troops from Russia?"

Petrie joined me and traced his finger along a thin line from Stalingrad to Warsaw, much further north than Tankow.

"That is the alternative. It adds an extra day to the journey. And if my agents are correct, the Germans cannot move any more troops from the battlefield for at least two weeks. There is a big push on and Hitler needs every man he can get in the fight. That gives the Navy enough time to get into the Med. It will be tight, but it's the best we can do."

After Petrie left I called Pound at the Admiralty.

I have just spoken to MI6," I told him.

"Yes, he telephoned earlier, just before he came to the War Rooms. Provided there are no setbacks our boats will be in position as the German convoy closes on the North African coastline. The problem is that our own convoy is under attack as we speak."

## Chapter 64    Scotty in the North Atlantic

The first clue that we were in U-Boat waters came with the dawn, their favourite time to attack.

We were seven days from Devonport and the voyage up to now had been quiet, verging on the tedious. *Ganges* and her Battle Squadron surrounded our eight merchant ships using their combined experience of the many battles they'd fought in the North and South Atlantic during the last three years.

And not only were they able fighters; the corvettes, deployed at the edges of the convoy, used their Asdic and Radar to pick up any threats from submarines and surface ships. There would be no enemy aircraft this far from land.

The explosion was strangely subdued and we all rushed to the ship's side to see whence it came.

"There, just off the starboard quarter," I said to James who stood beside me.

"Which of the merchantmen would that be?"

I sensed him shaking his head.

"Could be the *City of Cardiff*. She had six of our MGBs on board. Or it could have been *Clan McEwen*. She was one of those stopping at Cape Verde."

Whichever ship it was, she seemed to still be on the move. I felt the vibrations as our own ship heeled over to port and increased speed.

*"Ganges* must have ordered a change of course or a change in zigzag pattern," I said aloud, desperate to go up to the Bridge to find out what was happening. But, that would have been a mistake. Our own captain had enough on his plate right now without one of his passengers getting in the way.

We watched as dawn turned to early morning and the sun gradually climbed above the horizon. Through our binoculars we saw one of the corvettes approach the torpedoed vessel. It was the *Clan McEwen* and I cursed myself for feeling relief that it wasn't a ship carrying our MGBs.

James looked at me and I smiled.

"I was just thanking God that it wasn't one of our ships over there," I said.

He nodded.

"I had the same thought. I bet everyone in the flotilla did."

Our captain arrived at that moment and lit a cigarette.

"Thought you might want to know what's going on," he said, inhaling the smoke deeply.

"Bloody U-Boat got inside the screen in the early hours, waited for dawn before surfacing and firing a salvo of torpedoes. One and only one hit. It's done some damage, but we're barely six hours steaming from Cape Verde so *Ganges* has sent the corvette and a destroyer to escort the *Clan line* boat and the *City of Exeter* in. *Exeter* was the other ship carrying cargo for the islands."

"Cape Verde's part of Portugal isn't it?" James asked and the captain nodded.

"Supposed to be neutral, but they've always had a soft spot for us. They're sending a couple of their big tugs out to meet them."

"And the rest of us carry on?" I asked and he nodded again.

"Ten days to Cape Town, Harry. A quick bunker, fill the tanks with oil and water. Then up to Suez."

He turned as the ship's Senior Radio Officer joined us.

"For you, Commander, just arrived. In code, so I've no idea what it is," he said, passing me an envelope.

I looked inside and groaned.

"Fetch Morrison, James. This'll take some deciphering."

In fact, Morrison decoded the message in less than twenty minutes and handed it back to me. It made for some grim reading, yet was also not to be unexpected.

*"To Commander, 18th MGB Flotilla,"* it read, "*Top Secret. Your targets are expected to depart Trieste in nineteen days time. The convoy will consist of seven merchant ships and twenty one escort vessels. The escorts are currently in the North Atlantic and we anticipate them entering the Mediterranean Sea past Gibraltar in the next three days. Your orders remain unchanged and you will commence preparations for your attack immediately after refuelling at Alexandria. The first train carrying enemy troops left Russia five days ago and was destroyed when a tunnel collapsed on it near the Polish border.*
*Copied to Admiral 5th Battle Squadron, HMS Ganges. Message Ends.*"

I read it again and interpreted the message for what it really said. This was going to be tight. The Mediterranean Fleet had their work cut out escorting our own ships from Gibraltar to Malta and all points in between. They would not be able to harass the German Escort Group on its way to Trieste.

The deck below my feet vibrated again. We were speeding up again. Once we refuelled at Alex we would go straight out to sea to meet the convoy on its Southern run. No time for practice shoots, no time for mistakes. I showed the message to James.

"How easy will it be to refuel the boats where they are?" I asked.

"No idea, Sir. CPO Shaw's the man to ask."

"Go ask him, James. Tell him to let me know what we'll need to refuel the whole flotilla between Cape Town and Suez."

As he opened the door I called him back.

"And tell Morrison to come by in about an hour. I want to send a message to all our skippers and he can code it up."

Our original plan gave us twelve hours in Alexandria to refuel and top up the water tanks. I suspected that those twelve hours would be better spent getting into position to greet the German convoy. I uncapped my pen and started writing a list of what had to be done. It wasn't a long list. Food, water and fuel were clearly critical items.

But, target practice would be important, which meant that we would also have to replenish whatever ammunition we used. Morrison was in for a busy few hours with his code books.

# Chapter 65    Annie at Newlyn Police Station

Carol and I arrived at the front desk just after tea and watched as the sergeant wrote something in a huge journal. He didn't even look up, which I found irritating. At last I could take it no longer.

"Sergeant, we have been standing here for three minutes and you have ignored us. You haven't even looked up to acknowledge our presence and you haven't had the grace to apologise for being so ignorant."

I heard Carol inhale deeply beside me, but our men were off fighting a war and this officer was doing his best to be rude. And succeeding.

Some of us have important work to do, Miss. I'm about to go off duty and am finishing my report for my relief."

As he said this a door behind him opened and another, younger, sergeant walked through.

"How can I help you, Miss?" he asked immediately.

We wish to see Sammy Smith. He is in your cells."

"Are you family?" he asked.

"No, we are friends in a way. But I represent Captain Dennis, Port Commander."

"Do you have identification? You would be surprised at what people say to get into the cells. We have to be careful."

The older sergeant finished writing his report and stared at me through hooded and narrow eyes.

"We don't allow visits in the evenings. We don't have enough men on duty to stay with you in case Smith attacks you," he ground out through clearly clenched teeth.

The younger man laughed and smacked his older colleague on the shoulder.

"You're a card sometimes, Bert. Sammy's not going about assaulting women. Good God, if you blew hard he'd keel over. Get on your way."

He turned and opened the door behind him.

"Penrose, show these two ladies down to the cells. They're visiting Sammy. And offer them a cup of tea while you're at it."

The older sergeant snorted and stalked out of the station.

"Sorry, Miss. Old Bert should have retired last year but we're short-handed. All the young lads have been enlisted. Army mostly, they're always on the lookout for Redcaps."

Carol looked bemused at the expression and I explained that Military Policemen were referred to by the colour of their caps.

PC Penrose showed us through to the cells and unlocked Sammy's door.

"Milk and sugar, Ladies?" he asked before leaving us to ask Sammy some more questions.

I started with the pleasantries. Sammy certainly looked brighter than he had the last time we were here. And his cough was nowhere near as bad.

They let me out three times a day to walk around the exercise yard," he explained. "And the doctor gave me some medicine. It seems to be working. Did you find Eileen?"

"Yes, but she wasn't that helpful," I replied. "She couldn't tell us anything about the man that Madge was with. Though she did confirm that it was impossible to earn the sort of money that Madge had when she died."

He nodded and his head sank to his chest. I thought he was going to cry but instead he whispered something.

"What did you say?" I asked him.

"There's been something bothering me, Miss. Ever since we spoke a few days ago."

PC Penrose brought the tea back in and placed the tray on a small table.

"I'll be just outside. Shout when you're ready to leave," he said, picking up the fourth mug and closing the door behind him.

"Madge didn't know the name of the man who gave her the money. Just that she met him in Plymouth. That's what I remembered after you left. All he told her was that she was to call him Will."

"Will, short for William?" I said, rather foolishly as there was no other name it could stand for. I was thinking hard, though.

"Can you think of anything else she said?"

He held his head in his hands and I suggested he take a sip of tea. He did so and sat upright.

"She thought he spoke with a Welsh accent. And she said he was big."

It was clear that this was the limit of what he knew and a few minutes later we left.

"Does that take us any further forward, Annie?" Carol asked as we walked back to the harbour.

"I don't think that we have any sailors with the first name William, but I can't remember all their names. I'll go through the files tomorrow. I do remember Harry saying that he joined his first ship in Plymouth. And that CPO Williams was just a junior petty officer on board at the time. He's rather proud of the fact that they've served together ever since."

"I've never spoken to him," Carol said. "Where's he from?"

I looked back at her and felt my lips form into a grimace.

"Wales. He went back to Cardiff to see his wife after their friend died a few weeks ago on Lieutenant Roberts' MGB."

"The wife that disappeared, you mean?"

I nodded.

"I think that I may have to phone the police officers who came down here to see him. Check if anything has developed in their case."

Which I did the following morning.

"Funnily enough, one of our local trawlers was doing some bottom trawling close in-shore," the constable told me. "At this time of year the herrings run close to land because there's lots of food for them in the shallow waters. Unfortunately their nets snagged on something on the sea bottom and when they finally freed them and hauled them in there was a load of old anchor chain."

"Is that so unusual close to a harbour. I've heard Newlyn fishermen saying that they've lost anchor chains in heavy seas and gales," I replied.

"Same up here, Miss Lenton. But it's unusual for the chain to be wrapped around two bodies. Two human bodies, that is. They're in the Morgue as we speak. Doctors haven't identified them yet. The sea isn't kind to bodies, Miss. Nor are the fish."

I shuddered as I asked him to let me know if they managed to identify the two bodies.

# Chapter 66    Braun approaching Gibraltar

"Signal all ships," I told Klopp, "*All captains to check that no lights are showing on their ship nor on any ships around them. Maintain strict radio silence until otherwise ordered. Form line astern and go to Action Stations in one hour.*"

I watched as the signal flags fluttered high above the decks and listened as my Petty Officer reported each ship's response.

"All acknowledged, Sir. Permission to leave the Bridge and check *Der Condor*?"

I nodded at Klopp and saw his colourless face stare back at me. I wondered if his stomach was churning like mine. Nineteen ships left in my flotilla and I needed them all to stand any sort of chance of escorting Rommel's reinforcements safely from Trieste to North Africa.

I knew now how the Admirals of old must have felt going into battle. Men like Nelson, English though he was, and before him Drake, my own Donitz. Did they feel like this?

I was relying on speed and surprise to get past the British fortress of Gibraltar. Right now our heading was due South but as we approached the Straits of Gibraltar we would make a sudden turn to pass between the infamous Rock to port and Tangier to starboard.

The Straits were barely twenty miles across at that point. We would be visible to observers on both sides. I hoped that the time of day would favour us. Well, time of night as we would pass into the Med at just after midnight, so land-based observers would know only that a small fleet of ships was going by. And our speed should help: maximum speed would be sixteen knots. Frustrating because *Der Condor* was capable of closer to thirty. But I wanted to keep us together, to protect some of the slower and smaller ships like the corvettes. I needed them for convoy duty.

"All closed up, Sir, no lights showing on *Condor* and none out there either," Klopp pointed to port and starboard. I knew my ships were there, but could see nothing.

"The weather's helping us tonight. Maybe the Gods want us to get through unscathed," he continued.

"The hell with the Gods, Johann. Germany needs us to get through unscathed."

I looked at my watch. Thirty minutes to the turn. Why does time go so slowly when you want it to fly?

"This is the second time I've been in the Mediterranean," I told Klopp. "When war broke out I was a junior officer on a U-Boat down here. Worst posting I ever had. Took us four weeks to get back to Germany. But we sank three ships on the way."

"I didn't know you were in submarines, Sir. I've always believed that to be the toughest of assignments. No room for error, and quite a horrible death."

He turned and his hand rose to his mouth.

"What was that?" I asked.

"A sweet, Sir. I find chewing helps me relax."

He was rubbing his upper leg and I heard an indrawn breath.

"Is it your leg, Johann? You really should go ashore and let someone look at it."

"It hurts sometimes more than others. Its been worse, Sir."

"Do you take anything for it? Any pain killers?"

"Yes. The doctors prescribed them and I get a new batch when I'm in port. They help, but they do not remove the pain entirely. I'll go and check our course and prepare for the turn if I may, Sir," he said, clearly wanting to change the conversation.

Once or twice recently I sensed that Klopp was not himself. A little too casual, a bit too relaxed when times were tense. I wondered if his pain tablets affected him more than he let on.

"Almost time, Sir," he called from the chart table and I gave the orders.

"Port fifteen, steer course 090, due East. Make revolutions for sixteen knots."

I watched the Radar screen as nineteen ships slipped smoothly into three lines astern. Each steering the same course as *Condor* but at fifty yards distance from another. As Klopp said in relation to submarines, absolutely no room for error. If one ship slowed down there was no time for the one behind to avoid her. Twenty minutes later we were through. No explosions, no excitement, plenty of tension and probably a lot of anxiety. But we were all through. The Radar screen showed the group spreading out into our usual arrowhead formation once more.

*"Radar, Bridge, contact five miles ahead. On the surface, low profile, could be a submarine."*

Klopp joined me at the repeater screen.

"Bridge, Asdic, any contacts dead ahead," he asked.

"Bridge, Asdic, nothing on screen."

"Could be one of ours," Klopp said as we both stared hard.

"Unlikely, Johann. We have no reported positions of submarines this close to Gibraltar. All ours are closer in towards Malta. Gibraltar Radar must have spotted us so they know there's a large force of ships, probably German ships, heading East. We'll send two destroyers to attack the submarine."

I turned to our radio operator.

"Signal *Meteor* and *Comet*. *Radar contact five miles ahead. Probable British submarine. Attack and destroy.*"

I heard the acknowledgements and ordered the men to remain at Action Stations. We would soon know if the attack was successful. If the destroyers could make the most of their superior speed they would witness the fastest crash dive of an English submarine in history. Ten minutes to arrive at the position. Which meant that we should see their guns firing in less than five.

I felt the old tension mount again. Much better to be attacking, not waiting. But I wouldn't make that mistake again. My responsibility lay here with the Group.

"Gunfire dead ahead, Sir," a lookout reported and I followed his arm, pointing out across the foredeck and over our own mighty guns.

*"Asdic, Bridge, contact eight miles due East. Diving."*

"Report depth and course every twenty seconds," I ordered.

"Radio Operator, relay the information to *Meteor* and *Comet.*"

"Their Asdic won't be as effective as ours because of their speed and their depth charges. Both will disrupt the readings," Klopp said.

"Bridge, Asdic, underwater explosions, Sir. Same bearing."

The Asdic operator continued to call out the depths and course alterations as the submarine fought for her life. We must destroy her, I thought. She stands directly in our way.

## Chapter 67    Scotty En route from Cape Town to the Suez Canal

We stopped in Cape Town to refuel and fill our water tanks and food stores for the next stage of our journey North to the Suez Canal. As our convoy turned into Table Bay and steamed in towards the colossal Table Mountain I couldn't help but shake my head.

"There are some harbours that never fail to impress and excite," I said to James, "and this is one of them."

"Been here often?" he asked and I nodded.

"Before the war I was Third Mate on an old tramp steamer. Six thousand tons, built before the first war, an old rust bucket. We carried general cargo around the east and west coasts of Africa. I was out here for almost a year and this was always the most magnificent sight of all the harbours."

Amazingly, it hadn't changed. It was like being back in 1938, no worries, just long, hard days, loading and unloading cargoes of crops straight out of the fields, fruit off the trees, timber, stone, everything and anything.

We stood at the rail as our convoy steamed across the bay and followed miniscule pilot boats to pre-booked berths along the waterfront. I could almost sense the spies peering through their binoculars at us. What were these ships carrying? Why so many warships and so few merchant ships?

Knowing that Cape Town was a hotbed of German agents, our escort Leader, Admiral Turner on board *HMS Ganges*, ordered half his escort group to leave us and steam on to Port Elizabeth to bunker before we were in sight of the shore line.

Even so, questions would be asked and radio lines would be humming with coded messages flying across the ether to Berlin.

For our part, we told all our crew to stay in their cabins and not venture on deck. It was only for twelve hours, so not a hardship. James and I were in civvies; shorts and vests, looking like off duty crewmen. Rank hath its privileges, they say and we wanted to watch as *Pacific Liberty* edged ever nearer the jetty.

"The captain's good at this," James said as we saw the Captain leaning over the bridge wing giving orders to the tug gently pushing us into position.

"He is all of that, James," I replied, in a tone that was at once envious and respectful.

Twenty four hours later the Captain reversed the manoeuvre and led his ships back out to sea to meet our reduced escort group. And four hours after that the other escorts steamed over the horizon. We were back in the midst of our Royal Navy guardians for the last part of our epic voyage.

During that night our two Royal Navy stragglers joined us from their detour to Cape Verde. We were back to full strength. We now faced two weeks at sea, heading north along the eastern coast of the great African continent, always out of sight of land.

Germany had fewer vessels out here, but the convoy steamed as if we were in the mid-Atlantic surrounded by U Boats. Strict zigzagging by day and by night. Lookouts constantly on the Bridge, Radar sets permanently manned.

We used the time to get our MGBs ready for battle. In Cape Town we'd loaded hundreds of barrels of fuel and the Coxswain seemed to regain much of his old humour and warmth as he and the other Coxswains supervised crews as they refuelled the six MGBs on *Pacific Liberty*.

With less than two days to go before we arrived at Port Tewfik at the southern end of Suez *HMS Ganges* changed course and steamed back towards us. She performed a racing turn and settled on a course parallel to ours, barely fifty yards off our starboard side.

*"Good morning Pacific Liberty. Would you ask the Convoy Commander to have a word with Admiral Turner?"*

As it happened, ComConvoy and I were finishing breakfast in the officers' saloon and heard the PA so both climbed the companionway to the bridge wing. "ComConvoy here, Admiral. Do we have a problem?" he said into the PA microphone.

*"We do, Sir. We've had word of an enemy battle fleet ahead. Right across our course. No chance of avoiding them, I'm afraid. Wanted to warn you so you can alert the convoy. Don't want to use the radio - they may not know we're in the area. But they'd soon pick up a radio message in these waters."*

He explained that he was despatching two destroyers and two corvettes to act as decoys and lure the Germans away while we altered course in the opposite direction to try to slip by. I knew that there was no other option open to the Admiral but an idea began to form that there was an alternative.

"Captain, may I have a word with the Admiral?" I asked and he passed me the microphone.

*"Good morning, Sir. This is Commander Scott, leader of the flotilla. I wonder if I might make a suggestion, Sir."*

I didn't know the Admiral personally but his reputation was that of a man who liked a direct approach.

"Go ahead, Commander. I served with your Captain in the last war and assume that he wouldn't have you in his fleet if you were hare-brained," he boomed back.

"What if we used three of our MGBs to attack the Germans while your destroyers were acting as bait? We did it off the Irish coast a few weeks ago and destroyed a German convoy in the process."

I explained our role in destroying the German ships carrying the latest in explosives back to Germany in more detail. At the end he said, simply, "Commander, I've been ordered to get you safely and in one piece to

Suez. Their Lordships would separate my head from various other of my body parts if I took such a risk."

"Only if you told them, Sir. As you said, we're under complete radio silence. We could launch when we're still outside the enemy's Radar range, say a hundred miles from them. Sea's calm, it'll be pitch dark, they won't be expecting an attack. Your destroyers could already be on their Radar and the Germans'll be focused on them."

I went on a little more about tactics and returning to the convoy before I stopped. There was a silence for a few seconds before the Admiral replied.

*"Commander Scott, you have your wish. Be ready to launch by 0200 hours tomorrow morning. Rendezvous with us after your attack. Pilot will give you the estimated position. We'll radio you an exact location at 0500 and 0515 hours. Short transmission only. In code."*

"Things have changed since my day in the Navy," ComConvoy said as we resumed breakfast.

"In those days you never volunteered."

I smiled and shook my head.

"No, it's just the same. But, it's the greatest good for the greatest number. Once we get past that fleet they won't stand a chance of catching us. We're too close into shore and not that far from Suez. And my boats are low enough in the water to get to within a few hundred yards of the fleet before they know we're there."

I hoped that I was right and wasn't risking my crews unnecessarily. But I had no time to dwell on those thoughts as we worked through the evening and night to get *Dotty, Boxer and Terrier* ready. Just after midnight ComConvoy slowed *Pacific Liberty* to Dead Slow and we launched my three MGBs.

Before I climbed down the ladder to Dotty, now bobbing up and down in the water below my feet, he took me to one side.

"Godspeed, Harry. I'll be waiting for you. No heroics, get in, fire your torpedoes and get out."
He turned and climbed back up to the bridge.

# Chapter 68    Klopp in Trieste

I stood next to the Captain as we led Gruppen 158 through the boom guarding the entrance to the old port of Trieste. Our bridge lookout waved across to the tug operating the boom and Captain Braun ordered him to the other wing.

"You are on look-out, not on holiday, Kohler. Keep your eyes peeled. The British have been known to send mini submarines into a harbour when the boom's open."

"Have you been here before, Sir?" I asked, feeling a little sorry for Kohler. He was wrong, but he was barely seventeen years old and this was his first trip. I made a mental note to talk to him later and remind him that the Captain liked everything just so.

"Once, before the war. Most of my service has been in the Atlantic and Arctic Oceans. Never had the chance to feel warm and see the sun for much more than a few weeks."

"Signalman, make to all ships, *Captains to meet on board Condor at 1700 hours*."

"Commander Klopp, please take *Condor* alongside."

"Very good, Sir."

I felt a thrill at the prospect of berthing the ship. At almost 12,000 tons fully loaded with fuel and ammunition she was classed as a heavy cruiser. For all her weight I knew her to be highly manoeuvrable, which was important for a vessel over six hundred feet long - twice the length of the American's Statue of Liberty.

But her four great propellers gave me the benefit of turning her in towards our berth with remarkable ease. I felt Braun's eyes on me the whole time, but refused to look at him. This was one of the reasons I loved the sea: to be given the opportunity to navigate my way through a crowded anchorage to a waiting berth.

"Ring Finshed With Engines, Kohler," I told the young seaman as the deck crews secured the moorings.

"Well done, Commander Klopp. Very smooth. I doubt if I could have done better," Braun told me before he left the Bridge. "No shore leave. We have much to do to prepare for our journey south in two days. Pass the word to the rest of the Group."

The First Lieutenant arrived on the Bridge from his station at the bow.

"Did I hear right, Johann?" he said. "No shore leave and we're in one of the most beautiful cities in the world. Ah well, at least that means no drunks coming back on board tonight."

I laughed out loud.

"Join me for a schnapps after I've finished here. It'll help dinner go down," I replied before sending for the Coxswain. He was not as understanding as the First Lieutenant but would make sure no sailors tried to climb down the mooring lines to get ashore.

After dinner I stood on deck breathing in the night air. Trieste was a central port for much of Asia and Eastern Europe and welcomed ships from many nations carrying many different types of cargo.

Tonight, with the breeze off the land I smelt spices, Turkish tobaccos and local fish being cooked. But even that combination couldn't completely mask the smell of diesel, raw sewage and dirty harbour saltwater.

I lit a cigarette and felt someone next to me. I turned and was surprised to see Captain Braun.

"Good evening, Sir, I thought you had gone to bed."

"I had, Johann, but sleep is impossible in this heat. Even with the porthole wide open and the ceiling fan at full blast it's still hot."

I offered him a cigarette and he lit it with his own lighter.

We stood quietly and I was about to suggest he could take a sleeping tablet when he said something that made me shiver.

"You chew a lot, Johann. Why is that?"

"It helps me relax, Sir. It's nothing, just some sweets that I buy when I'm ashore. They mask the flavour of the painkillers."

"May I have one?"

I swallowed heavily and was glad of the darkness.

"I will be pleased to give you some, Sir. But I don't have any on me just now."

Without warning a huge explosion rent the air and we both looked towards the source.

"There, over there to starboard. Jesus, look at those flames," Braun said. "Quick, Johann, to the bridge. All Hands to Action Stations."

I watched the flames licking up the side of the stricken vessel.

"Looks like a tanker," the lookout said when he arrived. "Noticed her when we came in. According to one of the dockers who moored us she's bound for Greece. Won't be going far now."

Within minutes the flames were as high as the funnel and three more explosions split the evening air. The smells of spices, cooking food even diesel were now smothered. All I could smell was burning oil.

Two tugs appeared and threw ropes up to the burning vessel to pull her away from the pier.

"Asdic Bridge. Contact four hundred yards due east, depth one hundred feet, moving towards the harbour entrance."

"Commander, take the ship's motorboat and crew with a load of hand grenades. I will radio you directions from here."

I ran down the companionway to the boat deck calling the Coxswain and boat's crew as I went. We scrambled into the boat and the duty crewmen lowered us quickly to the sea below. Two sailors released the falls and we sped towards the harbour entrance.

"Jesus, that's a ship coming in," the Coxswain swore. "If we're not quick that sub'll slip out while the boom's open."

# Chapter 69    Scotty aboard *Dotty* in the Red Sea

We steamed at full speed away from *Pacific Liberty* towards a fleet of German naval ships. We had no idea how many there were, nor how good their lookouts would be. Neither of these things mattered. We had to make the most of our speed and pray that the enemy would not see us until the last possible minute: an advantage of being low in the water.

Two hours separated us from the German ships, two hours during which every man aboard would deal with his own thoughts. The sooner we were in action the better for us all.

"Cocoa, Sir. Think we could all use it," the Coxswain said, handing me a huge mug that looked more like a bucket than a cup.

"Thanks, Coxswain. Pipe Up Spirits. Half measures only in the Cocoa. Help to take the men's minds off what's coming."

After he'd handed out the Cocoa with a half tot of rum he came back into the wheelhouse.

"Heard anymore about your wife?" I asked and he shook his head.

"No mail at Cape Town, Sir. Not that I was surprised. She never wrote much anyway. But a letter would have been nice."

"Nothing from the Police I take it?"

"No, Sir, nothing from them either. I hope she's happy wherever she is. How's the Kye?"

I laughed and sipped at the hot drink. This was not civvy-street cocoa. Williams made his, like all good sailors, from tinned milk and slabs of chocolate. Occasionally, on freezing cold nights and at tense times like tonight, he added a small dash of rum to help settle the nerves.

"Perfect, Coxswain, perfect."

We steamed on into the blackness, the nearest land over seventy miles away on either beam. Egypt to port,

Saudi Arabia to starboard. And ahead of us, two days away was the start of the Suez Canal.

"Sound Action Stations, Number One. Time to go back to war."

The bells rang throughout the boat and men quickly arrived at their station.

"Fore gun closed up," Sub Lieutenant Hawes reported from forward.

"After guns closed up."

And so on. Depth Charges, Torpedoes, Engine Room. The last to report, as tradition dictated, was the person standing next to me.

"Coxswain at the helm, Sir. Course $340^0$, revs for 45 knots."

On either side of me *Boxer* and *Terrier* would be replicating our actions. We'd agreed our plans before leaving *Liberty*.

I looked at my watch. Almost 0500 hours.

A set of co-ordinates blasted across the wheelhouse and I looked at the Coxswain.

"Dead on time. The Admiral's a stickler for punctuality, Sir."

Morrison wrote them on his signal pad and followed me to the chart table.

I plotted the position on the chart.

"More or less where we thought, Sir."

"A couple of degrees out, Morrison. Coxswain, alter course to $342^0$. Maintain speed."

A few minutes later the position of the German fleet was confirmed.

"Radar Bridge, contacts Dead Ahead, bearing $342^0$. Six, no seven ships in formation. Steering towards us on $145^0$." A pause before, "Estimated speed sixteen knots, at our present speed we will be up with them in eleven minutes."

There it was. We were within their Radar range now. We'd know soon enough when they saw us through the medium of six, seven and eight inch shells raining down on us. We ploughed on, our bow waves the only indication we were even here.

I said one word into the radio and we slowed to half speed.

"Radar Bridge, *Boxer* and *Terrier* have slowed. Enemy now dead ahead, range one mile, one minute to target."

"Stand by fore gun," I told Sub Lieutenant Hawes.

"Number One Stand by depth charges."

We roared on into the semi-darkness and I saw the silhouettes of the enemy ships for the first time.

"Fire at will, Sub," I shouted through the open windscreen, feeling the warmth of the early morning Mediterranean air on my face.

The roar of the five inch gun was nothing compared to the firepower of a battleship. But we'd loaded with high explosive and we saw hits on the German vessels ahead of us with a few small fires breaking out.

"Half Ahead, hard astarboard," I told the Coxswain.

"Fire all racks, Number One," and I sensed the depth charges flying through the air towards the nearest ship; from what I could make out, a destroyer.

We weaved through the ships ahead of us and turned for our second and final run. There seemed to be gunfire all round us, but light shells only. We were too close for the Germans to lower their muzzles.

I told the Coxswain to head towards the sole aircraft carrier and as we raced towards her, Sub Lieutenant Hawes fired round after round.

"Stand by Number One."

We were almost up with the carrier when I gave the order for full astern and hard a port. *Dotty* swung round immediately.

"Fire both racks. Full Ahead, steer 090$^0$."

And we were through and heading away on a course opposite to one that would take us back to *Liberty*.

Hopefully, the Germans would follow us and I hoped even more that our destroyers were waiting.

A series of banshee like screams sounded overhead as our destroyers opened fire on the German fleet. Shell after shell passed over us.

"They must be hove to broadside on to the Germans. That's the only way they can use all their guns," one of the lookouts said.

And so it was. We were up with them in no time and I flashed my signal lamp to let them know who we were. By now the sun was rising above the horizon almost directly ahead of us and as we passed the waiting destroyers they sounded their sirens.

"Stand down from Action Stations. Normal watches," I ordered.

"Looks like a nice day, Sir," James said as he came back into the wheelhouse. "My watch, I believe."

"Did you see what damage we did?" I asked.

He shook his head.

"Ah well, looks like the convoy's had time to slip through. Morrison, make to *Boxer* and *Terrier*, *Time to go home, course 295 ° full speed ahead*."

# Chapter 70    Annie in Newlyn

"We're sure as we can be that the bodies are those of Agnes Williams and Leonard Dixon," the officer said. His voice was musical as so many Welsh voices were but the words were anything but.

"How can you be sure?" I asked.

"Unfortunately we can't be one hundred percent certain because they've been in the sea for so long. There are no fingerprints, see, and not much left of the faces either. Horrible sight they were, lying on that cold metal table in the morgue. Even the doctor almost lost his breakfast."

I shuddered at the thought of what they'd seen.

"So how can you be sure?" I said again.

"The man had nothing on, no clothes at all. But he did have the remains of a tattoo on his chest. It was a large tattoo. We asked his ex-wife and she described it almost perfectly."

I found myself visualising them tied up in chains beneath the sea and wondered aloud if they were alive when they went in.

"No, they weren't. Well, we don't think so. The thing is whoever did this horrible thing was good with a knife. In some cases there were chips out of bones like the murderer used it like an axe."

"Used what like an axe?"

"The knife. Doc reckons whoever did this was a strong man. Fit, too, to kill two people like this."

Oh God, how much worse could this get?

"Do you have any suspects?"

"Well, the barman said that the only people in the pub that night were locals. Apart from one stranger. Bit scruffy, he said, dark coat like a navy greatcoat he reckoned. Over six feet tall as well."

"That could match thousands of people."

"Yes, it could. But he also stared at the woman when he first came in as though he recognised her."

"What about the woman. What makes you think it's Agnes?"

"She was also naked. No marks or tattoos," he sniggered. I stayed quiet.

He coughed and resumed the conversation.

"Agnes broke her leg last year according to her doctor. Emergency it was, fell down the stairs. He said she was drunk. Doc pointed out a break in her shin - he said the bone came all the way through the flesh and couldn't be repaired properly."

And there you have it. Agnes and this man dead.

"There's something else," the officer said.

He explained that they'd spoken to Agnes' neighbours along the street, hoping that someone could add something to the sad tale.

"You always get some busybodies poking their nose in. And good job, too, or we'd never solve any crimes," he said.

And they did strike gold. One of them wrote to Williams saying that his wife was having an affair. He'd written twice and Williams had travelled home after the first letter, around two or three months earlier. I thought back to that time. It was about the time we all came down to Newlyn. I was aware that the officer was still talking.

"I'm sorry, could you say that again?"

"I said that this neighbour wrote a second time the week before Agnes disappeared. It is possible that Williams may be involved in the deaths of these two people."

He said that a local magistrate had just issued a warrant for Williams' arrest.

"That's really why I telephoned this morning. Can the Navy hold on to him down there until the local police come for him? I'm catching the midday train out of Swansea."

I explained that Williams was on active service away from England and we weren't sure when he would return.

"But I'll see what I can do and phone you back when I've spoken with my senior officer."

I explained the whole story to Captain Dennis and returned to my desk.

A little later he called me in.

"Do any of your Wrens know anything about this?"

"No, Sir. They may have overheard the conversation, but I don't think they know who I was talking about."

"Write it all down, Anne, then code it up. Send it to Harry on the *Liberty*. We'll let him decide whether to alert the authorities in Alexandria."

I felt a sense of relief at that because Harry could decide when to tell Williams. Somehow, the eve of going into battle didn't seem like the right time to change Coxswains.

I started writing the signal up but put it to one side as other, more pressing tasks crossed my desk. Finally, I left the office, met Carol Crebo and visited the Fishermans Arms.

Pat, the landlady was in her usual place, sitting on a stool at the end of the bar.

"Evening, ladies, what brings the Navy into the Fish this evening?" she asked in that delightfully soft Newlyn accent of hers.

"We were looking for Eileen. Has she been in?"

"No, but it's a bit early for her. Usually drops in a bit later."

"Oh, well in that case we'll have two gins, please and wait for her."

We sat at the window overlooking the harbour.

"Do you think Williams really did kill his wife and that man?" Carol asked.

"I don't know. The police are very keen to talk to him. I rang them back later and gave them the gist of what

I'd done and they said that they suspected the fire in the pub was arson."

They'd gone further, I told Carol, and said whoever killed the two people tried to hide their tracks. They also said that they found fingerprints on the anchor chain but couldn't identify them so sent them off to Scotland Yard as they had more sophisticated equipment.

Eileen turned up a little later and didn't look at all happy when she saw us. I didn't blame her as she had a man with her and probably couldn't afford to lose a night's earnings. So we finished our drink and as we left I asked her for a quiet and quick word outside. When I'd finished telling her what we knew she looked thoughtful before replying.

"If he killed them what's to stop him killing Madge?"

The next morning I stopped at Newlyn police station on the way to work and asked if they had taken finger prints in Madge's bedroom. They had not. The older sergeant was back on duty, which meant that my suggestion would not be well received. But I gave it to him anyway.

"I've checked with her landlady and the room hasn't been touched since she left," I told him. "It might be an idea to get your people along there and look for finger prints."

He heaved a sigh and scribbled something on a scrap of paper. Somehow, I didn't think he would do anything else about it.

When I arrived at the office I told Captain Dennis what I suspected and he phoned the police immediately. When he was angry, which was thankfully a rare occasion, his voice was very soft. But the feeling he injected into it when he told the sergeant that he would be talking to the Chief Constable had the desired result.

The next day, the sergeant told me that they'd found Sammy's prints, which was to be expected. They'd also found some other prints, but had no records of them. I wondered if they could be Williams' but there was no way of telling. And, he told Harry that he'd only been inside Madge's room once, several months earlier. Did fingerprints last that long I wondered. I added this latest twist into the coded message and sent it to the Admiralty for onward transmission to *Pacific Liberty*.

# Chapter 71    Klopp in Trieste

Seaman Ryker steered the motorboat away from
*Condor* towards the last known position of the enemy
submarine.

"How big are these submarines, Sir?" he asked as we
navigated through the ships at anchor towards the
harbour entrance.

"Mini-subs aren't huge, maybe twenty feet long. And
not fast, either according to our Identification Manual
of enemy warships. Barely three knots at most. But,
they're difficult to spot."

The radio blared at that point.

"Alter course, Ryker, steer straight for the entrance and
slow ahead. We are getting close to her."

The Coxswain and three of his men were at the
motorboat's sides, each with a supply of hand
grenades.

"Fuses set for six seconds," he said, anticipating my
question.

The radio blared again.

"Fire," I said simply and each man pulled the pins
from two grenades and dropped them into the sea.

"Full Ahead, Ryker," and we sped off out of the
immediate area.

The sea boiled a little as the grenades exploded and we
watched, drifting ever nearer the entrance. Another
message from *Condor* and we manoeuvred gently back
into position, preparing another eight grenades.

"Stand by, men," I said and waited for the message.
"Fire."

We raced out of the area again and turned sharply. A
cigar-shaped craft rose from the sea bow first, bearing
two men in frogman's rubber suits with oxygen tanks
on their back. It was the first time I'd seen one of these
vessels and it was ugly. All black, and with part of the
bow missing.

One of the men sat astride the vessel as though he was riding a fat, legless horse. The other hung down the side, almost in the water.

"Quick, back alongside, let's try to capture it" I told Ryker and we hurtled back in towards the submarine. As though he knew what we intended the enemy sailor sitting astride the ugly craft pulled at a lever and the thing exploded, the force lifting our boat literally out of the water. When we landed, and that was not a pleasant affair, the jolt ran up through my body, with much of the pain centred around my leg. Or where my leg used to be.

Ryker regained control and I told him to head for *Condor* as fast as he could. Water was coming in through a number of seams and the Coxswain and his men were busily bailing it out. But it was gaining on us all the time.

We made it back to the *Condor* and managed to hook on to the falls. Another minute and we would have sunk.

"Well done, Commander. Shame you couldn't capture the submarine. It would make a fine trophy," Braun said when I reported to the bridge.

"Yes, they had some sort of self-destruct lever on the side. I saw one of the sailors pull it immediately before the explosion."

"You'd better write it all up in a report. Headquarters will be interested. We don't have much information about these things. They're still new."

He paused while he lit a cigarette.

"The Gestapo are in the wardroom. A few loose ends about Zirk, they said. They want to see you. They've already seen me. I said that I could tell them nothing more than I had already. They were angry, I would say. They don't believe our story. They also want to see Ryker."

"Why Ryker?" I asked. God knows I could lie for the Fatherland, but I wasn't sure about Ryker, a view I shared with the Captain.

"Was he hurt in the explosion? Concussed, knocked out perhaps?" he said and I smiled when he told his steward to escort the ship's doctor and Ryker to his cabin.

The doctor arrived first and the Captain told him what he wanted. At first the doctor refused, saying it went against every part of the oath he swore when he qualified. The Captain pointed out that they were short of doctors on the Russian front and he couldn't really say that a doctor was absolutely necessary on a cruiser like *Condor*.

At which point the doctor said that in cases where a man suffered an extreme explosion, sometimes a long sleep prevented any future problems. Ryker listened to the exchange with his mouth wide open so I took him to one side and explained that the Gestapo were keen to talk to him before we left Trieste on the tide the next morning.

Ryker and the doctor left for the sick bay a few seconds later. I called in there on my way to the wardroom and raised an eyebrow at the Doctor.

He pointed towards one of the beds where Ryker was already sound asleep and snoring for Germany.

"Ten hours, possibly even twelve before he comes round," he said.

"Well done, Doc. We'll be at sea by then. How will he feel when he comes round?"

"A headache, rather like a slight hangover."

"He's a sailor. He doesn't know what a slight hangover is," I replied as I closed the door and walked down the alleyway.

The Gestapo interrogated me for over an hour. The same questions repeated in a different way. I stuck to my guns and told them that we'd warned Zirk about the decks being slippery when we were under attack, but he hadn't listened. There was nothing more to add.

"And seaman Ryker. Bring him here," they ordered.

"He was injured when we attacked the enemy submarine earlier this evening. He's in the sickbay with the doctor. He's unconscious, the doc thinks it's concussion and he's likely to be out until long after we sail."

The men bristled and one stood up.

"You will bring him here or I will fetch him myself," he screeched at me.

I stood and looked him straight in the eye.

"We are under orders from Berlin to sail on the morning tide tomorrow. With a full complement of men. Those orders came from The Bunker, do you understand?"

He had the grace to step back.

"We have a busy day tomorrow and I need to get some sleep before that. If there's nothing else I will have the steward escort you to the gangway. You have taken a lot of our time."

He made to speak.

"If you want to waste any more of our time, gentlemen, I will ask the Admiral to telephone The Bunker and ask if we can delay sailing because two junior gestapo officers are interrogating us and want to interrogate another sailor tomorrow morning."

I picked up the telephone on the wardroom bar.

"Mueller, please connect me with the Admiral," I said into the phone.

Mueller, our shipboard operator asked me to repeat what I'd said and was clearly of the view that his Commander was mad. We had no Admiral aboard Condor and no telephone communications with the shore.

"That's right, Mueller, the Admiral in Trieste HQ."

"Commander Klopp, we've taken enough of your time. We will go now. But will want to see you again when you return."

And that was that. They left, and I have to say they left in a hurry. By the time we returned to Trieste I doubted that Zirk and his death would be anything other than a distant memory to those scum. They would have focused on something else. But just in case, I would suggest that the Captain contact the Admiral himself before we sailed.

# Chapter 72    Annie in Newlyn

Sammy looked the same when I visited him in his cell to introduce him to the solicitor who had agreed to take on his case. His face was pale, his skin pock marked and his clothes quite smelly.

I explained that though we wanted him to be released, the police were against it. But a local magistrate was due to hear the case later that morning and had already spoken with the Welsh police about their suspicions concerning Chief Petty Officer Williams and the death of his wife and her lover.

Carol Crebo would also be in court to testify that she had seen Williams giving Madge a wad of money. Whether all this would secure Sammy's release we didn't know, but it was the best we could do.

"Where's Williams now?" he asked and I explained that he was overseas on active service.

He was silent for a moment before asking if he could freshen up before appearing in court. The solicitor called for the sergeant and, with a degree of reluctance, the sergeant agreed.

"He'll need a change of clothing," I told the officer.

"He's wearing the same clothes he had on when you arrested him. That's a dreadful way to treat an innocent man."

"How do you know he's innocent?" the sergeant asked at which point the solicitor stepped in.

"Because unless they changed the law after I entered this cell everyone in this country is innocent until proven guilty. You, my dear sergeant, have arrived at your own decision and that is against the law. Miss Lenton placed a suitcase with your constable behind the desk. It contains the prisoner's clothes. I strongly advise you to allow him the privacy to change."

And the sergeant, with a large scowl on his face, did just that.

Sammy returned to the cell shaved and changed and I must say that he looked, and smelt, the better for it, though his eyes still held the pain of losing his wife. And he still coughed more than a normal person, the effect of the gas entering his lungs I assumed.

I left him with his solicitor and walked to the court with Carol where we sat in the waiting area.

"I've never been in court before," she said, her foot tapping erratically against the chair leg.

"Just tell the truth, Carol. That's what the solicitor said to tell you. Tell what you know, nothing more, nothing less."

She was in the courtroom for a long time. When she came out she was as white as a sheet.

"I almost fainted," she said. "The magistrate was very nice and gave me a glass of water because I was so nervous. But I did what you said and told the truth."

An usher came over to me at that point and told me that it was my turn to give evidence. The room was smaller than I had imagined. Three magistrates sat high up behind a huge oak bench and Sammy sat in the dock behind iron bars. His solicitor sat a table below the magistrates and another table alongside housed what I assumed were the police solicitors.

The usher guided me to the stand where I placed my hand on the Bible and swore to tell the truth.

Sammy's solicitor asked me how I had become involved in the case and I explained my position as the Assistant to Captain Dennis, Officer Commanding this area. At his request I described how CPO Williams had returned home on leave when he had received word from a friend that his wife was seeing another man. And went on to describe how he seemed different according to a number of witnesses after his return to duty.

The police solicitor said that this was entirely hearsay evidence and not relevant but the magistrate held up a piece of paper.

"My Clerk spoke to Swansea police earlier this morning and they confirm what Second Officer Lenton has told us. Go on, please Second Officer."

And I continued, finishing with my own encounter with Williams outside my office when he acted in a highly aggressive manner.

After that I was allowed to leave and the solicitor told me later that the police sergeant admitted that amongst the fingerprints they found in Madge's room were several sets which were unidentified, but they would need to collect Williams' prints in order to exclude him from the enquiry.

With so much evidence pointing away from Sammy, the magistrates released him, though told him to report to the police station every day. And asked that the police contact Harry's senior officer to ask that Williams be returned home at the earliest opportunity. Later that day the police released Sammy and I drove him to Madge's old boarding house.

"I checked with the landlady and she said that if you wanted you could stay here until you find somewhere else," I told him.

He swallowed and it was a few minutes before he could speak.

"Thank you, Miss Lenton, for all you've done. But I don't think I can stay here. Too many memories," he said.

I understand, Sammy. If you prefer, the landlady at the Fishermans Arms has two rooms, one of which is vacant. Shall I drop you there? You could always arrange to see Eileen, she has the other room."

He nodded and I left him at the pub doorway looking out over Newlyn Harbour where so much had happened to him in the recent past.

And to me, too, I thought as I drove back to the office. I wonder how Harry is. Where is he? Please God bring him back safely.

# Chapter 73    Klopp in Trieste

After the Gestapo left I spoke to the Captain before returning to my cabin. I doubled my dosage of painkillers, washed down with a stiff Schnapps and slept solidly for five hours. I woke as the Coxswain's voice blasted across the ship's tannoys.

"Hands to stations for leaving harbour. I repeat, hands to stations for leaving harbour."

All round the ship men walked briskly down alleyways, climbed companionways to the open decks above or to the steaming hot and smelly engine and boiler spaces below.

I donned my uniform and heavy coat and climbed to the bridge, my leg throbbing slightly.

"Good morning, Sir," I saluted the Captain. The old fashioned salute which he now accepted, not the Nazi salute with a clicking of heels. It was another in the subtle changes in our relationship.

"Good morning, Commander. The Admiral sends his best wishes and tells us that Berlin have told the Gestapo to stop wasting their time and ours on this Zirk fellow. They are to remove all trace of his stupidity from their records and get back to work."

"Good news, Sir. Thank you for telling me. I shall take reports on our readiness for sea."

I stood at the bridge telephone and voicepipes as every department reported in and was able to report to the Captain.

*"Der Condor* is closed up and ready for sea, Sir. Special sea duty men at the bow and stern. All other crewmen at Action Stations as ordered."

He nodded and walked out on to the bridge wing. I stood for a moment and marvelled at the speed and efficiency of this crew. Many were enlisted, neither volunteers nor permanent sailors. Men recruited for the war and ordered to sea. No choice, and little chance to see families and friends for months on end. Sometimes more than a year.

I had no family to speak of. Distant relatives somewhere, though I had no contact with them. And most of my friends, like me, were at sea. Somewhere. It could be a lonely life, but I loved it. Apart from the pain. But that was manageable provided I didn't run out of painkillers.

I stood in the centre of the bridge, my own station for leaving and entering harbour.

"Single up fore and aft, Commander," the Captain ordered and I repeated it into the phone, watching as the First Lieutenant oversaw his men at the bow casting off all but one rope. I had no doubt that his deputy was doing the same at the stern.

"Let go forrad," Braun ordered, "slow astern port engine, half ahead starboard."

The ship's bow gently eased away from the land.

"Stop engines," Braun ordered and when the screws had stopped turning, "Let go aft."

The lieutenant on the after deck called, "All clear aft," and Braun took us out to sea.

All around the harbour Escort Group 158 replicated our manoeuvres and we soon formed up in line astern, leaving the harbour entrance to wait for the six merchant ships we were to guide south to the North African coast.

As those ships left Trieste and joined us in the huge Gulf outside the harbour we chivvied and shepherded them until they were in the centre of our huge escort group. Surrounded by warships, the twenty thousand troops and hundred of tons of armour would remain enfolded like this until we arrived at our destination, the port of Marassi, a short drive from Fieldmarshal Rommel's HQ.

The weather held fine all the way south through the Adriatic Sea. We went to Action Stations twice each day, not because we were in danger, but to keep the crew on their toes.

"When we move from the Adriatic into the Ionian Sea the risks will increase," I told Ryker who stood watch with me during the night. "Enemy submarines and surface ships operate there, though not in great numbers."

"And after that, Sir, when we get closer to Egypt?"

"Once we're in the Mediterranean Sea, everything changes, Ryker. The enemy are there in greater numbers and though we will head east and their focus will be to the west towards Malta, they will know that something is happening. That a German convoy is on the move."

"What then, Sir?"

"Then, Ryker, they'll throw everything they have at us. When they know where we are."

I wondered how good their intelligence was and whether they knew we were on our way. And if they knew, what was their true strength in this part of the Mediterranean? Our agents reported that their great fleet had no stomach to leave Malta to protect their ships, but was that true? We received reports twice daily that they stayed in Valetta Harbour, the British naval base on Malta.

I walked out on to the bridge wing, away from the lookout and took a sip of coffee to wash down three painkillers. Ten minutes and relief would come. I looked at my watch. Two hours before I was back in my cabin. I still had plenty of tablets. Enough to last me back to Hamburg.

I finished my drink and walked back inside.

"Do you think we'll get them all to Egypt, Sir," Ryker asked.

"If we don't, I'm told that Rommel is finished. The British will throw him out of Africa. Before starting to attack Italy and the southern European areas that we hold. We must get them all there, Ryker. The war may well depend on it."

# Chapter 74    Scotty at Suez

"Morrison, you obviously know what is in this message as you've decoded it."

"Yes, Sir. Couldn't believe my eyes, Sir. It's not the Coxswain I know."

I shook my head.

"Nor me, Morrison. I know that I can trust you to say nothing to anyone about this."

"Yes, Sir, of course. What will you do, Sir?"

And that was the clincher. I didn't know. Annie's message was clear. It was my decision if and when to tell Williams that he would be placed under arrest and taken back to England. Not the Admiralty, not the Old Man. Mine.

"Ask the First Lieutenant to join me on deck, Morrison."

I walked outside on to the lifeboat deck and leant against the rail. All around us sat our escort group with *HMS Ganges* barely a hundred yards away, swinging gently around her anchor. The other five merchantmen were nestled inside a cocoon formed by our Royal Navy guardians. Ahead of us was the port of Tewfik, the southern entrance to the Suez Canal.

"You wanted me, Harry?" The informality had started after our attack on the German fleet. I was pleased. As it marked a distinct change in our relationship.

"Thank you, James. Yes. Did Morrison tell you anything?"

"Not a thing. He was quite pale, not at all like him. No bounce, almost sad."

I told him why that would be by explaining the details in the message from Newlyn.

"Good God, his wife and her boyfriend and the prostitute in Newlyn? I can't believe it, Harry. It's not possible."

I gave him the message that Morrison decoded just a few minutes earlier. Two pages of neat handwriting laying out the facts as Annie and the Old Man knew them.

"Well, what are you going to do? The Old Man's put the ball squarely in your court."

"I really don't want to go into battle with a new Coxswain. I know that he hasn't been right for some time now and this probably explains it. On the other hand it's entirely possible that he didn't do these things. We'll get the job done first and I'll tell him when we're on the way back to Alex," I replied, wishing as always that we were on that journey back to Alexandria already.

After that I told James to make sure that all crews stayed below decks for the journey through the Canal. The crews on the other ships would do the same. Though Egypt was, largely, in British hands, there were many spies throughout the land and some of them would be studying the ships transiting Suez very carefully indeed. I didn't want any of them wondering why so many British sailors were on merchant ships. *Ganges* and over half the escort group went through in one batch first. They would wait for us at Port Said to guide us on to Alexandria. The rest of the group would transit with the merchantmen, looking more like a normal convoy with its escort.

I walked up to the Bridge and asked ComConvoy if I could watch the start of the transit from there. We watched as *Ganges* and her group left the anchorage and made their way in line astern to the southern entrance. An hour later we received the order to proceed and ComConvoy led the other five ships towards the entrance.

"No locks on Suez, Harry. Not like Panama where you have to carry one of their pilots and navigate locks at each end. Here the Red Sea and the Med are the same heights, give or take, so we just sail right through. Slowly, though, the Egyptians don't like the canal banks washed away by speeding merchantmen."

So it was that we steamed at seven knots the ninety miles north to Port Said. *Ganges* timed our arrival at the southern entrance to enable us to leave the Canal and arrive at Alex under cover of darkness.

Having seen enough of the canal, and with darkness already falling, I went back below and asked James to join me for a drink. As we sat on deck with beers in our hands Morrison came by with another message.

"Just arrived, Sir. The ship's radio officer's a good sort. As soon as he saw your name coming in he sent a sailor down to fetch me. Looks like we'll have company for our attack."

I read the message and passed it to James.

Well I'm damned, the Brylcreem boys are going to act as decoys for us. And there's me thinking the RAF didn't want any part of this," he said.

"That's what we were told. I wonder what changed their mind. Not that it matters. If they can take the Germans' attention away from us it gives us a better than even chance of hitting them hard while they're looking elsewhere."

"If the convoy's on time we'll be back in Alexandria by this time tomorrow," he said. "Any idea how we're getting home?"

"Not a clue, James. I daresay they'll have something arranged for us at Alex. Be nice to think that they'll have us aboard a fast convoy straight out to Gibraltar."

I didn't add another possibility. That they didn't expect all my MGBs to make it back. But, James was nobody's fool. He would have worked that one out as well.

## Chapter 75    Klopp in the Adriatic Sea

Somewhere off our port side was the Greek island of Crete, though we couldn't see it. For a start it was dark. But more important it was over three hundred miles away. And we were within twenty four hours of achieving our goal: safe delivery of our merchant ships to Fieldmarshal Rommel's nearest port.

Captain Braun was on the bridge and had been for the last two hours. Egypt was still some way off, but land-based aircraft could now reach us for the first time since we left Trieste. We'd doubled the lookouts on the bridge and relieved the Asdic and Radar operators every two hours. We couldn't allow anybody to let their guard down.

"Asdic Bridge contact bearing 090 distance seven miles. Low in the water, probably a submarine."

Braun's hand closed on the Action Stations klaxon and the ship quickly closed up.

"Commander Klopp, order *Breslau* and *Mainz* to attack. Destroy if at all possible. If not possible keep her out of the way until the convoy has passed."

I gave the necessary orders and acknowledged their replies. The sun was just rising over the horizon, shedding enough light to see the two destroyers racing away from the convoy. I gave instructions for the rest of the escort group to close up to fill the gap and walked out to join the captain on the bridge wing.

It seemed no time at all before the first waterspouts rose high in the air as our two ships dropped their first rack of depth charges. Braun was tapping his hand impatiently on the wooden taffrail that surrounded the bridge wing as though he was keen to join in the fight. But our place as leader was here with our flock. Braun learnt that lesson the hard way when we lost Zirk overboard.

"They're going in again," I said, peering through my binoculars. "Looks like *Breslau* is standing off while *Mainz* attacks."

"Our captains are learning, Johann. No point both going in unless there's more than one submarine. *Mainz* won't see a thing underwater once she's dropped her charges. But *Breslau* will have a better view from further away. They'll reverse roles and keep on doing it until they have a result."

For the next hour and a half they played that game. We lost sight of them as we steamed past, Braun giving orders to increase to maximum speed to put more distance between the enemy and ourselves.

It was almost four hours later before *Breslau* steamed alongside us with *Mainz* resuming her place at the stern of the convoy. *Breslau's* captain stood on his bridge wing with a loudhailer in his hand.

"We have a Probable only, Sir. Lots of air and oil bubbled to the surface along with some rags and pieces of timber. But if we didn't sink her I reckon we did her some damage."

"Well done, Commander, at least you gave us the chance to get the convoy through. Resume original station on the port side of the convoy."

The sun was now high above us and I watched as the Navigator and two midshipmen took the noonday sun sights. I smiled as I recalled my own days as a midshipman. You were neither an officer nor a rating. You were somewhere in between, looked down on by both until you sewed that thin golden stripe to the sleeve of your jacket.

Every day at noon you stood on the bridge wing and measured the height of the sun above the horizon with a sextant before labouring through tables of figures to determine the ship's exact position through a page full of calculations. At first it was impossible, but I soon got the hang of it and on my last ship as a midshipman completed the calculations before the Navigator.

Back at the chart table I listened as the Navigator asked each Middie to note their position on the chart. He nodded and smiled, a sign that they were spot on. "What is our Estimated Time of Arrival, Pilot?" I asked him.

He pencilled in the final leg of our journey and used his dividers to work out the distance.

"Noon tomorrow, Commander. If we maintain our current speed. And if nothing else gets in our way." There was every likelihood that we would maintain this speed. The captain was keen to get us there as soon as possible. It was equally possible that the British would try to stop us. They must know that a convoy of this size was on its way. And that it would in all probability be carrying reinforcements, either men or equipment."

"Commander Klopp, tomorrow will see us in easy distance of the enemy's aircraft and surface ships. Stand as many of the men down as you can for now. Tell the petty officers that we go to Action Stations at midnight. I believe we will need to be refreshed and ready for whatever they throw at us."

## Chapter 76    Scotty at sea between Suez and Alexandria

We were on the last leg of our journey aboard *Liberty* and it was a fast one. With *Ganges* and the group all round us we sped through the early evening into the pitch black of night. During wartime no ships showed lights at sea unless the fog came down and they needed to stream lights off their stern to, hopefully, stop ships behind from ramming them.

There was no fog tonight, though, and none in our forecast for the next twenty four hours. Which was a shame as it would have been to our benefit in the run up to our attack. Our boats were loaded, fuelled and ready to go as soon as we received confirmation that the German convoy was on time.

The plan was simple. We would leave Alex under cover of darkness and steam due north. Eight boats would attack from the stern, eight from ahead and I would lead the rest in from the west. The RAF would attack from the east and give us a fighting chance to be amongst the merchant ships before the German Naval escorts realised we were there.

That was the theory. But, plans are made to be changed and we would change them if needed. In my mind I visualised the Mediterranean Sea. A convoy of this size would be spread across three square miles of water with the merchant ships surrounded by the twenty or so escorts. Three warships for each merchant. A very expensive convoy indeed.

I sat at the table in my cabin and composed another letter. I'd written to Annie every day of the voyage and the letters were piled up in envelopes in my sea bag. But this one was different. This was the letter that we all dreaded writing because we never wanted it to be read. I finished and read it through one last time.

*"Dear Annie,*

*This is the last letter that I will write and it's to you
and you alone. When we first met I thought you were
aloof, somehow apart from the rest of us. But in the
few months we had together I realised that this was far
from the case and that you are the warmest, kindest
and most beautiful person that I've ever met. I started
to fall in love with you that night at the end of the
harbour, the night you held me while I cried like a
baby. Tonight as I sit writing this en route from Suez to
Alex, I can honestly say that I love you with all my
heart.*

*I wish I was there with you now. Not because I fear
what we're about to do. But because that's where I
want to be for the rest of my life.*

*You gave me hope when I had so little. You gave me a
reason for living when I thought that I had no reason.
And you gave me your love when I thought that I
neither had love to give nor deserved receiving any
from someone as beautiful as you.*

*Do not mourn me for long. I can't tell you the
impossible - not to grieve at all. Because I can't begin
to understand how I would feel if our roles were
reversed. Live your life, I hope and pray that it will be
a long and happy one. You deserve much happiness. I
wish that I was there to share it with you.*

*With all my love
Your darling Harry."*

I folded it once, placed it in an envelope on which I'd
written Annie's name and address, sealed it and added
it to the pile in my case.

A knock sounded at the door and James came in. He
handed me a beer and we both drank.

"Written to Carol?" I asked and he nodded.

"First time that I've written to a girl, Harry," he said.
"Didn't think I'd have much to say at first. Funnily
enough I almost ran out of paper."

We both laughed and I raised my bottle.

"To us, James, you, me, *Dotty* and crew and all our boats and people. God willing we'll all come through the other end."

We clinked bottles and looked briefly at each other. Words between us were unnecessary. James knew how highly I regarded him and shared many confidences with him that I would not have shared with anybody else.

We finished our beers and I stood.

"I'm going to see the Coxswain. I think it's only fair. He's been a good man and I believe that he may be innocent. Only a trial can tell and he should know what is suspected."

I walked down the companionway to the mess deck, stopping in the Officers' Bar to collect more beers. The Coxswain was in the crew mess playing chess with our Chief Mechanic. Perhaps things were getting back to normal.

"Coxswain, I wonder if you could spare me a minute." We walked out on to the deck and I sat with my back to the superstructure while he sat with his back against the ship's side. I passed him a bottle and took a sip from mine.

"Dave, I received some news from Newlyn just before we arrived at the canal. It's about Agnes."

He looked down and tightened the grip on his beer. I started to tell him about the two bodies and when he looked up tears flowed down his cheeks. I stopped and sat quietly, unsure what to do.

"I'm sorry, Dave," I said at last. "Very sorry."

"What else, Sir? What else do you know?"

I told him about the prostitute in Newlyn, a stranger's fingerprints in her room, the pimp, Sammy almost dying. Everything that was in the report. He took a deep breath.

"What happens now, Sir? Shore Patrol waiting at Alex for me, I suppose."

For the first time since receiving Annie's message I knew what was next.

"No, they're not. Nobody except the First Lieutenant knows about this. Well, Morrison obviously because he decoded it. Captain Dennis left it to my discretion to decide what to do."

"And what will you do, Sir? I'd like to know. You see, I did kill them. All three of them. I was mad at Agnes for two timing again. It's not the first time. After that I panicked. Madge was going to blackmail me and I'd already given her all I had. I didn't have any more money."

"Why didn't you tell me? I could have helped? Good God, man you saved my life at Dunkirk."

We talked for another hour and I still didn't understand what turned this pleasant but tough man into a murderer. I looked at my watch.

"We'll be in Alex in an hour. I'm not going to ask for your arrest. I need you and *Dotty* needs you. We need our Coxswain at the helm when we go into battle. When we get back to Alex afterwards we'll be exhausted, too tired to see the authorities. I'll probably sleep for a few hours."

I smiled at him and he smiled in return. He wouldn't be the first sailor to abscond from Alex. There were plenty of ships coming and going. Not all of them went to England, either. He could take his chances.

# Chapter 77    Winston Churchill at the War Rooms

Harding, my valet, came into my bedroom when it was still dark. I hate being woken part way through the night. I'd barely even got to sleep.

"I'm sorry to disturb you, Sir. It's Sir Sholto Douglas, Marshall of the Royal Air Force."

"Yes, yes, I know who Douglas is. What does he want?"

"He said that it was vital that he talked to you this very minute. He has news from the Mediterranean Sea, Sir."

I snatched the phone from Harding's hands and told him to leave.

"Prime Minister here. What's so damned urgent that you had me woken in the middle of the night?"

"Actually, Winston, it's six in the morning in Alexandria, far from the middle of the night. Which means that here it is now......."

"Dammit, Sholto, I don't want to be woken up to be told the time. That's like being in a bloody hospital bed."

"Quite, Winston. We have some bad news, I'm afraid."

I felt a chill run through my body. Today was the day of the attack on Hitler's convoy.

"Are you there?" Douglas asked.

Yes, yes, of course I'm here."

"We had hoped to conduct a fast, feint air attack on the convoy. We can't. Thick fog. Can't even get the planes off the ground. It's impossible. Came out of nowhere. The Met Office people didn't see it coming. Nothing one minute, thick as pea soup the next."

"And have you told everyone who needs to know?"

I was vague as we had to be so careful what we said on the telephone. We just never knew who may be listening in so conversations sometimes sounded obscure.

"Yes, their Lordships have already relayed the news to Alex."

I thanked him, though still did not appreciate the ungodly hour and reached for my cigar. Part smoked before I went to sleep, it might help me regain some sleepiness. Though I doubted it. My mind flew across the seas to the Med. The flotilla of MGBs would already be speeding towards the convoy. God help them

When Sholto first aired the idea of a feint attack, leaving the Navy more time to carry out the real thing, I was overjoyed. Now that hope was dashed. How many young sailors would die this day in foreign waters? How many would make it back to Alex?

And most important of all, how many of Rommel's reinforcements would get through? Not enough, I prayed, to allow him to venture any further into Egypt. Not enough, I prayed, to prevent the Auks' successor destroying the German battalions.

I stubbed the cigar out and lay back down to sleep. When it finally came I dreamt of blood red seas, English sailors floating face down and burning ships.

# Chapter 78    Scotty in Alexandria

Alex was like no other port I ever visited. It wasn't as big as Devonport or Portsmouth but it was crowded. Ships from all over the world called here, even during wartime. Many flew the flags of neutral countries, a symbol which German submarines often respected. But not always.

This evening as we arrived I could see the Merchant Navy's Red Ensign on many vessels: freighters, tankers, old tramps. But there were also Dutch, French, Norwegian, Brazilian, American and many other flags. ComConvoy led his brood of ships directly to a secure area used only by the Royal Navy. On the voyage from Port Said his crew, and the crews of the other merchant ships, had opened the hatches and prepared the MGBs for unloading. The sailors placed great strops of rope around each boat and while the Captain navigated his ship to her berth the crew hoisted the huge derricks into place ready to lift the MGBs out of the hold and lower them gently into the water.

I stood at the side of the hatch and looked at *Dotty* just a few feet below me. From this angle she looked huge. But, in reality she was small. Which was a double edged sword as ever. Low enough to creep under the enemy's Radar but small enough to be sunk by a single lucky shell. Or unlucky depending on your nationality. Morrison walked up to the hatchway and whispered in my ear.

"Ship's Radio Officer says that the Shore Patrol are waiting at the berth. He's had a message from them saying they want to see the Coxswain, Sir. I've just decoded this."

He passed me a single sheet of paper and I cursed fluently as I read the words.

The Police had bypassed the Old Man and contacted the Admiralty. Suspected Murder trumped a mission to destroy a German convoy.

*"Leader 18th Flotilla is to hand CPO Williams to the Shore patrol at Alexandria before departing on mission."*

"Dammit to hell, we can't do this."

"It's all right, Sir. Sparks and I got quite pally on the way out. Played cards most nights and had a few beers. He replied and said that they can't come aboard till the Q flag comes down cos we've got a case of fever."

I ran up to the bridge where ComConvoy was peering over the bridge wing at the Shore Patrol, the Navy's very own Police, below.

"What do they want, Harry?"

"My Coxswain, Sir. Can you delay lowering the gangway till we've left? I need him for this trip. Can't make anyone else up at this late hour."

"It's a pleasure. Never liked the Shore Patrol when I was in the Andrew. Too handy with their fists for my liking."

"Can I ask another favour, Sir?"

"Of course."

I told him that in my cabin was a pile of letters home.

"Just in case, if you know what I mean, Sir."

He nodded and held out his hand.

"Somehow a salute just won't do, Harry. Fair winds, a following sea and safe home. That's all any matelot asks for."

I ran back down to the main deck as *Dotty* appeared from the hold and the ship's derricks lowered her gently to the water below. The Coxswain and Morrison were standing on her deck and as she dropped back into her natural habitat they slipped the strops off and secured her to *Liberty's* side while we all climbed down into our beloved boat once more.

"Well done, Morrison," I called as I entered my wheelhouse for the first time in almost a month.

"Quick thinking. We'll make a sailor of you yet."

"I think we've already done that, Sir," the Coxswain replied "He's just told me about *Liberty's* Radio Officer."

For the first time in many weeks the man smiled. And for the first time in months I felt as though we had *Dotty's* Coxswain back. I told him.

The radio blared out at that moment.

"Alexandria Command to *HMS Beagle*. Are you receiving?"

What next I wondered.

*"Beagle* to Alexandria. Receiving. Over."

"I have a message from the Shore Patrol ordering you to berth at Pier Six before leaving Harbour. Acknowledge. Over."

The smile disappeared from the Coxswain's face.

*"HMS Beagle* to Alexandria. My orders are to proceed directly to sea on operations. Please confirm that your order has been approved by the Admiralty in London."

There was no response for several minutes.

*"HMS Beagle*, you are ordered to remain in your current position until the Admiralty reply to our urgent, repeat urgent message."

I looked at our flotilla as each boat made its way to our side.

"How many, Number One?"

"All accounted for, Sir. All boats in the 18th MGB Flotilla present and correct."

I picked up the handset.

"18th MGB Flotilla. Proceed to sea as instructed. Do not acknowledge. Over and Out."

The roar of twenty-four boats' engines, each delivering over 4,000 Horse Power, drowned out any further broadcasts from Alexandria Command. We made our way out of the harbour, three boats in each line, eight columns in formation. As we passed the breakwater I gave the command we'd all been waiting for.

"Full Ahead all engines. Coxswain, steer course $060^0$."

"Alex Command to *Beagle*. Acknowledge."

The voice sounded familiar. What the hell was the Old Man doing out here?

*"Beagle* to Alex. Receiving, Sir."

A chortle sounded down the line.

"Alexandria Command are a bit annoyed with you, Harry. Can't say I blame them. Anyway, convoy is on schedule and currently estimated to arrive on the Egyptian coast at midday today. That's in eight hours' time, Harry. Take down the co-ordinates."

I wrote them down and passed them to Hawes who pencilled the position on the chart.

"Alex to *Beagle.* One other point. There will be no RAF involvement. Too much fog over their bases. Over."

"Yes, we received the message earlier. We always thought it would be down to the Navy, Sir. Is that all?"

"Alex to *Beagle.* Yes. No further communications until after the attack. Good luck. Over and Out."

We steamed on into the early morning. It wasn't the best time to attack, but beggars never could be choosers. The sun would be barely above the horizon when we came up with the convoy. Not that we would see it. The fog that kept the RAF on the ground was already spreading over the sea.

"At this rate we'll be looking for the convoy on Radar," I told James.

I rearranged my plans mentally and radioed fresh orders to the flotilla. Four separate attack teams. One from each point of the compass. First targets would be the merchant ships. After that, well, who knew? We'd take our chances.


## Chapter 79    Scotty in the Mediterranean Sea

Eighty miles and we'd have the convoy in sight. Two hours at our present speed.

"Radar Bridge contacts 260$^0$ twenty miles. Lots of contacts, Sir. At least ten."

A minute later, "They're fast, Sir. Could be E Boats."

I pressed the alarm for Action Stations and unhooked the PA handset.

"Captain to Crew. We have a large force of E Boats heading towards us. Stand by."

My next call was to Group A, my unit of six MGBs and Group B, led by Lieutenant Brown in *HMS Collie*.

*"Beagle* to Groups A and B. Ten E Boats heading in towards us. Bearing 260$^0$. We will head them off and let Groups C and D make their own way to their attack points. All leaders acknowledge."

I listened to their replies and gave the orders for our new course.

"Line abreast."

The Radar repeater in front of me showed my twelve MGBs spreading out to either side. The Germans came on as though they didn't know we were there. But that couldn't be true.

Their E Boats were similar to my own MGBs. Small, powerful craft, twin engines unlike our three engines. Three 20 MM machine guns on the fore deck and a 30 MM cannon on the after deck. Their best weapons were the depth charges and torpedoes they carried for use against coastal shipping.

"Number One," I called through the loud hailer to the First Lieutenant at his station beside our own 20 MM cannon on the fore deck. "When we're a mile away exactly I'll give you the order to open fire. After that look for their bow waves."

He waved back.

"All Boats, open fire on my command. They won't be expecting a heavy attack."

We sped on into the mist and darkness, all the time watching for the tell-tale white bow waves.

"Radar Bridge contacts dead ahead. One mile."

The rest of the message was drowned out as the foredeck guns on all our boats opened fire almost simultaneously. As my boats raced through the small German fleet, we fired our depth charges as well. The early morning was a cacophony of explosions, gun shells and machine gun fire.

We were through and out the other end.

"Reverse course, Coxswain, let's get after them."

*Dotty* skidded around at almost her top speed. Forty knots and turning was not for the faint hearted. I heard the sound of smashing crockery in the galley below. We'd clear that up later.

"Radar Bridge, E Boats remaining on course. They have not, repeat not, turned around."

"We'll never catch them, Sir. Their top speed's only a knot or two below ours," the Coxswain said.

"Dammit. They'll warn the convoy we're here. That'll scupper any chance of a surprise attack," I replied.

"Radar Bridge, I count only eight contacts, Sir. We must have got two of them."

I stood the crew down from Action Stations.

"Coxswain, we've got about an hour before we're up with the convoy. Make sure the crew get a hot drink and a sandwich."

The First Lieutenant came into the wheelhouse.

"Change of plan?" he asked.

"It'll be suicide attacking from the front of the convoy, James. They'll be expecting that now."

I walked back to the chart table and plotted their position as it would be in an hours' time.

"The E Boats will have radioed our position. They'll expect us to attack from the West as that's where we are now."

I did a few calculations and thought for a few seconds.

"18th Flotilla from Leader. Group C and D alter course. New plan of attack from the North East. Leaders, please advise your ETA."

I waited until the commanders recalculated. An hour, they told me. It would take us about an hour and five minutes to reach our new attack position. My other Groups would attack first and take some of the heat off us. And from that direction they might not be spotted until they were very close.

"The Germans might not consider that there are two groups of us, Sir," James said and I looked at him with a raised eyebrow. He walked back to the chart table and I followed.

"Well, we attacked the E Boats here, forty miles west and in front of the convoy. That's what the E Boats will tell the convoy. But Groups C and D will attack from behind and from the north east."

I smiled and slapped him on the shoulder.

"When C& D attack that'll be surprise number one," I said.

"And when we attack from the other side, that'll be surprise number two," he said.

"And there's another factor, James."

I peered through the windscreen. I could barely see the foredeck.

"Convoys get very confused in fog. And this stuff's getting worse. The escorts will have their work cut out keeping the convoy in their rightful positions. We might have some luck on our side after all."

It was all coming together. I gave the necessary orders and sat in my chair. The Coxswain returned with a sandwich and a huge steaming mug. I took a small sip and smiled.

"I don't recall asking for a dash of rum, Coxswain."

"Thought you'd need it, Sir. Anyway, I haven't had the chance to thank you."

"After what we've been through together since the start what did you expect me to do? Hand you in to that lot? What will you do when we get back?"

He stared out of the windscreen without replying before turning towards me.

"I don't know, Sir. I don't want to spend whatever's left of my life always looking over my shoulder. But if I hand myself in I'll hang. I killed them in a moment of madness. Almost killed the pimp, too. That's not a good way to live."

"I'll do whatever I can, Dave. It may not be much but I'll tell the court how good a man you are."

He nodded but we both knew what the outcome would be. Whether he was hung or shot, he would be executed.

"OK, Morrison, go and get your sandwich and Kye," he told the sailor at the wheel. "Coxswain at the helm, Sir. Course 030$^0$, engines Full Ahead."

I walked to the front of the wheelhouse and stared at the mist swirling around the guns and crew on the foredeck. *Dotty* flew through the waves, barely pitching or rolling. It felt as though she couldn't wait to see the German ships, couldn't wait to race through them, depth charges, torpedoes and shells exploding all around us.

I looked at the Coxswain and he turned and smiled. "Not long now, Sir. We'll sort those bloody German sailors out.""

## Chapter 80    Klopp aboard *Der Condor* in the Mediterranean Sea

The sun was probably just above the horizon, yet the darkness mingling with the fog stopped us seeing any further than the forecastle. I willed full daylight to come sooner, so we could see what we had to deal with.

The E Boat squadron leader spoke of a huge force of fast attack boats. We didn't know that there were such vessels in the Mediterranean. Another mistake by our so-called Intelligence units.

Captain Braun picked up the PA handset.

"This is the Captain. Very soon a large group of enemy MGBs will try to attack us. They are small, very agile and deadly. We may get little warning. All of you on deck and above must keep a sharp lookout. We must get our merchant ships to Fieldmarshal Rommel. Nothing must stop us."

His orders to our escort captains were simple. They were to destroy any enemy gunboat. No survivors, no rescues, just destroy them.

"Four hours to go, Johann. Just four hours and we can hand over our charges and go home."

"Where do you think they'll come from?" I asked.

He shrugged his shoulders.

"The E Boats said they were to the west of us. They won't have time to do anything fancy. Though if I was in their shoes I would want to at least try to spring a surprise. Perhaps from the north west."

He shrugged again.

"Who knows, Johann. You should go to your station. We may need your depth charges before the morning is over. I fear we may get just one shot at this. This fog is thick and getting thicker."

He picked up the handset.

"Radar this is the Captain. Keep a good watch on that screen. We can see very little in this mist."

"Good luck, Sir. See you when it's over," I said as I left the Bridge.

I walked to the after deck where Ryker was already at work.

"We have six racks of charges on each side, Sir. Full load. We can do some damage with these."

I lit a cigarette and used the gesture to place three painkillers on my tongue. God knows I'd be needing these in the hours ahead.

"Where do you think they'll come from, Sir?"

I peered astern. Perhaps Braun was right and the British boats would try to creep up on us from astern.

"Keep looking astern, Ryker. Here, take my binoculars. Tell me if you see anything. Or even think you see something. Not that you'll be able to see much in this."

The fog actually seemed to encircle the ship, little wisps blowing in the wind around us. I could see neither our charges nor our escorts. I hoped that the Radar operator could.

The sun was over the horizon now, though it was of no help in lengthening our line of vision. I finished my cigarette and threw it over the side before checking the depth charges. If we needed them it would be in a hurry.

"If we fire one of those anywhere near one of those MGBs they won't stand a chance," Ryker called watching as I double checked the depth settings.

I started to remind him to keep looking behind us but never finished the sentence. One of the destroyers in our outer screen was slewing across in front of one of the merchant ships. I felt rather than heard the collision as they were over half a mile away.

"What the hell was that?" I shouted when I saw the wake of a torpedo coming towards us.

"Bridge, hard a port, incoming torpedo," I screamed down the telephone.

I give the Captain his due. We were turning before I replaced the handset in its cradle. We heeled over to one side and two torpedoes raced down our side, parallel and barely a yard away.

I should have heaved a sigh of relief but when I looked up I saw that one of the corvettes was directly in the torpedo's path. This time I did hear the explosion. It wasn't loud, but the effect was stunning.

A huge flame shot out of the funnel and a waterspout over a hundred feet high followed. I looked away as the corvette rolled over on to her side and sank. One hundred and fifty sailors vanished in an instant.

Another explosion, this time from the destroyer and I looked towards the two ships locked in an impossible embrace. The bows of the merchant ship had simply cut through the destroyer leaving the warship's bow floating free while the after part of the ship gradually settled deeper into the water with the freighter's bows embedded into it.

There were more explosions as the enemy MGBs weaved through the screen of warships towards our freighters. One of the explosions seemed to come from dead ahead.

"That's the ammunition carrier," Ryker said. "I watched them loading her. Tanks, artillery, guns and ammunition."

"And men, Ryker. Don't forget the men.""

"Bridge Depth charges. Acknowledge."

"Bridge, Klopp here, Sir."

"Fire at will, Commander. As soon as you get the chance."

One of the MGBs was heading straight for a freighter just a few hundred yards away. Ryker was already at the firing controls.

"On my command, Ryker," I told him, gauging the distance between us. He would have to come close to us to get to the freighter.

"Stand by, stand by," I ordered.

I judged the MGB to be less than fifty yards from us when I gave the order. The two depth charges sailed into the air before dropping in front of the boat. Two loud explosions, the usual geyser of salt water rising into the air then nothing. The boat was no longer there. The freighter sailed on oblivious to the mayhem all round. I counted six or seven MGBs all speeding madly, insanely between the warships, firing depth charges and torpedoes as they went. All homing in on the centre of the convoy. But one by one our warships were destroying them.

I watched as another of the small craft disintegrated. Another one flew into the air and broke up when it landed back on the surface of the ocean. Seven sped off into the distance and I relaxed for the first time in almost an hour.

Thank God that's over," Ryker said, lighting a cigarette.

And that's when the freighter nearest us broke in half.

# Chapter 81    Scotty in the Mediterranean Sea

The radio waves were full of messages from my MGBs attacking the convoy. So far we'd sunk at least three of their merchantmen and badly damaged two of their warships, one sinking. And now we had the convoy firmly in our sights.

"All boats fire at will. Top priority the merchantmen." It was literally every boat for herself as we raced past the stern of the first warships in the convoy screen. Sub Lieutenant Hawes took it on himself to launch three torpedoes as we passed by and from the explosions a few of my other boats did the same.

"Aim for the merchantman dead ahead, Cox," I ordered and he swung the bow gently to one side.

The ship was barely four hundred yards away.

"Dead Slow Ahead, hard a port."

James was at his post next to the depth charges and he timed it perfectly, firing a rack of three barrel-shaped charges into the side of the freighter.

"Full Ahead, wheel a midships," I shouted above the explosions.

I didn't bother looking back. One of my boats, I though HMS *Collie*, headed directly towards another German ship, this one clearly more of a passenger liner.

Lieutenant Brown, *Collie's*, CO knew exactly what he was doing. He kept his boat close to the liner, stopping the warships from firing at him. Any stray shells would destroy their own ship.

His aim was perfect and three torpedoes left their tubes at point blank range as he pulled away into the centre of the convoy. Four merchant ships destroyed and we were barely fifteen minutes into battle.

We roared back into the fog, the Radar operator calling out positions of the closest ships then we turned back to join *Collie*, passing quickly through the centre of the convoy to turn towards the two remaining troop carriers.

Smoke streamed from burning ships, German and British. I couldn't afford to think about my own boats. If even these two ships arrived in Egypt our forces could be doomed.

The gun crews kept up a solid barrage as we steamed in towards the Germans, but the small anti-aircraft shells were of no use against metal freighters. Though I could see sparks flying as they hit the wheelhouse and bridge wing.

"Sir, enemy warship astern. Looks like a destroyer," the bridge lookout reported.

"Number One, lay three mines astern," I shouted and told *Collie* to do the same.

I turned back to the two ships ahead. One was another troop carrier, the other looked like a passenger cargo ship judging by the huge superstructure.

*Collie* was closer to the troop carrier so I focused on the passenger liner.

"Steer for the liner, Coxswain," I ordered.

"Mines away," I heard through the PA and wondered if they would do any good. Normally at that distance, the German destroyer would see the barrels rolling over the stern. But, in these conditions we might give them a nasty surprise. There was certainly no chance of the enemy lookouts spotting the mines in the water.

"Stand by Torpedoes," I told Sub Lieutenant Hawes before running back to his position.

"Alfie, you'll have one shot at this. Wait for my command. You've done well."

Back in the wheelhouse I looked all round. It was like an inferno with ships ablaze all round me. And those that weren't ablaze were belching black smoke from their funnels adding to the lack of visibility. We were still keeping the German ships off guard by staying in the middle of them.

But we couldn't stay like that for long. Soon we would have to make a break for it. And I doubted that many of us would survive the retreat. If only the RAF could give us cover, but there was no chance of that happening.

"Stand by," I told Hawes through the radio and he waved in acknowledgement.

The freighter looked massive as we raced towards her. I wondered momentarily how many troops she carried. Not for long, though, as memories of Dunkirk came back. That day German aircraft flew along the shoreline bombing and strafing our soldiers. This was what war did and there was no glory in it.

"Fire," I called out and saw the three fish dropping vertically into the water before their tail fins drove them towards the convoy. We were barely a hundred yards from our target and the torpedoes travelled at almost a hundred miles per hour. The Coxswain turned the bow away and we started to head away from the convoy.

The first explosion almost turned us over, but the Coxswain handled the wheel well and I pushed the two outer engines to astern to counteract the wave that hit us in the rear.

The next two explosions were even bigger and I risked a quick look. The steamer was alight from her stem to her stern and already listing badly. I looked across at *Collie's* victim. She was already going down by the head, though slowly.

Of *Collie* herself there was no sign.

"Anyone seen *Collie?*" I shouted.

"There, Sir, coming out from behind the ship," James reported, pointing to the sinking freighter.

All the merchant ships were either sinking or badly damaged. And damaged just wasn't good enough. I couldn't let any of them get to their destination. But, we were running short of torpedoes and depth charges. I told the lookouts to check how many of our boats they could see. Twelve they said. Half of the flotilla already gone.

"All boats, one last pass through the convoy. Depth charge and torpedo all remaining troopers."

As *Collie* and *Dotty* turned another explosion came from one side.

"It's that destroyer, Sir. Must have hit one of our mines or one of *Collie's*."

"One more pass, Coxswain, then we head for home. Let's finish off the liner."

I picked up the handset.

"Bridge Torpedo," and a matelot's voice answered.

"Sir, the Sub's been hit. Flying metal when that destroyer blew up."

"Take over aft, Coxswain. I have the wheel," I said, praying that young Hawes wasn't badly injured.

I turned and looked ahead. Less than a minute and we would be up with the liner. And as I looked a huge warship came out from behind her and raced towards us. A cruiser, and all her guns were pointing towards *Dotty*.

# Chapter 82    Klopp On board *Der Condor* in the Mediterranean Sea

I had never seen such carnage. Even in the thick fog, I could see ships burning, ships sinking, bodies in the water, lifeboats upturned. From my position on the after deck I looked around the convoy. Two of our charges were still afloat and looked in little danger of sinking if fire control parties did their job.

Our escort screen was all over the place. Hardly surprising given the severity of the attack. What was surprising was how we had been taken unawares. There were so many of these attack boats, zig zagging through the convoy keeping close in to our own ships so we couldn't fire at them.

Captain Braun stood on the bridge wing directing his ships, as well as *Der Condor*, but there was little that we could do.

"Bridge Depth Charges," the PA sounded.

I answered and Braun gave his orders.

"We will attack these boats with depth charges. Fire from port and starboard racks, Commander, as we pass. And fire at will. Do not wait for my command."

Ryker and I sat at the controls, him on the port side, me on the starboard.

Wait for my command, Ryker," I said as *Condor* moved out from behind the burning liner.

"Dear God," I heard Ryker say aloud. "What a mess." Explosions all round us made the usually calm Mediterranean Sea look like a scene from hell. We passed a lifeboat with a handful of soldiers sitting, staring at nothing. They were less than fifty yards from us and our bow wave capsized the boat. None of the troops wore a lifejacket.

"Oh, Dear God," Ryker said again, tears streaming down his face.

I knew the feeling and slipped another three tablets under my tongue. Funnily enough for the first time in a long time I felt no pain. Just a quiet torpor. I wondered if I had taken too many. Before *Condor* turned on to a new heading I saw two attack boats heading towards us. As Braun turned the ship they were hidden from view momentarily.

"Safety catches off," I told Ryker. "Any moment now."

I judged it to a nicety and as we passed between two of the boats we fired three depth charges on each side. They were set for immediate detonation on impact, the only way to deal with these little craft.

My mouth dropped open when both boats rose into the air, almost as high as the deck on which I stood. When they landed they broke up, simply fell apart in front of us. I walked to the rail and leant outboard. Another two boats headed towards us, further apart than their comrades. And they made their first mistake because there were none of our ships behind them. Our foredeck guns lowered towards the surface of the sea and I felt a moment of elation.

Braun would exact what revenge he could and destroy these two British boats. There was no escape. The first salvo of shells landed behind the two boats as they zig zagged onwards. The next salvo landed in front. The next would do it. Bracketed, excellent gunnery.

But, before we fired again, the two boats parted company and steamed outwards, away from us. Our shells landed where they had been, which was of no use at all.

They passed down our sides, too far for our depth charges to be of any use. As they passed I saw the huge wake building up behind them. Our after deck guns roared out but we were too late. The small boats headed in towards the two remaining merchant ships. As they disappeared into another bank of fog I heard more explosions and saw flames shooting into the sky. Both ships must have been damaged even further. I felt something on my cheek.

"A breeze, Ryker. Look, the fog is lifting."

And all round us the breeze blew the fog further and further away. The deck tilted as Braun turned the ship to go after the attack boats. Now we really had a chance. Visibility improved by the minute.

One of our junior lieutenants arrived.

"Captain wants you on the bridge, Sir. I'm to take over here."

I ran as best as I could up the companionway and on to the bridge itself.

"Commander, we will chase the enemy down and destroy them all. I have ordered all but three of our escort group to join in the chase. The other three are to search for survivors."

I looked ahead and realised that there was a world beyond the forecastle, two hundred yards beyond. And getting clearer all the time.

I stood at the front of the bridge and watched the swirls of fog get thinner and thinner. Perhaps we would have the chance to destroy the enemy after all. Although what good it would do for Fieldmarshal Rommel I had no idea. I half listened to the radio operator as he called up ship after ship.

Not a single merchant ship answered. And seven of our escorts either failed to answer or reported themselves too badly damaged to join with us in the chase.

"Radar Bridge, I have ten contacts bearing $180^0$ estimated speed forty knots."

Ten to our fifteen. Put another way, thirty heavy guns against mere pea shooters.

"Let the chase commence," Braun said. "Form pattern five."

And our remaining escorts moved into their new positions: three columns, five ships in each column. Perfect for attacking.

# Chapter 83    Scotty aboard *HMS Beagle* in the Mediterranean Sea

I was as sure as I could be that we had completed our mission. *Collie and Dotty* certainly destroyed the two remaining merchant ships. There was no way they would ever make it to Egypt. And piecing the reports together from the surviving MGBs it seemed that all the other enemy merchantmen were sunk or sinking. I refused to think of the thousands of men who died because of our actions. You couldn't think like that in war. We didn't start it, but we had to end it and that meant that people died. The Coxswain came back into the wheelhouse and shook his head.

"Nothing to be done, Sir. Mr Hawes died instantly, I reckon. Shard of metal across his throat. I'm sorry."

The First Lieutenant and I exchanged looks. There was nothing to be said.

"Radar Bridge, contacts dead astern, Sir. Fifteen of them. Bearing due North, distance six miles, speed estimated at thirty five knots."

"They can't catch us, James. But I wonder how good their own radar is?"

"If it's good they can use use it to find our range, Sir, that's for sure. They don't need to see us. Problem is that the fog's lifting quickly now. We won't be hidden for much longer."

As he said that a salvo of shells streamed overhead and into the sea a mile ahead of us.

I picked up the handset.

*"Beagle* to flotilla, line abreast. Smartly now. Report when in position."

Another salvo flew overhead, this time landing half a mile astern. All ten boats were now running parallel to each other in a perfect line across. I gave the next order and we went to Emergency full Ahead.

We carried on like this for another minute or so before I gave what I hoped to be the last order before we turned for Alexandria.

"All boats, heave to."

We gradually slowed and to help the process put engines full astern, pushing the boats back towards the pursuing German ships. I wanted to put them off their aim as much as possible until I could turn for home.

I looked at the Coxswain. Funnily enough I had put all thoughts of this man being a killer out of my head.

"Coxswain, a word on deck, please."

When I finished I walked back into the wheelhouse and Williams took Hawes' place at the torpedoes.

"All boats slow ahead," I ordered and we started to move forward.

Another salvo of shells, the closest yet, landed barely thirty yards off our port bow. The cascading water soaked the gun crew on the foredeck.

"Flotilla, Full speed Ahead, course $090^0$."

We turned and headed away from Alexandria to bring us almost abeam of the German ships, but a mile away. Because we were moving so quickly I hoped that they would lose their bearing on us. We saw flames coming out of the fog ahead as I brought the flotilla to a halt. In line abreast again.

We fired what remained of our torpedoes into the thinning fog. I judged that most of them would miss. But combined with the mines that we laid while the fog was still thick, we could give the enemy food for thought before they resumed their hunt.

I counted six explosions, as did James and Morrison. Nobody disagreed.

We turned on to our original course and started the voyage back to Alexandria, two hours to the south.

"We should be out of range soon," James said as he came into the wheelhouse. As he spoke a shower of shells flew overhead, followed by another immediately behind us.

"Zig zag, Morrison," I ordered as the boat bucked up and down like a wild horse. Water spouts erupted around us. One of the MGBs caught a direct hit.

"Nobody's getting out of that," I said holding on to rail to stay upright.

At last the shelling subsided and soon stopped completely.

"Go round the boat, Number One. Make sure you can account for everybody. Morrison take the wheel until the Coxswain returns."

"Two casualties, Sir," James reported when he returned. "Depth charge rating looks to have a concussion. Says he doesn't know how he got it. Must have been when *Dotty* started acting like an aeroplane and took off from the water, he says."

"And the other?"

"I can't find the Coxswain. Nowhere aboard. He was at the depth charges then he wasn't. I have looked all over, Sir. He's not aboard."

I looked at the man who had been my deputy for much of the war and raised an eyebrow. He shook his head.

"Well, we're not leaving him," I said and ordered the flotilla to turn round. An hour later it was as clear as day that we wouldn't find him.

## Chapter 84     Klopp Aboard *Der Condor* in the Mediterranean Sea

We were the lead ship in the centre column and Braun was determined for us to be the first to engage the enemy. He told the Gunnery Officer precisely what to do and I thought his tactics were very clever.

"Lull them into a false sense of security, bracket them, but not too closely. Let them be the clever ones," and more in the same vein.

When we fired our first shots we had no means to see where they landed, but our Radar screen showed the ten little dots continuing to move apace towards Egypt.

"We have them, Commander. Look at how they zig zag. Another few minutes and our Gunnery officer can land his shells even closer. Let's play with them like a cat with a mouse for a little while longer."

"Sir, do you think that's wise? Wouldn't it be better to just finish them off now?" I asked, wondering why he was holding back.

"Commander Klopp, I told you once before not to argue with me. Have you forgotten?" he ground out looking at me with such venom in his eyes that I stepped back."

"They have ruined my reputation. I should have landed twenty thousand men with all their equipment on the Egyptian beaches and they should have joined Fieldmarshal Rommel and pushed the British into the Mediterranean. They have ruined all that. So now I will teach them a lesson. Go to your station. We may yet need your precious depth charges."

I left the Bridge and returned to my normal station, telling the First Lieutenant to go to the bridge. Ryker looked at me, saying nothing.

"Are the charges ready, Ryker?" I asked and he nodded.

"All safety catches off, Sir."

I lit a cigarette and took a tablet from my pocket. I looked at it and replaced it. For some reason I did not want it. I don't think I even needed it.

The explosion came from our port side and I looked towards the sound as it rolled across the calm sea. At last I saw what caused it.

"It's one of the destroyers, Sir. Why is she slowing down?"

"I don't know. There are no mine fields out here," I replied when I saw a mine floating on a parallel course just yards from our port side. I picked up the handset and shouted into it."

"Mines to port. Possibly to starboard, too."

But I was wrong. The next explosion raised *Condor's* bow up and her stern, where Ryker and I stood, dropped into the sea. The water flowed all round us and we grabbed whatever rails we could to avoid being swept off the ship.

I ran up the companionway to the bridge, faster than I'd run since losing my leg. I was halfway up when another explosion sounded and scraps of metal flew through the air. Luckily I was protected from the blast but the bridge was not.

When I entered what remained of the wheelhouse there was nobody standing. Blood smeared the walls and decks, bits of flesh hid the compass from view. The ship's wheel was no longer there, nor was the Coxswain.

I heard a groan and saw the First Lieutenant trying to stand.

"Stay where you are, the doctor's on his way," I told him.

One of the lookouts entered the wheelhouse.

"Run as fast as you can down to the engine room. Tell the Chief Engineer we've been mined. Or torpedoed. Anyway, tell him to stop the ship, we have a huge hole in the bow. He'll know what to do."

Other ratings came up to the bridge and I gave the

orders necessary to move the command centre to the poop deck at the rear of the ship. I looked around for the captain but he was nowhere to be seen.

"Where is the Captain?" I shouted and a rating ran on to the bridge.

"Sir, he's down there," he pointed to the deck below. "It must have been the explosion that blew him off the bridge."

There was no more I could do. Not until the secondary steering position was operational so I walked over to the captain. I expected him to be a mess. But he wasn't. His face and features were intact. But I could see what killed him.

I lifted him away from the metal stanchion at the foot of the mast and checked. He had no back to his skull. The fall from the bridge and the force of landing meant that his entire skull was no longer there. Just flesh and, I assumed, brain matter.

Down on the poop deck the reports came in from all departments. The pumps were holding, power was restored, the auxiliary steering and command position was operational. With luck, and with the escort group around us we would make it to the port of Salvo in Southern Italy. And whatever enquiry awaited me.

# Chapter 85    Scotty in Alexandria

We arrived in Alex as night fell. I don't think any of us ever thought we'd be coming back after the hell of the last twelve hours. The battle was bad enough, but coming to terms with the loss of over half the flotilla affected us all.

Though we hadn't been together for long, somehow we'd become a close knit team. It was often the case in the Navy's smaller ships that friendships formed and strengthened more quickly than on the larger capital ships. Or perhaps I was romanticising it all.

We berthed and as I expected the Old Man was waiting.

"Congratulations, Harry," he began as we settled in the wardroom, each of us with a gin in hand. "A first class job. Sorry about your crews. We've lost a lot of good men."

"Almost two hundred, Sir. Seems a heavy price to pay. I hope it was worth it."

He removed a sheet of paper from his pocket and passed it across. I read it and had difficulty swallowing.

*"To Captain R. Dennis DSM, RN Cross,"* it started. *"Congratulations on job well done. Agents report no merchant ship survived the attack. Reports over twenty thousand troops dead. Seven enemy warships destroyed with further loss of life. No likelihood of replacements this year. Please relay my earnest thanks to Commander Scott and his men. Ends WLSC."*

"WLSC?" I asked.

"The Prime Minister, Harry. This mission was authorised at the very highest levels. You asked whether the sacrifices were worth it. I can't answer that. I do know that had any of the reinforcements got through they would have strengthened Rommel's hand and could have been the difference between victory or defeat. And defeat could well mean death for thousands of our desert troops. The trouble with war, Harry, is that we just don't know all the answers. So we do what we can with what we do know."

He took a sip of his drink and put his glass down.

*"Dotty* and the other boats go home the way they came. Orders from the Admiralty. You fly home with me tomorrow."

We discussed the arrangements for the rest of the crews and he stood to go.

"Bad show about your Coxswain, Harry. Any idea what happened?"

I shook my head.

"We went through the mill, Sir. The boat was all over the place. Surprised a few more weren't blown overboard."

He left and I returned to my cabin to pack. Morrison stopped me in the alleyway outside.

"What should I do with the Coxswain's stuff, Sir? I've packed it all in his sea bag."

"He has no family, Morrison. Hand the bag over to the quartermasters when you get back to England. And you'll need to sew your new stripes on, Petty Officer. *Dotty* needs a new Coxswain."

I packed my own sea bag and returned to the wheelhouse. The Coxswain hadn't been blown overboard at all. He told me that he couldn't go back to England to certain execution. Nor could he simply run away. He took the only other option open to him. Wherever he was, whatever he had done, I prayed that he might find peace.

We drove out to Alexandria Airport the following morning. A Handley Page Halifax heavy bomber waited for us on the tarmac. The seats were hard, the flight long and noisy, the food awful.

But we landed at RAF St Mawgan in North Cornwall three days later having stopped at Gibraltar en route. As we drove down to Newlyn I asked a question that I'd asked myself time and time again.

What happened when Annie met her husband? Would I be able to say goodbye to her? I hoped that I would. My time with her was the happiest of my life and nobody could take that away.

# Chapter 86    Annie in Newlyn

The phone call came out of the blue, as had the first of many letters. Roger was never a regular writer and it was many years since I received a letter from him. These past seven weeks more than made up for the dearth of letters over the past three years.

Whenever he was in port resting from the trials and tests of his new ship he found time to write. To remind me of the good times we had. To say how desperately sorry he was for not keeping in touch. To explain that he had affairs while he was away because he wanted me but couldn't have me.

The more he wrote, the more confused I became. Or the more he confused me. I spoke with my Mother who said what she always said.

"It's your life, Anne. We can't make decisions for you. It was your decision to marry Roger and we supported you. He seemed like a different man when he was here. He discussed business with your Father like he never did before. When this war ends there won't be jobs for everyone in the Navy. Many people, possibly Roger amongst them, will have to get new jobs. If he is family we will take him on."

I spoke to Carol who had become a very good friend since Harry and James left. She was sympathetic, but gave no answers.

"People do change in wartime, Annie," she told me as we ate lunch in the Fishermans Arms. Their pasties were to die for but I'd have to stop eating them or get a new uniform.

"Look at James. Look at Harry. Neither were looking for relationships. James had lots of difficulties because of his scar. He's changed completely. He bubbles now, he smiles and laughs."

I went back to the office as confused as ever.

"Miss Lenton, phone call for you."

My heart leapt. I knew the Old Man was flying back and should be here today. And he said that he would do his best to bring all the officers with him. But I hadn't heard anymore. I hadn't even heard from Harry. No letters, no messages. There should have been a way for him to get a message through.

But even when the Old Man rang from Gibraltar he gave me no message from Harry. And when I asked how he was, he just said that he was fine. I wasn't sure if I felt relieved or irritated.

I picked up the telephone and said my name. It was Roger.

"Annie, we've got our orders. Can't say anything over the phone but we leave Falmouth tomorrow morning. Can I see you this evening?"

I hesitated as I wanted to be at the office for when Harry came back.

"It'll have to be in the office. I'm on duty and can't get off," I lied.

"Righto. It'll be around five o' clock. I love you."

I couldn't remember the last time he said that. I said goodbye and stared out of the window.

"Miss Lenton, it's another telephone call. You're in demand today."

This time it had to be Harry.

I picked up the handset and said my name. It was Carol.

I listened to what she said. It didn't take long.

"Are you sure?" I asked.

She gave me a name and a telephone number. I walked through to the Old Man's office, dialled the number and asked three questions. The answer to each one was yes. I looked at my watch. Almost five o' clock. The door to the outer office opened and I walked though. Roger stood there in his uniform.

"Another stripe. You've done well," I said pointing to the door behind me. He followed me through and I sat in the Old Man's chair.

"This is a bit formal, Old Thing," Roger said as he settled into the chair that I normally used.

"What do you want, Roger," I asked in a voice as calm as anything. Though I certainly didn't feel calm underneath.

"I want us to have another chance, Anne. I told you that I haven't stopped loving you since we were last together. I want us to have that again. I will do anything."

"Before I give you my answer, let me ask three questions," I said and he smiled, sat forward and held my hand across the desk. I was so surprised that I neither said nor did anything. I just sat there.

And at that moment the door opened and Harry walked in. He had a huge grin on his face. A smile that disappeared immediately.

"I am so sorry, I didn't mean to interrupt. I was looking for Captain Dennis," he spluttered, his face turning redder by the second. He started to close the door.

"Harry, please wait. I can explain."

But he was gone.

Roger was staring at me.

"I said three questions," I repeated.

"Firstly, who is Alison Bennett?"

His face paled. I waited.

"I don't know any Alison Bennett," he said.

"She knows you, Roger. I spoke to her earlier this afternoon. Let me remind you. She's a nurse at Falmouth Hospital. How long have you known her?"

He looked down at the floor.

"You almost did it, Roger. I almost believed you, almost believed that you were a different man. But you are the same now as you have always been. My answer was always going to be No because when something looks too good to be true, it usually is."

I stood up and looked down at him.

"A friend of mine is a nurse here and she made a few enquiries of her friends in Falmouth. You've been seeing Miss Bennett since you arrived back two months ago. Promised her everything. As you did me. I won't waste my breath on the other questions but never contact me again. Nor my family. I have no wish to have anything further to do with you. Goodbye."

When I walked out of the office the Old Man stood at the door.

"Are you all right, Anne?" he asked.

"Yes, I am now, Sir. There's an officer in there who has been pestering me. It's my ex-husband. Would you ask him to leave?"

I didn't wait for an answer. If Roger didn't leave I suspected the Old Man would call the Shore Patrol in to have him locked up.

# Chapter 87    Scotty in Newlyn

I shouldn't have been surprised. I encouraged Annie to see her husband and we'd only known each other for a few months. Their marriage lasted a lot longer than that and must at some point have been based on love.

I walked to the end of the harbour as I had four months earlier. This time, though, to sit and think. Not too much as I would have plenty of time for that later. I sat on the wall and watched one of the fishing boats come in through the gaps, as the locals referred to the gap between the two piers.

So much had happened in the last few months. One tough but pleasant man who I thought I knew killed three other people and died himself.

James had found true love with Carol. He was thrilled when I persuaded the Old Man to let him fly back with us. I was so happy for him when Carol was there to meet him at the harbour gate.

I had found love, or so I thought, and now had lost it. He seemed a good looking chap, a Captain now. Off to war again. That is what I needed, another mission.

I lit a cigarette and took a long drag.

"Could I have one, please?" she said sitting next to me. I passed her one and lit it.

"Just for a moment, Harry, don't say anything. Let me tell you what I want."

She paused and took a drag before almost choking. The tears came to her eyes and she ground the cigarette out under her heel.

"I met Roger as you suggested. He said all sorts of things. All nice, loving, genuine. He wanted me to consider going back to him. That was seven weeks ago, the day you left."

She paused and the tears flowed down her cheek.

"I didn't know if you were coming back. Or when. I was lost without you. I didn't realise how much I loved you. And how much I cared if you died. He rang this afternoon and asked for my answer. By then I had already made my mind up. I had actually found out what love was with you. Carol called a few minutes after he rang and told me that he was seeing a nurse in Falmouth. I laughed. You see, I realised that I no longer cared. That is what I was telling him when you arrived."

She stopped and I took her hands in mine.

"When I walked into that office and saw you both there I thought the worst," I said. "I wasn't angry, because you gave me what nobody else ever has. You gave me love and I loved you back. I knew when we sat here all those months ago that something inside me changed. Something came alive that wasn't there before."

We hugged tighter than we'd ever hugged before.

"I love you, Annie. I can't think of anyone else I want to spend my life with. Will you divorce?"

She nodded.

"I phoned a local solicitor before Roger arrived. It will take time, but I have an appointment tomorrow."

We stood and walked back down the pier.

"When will *Dotty* be back?"

I shook my head.

"I have no idea. But Uncle Nick visited before I left for Egypt and said that he's finished repairing Mum's house. I wondered if you wanted to rent a room."

## Stay in Touch

Thank you for reading my book. If you enjoyed it, please take a moment to leave me a review at your favourite retailer. You can stay in touch via

http://www.kevedwards.com

Email: info@ Kev Edwards.com

Facebook: <u>Kev Edwards</u>

## Other books by Kev Edwards

The Killing Seas (Book 1 in the International Marine Police Series)

The Savage Seas (Book 2 in the International Marine Police Series)

Golden Seas (Book 3 in the International Marine Police Series)

African Storm (Book 4 in the International Police Series)

Diamond Storm (Book 5 in the International Police Series)

Power Storm (Book 6 in the International Marine Police Series)

## About the Author

Kev Edwards is a Cornishman born and raised with the sound of waves crashing against the shore below his bedroom window. From an early age he decided to join the British Merchant Navy as a navigator. Coming ashore some years later he now works as a free-lance consultant and author. Kev lives in Nottinghamshire with his wife, Rosie, and ten year old Border Collie, Ally.

## Acknowledgements

I thank Rosie, my wife, who has been the source of unending support throughout our marriage, and the more so during the writing of this, my seventh novel. I am also grateful to my sister in law, Fiona, for her design work. And I also thank Martin, Zelda and all others who proof read the final drafts: thank you for all your comments and suggestions. And to my Border Collie, Ally, for keeping me calm and my humour intact in moments of stress, thank you, too.

Printed in Great Britain
by Amazon